COME
AND
GET ME

COME AND GET ME

A CAITLIN BERGMAN NOVEL

AUGUST NORMAN

CROOKED LANE

NEW YORK

Norman

Published in the United States by Crooked Lane Books, an imprint of The Quick Brown Fox & Company LLC.

Crooked Lane Books and its logo are trademarks of The Quick Brown Fox & Company LLC.

Library of Congress Catalog-in-Publication data available upon request.

ISBN (hardcover): 978-1-68331-975-7
ISBN (ePub): 978-1-68331-976-4
ISBN (ePDF): 978-1-68331-977-1

Cover design by Andy Ruggirello

Printed in the United States.

www.crookedlanebooks.com

Crooked Lane Books
34 West 27th St., 10th Floor
New York, NY 10001

First Edition: April 2019

10 9 8 7 6 5 4 3 2 1

To those on the bottom, looking up:
You are not alone.

CHAPTER

1

"*I* SEE THE WAY *you look at girls,*" his mother had said. "*Like they're toys. Like you want to own them.*"

Almost ten years ago now, but the moment came back to him like the words to his favorite song, the way her lips wrinkled when she sucked the last of the menthol through her lipstick-coated Newport, the glazed-over stare from under her heavy, half-closed eyelids, the pointless, but repeated glances at the empty pill bottles on the table.

"*You can't own a woman. It's like trying to control a river.*"

After all this time, he still didn't know if she'd intended the irony.

Hadn't the pills owned her?

The men who sold them?

The creditors she couldn't keep up with, the repo men she hid from or—worse—invited in for her barter system?

Wrong choice after wrong choice, man after man, time after time. Maybe if one of the sweaty many had guided instead of giving in, taught instead of getting in—maybe she'd still be alive.

He'd been too young to help then. Too unsure.

Now he was sure. Strong, patient, firm, responsible, understanding, and above all, disciplined.

Not only could he own a woman, he'd have one in his basement by the end of the week.

2

"**A**RE YOU OKAY, Caitie? You look like you've been crying."
Caitie. Forty-two years old and Mary Lubbers-Gaffney still called her Caitie, like two decades hadn't passed since they'd stood in the same state.

Caitlin dabbed the last of the unexpected weakness from her eyes and motioned Mary into the hotel room. "Allergic to the Midwest, I guess."

"Maybe the recycled plane air."

"Probably."

Rather than meet Mary's unconvinced gaze, she studied time's gifts to her old friend. Mary's shoulder-length auburn tangle burned like a forest fire with a tinge of gray ash, and her smile flared like the match that set the blaze. Her power suit, assertive but feminine. Her makeup, flawless.

"You look good, Mary."

"You too, Skinny. They don't have carbs in LA?"

"I run a lot."

"From what?"

The only way to knock the awkward out of the moment was to concede to the hug. Caitlin took off her sport coat, then raised both hands. Mary did the rest. Somewhere past a ten count, Mary released her, reached into a bag, and pulled out a red graduation gown and matching mortarboard.

"Ready for your big day?"

Caitlin slipped the satin robe over her dress shirt and ran a brush through her hair. Brown and straight, down to the chin. Good enough for journalism.

Mary presented lipstick. Nothing had changed. Back in college, Lipstick

Lubbers wouldn't go to a party without half an hour in front of a mirror. Caitlin carried only powder and eyeliner, but rarely used either. She took the tube, puckered, dotted on a coat of Maybelline's Rebel Bloom.

"Wow, that is exceptionally pink."

Mary winked. "You're single, right? Keep it. Might help you make a friend at the after-party."

Caitlin made a note to trash the war paint at a less insulting moment, dropped the tube into her purse, and donned her pointy new cap.

"Lead the way, Dean Lubbers-Gaffney."

Mary guided her out of the hotel and into the halls of the student union. An April evening in Indiana meant hot-blooded students wearing T-shirts and shorts—anything to tease the spring out of hiding after a white winter, even if the temperature only hovered in the sixties. Caitlin's thin-blooded California body was thankful for the gown.

Mary paused at the entrance to a conference room. "Mind taking a few questions? My students need the practice."

"You want me playtime-nice or full-on bitch?"

"Just be you." She reached up, straightened Caitlin's hat. "Well, try not to swear."

They opened the doors to applauding students, faculty, and blue-haired literati. Mary walked to a podium and waited for the crowd to settle.

"Last year, for whatever reason, this esteemed university honored me with the title of Dean of the Media School. Since they've yet to come to their senses, I'm using my powers for good. Twenty years ago, a bright young student left campus four credits shy of graduation. Despite her lack of parchment, she went on to write award-winning investigative journalism for both print and broadcast media—"

With the crowd distracted, Caitlin wiped the pink lipstick on the sleeve of her gown.

"—and recently published a bestselling memoir about her work to expose corruption within the Los Angeles Police Department. Tonight, it is my pleasure to present the diploma she left behind. Please join me in congratulating our newest graduate, Caitlin Bergman."

Caitlin fought off a surprising blush and joined Mary at the podium for the ceremonial tassel turning and honest-to-goodness paper diploma she'd never felt she'd needed. She rattled off the required acknowledgments, then pulled the mic closer.

"I understand we've got some aspiring journalists in the house."

A young man's hand shot up. "Mrs. Bergman—"

"Miss."

"I'm sorry—Miss Bergman, where are you from?"

"Yikes. I don't mean to be an"—she shot Mary a quick smile, chose a PG abbreviation—"a-hole, but do a web search for background info first. Who's got a real question?"

Another hand, female this time. "Miss Bergman, with the decline of print journalism, what are our chances of finding a job after graduation?"

"Now we're talking."

She launched into a depressingly honest portrait of the modern world of journalism. Somewhere around the advice "learn to build phone apps or get into nursing," Caitlin wound back toward hope. "Good writers who present unbiased truths will always find work, but don't expect to strike it rich. Anyone else?"

A slight British accent broke through, the speaker a dark-skinned young woman. "Lakshmi Anjale from the *Daily Student*, Miss Bergman."

Caitlin smiled. She'd spent most of college in the *Daily Student* editorial office. "Miss Anjale."

"According to my research, this is your first return to campus in twenty years. With your successes, you could have come for a victory lap at any point. In fact, I understand you've been invited to lecture several times in the last decade. Why return now? Will you be working on a story while you're in Bloomington?"

The young woman's voice carried a weighted urgency, as if her question held an understood significance. Caitlin squinted against the glare of the lights but couldn't read her facial expression. "I'm always working on a story, but I'm not here on assignment, if that's what you're asking. Something about your tone leads me to believe you have a specific follow-up question."

The girl nodded. "Allow me to clarify. Are you planning to look for Angela Chapman while you're in town?"

The name sounded familiar, but Caitlin couldn't make an association. "No, my motives for being here are purely personal."

She looked over at Mary, saw her twenty years earlier, the apartment they'd shared, the fun. A flash of her last week on campus scared the nostalgia away. She squeezed the mic like it wanted to run too.

"The diploma, for one thing. Quite an honor after all this time. I also promised my agent I'd sell a few books, so here's a shameless plug for my signing tomorrow morning."

She could stop there, excuse herself by being witty and polite, but something about the girl's eyes said, *Embrace the moment*—and Mary had told her to be herself.

"You're correct, though. I am working on something. You see, twenty years ago, a boy—" She looked down, noticed the university's nearly two-hundred-year-old seal inlayed into the podium, returned to the mic. "Not a boy—a young man I knew and trusted took me to an abandoned limestone cutting facility five miles from here, raped me, and left me for dead. So I've returned to finish that story."

She gripped the podium, well aware of the serious silence caused by her admission.

"Plus, Mary said there'd be wine and cheese."

3

MARY CAUGHT UP with Caitlin fifty feet from the safety of her hotel room. "I left as soon as I could. Is that really why you disappeared? Caitie, why didn't you tell me?"

Caitlin kept walking. "You had the GRE, graduation, that Chris guy—pick one. Plus, I signed something."

Mary matched her pace. "Who cares? Let's talk about this."

Caitlin slid her keycard into her door lock. The light went green. She turned back to her friend.

"I'm fine, Mary."

Mary didn't have to say anything. The pity on her face did the job.

"Okay, I'm not fine. Thought I was—apparently not." She heard the mechanical whir of the lock, pushed too late. "Damn it." She worked the keycard again, pushed the door open. "I went straight to the hospital, did the kit, called the cops, and left town. He did two of his four years, got out, then killed a family in a car accident—drunk driving, his fault. He's back in prison where he belongs. So don't look at me like that."

"Like what?"

"Like I'm a victim, because I'm not. I'm a badass."

Mary sighed, laughed a little.

Caitlin wasn't ready for the laugh. "What?"

"We haven't even hit the bar, and you bust out college rape."

Caitlin opened her mouth, found an unexpected chuckle of her own.

"I missed you, Mary. Give me five minutes, I'll meet you upstairs."

"I can make an excuse, Caitie. You don't have to—"

"Five minutes, and we'll all act like it never happened."

Mary let her escape.

Safe in the room, Caitlin pulled off her ridiculous mortarboard and gown and slumped down against the door. Her jeans met paper.

"So much for framing your diploma, dummy."

She sat forward, then remembered her diploma and a handful of other papers lay to her left, safe and unwrinkled. She reached behind her, found an unsealed, unmarked, letter-sized envelope. She opened the flap, pulled out a handwritten note in calligrapher's cursive on hotel stationery, no signature.

You were very brave to come back to Bloomington, Caitlin Bergman.
I will keep you safe.

Caitlin stood, pulled the door open. "Damn, Mary, that was some fast pen work—"

She looked both ways, saw no one. "And I'm talking to myself like a jerk."

* * *

Seconds before the elevator doors opened, she heard the party. She straightened the black sport coat she'd thrown over her dress shirt and moved toward the sounds of inebriation wafting through an ominous set of walnut double doors. She checked the text message again.

Last door on the right before the party.

Easy enough. She exited through the door marked "Roof Access," found an unoccupied- ten-by-ten balcony under the clear night sky.

She walked to the metal railing, filled her lungs.

Soil, grass, wet leaves—the scents left from daytime rain evoked images of textbooks spread out on blankets over bright green lawns. Nine stories up, she could see half of the campus. Glowing orbs of streetlights over concrete paths through hundred-year-old trees linked the art museum, the theater complex, and the limestone towers of the library. So much limestone. She'd forgotten the old world beauty of the soft mineral, a feeling she'd only seen reproduced in Washington, D.C., much of the material pulled from the same local quarries.

A male voice interrupted her solitude. "You beat me here."

She turned to an older African American gentleman in a Kangol trilby-style hat and a rumpled sport coat. Even if she hadn't known Scott Canton, his outfit would have introduced him as a poetry professor.

"Thank you so much for doing this, Scott."

He joined her at the railing. "Not at all. It's a pleasure to see you in person rather than merely hearing your charming voice on the other end of the phone."

Caitlin had run into her old teacher ten years back at a writer's conference at the University of Southern California. Not only had they kept in touch since, she'd quoted him as a source in two articles: the first, a piece about veterans using art to overcome post-traumatic stress disorder; the second, only six months back, an argument in support of using marijuana to treat PTSD as well.

Scott reached into the lining of his hat and produced two hand-rolled joints. "As requested."

Caitlin stashed one in her purse and pulled out her lighter. "You're saving my life. Care to join me?"

Scott looked back toward the door. "Regrettably, I should run. Well before you let me know you'd be in town, I promised a lady friend a weekend at Lake Monroe. Said lady waits below."

Caitlin shook her head. "Ah to be seventy and horny. Come on, professor. It could be another twenty years before I'm back here. Remind me how this thing works."

He relented, took her lighter. "The things I do for my students."

Caitlin watched the joint's tip turn cherry-red.

Scott exhaled a cloud of pot smoke with a practiced sigh. "I caught your ceremony."

"Yep, I'm a graduate now." Caitlin took her turn, concentrated on the drug, not the reminder of her public admission. "This is great stuff."

"Those in need will always find weed." His palms bumped the railing, and a low, metallic tone escaped like a sigh. "I also caught the Q&A."

Caitlin looked back out at campus. "I thought you had a hot date, Scott."

"Not something you planned to talk about? Finishing that story?"

She groaned. "I don't even know how the words got past my teeth. Not only were they unplanned, but I have no idea what the hell I meant. Just verbal vomit, as they say."

He nodded. "You know, vomit is the body's way of eliminating toxins."

Caitlin genuinely liked the man, but this wasn't the time. "Or staying pretty. Let's not ruin a beautiful evening."

"Fair enough. How long are you in town?"

Caitlin took another hit, already closer to calm. "Two days, then back home."

"Alas, this must be the only moment we share." He handed her a business card. "In the event your two-day trip evolves into something more, come by my office, and we'll really get down."

On one side, his name, phone number, and office address; on the other, three simple lines.

If you have the words,
write them down, speak them often.
Your words are your strength.

Haiku format, but none of the expected reflections of nature. Caitlin liked a writer who didn't sweat the rules.

"This has truly been a pleasure, Scott." She tapped out the joint, tucked it in her purse, and put on her game face. "But we mustn't keep the ladies waiting."

* * *

Mary celebrated Caitlin's entrance with a full glass of wine and another vise-like hug. Scott's pot kept Caitlin social enough to shake a dozen hands and forget double the number of names. The Dean of Students popped by twice, once with a provost, again with the chancellor—all female. Each expressed their regrets for Caitlin's hard-to-believe-it-happened-here assault and pledged their support for an open dialogue. Their intentions felt noble, though Caitlin caught the subtle protective feelers.

The university takes every complaint seriously . . .
. . . complex issue all colleges deal with . . .
Will you be writing about the experience?

Caitlin assured those concerned she had no intention of making the school or herself poster children for campus abuse. She wasn't on assignment, nor did she have a deadline. The *story* she'd mentioned unintentionally would be a personal journey only, ending Sunday morning.

During a respite an hour in, the student with the slight British accent from the Q&A cornered her on a couch, with a full wine glass in each hand. "You're drinking the red blend, correct, Miss Bergman?"

"You certainly do your homework." Caitlin tapped the nearest cushion. "Lakshmi, right?"

The girl smiled, sat. "Lakshmi Anjale. I'm one of Dean Lubbers-Gaffney's students."

Caitlin took a glass. "What's on your mind? Looking for a mentor, perhaps a grad school reference? We can talk about anything you want as long as it's not sexual assault."

Lakshmi leaned closer. "I wanted to know if you had any theories about what happened to Angela Chapman."

Again, the name sounded familiar, but Caitlin didn't remember the context. Lakshmi reached into a bag, came up with an iPad. Caitlin took the tablet, saw a compilation of news articles and links to broadcast clips.

"Student Goes Missing, Presumed Dead."

"Statewide Search Underway for Missing Indiana Girl."

"Reward Offered for Information Leading to Missing Student."

Caitlin looked up, saw hope in the girl's brown eyes. "Your friend?"

"My best friend."

Caitlin knew she meant it, no hyperbole. "How long has she been gone?"

"Since our sophomore year, two years in May."

"I remember something about this, Lakshmi, but I'm sorry to say I haven't paid attention. If you've read my book—"

"Several times."

Caitlin smiled. "Then you understand I've had my hands full the last two years."

Lakshmi's shoulders dropped. "I knew it was a long shot."

Caitlin swiped at the screen, saw two photos of Chapman. The older, a shot from a family Thanksgiving, showed a makeup-less, medium-height teenager with long brown hair, wearing an Indiana Softball sweatshirt and a reluctant don't-take-my-picture smile. The second image, maybe two years more recent, featured the same girl lost in a search for herself. She had short, dyed-black hair in a tomboy cut, a nose piercing, and a tattoo of a hummingbird on her neck. Her hands held a lit cigarette and a red plastic party cup, and her mouth opened in what must have been laughter.

Mary Lubbers-Gaffney's arrival brought Caitlin back to the party. "There you are, Caitie. Got time to meet the Broadcast Department?"

Lakshmi reached for her iPad. "I'm sorry to have taken your time."

Caitlin saw the young woman's confidence losing its battle with hopelessness. "I'm sorry something took your friend."

She tapped the iPad's Mail icon, typed her personal email address in the "To" field, then handed the tablet back. "No promises, but send me what you've got."

The girl's smile went supernova, but Caitlin didn't have to dodge a hug. Lakshmi Anjale had the bearings of a pro. "Thank you, Miss Bergman."

"Please," Caitlin emptied the rest of her wine, "call me Caitlin."

After two generous refills and another hour of pleasantries, she found her way back to her hotel room and slept like she hadn't told a room full of people she'd been raped.

CHAPTER

4

B Y TEN THE next morning, Caitlin's pedometer app showed 2.2 miles, and her head no longer pounded.

She stretched her hamstrings, waiting at an empty stoplight out of habit from years of dodging angry Los Angeles drivers. The corner of Park and Second hadn't changed much. A row of single-story Craftsman homes built in the twenties for stonecutters lived on as rental properties. Green recycling bins overflowed with beer cans, evidence the local culture still studied the classics by lite lagers.

The green signal sent her two more blocks to Bryan Park. Noticeable improvements peppered the park, from the state-of-the-art playground to the huge public pool complex. She jogged southwest, leapt a tiny stream, and felt her heel dig into mud, the suction a reminder of the storms that had preceded her arrival. She stopped in a picnic shelter and caught her breath.

She knew she wouldn't make it to Tapp Road, wondered if she even should. Two and a half miles on the pedometer, two and a half back to campus. Coffee with Mary, then her book signing. Her showdown with the scene of the crime could wait. She started back toward the hotel.

She slowed when she saw the sculpture. An amorphous limestone rhinoceros looked to the east from atop a three-foot pedestal, and a good memory jumped back to life.

Twenty years old, blissful, half a bottle of Soft Rosé from Oliver Winery in hand, Caitlin helped Darren Thompson onto the smooth, cool stone. They straddled the surrealist beast, passed the bottle back and forth. She still felt the buzz in her head, the buzz in her pants from the night she got sex right. Darren Thompson, number two, the one right after the yearlong relationship that had never quite worked in the bedroom. Darren Thompson could move his lips, his hips, and his tongue.

God bless that stupid kid from Ohio.

After an hour and a half of ecstasy, they'd stumbled down to the kitchen, grabbed the bottle of wine, and ended up barefoot in the wet grass, then on top of the statue. When the wine ran out, they stripped naked behind a tree and started all over.

Forty-two-year-old Caitlin couldn't stop herself. She pulled her sweaty body onto the rhino that'd seen it all, wrapped her arms around its neck, and hugged the past. She leaned into the stone, not surprised to be a little turned on, but the tears running down her cheeks came out of nowhere and didn't stop until she'd run back to the hotel.

* * *

Attendance at her signing exceeded her expectations. A pair of girls in matching pink sweatshirts, both under Caitlin's height, five foot seven, stepped forward for signatures thirty-three and thirty-four. The last person in line, a young man with a goatee behind them, would make thirty-five. Off in a chair to the side, Lakshmi Anjale waited as well, though Caitlin didn't see a book in her hands.

Girl thirty-three started. "We loved your book."

She and her friend moved in tandem, copies out and open.

Thirty-four took over. "Totally. I read anything about angels. Vampires too."

"Vampires, huh?" Caitlin laughed. She'd finally figured out why thirty-five starving students had shelled out good drinking money for a book about LA police corruption. "You're students in Mary's class, right? How does the assignment work?"

The first girl looked relieved. "Extra credit if we bring in a signed copy of your book, one free retest on any of our exams if we write a summary."

Caitlin would have to take Lubbers out to dinner. Requiring her students to buy the book would sell all thirty copies she'd lugged along, plus the bookstore's pile.

"If you're doing summaries, here's a hint. The title *Fallen Angels* refers to both the victims of a prostitution ring and an ex-cop who had to expose his partner to save them. No actual angels make an appearance."

The girls giggled their apologies, then escaped with their grade boosters.

Mister thirty-five, the guy waiting behind them, opened his copy. "Would you mind?"

His thick goatee, darker than Caitlin would have expected from a man with sandy-blond hair, covered a series of unfortunate pockmarks near his lips. She caught herself staring and reached for her blood-red marker.

"Not at all. Who should I make it out to?"

His green eyes blinked away. "Just your signature would be great."

Caitlin noticed more scar tissue on his neck. Not from acne, maybe a burn. "Are you a collector?"

His eyes returned, brightened. "A collector?"

"Sure, autographs. I hate to say it, but I doubt my signature will make you any money."

He closed the book, held it to his chest. "You did so much without help from anyone, and I spend a lot of time alone. Maybe if I keep a piece of you, your strength will rub off."

"People mean well," Caitlin said, "but the only person I count on is me."

He thanked her and left, weaving through the bookstore's racks briskly, despite an uneven gait and slight limp, clutching her book like a religious tome. After last night's admission and the morning's crying jag, Caitlin wondered if he wasn't already the stronger of the two.

The bookstore event staff began their cleanup, and Lakshmi finally approached.

Caitlin started. "I'm sorry. I haven't had a chance to read any of the Chapman material—"

"I know. You would have rung," Lakshmi said, serious.

"Because?"

"Because you would be angry, and you would want answers."

Caitlin sighed. "Lakshmi, I like you, but that doesn't change what I'm about to say. Horrible things happen in life, to us and the people we love. Answers to questions this big take time, no matter how angry we are."

"I don't need you to find Angela, Miss Bergman."

"Good, because I'm sure the police and every news agency in the Midwest have already done exactly what I would do."

Lakshmi rolled her eyes the way only a young woman could. "No, they wouldn't, but that's not my point. A body's been found."

The words hit Caitlin in the gut. "Is it her?"

"I don't know. They said they'll only give information to *professional* news outlets."

The frustration in the girl's voice hit even harder.

Caitlin checked the time. "I can give you two hours."

CHAPTER

5

SUCH A WOMAN.

The young man stared at the signature, the book propped against his mirror.

Firm strokes, deliberate, practiced. Nowhere near as refined as the note he'd slipped under her hotel room door, but made by a sure and steady hand.

A woman. Not a girl acting mature, but sure of herself, strong, and confident. A survivor.

The note had been a risk, an unplanned, spur-of-the-moment aberration, but standing in that conference room, seeing Caitlin Bergman's naked pain, he knew he had to reach out and let her know she'd been seen. Even after the mad dash down the hall and the perfect synchronicity of happening upon the paper and envelopes, he'd almost dared to go one dangerous step further and sign his name. He'd calmed himself, content with the knowledge he'd meet her at the signing.

Seasoned, real mileage to her; sweat, not perfume; blood, not makeup; wrinkles everywhere. If you licked her skin, she'd taste like alcohol and daring.

How random. Six months back he'd heard an interview on National Public Radio about the reporter who had not only uncovered a human-trafficking ring run by cops but who'd had to fight her way out of the Hollywood mansion they'd turned into a brothel. He'd bought the book that week but had seen the notice for the signing on a campus light pole only two days back. Now he'd met the woman face to face.

Well, almost.

He stroked his goatee. He thought the facial hair made him look like a dork that spent time in coffee shops, loudly comparing whatever the baristas gave him to what he'd gotten that magical summer he'd spent in Italy—an easily forgotten man with some equally forgettable name—a real *Chet Watkins*.

He pulled the corner, slowly. The layer of latex under the hair came up as designed, leaving only his scars. He reached for the scar tissue on his neck, pulled it off, inch by inch. He hated to lose the last remnants of Chet, but he'd been seen and had to burn. However insignificant Chet's half-beard might've seemed to casual observers, the damaged skin beneath gave them an additional reason to look away. Even a young woman he'd recognized from campus had walked by at the signing, with no more than a passing glance.

Not Caitlin Bergman. She'd noticed the raised tissue and returned his gaze.

Are you a collector? she'd asked.

In that second he thought she'd peered through his latex camouflage and seen the real him, maybe even knew the answer. Maybe he was that obvious.

Was he a collector?

He wanted to be, but knew how collections worked. They started small with simple, elegant pieces, then built to top-shelf items through judicial choices, no room for greed.

He grabbed his copy of Caitlin's book, stared at her photo on the back cover, tapped his fingertip on her face. Might be a risk to keep the book, but he and Caitlin Bergman had shared a moment, and he'd learned that some moments meant everything.

Caitlin Bergman, I didn't expect you. Didn't plan for you. You're out of my budget—for now.

6

"You have a wraparound graphic on your car asking for information about Chapman's disappearance?" Caitlin didn't know cars but could tell Lakshmi's once-red Toyota Corolla was old enough to apply for its own driver's license.

"Angela's mom donated the car."

Caitlin did a quick phone search. "We can't roll up to a crime scene in this thing and be taken seriously. Take me to College and Third."

The rental chain gave Caitlin a deal—twenty-five bucks a day for a white hybrid that she could drop at the Indianapolis airport on her way back to California.

She threw Lakshmi the key fob. "Bring me up to speed while you drive. I need my hands for my phone."

Lakshmi pulled into traffic. "Right, the police found a body—"

"Which police? Campus, Bloomington PD, State?"

"The Jackson County Sheriff's Department."

"In a different county than we're in. And why do you know this?"

"The *Seymour Tribune*."

Caitlin searched the paper's website, found the one-line blurb.

> *The Jackson County Sheriff's Department confirms that hunters found human remains in a cornfield outside of Seymour.*

Caitlin held out her hand. "Stop. Where are we driving, and why?"

"The coroner's office in Seymour. I thought maybe we could—"

"See the remains? That's not going to happen. Pull over."

Caitlin scrolled through her contacts and hit the "Dial" icon.

Lakshmi edged the car onto the shoulder of the two-lane road. "Are you calling him?"

"Who?"

"The ex-cop from your book. Mike Roman. I loved how you described him: *a cop built on the frame of a marine grown from a boy scout.*"

Caitlin smiled, remembering the rest of the phrase her editor had trimmed: *Who'd do anything, legal or not, to earn his merit badges.*

She'd worked with Roman a few times since the events of *Fallen Angels.* He was a solid investigator and a better bodyguard, but without a badge he'd be useless with a dead body in southern Indiana. "Roman's a blunt instrument. I'm looking for a scalpel, particularly one that owes me favors."

She switched to speaker, heard the warm tenor tones of Jim Martinez's official FBI phone voice. "You don't usually call through the switchboard," he said, hushed.

Caitlin preferred the man's bedroom voice, a few notes lower and a lot less professional.

"I didn't want to give you the impression this was a social call, Special Agent."

"Ouch, my title even. Guess that means we're not getting sushi tonight."

That was Jim's joke. They'd met for "sushi" four times but had never actually gotten around to eating a meal together. The man had two kids, two ex-wives, and one of the most stressful occupations in America. Time was a commodity neither of them wasted.

"Sorry, I'm in southern Indiana, and I'm not alone. You're on speaker."

"You could have led with that."

"I know, but I like playing with you. Know anything about female remains found in Jackson County, Indiana, either yesterday or the day before?"

"I do not."

"But I bet you could impress a girl if you wanted to."

"You know I could. *Solo con mis manos.*"

"We're two thousand miles apart. What can you do with that big brain of yours?"

"Give me five minutes."

The connection ended. Caitlin caught the look of admiration on Lakshmi's face.

"That's right," Caitlin said. "I know an FBI agent."

"Sounds like you know him rather well."

Caitlin smiled. She wasn't exactly a bombshell, but she'd attracted a fine

range of intelligent men like Jim in her past. Had she used them for information, sex, and cocktails? Damned straight.

"Talk to me about the local law enforcement," she said. "I bet you know
the name of every official who's been involved in Angela's disappearance."

"I do. It started with Bloomington PD. Detective—"

Caitlin put her hand up again. "Not yet. My point is, there are multiple
agencies involved, right?"

"Right."

"Each with their own territory. Why would they tell us anything?"

Lakshmi's eyebrows went up. "Because we're the press?"

Caitlin lowered her window. High sixties out, a handful of clouds, nothing dark. "Not at this stage we're not. We're an annoyance they don't have
time to deal with. Do the people in Angela's case like you?"

"Like me?"

"How much do you call them, Lakshmi? How often?"

The girl shifted in her seat. "Probably too much."

"Who's the lead detective, which agency?"

"His name is Jerry Greenwood, Bloomington PD."

"Got the number?"

Lakshmi got out her phone, tapped on the saved contact, started the dial.

"Whoa—we're not using your phone."

Caitlin dialed the digits into her own phone, moved the call to speaker,
got an automated directory.

"You've reached the Bloomington Police Department—"

Lakshmi leaned over. "He's twelve-fifty-five, but I get his voicemail every
time."

Caitlin pushed zero and put a little country in her voice for the female
receptionist. "Sorry to bother you, but this is Cheryl over at Bloomington
Tire. I've got a cell phone here that I think belongs to Jerry Greenwood. Is he
in the office?"

"Hold, please."

A ringtone replaced the operator's voice until a male answered,
"Greenwood."

Caitlin hung up.

Lakshmi's jaw dropped. "Did you just prank-call a detective?"

"Start the car. They didn't find Angela Chapman."

"You're guessing."

"What have we learned?"

The girl gave a little laugh. "That he dodges my calls."

"More than that. One, he's on the clock, and two, he's at his desk. You're an aspiring journalist: How do I know he's at his desk?"

Lakshmi took a second before she smiled. "Because you told the receptionist you had his cell phone. She would have patched you through to his voicemail if he wasn't in the office. Now we know he's at work. So what?"

"How many homicides, or even missing persons cases, does Bloomington have each year?"

"Not many. Two, three at the most."

"If the lead detective gets a break on a two-year-old case with more national attention than he's ever likely to have again, he's not going to be sitting at his desk."

"How can you be so sure, Caitlin?"

"Do you know the Picasso napkin story?"

"The artist?"

"Goes like this: Picasso's at a garden party. A woman asks him to draw her portrait on a napkin, something she'll gladly pay for. He takes the napkin, draws for thirty seconds, hands it back, says, 'Five hundred francs.' Outraged, the woman says, 'Five hundred francs? You drew that in thirty seconds.' Picasso says, 'Yes, but it took me thirty years to be able to do that portrait in thirty seconds.'"

"That's a great story. Is it true?"

"Who knows—did you miss the point?"

Lakshmi reached for the car's ignition but stopped when Caitlin's phone rang. "Is it Greenwood?"

Caitlin answered; let Martinez show off.

"Your lady in the woods appears to be one Frances Danforth, buried in nineteen fifty-five. Hunters digging a latrine brought her up. Impressed?"

"Very," Caitlin said. "That's the kind of skill that got you promoted to anti-terrorism."

Martinez paused for enough time for her to validate her guess.

"Let me know when you're back in town, *hermosita*. I'll neither confirm nor deny your inference in person."

"I look forward to it."

She hung up, pointed to the road.

"Back to school, Anjale."

7

T HE NEED TO return Lakshmi to her car gave Caitlin a polite out but also left her facing an inconvenient truth. With access to a rental, she could easily drive down to Tapp Road. It was fifteen minutes to one, and her only appointment was dinner with Mary and her husband; she had plenty of time.

She parked at a curb, pulled up a map on her phone. Four miles south. Only two turns. She put a signal on, waited for traffic, watched the green arrow blink. Traffic thinned, then disappeared altogether, but Caitlin's rental didn't move an inch.

She closed her eyes, exhaled.

Troy Woods won't be there. The building might not even be there anymore.

She opened her eyes, unbuckled her seatbelt, took another deep breath.

Her phone rang. She didn't recognize the number but answered like she'd won a contest. "This is Caitlin Bergman. Thank you for calling."

The unfamiliar male voice gave a slight chuckle. "Did you just thank me for calling?"

She flipped her turn signal off. "Sure did. Who is this, by the way?"

"Detective Jerry Greenwood from the Bloomington Police Department, returning your call."

That made it Caitlin's turn to chuckle. "Good afternoon, Detective."

"Couldn't help but wonder why a Los Angeles–based reporter would be in Bloomington and looking for me on a Saturday."

"Sorry about that—dialed a wrong number."

"'Course," the man said, nothing but charm in his voice. "Since you've got me, anything you want to talk about?"

Caitlin tapped on the steering wheel. By five short minutes, poor

Lakshmi had missed a chance to grill the detective who sent every one of her calls to voicemail. Couldn't hurt to meet the man, maybe feed the girl some insider info before leaving town. Plus, Caitlin needed to do something about the pool of acid attacking her stomach, or she'd never make the drive south without barfing in her rental car.

"I was about to grab a bite to eat, Detective, and cops always know the best places. Have a recommendation?"

Greenwood took a second. "Lennie's on Tenth. Gourmet pizza and microbrews."

Caitlin smiled. "Interesting choice. I used to wait tables there."

"What's that word," he asked, *Serendipity?* I figured a big city reporter had called through the switchboard to see if I was in the office and assumed the next step would be a surprise interview; thought I'd call you back and beat you to the punch before I ducked out for a salad. Care to grab lunch with a man you met from a wrong number?"

* * *

Detective Jerry Greenwood scanned the room for less than two seconds before approaching Caitlin's table with a smile. From the slight gray in the temples of his otherwise full head of short brown hair, Caitlin guessed the tall, decent-looking man was in his early forties. She saw a cell phone holstered on the belt of his slacks, but no badge or gun.

"Thanks for meeting me," he said, taking a chair. "I hate eating alone. How long are you in town?"

"Short trip," she said. "I leave tomorrow afternoon."

A waitress stopped by. Caitlin ordered a beer and a sandwich. Greenwood went for an Arnold Palmer and a teriyaki chicken salad.

"No pizza, Miss Bergman?"

Caitlin shook her head. "Late night only. What's your excuse?"

"Spend a lot of time on the phone at my desk. Not a great way to work off dough."

Caitlin didn't see any spare dough on the man.

He reached for a water in front of him. "About that wrong number."

"Meaning you didn't leave a cell phone at a tire store?"

"Not lately, though wouldn't have put it past me two years back."

"Angela Chapman?"

Greenwood's dark eyebrows went up. "No, another reason entirely. To tell the truth, Miss Bergman. I've been expecting your call for years."

Before Caitlin could parrot his *years*, the waitress returned with the necessary liquids. Greenwood laced his fingers on the tabletop, waiting for her departure.

"You wouldn't remember me," he started. "I grew up here, went to Bloomington South, came back after the police academy. Even knew Troy Woods—well, his family. Older sister dated my brother in high school."

Caitlin reached for her beer but barely processed the taste. Jerry Greenwood commanded her full attention.

"I was a twenty-three-year-old patrol officer when Woods attacked you. My girlfriend at the time was Melissa Hartman. Later became my wife."

Caitlin didn't remember Melissa, but the last name got her on her feet. "Your father-in-law is Connor Hartman?"

Greenwood rose to meet her, a hand out. "I married Melissa. Chief Hartman came with her. Not something I'm particularly proud of."

"So when I called—"

"You made a big impression at your graduation."

"When I said I was here to 'finish that story,'" she said, nodding. Connor Hartman, a real son-of-a-bitch, had controlled the Bloomington Police Department in the spring of her senior year, and here was his son-in-law, worried about the implications of three simple words. Apparently two decades changed nothing. A voice inside said, *Run.*

Caitlin made a beeline for the door, heard Greenwood behind her.

"What about your lunch?"

"Get it to go—shove it up your ass."

He followed her outside. "Miss Bergman, wait. You stay; I'll pay for lunch and leave—least I can do."

She spun in the middle of the parking lot. "Your department did *the least they could do* twenty years ago."

Greenwood's confusion looked genuine. "Hey, you called me. I thought you wanted to talk about this."

Caitlin took two steps backward, bumped into her rental, her inside voice telling her to run once again, in primal, survivalist pleading, not caring that rational-adult-boss-bitch-reporter Caitlin Bergman had interviewed sleazy politicians and cartel hit men, even faced down men with guns, all without breaking a sweat.

"Wow." She slapped her hand on the hood, took a breath, centered herself like a professional. "Connor Hartman's son-in-law was the last person I expected to meet today."

"By marriage only, Miss Bergman. Like I said, I fell in love with the daughter, not the man. When you called, I assumed—"

A pizza delivery car paused in the lane between them. Greenwood stepped back onto the sidewalk, let the driver pass. "Wait, did you call about Angela Chapman?"

Caitlin crossed her arms. "What if I did? Would you have called me back?"

Greenwood walked through the lane, stopped at the passenger side of Caitlin's car. "You kidding? An award-winning journalist wants to look into a two-year-old disappearance that's stumped my entire department, the state police, and the FBI? Why would that bother me?"

"I can't tell if this is sarcasm, Detective, but I've known some police officers who keep their investigations private."

"I'm not saying I wouldn't normally do just that, but that girl's family could use help from someone like you."

Caitlin shifted her hips. "I'm not officially working on the story."

"Just curious?"

"A student asked for advice."

"Bet I can guess which."

Greenwood pulled twenty dollars and a business card from his wallet, left them on the hood. "Let me say this. I'll be glad to help any way I can, whether your story is set in the past or the present."

Caitlin watched the detective walk away, then went back inside and asked the waitress for a to-go box, even though her appetite wouldn't come back anytime soon. No way she was driving down to Tapp Road now. She retreated to her hotel room, smoked the last of Scott Canton's pot, and passed out.

*   *   *

At seven PM, she found Mary near the back of a Chinese place with a slightly plump but good-looking man of the same age with his own full head of red hair.

He got up from the table. "The great Caitie."

Caitlin put out her hand, but he pulled her near. No real surprise, Lubbers had found herself a hugger.

"Ease up, Aaron," Mary said. "Caitlin's not as touchy-feely as we are."

Aaron Gaffney squeezed harder. "Never too late to start."

"Honey, please."

On his release, Caitlin took a chair. "Never apologize for your creepy, touchy-feely love."

Aaron sat, nuzzled his wife. "I know we don't have long, but tell me every horrible thing you know about Mary."

Lubbers hit his arm. "I've told you everything I've ever done."

Caitlin looked at her friend's happy eyes and her friend's husband's happy eyes, and wondered if her own eyes had ever looked that happy. She knew the answer in the instant. Not since college. She found a smile.

"What have we got—a night? I might have to leave out Panama City."

Mary laughed. "Don't you dare. I've been told there's a monument in a Florida bathroom devoted to me. Well, at least to my boobs."

Caitlin started the tales and forgot all about the body in the field, the police chief's son-in-law, and the missing student.

8

By ELEVEN THIRTY, Aaron had them back at Caitlin's hotel.

"This is stupid." Mary threw her arms around Caitlin's shoulders. "I haven't seen you in twenty years. We should drink more."

Aaron had avoided intoxication. "Babe, you know I've got golf tomorrow, right?"

"Boo," she said. "You're no fun, Gaffney."

Caitlin surprised herself. "My room's got two beds. Sleepover, Lubbers?"

They released Aaron, bought another bottle of wine, and stumbled back to Caitlin's room.

Mary fiddled with a liquor store corkscrew. "What time's your flight?"

"Noon." Caitlin unwrapped a pair of plastic cups. "Figure I'll leave by nine."

"You're not making that."

"I don't really want to."

"Do you have to?"

"I have a signing this week."

Mary poured them each a cup. "No, you don't."

"I don't?"

"No," Mary said, not quite as a challenge, but Caitlin knew she'd been caught. "I talked to your publicist. You've got nothing for weeks. Plus, you told me you're between contracts, right?"

Caitlin nodded, took a sip. Her editor at the paper had given her a three-month window for book publicity. She could still pitch stories, but he wouldn't assign anything until she returned to full time. Between her savings and the recent film rights sale of *Fallen Angels*, she could afford time away.

"What about your rape thing?"

"What about it?"

"Caitie, you made a damn speech, freaked out the chancellor and everything. You're here to *'finish that story'*—remember? Are you saying you wrapped that up?"

"Not exactly." Caitlin doubted getting high and passing out in her hotel room counted as closure. "First off, calling what I said at the Q&A a *speech* is a tad generous. Words just came out in the moment. I never had an actual plan. I thought I'd come for the diploma, hang with you, sell some books, and if there was time, maybe go back to the place it happened and tell the rocks to screw themselves, maybe journal about the whole thing, but that didn't happen."

"You should stay until it does, Caitie."

Caitlin looked up at her old friend, saw the same expression of trust she'd counted on years ago. "Sure. I'll just drop a few grand on soul-searching. Not sure how much you know about publishing, but books don't exactly bring in lottery money."

"I've got a place you can stay for free, as long as you want."

"I'm not going to impose on you and Aaron, Lubbers."

"Think I want your single ass in my sex palace? You can't handle the noises I make. I've got a house south of campus—my place before Aaron and I shacked up."

"You kept it?"

"Hyphenated my name, kept my one-bedroom cottage. My marriage is great, but a little extra space never hurts."

Caitlin knew she could take her diploma back to LA in the morning, lose herself in some new assignment, even meet up with Jim Martinez for some sushi—all without ever having to feel as out of control as she had at lunch with Detective Greenwood—or as nervous as she'd been watching a turn signal blink. She could go back, run away . . . again.

She swirled the last inch of wine in the hotel's plastic cup, reminded of her father's favorite saying, something he claimed came from a pack of gum. He'd mumble his silly mantra every time he had to choose between doing something the easy way or the right way. Under a set of jack stands or a leaky sink, with a roll of duct tape in hand, she'd hear his nickel philosophy.

Could *don't mean* should,
but would *won't mean* did
—*unless you let it.*
Otherwise, you'll never forget it.

Did it mean anything?

Caitlin wasn't sure, but her dad never failed to drop his duct tape mid-project to run to the hardware store for the right part, even when short on money or time.

She *could* go back to LA in the morning, but it didn't mean she *should*, and if she didn't stay in Bloomington now, she never *would*. But she'd definitely never forget it.

Caitlin tipped back her last bit of wine. "Okay, Mary, I'll stay. Now less talk, more drinking."

*   *   *

They passed out next to each other and slept until checkout. No makeup, suitcase in tow, Caitlin followed Mary three blocks south of campus to a yellow and white cottage on Park Street. Rough concrete steps led from the sidewalk to a wide front porch shaded by a giant oak tree, probably older than the seventy-year-old house.

"Well, shit," she said. "This is perfect."

After Mary left, Caitlin ordered Thai. When the last spring roll was gone, she powered up her laptop, opened her writing app, and began typing.

Total word count after ten minutes: 752.

Telling the story of her rape proved harder than she'd imagined. Every time she started, the images came. Troy Woods, the rough pieces of discarded limestone, the dried blood on her thighs.

She tried a new sentence, found her hands shaking. She knew the caffeine in Thai iced tea could launch her heart rate into the stratosphere, but why the flop sweat? And the pressure against her chest? She pushed back from the table. Like the sweat and chest pressure, she recognized the overwhelming sound of blood rushing to her ears as one more symptom of a panic attack, and she wasn't going to have one.

She dropped onto the couch, gasping for air. Still too much pressure. She rolled off, crawled past the coffee table, felt the cool planks of polished hardwood.

She sat back over her heels, closed her eyes, breathed in through her nose. She held the breath, then exhaled as slowly as possible, despite the rough pulses that came with uncontrollable shudders.

Again.

She rested her arms at her sides, inhaled, held a five count.

Again.

She'd yoga this away, drink this away. If necessary, get a hold of Scott Canton and smoke this away.

Again.

She finished an exhale, breathed normally, opened her eyes. Her pulse no longer banged in her temples.

"There's a reason people go to therapists," she said aloud. She laughed, answered herself in a parrot voice. "Bawwwwwk. Yeah, cause they talk to themselves."

The advice she'd given to others, requested or not, seemed so obvious: *If you're smart enough to think the word "denial," you're smart enough to get help.*

She shut her laptop, grabbed her cell phone, and scrolled through her unread emails, happy for the distraction. Most could wait, but one stuck out. The sender: Lakshmi Anjale.

Caitlin:

I was thinking about an assignment we had last month regarding context, how personal stories are used in journalism to humanize larger issues. Obviously, you're not the only woman to deal with sexual assault on a college campus. You know my agenda, but I don't think the two issues need to be separate. I'd like you to meet Doris Chapman, Angela's mother. Her perspective on the safety of women on college campuses might bring a modern touch to your own tragedy.

Lakshmi continued with contact info and available scheduling. The girl's plea read heavy-handed on the page, but she fought for her cause. Caitlin's favorite part? Lakshmi's inference that she hadn't yet left town.

Her finger hovered over the "Reply" button.

If she said yes, the whole point of her trip would change. She'd meet the mother, hear the details, feel the pull. She'd been able to quit smoking, abstain from sex, even ditch booze when necessary, but when it came to a story no one else could tell, Caitlin fiended like any other junkie.

She knew her own assault—beginning, middle, and end—but wasn't sure she could write that story, let alone find an audience. This Chapman thing, though.

Might be a book in it.

Might even help someone.

Couldn't hurt to look.

She shot a message to a neighbor about her plants and mailbox, then typed her reply to Lakshmi. Unlike trying to tap into her assault, the response flowed like a river.

CHAPTER

9

10:13 AM. Thirteen minutes and still no sign of her.

Maybe she'd picked a different route from what she'd run yesterday. Maybe she hated Mondays, took the day off from her workouts. Maybe she wouldn't come.

He undid his lightweight cycling helmet, scratched his scalp where the sweat beaded. Ten more minutes and he'd be in trouble. The mailman would pass and he'd be seen. Not his truck; he'd parked up a logging road, fifty feet around a corner, near the gate with the rusted-over padlock. Still, even the most disgruntled postal employee would notice a solitary cyclist standing over a mangled bike with blood streaked from his spandex shorts to his foot.

Five more minutes and he'd give up.

He exhaled, shuffled back and forth. He'd missed this feeling, the unbridled anticipation, the moments before the taking.

"Don't get excited," he muttered, clicking his teeth together. Like he could control the sensation.

His body sizzled like a downed power line. Every hair stood at attention, every nerve amped to receive. He rolled his shoulders back, slapped his hands together, stepped onto the country road's asphalt surface, watched the bend that led uphill toward his position.

A breeze rustled the trees, but he couldn't hear any animals, not even birds. Made sense—nature knew a predator by scent. Humans were the only animals in the forest who'd grown complacent.

Speaking of which.

He put the helmet back on, snapped the clasp, then reached into his jersey pocket and pulled out the phone.

She'd be two miles in. Nothing challenging for her athletic physique, but she'd strain against the incline.

He clicked his teeth again, if only to stop them from chattering with the rush of adrenaline. The crisp pop of enamel on enamel competed with the heartbeat pounding on his eardrums.

He let out a groan, bent over at his waist, and exhaled. The window was closing. *Where was she?*

"Jesus, are you okay?"

He turned around, saw Paige Lauffer in running gear approaching from behind him, coming downhill. She pulled an earbud out, tapped on the phone inside the strap around her bicep.

He laughed. "You came from behind me. I didn't hear a thing."

The young blonde walked closer, squinting against the sunshine. "Do you need help? You're bleeding."

"Sorry." He limped two steps in her direction, pointed to the remains of his bike. "I'm a little shaken. I wiped out pretty hard."

"Looks like. Did you break anything?"

He'd loved Paige Lauffer's voice since the first time he'd heard her speak, now over a month ago. Sweet and caring, like a TV mom.

"I think I'm okay." He held up his phone, moved closer. "Do you have a phone? Mine's broken."

She nodded, reached for the Velcro of her armband.

"See, Paige," he said, now inches away. "The stupid thing won't even turn on."

She raised her head. "How do you know my name?"

He moved toward her. She may have heard the snapping noise of the personal defense stun gun disguised as a mobile phone he'd gotten online for twenty bucks, or may have only reacted to his movement and tried to pull back. Either way, the gun's contacts met the sweaty, bare skin of her chest above her sports bra before she could put distance between them.

Fourteen million volts in five seconds against the one-hundred-and-thirty-pound woman meant lights out—and twenty dollars well spent.

10

LAKSHMI RUSHED AHEAD of Caitlin to the front door of the three-story brick house and rang the doorbell. "Thank you for doing this."

"Stop thanking me, Lakshmi. I haven't done anything."

Caitlin counted three gables, two cornices, some latticework. Different vibe from a Hollywood mansion, but the size and style of the Chapman home read Midwestern rich.

"Here she comes," Lakshmi said.

Caitlin saw Doris Chapman approach through the window next to the doorframe. Even through the glass, she exuded power and wealth. A slight frost dusted her otherwise jet-black, straight hair. The quality of her sky-blue cardigan seemed more Manhattan boutique than the nearby mall. But when the door opened, Caitlin saw a woman in her mid-fifties who didn't sleep.

"Lakshmi," she said, opening her arms.

Lakshmi dove into the hug. The embrace looked like the real deal.

Doris let go and held out her hand. "Thank you for coming, Miss Bergman."

Caitlin shook her hand. "You have a beautiful home, Mrs. Chapman."

Doris sighed. "A home is where your family lives. This is my hell."

* * *

What had once been a basement home theater now housed the Find Angela Chapman headquarters. Couch, love seat, end tables—all shoved against a wall. White poster board covered any available wall space, and theories, suspicions, and questions covered the sheets of sturdy material like a science fair project no one wanted to work on.

Caitlin began a slow walk around the room, noticed a section of photos and detailed entries under the heading "Time Line."

"It's very—"

"Manic?" Doris finished.

Caitlin turned back. "I was going to say 'thorough.' What do you do for a living, Mrs. Chapman?"

"Look for my daughter. I used to be a patent attorney for a pharmaceutical company in Indianapolis. I've had a hard time writing intellectual property arguments about erectile dysfunction since Angie disappeared. Seems so pointless."

Caitlin laughed loud enough for Lakshmi to turn in her direction.

Doris smiled. "Thank God, someone finally laughed at that."

"Did you do all of this?"

Doris nodded. "Me, Lakshmi, the Chapter."

"The Chapter?"

The woman crossed the room to a computer and opened a browser. The words *Chapman Chapter* appeared above a discussion board. She scrolled through hundreds of posts.

"Angie's friends, amateur private eyes, retired law enforcement, and straight-up lunatics."

"The well-intentioned masses," Caitlin said, her eyes on a board titled "Suspects." She tapped on the two photos of young men hung directly below. "These two?"

Doris nodded. "The last to see Angie. They lawyered up immediately."

Lakshmi joined in. "They're the ones, Caitlin—Kieran Michelson and David Amireau."

Caitlin focused on the photo to the left, Kieran Michelson. She couldn't tell if the brown-haired, lightly stubbled, blue-eyed man looked twenty-one or thirty-one. Either way, he could be a model, even in the lighting of the Bloomington Police Department. The other, David Amireau, had beady eyes, a hawk nose, and an abundance of dark moles on pasty white skin.

Lakshmi gestured around the room. "If you look at our time line—"

Caitlin turned away. "I'm not ready for all the facts."

Doris raised a hand. "Lakshmi, don't scare her." She arranged a pair of rolling chairs in front of the computer. "Please, Caitlin, sit with me."

They sat. Doris leaned in, gentle. "I understand you'll be staying in Bloomington to work on a project."

Caitlin shook her head. Her three small words had turned into a full-on project. Might as well go with it. "Sort of a personal story, maybe another book."

"About rape."

"Sure," Caitlin said, glancing at Lakshmi. "And other things."

"I was raped," Doris said, all business. "Twenty-five years ago in Chicago. Want to hear the story?"

Caitlin's first reaction—*God, no.* The second after, she felt shame blush her cheeks. Doris didn't give her time to answer.

"Books, movies, TV shows, I can't watch any of them if the *R*-word comes up. But I obsess about abduction. Perverts in vans, the *Law and Order* episodes about the heinous things done to kids, the women in your book."

"My book?"

"Fallen Angels. A reporter working with the ex-cop she once sent to jail for corruption uncovers an underground prostitution ring run by LAPD officers."

"Wow," Caitlin said. "Where were you when my publisher wanted a synopsis?"

Doris continued, "I gobble up stories of abduction. Do you know why?"

Caitlin nodded. "Because you want to believe Angela is still alive."

"Because I know Angie is still alive, Caitlin. I *know* it."

"What about your suspects?"

"Yes, I suppose I should say I *feel* Angie's still alive. The facts indicate that my daughter died of alcohol poisoning or a drug overdose. Both of those boys—her boyfriend and the other one—were into cocaine, pot, and God knows what else. Both Lakshmi and the police assume they panicked and disposed of Angie's body. It's the logical conclusion."

Doris rose to stand in front of a three-foot-high photo of Angela, the kind police would use at a press conference. "My husband thinks Angie's dead. You don't see his handwriting anywhere in this room, at least not on anything in the last year."

"Separated?" Caitlin said softly.

"Not legally. He keeps an apartment near his office, claims it's better on his commute. It's really so he can move on, and I won't let him do that here. Because someone, somewhere, knows what happened to Angie, and I'm going to spend every last second, dollar, and tear I have to find out."

She turned to Caitlin. "I don't need you to find my daughter, Caitlin. The media stopped caring a year ago, the police ran out of options, and I'm too close to stop my bias from blurring my vision. I only ask you to look with fresh eyes."

Lakshmi put a hand on Doris Chapman's shoulder. Doris covered the hand with her own and looked back to Caitlin.

"We're the only ones who still care, and she could be out there fighting all by herself. I won't stop fighting until she tells me to."

*   *   *

Lakshmi gripped the wheel more firmly than needed. "You won't use any of our notes?"

The drive from the south side of Indianapolis to Bloomington would take forty-five minutes, and they'd only gone five.

"Lakshmi, I have a certain way I approach a story."

The deep valley of the girl's furrowed brow relaxed into a flat plain. "Brilliant, how do you work?"

"Alone. I trust no one, not even my own suppositions. Let's face it: you've just shown me a wall covered in suspects. It's going to be hard for me to ignore those faces and not assume they're guilty."

"They *are* guilty."

"And that's my point. You telling me they're guilty doesn't make them guilty. I've got to concentrate on what can be proven with facts."

"But I know things no one else knows, Caitlin."

Caitlin checked the car's clock. Thirty-nine minutes left. Better let the girl talk.

"Fine. What are you dying to say?"

"Really?"

"Go for it."

Lakshmi took a deep breath. "Kieran Michelson was *not* Angela's boyfriend."

Of all the possible threads involved in Angela's disappearance, Lakshmi's chosen topic reminded Caitlin that the girl had only recently hit twenty-one. Time for a patient lead, casual and caring. "No?"

"Everyone calls him Angela's boyfriend—her mom, the cops, the press. They weren't boyfriend and girlfriend. They just got drunk or high together, hooked up every once in a while."

Caitlin paced her. "Why is that important to you?"

"Because it shows how little they knew her and how little they've tried to get to know her since."

"Her mom calls her Angie."

"Angela hated that. I love Doris, but she still sees her daughter as a thirteen-year-old. Kieran wasn't her boyfriend, just a—" She stopped.

Caitlin wanted more and knew the words to get there. "A fuck buddy?"

Lakshmi blushed, looked away. "Yes, that."

"Did Angela have a lot of fuck buddies?"

Lakshmi hesitated again.

Caitlin tried a guess. "It's college. Nothing too serious?"

Lakshmi nodded. "She wasn't a slut or anything. She was just trying out some things."

"What about you, Lakshmi? Do you have a boyfriend?"

Lakshmi matched a serious headshake to her words. "No, not me."

"What about a fuck buddy?"

Again, the emphatic head shake. "Nothing since Angela disappeared. No time."

"When will it be the right time?"

"For a fuck buddy?"

Caitlin really enjoyed Lakshmi's accent. She felt tempted to see how many times she could make the girl say *fuck buddy*, but moved on. "For you to think more about your relationships than Angela's."

Anger darkened the girl's face. "I'll move on when someone catches the monsters that took my best friend."

C H A P T E R

11

Near campus, Lakshmi stopped in front of the bars on Kirkwood Avenue. "Are you going to start working?"

"It's Monday afternoon. Don't you have any classes?"

"What do classes matter?"

"Lakshmi, I will definitely need your help in the future, but please go to class."

Caitlin got out and walked to a Tibetan restaurant crammed into an old two-story house. She settled at an outdoor table, then noticed a familiar face.

Scott Canton sat two tables away with a young man. His muscular companion wore an olive-green T-shirt tucked into neatly pressed khakis. An old poet and a young warrior, talking over green teas.

Caitlin walked over. "Guess who didn't leave town?"

They turned like she'd caught them conspiring, but Scott broke into a smile. "What a lovely surprise. Caitlin, my friend and I are finishing up a private conversation. Mind if I catch you in a second?"

She nodded, stepped back. "Please do—sorry to interrupt. I've got work to do anyway."

She returned to her laptop, powered up, created a folder named "Chapman," and started her notes.

> *Angela Chapman. Missing two years. Sophomore at the time. Would be a senior now.*

"Two years," she said, drew a thumb across her lip.

"I'm sorry?"

She looked up, saw the waitress, ready for a drink order.

"Beer," Caitlin said to the woman with the ponytail to her waist. "Do you have Singha?"

The waitress nodded, left a menu. Caitlin went back to work.

> *Two persons of interest. Ex-boyfriend and friend, both older, now graduated. Not enough evidence to bring to trial.*

She noticed a brown bottle of Thai beer that had materialized without interruption, took a sip.

> *Who was Angela Chapman? Big change in personality from high school. Party girl with Goth style.*

"Are you ready to order?"

The waitress again. Caitlin sent her on a mission for dumplings and a house salad, then started a new paragraph.

> *If Angela died, why hide the body? Drugs, evidence of sexual abuse? Could the suspects afford to pay someone to make things go away? Could they do it themselves, as in physically, logistically?*

She started another thought.

> *If Woods had killed me, could he have made me disappear?*

She stared at the screen, her finger over "Delete."

"Here you go." The waitress delivered a plate of warm dumplings.

Caitlin could smell the garlic, onion, and hot oil of the sha-shas. "What happened to the salad?"

"I dropped it off five minutes ago."

The waitress left. Caitlin tilted the screen, saw mixed greens. She hit "Save" and went to food enlightenment.

Scott Canton tapped on the end of her table. "She lied about the salad."

Caitlin smiled through a swallow and gestured to the empty chair. "So sorry I interrupted. Please, sit."

He did. "I heard your waitress say your salad had been there for five minutes, but she brought it with the dumplings."

"Smooth move on her part. I don't notice the outside world when I'm in my tunnel."

"Your tunnel." He scratched at his nose. "Funny you should say that. I was speaking with my young friend about one of my own tunnels when you approached."

"Your time in Vietnam?"

He nodded. "And coming home. He's about to finish his first year in college after two tours in Afghanistan. Life on campus can seem a bit surreal."

"I'm sure. Better or worse?"

Canton shrugged. "I believe the only word that fits is *different*. So how long do we have you in our alternate reality?"

Caitlin went for another dumpling, tried to get a few chews in before she spoke.

"For the duration." She pointed to her laptop. "I've started a project."

"Fantastic." He stood. "I have a class in fifteen minutes, so I must let you return to your tunnel. Of course, this means you're expected at my office hours on Wednesday. Think you can find it?"

"I can find anything." She reached for her wallet. "If I were to give you forty bucks—"

He waved the cash away. "I'll make the arrangements, but save your money. Your company will be payment enough." He left with a smile and a hat tip.

Caitlin felt herself relax. She'd have more of Canton's weed in two days. She looked back to her laptop, made a note, then reached for her phone. Detective Greenwood had said he'd help with anything. Time to test the man.

CHAPTER

12

THE WATCH COMMANDER asked Caitlin to wait in the otherwise empty lobby of the Bloomington Police Department. A sturdy woman, near retirement age, in a well-fitted suit appeared seconds later.

"Miss Bergman, would you come with me?"

Caitlin recognized her from the department's website. "Sure thing, Chief Renton."

"Call me Abigail. Detective Greenwood's busy at the moment, so I wanted to take the opportunity to introduce myself."

They passed into the chief's office. Caitlin took one of the chairs in front of the large desk. Rather than taking the desk chair, the chief sat next to her.

"Is this okay? I find the distance created by that desk to be far too impersonal."

"Your office." Caitlin angled her chair to face the woman's not-quite-welcoming smile. Could a smile be nervous?

"I hope you find the modern BPD to be much better than your last inter-action with the department. Twenty years ago, this was a small-town shop. Today I've got twelve detectives and one hundred officers, all trained by the state, with additional certifications by the FBI and specialties in search and rescue, SWAT—even anti-terrorism. Almost thirty percent of my staff is female."

"Impressive, Abigail. Sounds like the right woman's in charge."

Renton relaxed a notch. "Better days all around. How can we help you today?"

"Not sure if Greenwood told you, but I asked if I might get a copy of the files."

"Yes, of course. I have them here." She went to her desk, handed Caitlin a sealed document folder.

Caitlin glanced at the description, saw her own name. "Nice, even customized for me."

"I'm sorry?"

Caitlin looked again, saw the date: *1997*. She held her own sexual assault file. Caitlin felt the weight of the private history in her hands. Light. About what she expected.

"This will be very helpful, but I was asking for the Chapman files."

"Oh." The chief sat down behind her desk. So much for the personal feel. "I'm sure you're aware we can't release the files from an open investigation to anyone, let alone a member of the press—not without a court order."

"That said," Renton continued, "I understand Doris Chapman has asked you to look into Angela's disappearance, and I'd like to help keep that woman's spirits up."

"Chief, I told her I saw little chance I'd find anything your detectives haven't, but she sounded desperate."

Renton's concern seemed genuine. "After two years, we all are."

Her office phone rang. The conversation ended after a few words.

"They're ready for you, Miss Bergman. Let me show you the way."

Caitlin rose. "Thanks for your time. And thanks"—she tapped on her assault file—"for this."

Renton squinted. "I'm not proud of what's in that folder. I wasn't here at the time, so I can't pass judgment, but I can say *my* department works in a very different way."

Caitlin nodded. "Hopefully, we all work in different ways now."

*   *   *

Detective Greenwood had his own desk in a four-cubicle bullpen. Besides a framed picture of himself with his arms around an attractive brunette, his workspace looked clean and efficient: no kids, no headlines. Caitlin felt the urge to open drawers, see if the man's interior matched his exterior, but he popped in behind her.

"We're good to go, Miss Bergman."

She rose from the visitor's chair. "Where to?"

Once again, he looked good in a fitted dress shirt, navy-blue slacks, and smooth brown dress shoes. "Crime lab."

"Seriously? The 'crime lab'?"

"Sounds cooler than 'conference room,' right?"

Caitlin followed him into the uncool conference room. A squat woman in a BPD polo and slacks worked a laptop, her hair in a ponytail so tight it gave Caitlin a migraine. The enlarged image of her computer's desktop appeared on a wall-mounted television.

Greenwood did the honors. "Caitlin Bergman, this is Detective Jane Maverick."

"That's a great name."

Maverick looked up like she smelled dog poop. "Need me to spell it?"

Caitlin guessed Maverick was in her fifties. "Did someone get that wrong?"

Greenwood lightened the situation. "Jane's not a big fan of the press."

"Vultures," Maverick muttered, reaching for an empty coffee cup. "I'm getting a fresh one." Her walk out the door blew a day's worth of cigarettes Caitlin's way.

Greenwood motioned toward the chairs.

Caitlin sat. "You two partners?"

"There are eleven of us on rotation. We all work together."

"Chief Renton said you have twelve detectives."

Greenwood shook his head. "Should be back to twelve next month. We're down one, and the vetting process is extensive."

"You lost someone in the line of duty?"

"No, just everyday life."

Behind them, Maverick swore through a mouthful of fresh coffee. "Bullshit. Shepherd ate his gun. Nothing everyday about that."

Greenwood remained the master of tact. "True, but no big conspiracy there. The man was diagnosed with early-onset Alzheimer's, and he didn't feel like losing the fight."

"Pussy." Jane returned to her seat at the laptop. "I had a double mastectomy. You see me check out early?"

Changing the subject, Greenwood opened his hands. "We have some dirty laundry, Caitlin, but nothing too bad. You're welcome to all of it."

Maverick laughed, then fired a shot Caitlin's way. "Is that why you're here? You gonna do an expose on BPD like you did in LA? See how many 'fallen angels' we have? Maybe see how we small-town amateurs botched the Chapman disappearance?"

Caitlin met her head on. "Actually, I'm writing about sexual abuse on college campuses, contrasting my own experience twenty years ago with attacks on women today. I chose this town because I went to IU, and yes, part of my piece may include Angela's disappearance. But I'm not looking to

embarrass anyone or focus on the day-to-day policing in this department."
She leaned forward. "Why? *Did* you botch the Chapman disappearance?"

Jane whistled low through her teeth. "What a bitch. I just might like you,
Caitlin Bergman."

Caitlin smiled. "I had no doubt, but that's not an answer."

Greenwood jumped back in. "About Chapman, did Chief Renton explain
the guidelines?"

Caitlin started her cell phone's audio recorder. "No photos of anything
you show me. I can record, but audio only, and I'll supply you with a copy of
the recording before I leave today. That way, in the event I take anything
from this exchange to print, there's no chance of misquotation."

"Great," Greenwood said. "Jane's going to cover the basics. It's my case,
but it helps to hear someone else talk through it."

Caitlin slid her phone closer to Detective Maverick. "And you're familiar
with the time line, Detective?"

Maverick nodded. "From patrol to K9, there's not a BPD officer who
doesn't have the Chapman time line memorized."

CHAPTER

13

DETECTIVE MAVERICK HIT the lights and began. "Two years ago, Angela Chapman was wrapping up her sophomore year. Know where the Varsity Villas are?"

Caitlin nodded. "Big townhouses near the stadium, known for party-friendly types?"

Greenwood, seated at the laptop, pulled up a satellite map on the extended screen.

Maverick pointed out a group of apartments separated by a strip of forest. "Chapman lived in Cedar Creek, the smaller complex directly north. She woke up there the day in question, a Friday two weeks before the end of the spring semester. Her roommate, Devon Miller, saw Chapman grab a granola bar around ten AM on her way to the gym. All smiles, no worries."

Greenwood switched from the map to a spreadsheet. "We traced two text messages from the Student Recreational Sports Center between eleven and noon."

Names and places came back to Caitlin. "The big gym down by the train tracks?"

"Right," Maverick continued. "Chapman does a cardio class, hits the showers."

Caitlin tried to decipher the spreadsheet. "Who did she text?"

"First was a reply to a friend, Lakshmi Anjale, journalism student. Need me to spell it?"

Greenwood zoomed in on the first exchange. "Caitlin's familiar."

"Lucky you. As you can see, Anjale posts, *Happy hour?* Chapman replies with a thumbs-up emoji."

Greenwood switched to an image of a pale young man Caitlin recognized from the wall in Doris Chapman's basement, David Amireau, then pulled up the first line of a second text exchange comprised of only emojis.

Maverick pointed to a crescent moon, a beer bottle, a smiling monkey, and a white triangle. "Obviously these kids weren't majoring in English. We're interpreting this as 'Come out for a beer tonight, and we'll do cocaine.'"

Caitlin had to agree. "Did Chapman reply?"

Greenwood scrolled down to the text-only answer: *F-balls yes.*

Maverick moved on. "Anyway, a camera shows Chapman leaving the gym at twelve fifteen. She got to her class in the theater building at one. We assume she walked; it's less than a mile."

"What about emails or messaging?"

Greenwood sat back, arms folded. "We have her laptop and tablet. Both were synced to cloud services, so if she used the email from her phone—"

Caitlin knew the answer. "You'd at least have a record."

"Exactly," he said, "but no phone was found."

Again, Maverick pushed forward. "Anyway, Chapman finishes class at three and meets intramural basketball friends at Bear's Place around five. All girls, Chapman, Anjale, and two seniors—Dolores Garcia and Mary Pavlos."

Caitlin checked the notes she'd made so far. "Not her roommate, Devon Miller?"

"Miller drove up to Purdue to visit her boyfriend, leaving our ladies knocking back cocktails courtesy of the upperclassmen and Chapman's fake ID. Around eight, Anjale and Chapman go back to Anjale's place to smoke pot and watch a movie. At ten, Chapman tells Lakshmi she's going to hit the bars with Amireau and her regular hookup, Kieran Michelson. You have the image, Jerry?"

Greenwood brought up another face Caitlin knew from the Chapman basement of horror—the good-looking one.

Maverick gave a whistle. "There's our handsome devil. Quarter to eleven, he and Amireau knock on the door. Lakshmi tries to keep Chapman in, says they're too messed up, but Chapman heads out."

"Why didn't Lakshmi go along?"

Greenwood handled that one. "Claims she didn't feel like going out. Too high."

Maverick finished her coffee, tossed the cup in the trash can. "So the threesome heads to Kilroy's Sports Bar, the home of late-night mistakes, and get there by eleven fifteen."

"Were they walking?

"No, Amireau and Michelson were live-out frat boys. A pledge chauffeur dropped them off. A kid named Fodor, like the guide. They called him Frodo."

Caitlin laughed. "How could they not?"

"Frodo spent the night driving drunks around and is accounted for until five AM. Where was I?"

"Kilroy's Sports," Caitlin answered. "Why'd it take so long to get there?"

Greenwood returned the screen to the text message spreadsheet. "Amireau and Michelson said they stopped for a street dog. Also confirmed by a text Chapman got from Anjale. She asks *OK?* Chapman replies, *F'd up, Going to Sports, Gonna eat some SAUSAGE first.* As you can see, these two were fast exchanges, both within the minute. No reply from Anjale until eleven twenty-one. She came back with, *It's ur body.* Eleven twenty-three, Chapman replied with, *We'll talk 2mrw.*"

He opened a video clip. "They entered Kilroy's at eleven thirty-two. Second bouncer that day that didn't flag Angela's fake ID."

The brief video showed Angela Chapman and her two male escorts walking happily into a crowded bar.

Maverick leaned against the wall near the TV. "They blend in until one fifteen AM, when our girl goes all Sleeping Beauty near the beer garden and hits the ground. Security kicks them out."

Caitlin looked to Greenwood, but saw no action. "No video?"

He shrugged. "Witnesses said it happened too fast to get their phones out, and the security cameras pointed the other way. We've got them on the way out, though."

He clicked another clip taken from an external camera. Michelson argued with a bouncer, while Amireau dragged Angela Chapman out the door, her arm draped around his shoulder, her eyes barely open. She might have been sixty sheets to the wind, but she laughed the whole way out.

Maverick pushed off the wall and sat on the edge of the table near Caitlin. "Okay, she's drunk as hell, safe to assume coked up, and out with a guy she regularly had sex with and his coke-snorting friend. No car. What do they do?"

Caitlin checked her notes, didn't see an answer. "Where do the boys live?"

Greenwood pulled up the map they'd started with. "Less than quarter of a mile from Chapman's place. The Varsity Villas."

Caitlin put herself in the same location twenty years earlier. "They walk home—unless they went to another party?"

Maverick tapped on the table. "Right on both counts. They walked to the boys' place, hit the bathroom, then went two streets over to an apartment party. Other guests said they arrived around two."

"Why do people remember that?"

Maverick reached into her pocket, pulled out a pack of gum, and popped a piece in her mouth. "Amireau brought a bottle of vodka when supplies were low. Plus, there was a fistfight."

"Do tell."

Greenwood took over. "The party host, Genevieve, and our kids lined up for shots. Genevieve says Chapman's eyes barely focused, and her balance was shit. She cut Chapman off, had her brother usher the trio out, but Amireau wouldn't leave without his bottle of Stoli. Whole party ended up on the grass out front to watch big brother drill Amireau twice in the face."

"Where's Michelson in all of this?"

Maverick tilted her pack of gum in Caitlin's direction. Caitlin reached for a piece, then declined with a wave when she read the label: Nicorette. From cigarette to coffee to nicotine gum, Maverick stayed alert.

Greenwood continued. "According to Genevieve, trying to help Chapman back to her feet after she fell down the front stairs."

Maverick pocketed the pack and tagged back in. "Finally, Chapman makes her way to Amireau, stops any further fight, and she, Amireau, and Michelson stumble back to the boys' apartment. First thing in the door, Amireau yells at Michelson for not having his back. Next-door neighbor confirms yelling between two and two thirty. No distinct words, just obnoxious, like most other nights that year."

Caitlin could imagine the fun of having coked-up frat boys as neighbors. "What about Chapman?"

Maverick shoved off the edge of the table and stretched her neck. "They claim vomiting. Michelson says the whole time he hovered over her in the bathroom, she was talking about going home between hurls. That's when he hears a crash from the main room. Have you seen *Tommy Boy*?"

Caitlin smiled and opened her palms to the sky. "You mean the Chris Farley-David Spade movie I know better than the Constitution of the United States?"

Maverick nodded. "You really are growing on me, Bergman. You know that scene in the frat house when Chris is talking about the future—"

Caitlin didn't need a reminder. "And he passes out mid-sentence and shatters a glass coffee table?"

Maverick snapped her fingers. "Right. That's what they say happened to David Amireau. He takes a header into their coffee table. It's pressboard, not glass, but he flattens it. So Michelson leaves Chapman in the bathroom— which is right inside the front door—and goes to deal with Dave. After ten minutes, he goes back to the bathroom. Chapman's gone, and the front door is wide open. He assumes she walked home on her own, goes back to tuck Amireau in on the couch. Neither wake until eleven the next morning."

"Nothing more about Chapman?"

Greenwood shook his head. "Last person who claims to have seen her was Michelson, followed by Amireau. She didn't make it home, and no one thought it was weird until the next day."

"Michelson?"

"Guess again."

"Lakshmi?"

"Bingo." Greenwood went back to the keyboard. "She started texting around ten AM. They came every half hour."

He showed the first: *All right?*

The second: *Still alive?*

The third, around eleven forty-five: *Starting to freak out. Not sure if you're mad at me or still passed out. Text to let me know you're alive, and I'll leave you alone.*

Maverick walked in front of the video screen and faced Caitlin. "Then the phone calls start. Lakshmi tries Chapman's cell, her roommate, Amireau, Michelson, gets no answers, so she drives over to Chapman's at two. Angela's car is in the lot, but no answer at the door. She goes to the boys' place, knocks, Amireau answers. Lakshmi said he had a black eye and a swollen nose and wouldn't let her in. He told her Chapman walked home last night, slammed the door in Lakshmi's face. You've met the girl. Think she took no for an answer?"

"Not at all."

"Right, she walks around the place, peeps in the windows."

"Did Lakshmi see anything?"

Maverick placed both palms on the edge of the table and leaned in. "Only Michelson cleaning up the main room with several big trash bags and a shop vac. So she knocks on the window. Michelson looks up—she says shocked—then opens the back door. He gives her the same answer, *Chapman left last night.* Lakshmi dials the Bloomington PD and shits this sordid mess into our laps."

Maverick leaned back, resting her case.

Greenwood unhooked the laptop and turned on the lights. "Any questions, Caitlin?"

They'd given a polished presentation of a solid narrative. Had they tailored it for the big-city reporter? Probably. Was she going to take their word for it? Definitely not.

She stopped her voice recorder and gathered her things. "How late does happy hour go at Bear's Place?"

CHAPTER

14

LAKSHMI SETTLED INTO a corner booth beneath tin ads for Pabst Blue Ribbon and Old Style. "We used to sit here every Friday, our French Fry Club. Did you come to Bear's Place with your friends as well?"

"Oh yes." Caitlin saw a waitress en route. "Here's an opportunity to repeat those mistakes."

She ordered a bacon cheeseburger, steak fries, and a Hairy Bear—the local bastardization of a Long Island Iced Tea. Lakshmi substituted hot wings for the burger, but matched starch selections.

Once the server left, Lakshmi called Caitlin's bluff. "I want to hear everything about your meeting with Greenwood, but first, why suggest the place Angela and I ate together the night she disappeared?"

The waitress returned with two pint-sized plastic pitchers filled with light peach liquid.

Caitlin took a sip. Gin, rum, tequila, vodka, whiskey, and fruit juice all wanted her black-out drunk as soon as possible.

"If you'd said, 'anywhere but there,' I would have learned something."

"Which would be?"

"That you're so traumatized by Angela's disappearance, you can't retrace the steps."

Lakshmi sipped through her straw. "But I'm not. You're feeling me out, right? Trying to gauge whether you can trust my statement versus what you learned from the police?"

Caitlin nodded. Despite her age, Lakshmi didn't miss much.

Lakshmi shook her head. "It's hard to break down how you're manipulating me without being offended."

"I've lost several boyfriends this way."

"Okay, if a person is comfortable in a place that caused them trauma, they either have nothing to hide or wish to appear as though they have nothing to hide."

Caitlin smiled. "Right. Putting someone back in a location can take them back in time emotionally. Like Homecoming Week."

"Have you been back to the place you were attacked?"

Caitlin crunched an ice cube. "It hasn't exactly been on the way anywhere."

"Will you?"

She raised her cup. "Let's see if I survive the night."

Lakshmi tapped plastic to plastic. "Thank you for manipulating me into coming back to Bear's Place."

"Here's to drinking on a school night."

"Not for me. No classes on Tuesday or Friday. Best senior schedule ever. Do your worst."

"Fine. Say *fuck buddy*."

Lakshmi laughed. "Fuck buddy."

Her accent got thick on the back of her tongue each time she hit the *k* sound.

"Leeds?"

Lakshmi leaned forward, her out-of-practice smile bigger than ever. "Birmingham. You spent time in England?"

"That's a story for another night. First, tell me how a British-Indian girl from Birmingham ended up at Indiana University. Give me the billboard for the Lakshmi bio piece you have to write for the *Daily Student*."

Lakshmi scrunched her face, blushed. "Right. Lakshmi Anjale, graduate of the prestigious Hackley School, Westchester, New York, chooses Indiana University Kelley School of Business over Princeton to fulfill father's dream of degree in statistical analysis, only to find direction, passion, and mentorship as an Ernie Pyle Scholar in the School of Journalism."

Caitlin made eye contact with the waitress, pointed to their near-empty cups. "You only mentioned your father. Your mother doesn't dream of stats?"

Lakshmi shrugged. "She died in a car accident in Birmingham when I was ten. My father moved us to Westchester."

The waitress brought their second round and enough meat and potatoes for four. Once the ketchup was poured and the consumption began, Lakshmi returned the favor.

"Are your parents alive, Caitlin?"

Caitlin noticed a slight smile. How much research had the girl done?

"My father passed ten years ago. My mother wasn't in the picture. You and I have a lot in common."

"What a horrible thing to have in common."

"Better than crabs." Caitlin dipped a fry into the ketchup mound. "Tell me how you and Angela got together."

"We met second semester freshman year. I transferred dorms and Angela invited me to a party."

"Why change dorms?"

"My roommate was mental. Anyway, Angela and Devon, her roommate, lived down the hall. We all played softball together. Angela and I also joined intramural soccer. By the end of the semester, she was my best friend."

"Why didn't you live together after the dorm?"

Lakshmi looked down at her hands. "My father doesn't like the idea of me living with other girls. I live in a one-bedroom apartment two blocks from here."

"Which is where you and Angela went after Bear's Place that night?"

"The other girls had plans, so Angela and I went to my place to watch a film."

"On a Friday night?"

"Once a month we had girl's night at mine. Plus, that close to finals I had a pile of homework and didn't want to be a zombie the next day. My classes were harder than Angela's."

"What was her major?"

"Hospitality. She loves helping people."

Caitlin noticed the use of present tense. How long would the cord between Lakshmi's optimism and sanity stretch before it snapped?

"It sounds like she helped you find a place in the world."

Lakshmi gave a slight nod, solemn. "And now she's gone."

Caitlin raised her mug. "Here's to Angela Chapman."

Lakshmi raised her own. "To *finding* Angela Chapman."

"To finding Angela Chapman," Caitlin corrected. "And helping her the way she helped everyone else."

Caitlin moved the conversation toward lighter fare, eventually confessing her guilty pleasures—dark rums, mint ice cream, and tall men with scruff. Lakshmi admitted spending more time than she should with reruns of *Friends*, intramural soccer, and red wine. Caitlin didn't pry into what she'd left out—sex, drugs, and rock and roll. Still, Lakshmi's version of Angela's last night matched up with the BPD's account enough to earn Caitlin's trust.

Her alcoholic buzz now a throb, Caitlin called the night. "I'll pick you up tomorrow at nine thirty, and we'll get started."

*   *   *

Caitlin walked along Third Street. Arc lamps lit the sidewalk every two hundred feet, but otherwise the path fell under the shadows of tall oaks. Two blocks from her turn south, she noticed a figure hunched over a low rock wall. Her gut told her the person was male and bigger than her. She could cross to the other sidewalk or barrel through.

She kept going. Fifty feet away, she saw that it was actually two people, waiting. Tension squeezed her shoulders, adrenaline kicked in. At twenty-five feet, she heard a female voice.

"Help, I'm freaking dying."

Caitlin left her tension behind and ran toward the sound.

A campus police officer in a blue top and bike shorts turned a flashlight her way.

"Whoa there, ma'am. You okay?"

"I'm fine," Caitlin said. "Is she?"

The girl in question lay on a berm behind the rock wall, one arm over her face.

The cop's light hovered over a pool of vomit. "Someone had a few too many shots. What'd you call it, miss?"

The drunk girl dropped her arm with the exaggerated motion of a six-year-old's tantrum.

"Five for five. I'm gonna die."

The officer turned back with a smirk. "Five shots in five minutes—that'll do it."

Caitlin noticed a bicycle against the wall.

"Where are her friends?"

"My guess is they saw me coming and hid."

Caitlin looked at the bike, then the officer, then the girl. Nothing about the mountain bike screamed police department. His uniform looked like something anyone could buy at a costume store. The girl looked incapacitated.

"Where are *your* friends, Officer?"

"Ma'am?"

"Don't you have a partner?"

He nodded. "Checking the block for her friends, ma'am."

A third ma'am. Caitlin forced a smile. "It doesn't look like she'll fit on your bike."

"No ma'am, but help is on the way. Please continue on to your destination."

Caitlin crossed her arms. "I'll wait right here until this *help* arrives."

She had the officer's attention. His smirk, long gone.

"Did I do something to you, ma'am?"

"You could lay off that *ma'am* shit, for starters."

"Well, I don't know your name."

"All you need to know is that I'm going to sit here until I see either your partner return or someone in an official police vehicle escort this woman somewhere safe."

"Why would you do that?"

Caitlin clenched her fingers into fists. "Angela Chapman."

The officer looked like he might say something, but stopped.

A breathy voice spoke from behind Caitlin. "What about her?"

She turned, saw a female officer on a bike come to a stop. Fifty feet further down the street, a white Dodge Charger with low profile lights and iridescent decals approached, its flashing lights highlighting the word "POLICE."

Caitlin turned back to the original officer. "Nothing. I'm sorry. Have a good night."

The male officer's smile returned. "You too, *madam*."

Madam? Caitlin would have laughed, but she remembered the drunk girl. "What's your name?"

The girl opened her eyes. "Laura Baker."

"You shouldn't be out here alone, Laura Baker. Feel better."

"I'm gonna die," she replied in a wail.

Caitlin shook her head. "Not tonight."

She walked past the officer's parked bike, noticed saddlebags stenciled with iridescent police decals, and wondered how she'd missed them the first time. Her heart pounded. No matter how hard she tried to control her breathing, her punk-rock heartbeat didn't turn to easy listening until she hit the sheets of Mary's bed.

15

Los Angeles

MIKE ROMAN CIRCLED the heavy bag, repeating a three-punch combination: two jabs with the left, one cross with the right, then a side step. His punches landed in time with the third song of his workout mix—"You Know You're Right" by Nirvana. The less-than-current song played through the tiny speakers of his phone. At six AM, no need to piss off the neighbors.

He stepped up his game, changed to a five-punch combo. "Bone Machine" by the Pixies came on. Mike added a little bounce to his hips.

The music cut out and his phone rang.

He grabbed a towel, wiped his forehead, and used his teeth to pull the Velcro of his wrist strap.

He swiped the phone screen. "You've got five seconds to explain how you got Caitlin Bergman's phone, and if you know what's good for you, you'll spend that time running from me."

The voice on the other end either cleared its throat or laughed. In either case, he recognized its hungover timbre. "Down, boy. It is I, mostly."

Two years ago a call from Caitlin Bergman would have sent Mike on the first train out of town. Now he answered on the first ring, every time.

"Just getting in? You do know it's six in the morning?"

"Not here," Caitlin said. "I'm three hours ahead."

"Still surprised." Mike pulled his other glove off and leaned against the counter.

Another hungover laugh came from Caitlin's end of the line. "You free to make a little money, same rates as last time?"

Mike smiled and looked around for a pen. "Who do you need killed?"

16

The hybrid's clock read 9:26 am when Caitlin parked outside Lakshmi's apartment building, a single-story, six-unit, red-brick building. She ended her call with Mike Roman, then texted him the business address she'd found for Kieran Michelson, not five miles from her own place in Los Angeles. Like herself, Kieran had moved to Hollywood the week after he left IU. Unlike Caitlin, the now twenty-four-year-old had his own business. His relocation must have involved a lot less crying.

Lakshmi came outside, locked the door to her apartment, and waved.

Caitlin lowered the window. "Was I the only one drinking last night?"

The young woman bounced into the passenger seat. "I pounded a coconut water. Want one? I have more inside."

Caitlin pulled into traffic. "No, I earned this feeling. Remind me how to get to Cedar Creek."

"Angela's apartment? Why?"

"You and I are going to recreate the day she disappeared."

Lakshmi smiled. "Turn north on Jordan."

Caitlin drove slowly through the campus, stopping more than once for students crossing the street without bothering to look, as if being on campus made them untouchable.

"Do you know the time line, Lakshmi?"

"Of course. Angela woke up that morning and talked to her roommate, but Devon doesn't live there anymore."

Caitlin turned north past the library. "I know. I just want to get a feel for the place. We won't bother the residents."

"There aren't any. After the investigation, Doris took over the lease."

Doris Chapman rented her missing daughter's apartment to keep it intact, even two years later? Brilliant.

Lakshmi pulled a set of keys out of her backpack. "We can go in anytime."

*   *   *

The Cedar Creek apartment complex consisted of six gray two-story buildings divided into clumps of four units, two down, two up—sixteen per building.

Lakshmi stepped onto a wooden-planked walkway. Caitlin followed, noticing several black-domed security cameras.

"Those work?"

"They added them after."

Caitlin pointed toward another complex past the walkway's end, maybe two hundred feet of thin forest away. "Is that the Villas?"

"Yes. There's a path through the woods on the other side of the complex."

Lakshmi opened Chapman's door and stepped inside. Caitlin followed. She saw a room to the left, maybe fifteen by twenty, with a secondhand couch and TV setup, a cocktail table with two chairs, and a sliding door to a wooden deck. On the other side of the wall, a kitchen.

"It still smells like her," Lakshmi said.

Caitlin hoped the girl's memory, rather than actual senses, had spoken. The place smelled like rotten carpet and stale beer.

She walked the other way, saw a narrow half bath on one side of the hall, a longer full bath on the other, then two doors at the end, both closed. Caitlin opened the one on the right, found an empty room, no furniture. Devon's room.

Lakshmi opened the door on the left and walked in. The pressure change rattled the posters on the wall. The whole room seemed ready to yell, "Welcome home." Angela's desk, an imitation-beech particle-board concoction, still looked new. Caitlin studied a plastic frame that held five photos: Angela and a soccer team—Lakshmi one of four in the shot. Angela and a basketball team—Lakshmi one of five in the shot. Angela next to Lakshmi at a party, a cigarette in one hand, a beer in the other. Angela in a cap and gown with her parents, high school–graduation style. Angela seated in a tattoo parlor chair, showing off the new hummingbird tattoo on her neck.

"I come here sometimes," Lakshmi said, quiet, like someone in a funeral home. "To be with her, to see if there's anything I missed."

Caitlin looked at the bed in the corner, a queen-sized mattress on a simple frame, the sheets a neutral cool gray. A two-year-old poster of the US Women's National Soccer Team hung on the wall above.

Lakshmi continued, "I don't know what I expect to find."

Caitlin opened the closet, saw two rows of hanging clothes, shoes on the floor, a three-drawer dresser on the far right, a laundry basket on top. She opened the top drawer, found underwear, nothing too frilly.

The top row of the hanging clothes were T-shirts and jerseys. The bottom row, skirts, jeans, and dresses. Two rows for two different Angelas.

"Not very girly," Caitlin said.

"She could be when she wanted to be."

Caitlin's image of Angela started to flesh out. There was the Angela the world expected her to be and the Angela she was trying out.

"I made a spreadsheet," Lakshmi said. "All of her clothes—the ones from the closet, anything I found in pictures in the room, on social media."

"Why?"

"In case she came back or someone came back for her, grabbed more clothes than what she was wearing that night."

"Anything missing?"

Lakshmi shook her head.

Caitlin saw the weight of the guilt Lakshmi carried on her shoulders, but telling the girl to let go of her dead best friend in the dead best friend's apartment wouldn't help anything.

"What time is it?"

Lakshmi checked her phone. "Ten thirty-two."

Caitlin turned for the door. "Let's hit the gym."

* * *

Caitlin followed Lakshmi up the thirty steps into the Student Recreational Sports Center. Even the entrance was a workout. The building not only housed a full-size gym every bit as modern as a Hollywood health club, but also basketball and volleyball courts and Pilates, spin, and yoga rooms. After twenty minutes of dodging young, sweaty bodies, Caitlin had seen enough.

A fifty-dollar parking ticket waited under the windshield wiper of her rental.

"Might as well leave it here. Which way would Angela have walked?"

Lakshmi pointed south. A concrete path led to the railroad tracks.

"Perfect," Caitlin said. "Takes us right by Lennie's at lunchtime."

* * *

Caitlin dipped her stromboli in marinara and got a nice chunk of Italian sausage and cheese. She was enjoying the experience much more than her previous visit there with Greenwood. "So Angela liked acting?"

Lakshmi munched on a roasted carrot. "She liked the people we met in the Theater Department. She didn't find a lot of creativity in her other courses."

"Were you in her class?"

"No, I took the first level my freshman year. I thought it might help if I ended up in broadcasting. Each class started with a massage circle. Who doesn't want that? Plus, great professor. One of those brooding grad students, you know?"

"Did Angela get the broody professor?"

"Totally. Chad Branford. So cool."

"Is that where she met Kieran and David?"

Their names transformed the relaxed young woman into a defensive tiger. "No, she met them where you meet all the d-bags—the gym. They were playing on the girl's basketball court."

"There's a girl's court? Like segregation?"

"Sort of. There's a limited number of courts, so they reserve one as a priority slot for women. Anyway, we showed up ready to play, and they didn't want to leave, so Angela challenged them to two on two—whoever won got the court."

Caitlin could see who won in the smile growing behind Lakshmi's frown. "A blowout?"

"Kieran had a foot on both of us but couldn't handle the ball. Dave's only contribution was smack talk. We destroyed them, so they upped the bet. Whoever lost had to buy pizza and wings. We probably gained five pounds that night."

"You all hung out?"

Lakshmi took a deep breath. "They were fun."

"Does it hurt to say that?"

She nodded. "They didn't seem like monsters."

"It doesn't sound like they are."

Lakshmi started to respond, but Caitlin didn't give her the opening. "Look at this from my perspective. A college girl goes out with two male friends. From all reports, she gets drunk—way too drunk—and possibly high on cocaine, but maybe something else, that makes her lose control of her body. Her friends don't notice, which means they're either just as drunk or riding the same high."

"They could have—"

Caitlin held up her hand. "So they all go back to the apartment to pass out. The natural assumption is something awful happened. How awful do you think these guys made it?"

"What do you mean?"

"These were her friends—your friends, even. Isn't the likely conclusion something accidental? Alcohol poisoning, an overdose, a slip and fall?"

"Yes, of course, but that's not the crime."

"I know," Caitlin continued. "The crime is covering up what happened to her."

"Which makes them monsters."

"Well, assholes, sure. Scared college kids, high out of their minds, afraid of losing everything because maybe they bought the drugs—maybe even thought they'd be culpable for her death. Probably could be, but there's plenty of evidence that Angela participated willingly. To me they sound like scared kids who made the wrong choice."

Lakshmi pulled her posture out of beaten-dog pose. "I see your point."

"I'm not saying they aren't guilty, Lakshmi, but the best journalists in the world can interview drug smugglers, dictators, and serial killers, and leave themselves out of the story."

"Could you sit down with the man who raped you and stay neutral?"

Caitlin thought about seeing Troy Woods again. Professional as she was, she couldn't say. Last she checked, he was confined in the Miami Correctional Facility in Kokomo, north of Indianapolis—two hours away.

"Fair point," she said. "But that crime's been solved. Let's concentrate on yours."

* * *

Heading west down a tree-lined concrete path, the first beads of sweat appeared on Caitlin's brow. A beautiful Indiana afternoon in the seventies still carried more humidity than the rainy season in Los Angeles.

"So, this Professor Branford?"

"Chad," Lakshmi answered.

"Right, Chad Branford. He was a grad student at the time. Any chance he's still in the program?"

They crossed the street with a handful of students on foot and bicycles, headed toward the theater complex.

"Are you kidding?" Lakshmi sped up. "I think that was him."

Caitlin jogged to catch up. Lakshmi cornered a cyclist near the bike racks. He took off his helmet and smiled.

Chad Branford had great teeth, straight and white, just like the commercials. Under thirty, clean-shaven, short brown hair, maybe six foot, with a lean physique, he looked like he cycled other places than campus. Hardly what Caitlin would have called dark and brooding. He even had blue eyes.

Lakshmi motioned her over. "Caitlin, this is Chad Branford."

He strapped his helmet to his backpack, held out his hand. "Hi."

Caitlin shook his hand. "And the devil appears. I asked Lakshmi if we might see you today, and you rode right past us."

He laughed. "Finally, someone asks me to play the devil."

Lakshmi laughed harder than the weight of the witticism. Caitlin had a feeling most of his students would.

"Why would you ladies be talking about me?"

Lakshmi put her arm around him. "She wanted to know who the best professor I've had at IU was."

"And when you couldn't find that prof, you talked about me?"

Lakshmi, a little color to her cheeks, laughed again. "Didn't I tell you, Caitlin? He's the coolest."

Caitlin addressed him. "Lakshmi's giving me the campus tour today. I'm working with her as part of a mentorship."

"So, not an acting student?"

"There's some crossover. Where are you headed?"

"Acting 101." He checked his phone. "Shoot, I'm running late, but it was so nice to bump into you." He gave Lakshmi a little hug. "Don't be a stranger."

They watched him jog up the steps into the building.

"Fun guy," Caitlin said. "Great teeth."

"Plus he owns Pizza Monster."

"Pizza what?"

Lakshmi didn't get to answer. A window above them slid open, and Branford popped his head out. "Any chance you ladies want to audit my class?"

Lakshmi turned to Caitlin. "Do we have time?"

Caitlin's phone rang. "Hold that thought."

The caller ID read Bloomington Police.

She answered. "This is Caitlin Bergman."

"It's Maverick. You busy?"

"What's up, Detective?"

"Campus PD's got a student who claims she was sexually assaulted. Your name came up."

Caitlin apologized to Lakshmi and Branford. "Change of plans."

17

CAITLIN SAT BACK in the hardwood chair. "Is this where you break them, Jane?"

Maverick took the opposite seat. "That's right, Bergman. Now talk."

"Oh no, you have to trap me with seemingly meaningless questions, let my lies trip me up. You'd better start."

Maverick set a folder on the table. "A female student under the legal drinking age claims a male campus police officer sexually assaulted her last night."

Caitlin recalled the name. "Laura Baker?"

"That's the girl."

"Is she okay?"

"Nothing a stomach pump and a Pedialyte couldn't improve."

"There's no evidence of assault?"

Maverick answered by placing a recorder on the table and hitting "Start."

Caitlin leaned toward the gear. "You are listening to the one and only Caitlin Bergman."

Maverick's lips might have curled a millimeter. "Miss Bergman, could you describe what you saw take place on Third Street last night?"

Caitlin recounted her walk while Maverick jotted notes on a pad.

"One last question. How long would you say it was from when you started talking to Miss Baker and the male officer to when the female officer arrived?"

"One, maybe two, minutes tops."

"Great." She stopped the recorder. "Greenwood wants to know if you want to get lunch."

"Just ate."

Maverick stood, opened the door. "You should watch him eat. It's walking distance."

Caitlin took the cue and followed her out.

*   *   *

She found Greenwood on a park bench. "So the bike cops wear body cameras?"

He combined a nod with a swallow of grocery-store salad.

"Why bother me if you knew Laura Baker lied?"

"Video footage is fine, but an eyewitness is even better. Plus—"

She took over. "Plus, you wanted to see if I'm biased against law enforcement in the town where I was raped. I'm a professional, Greenwood."

"So are we." He laughed. "And you looked pretty drunk."

Caitlin shook her head. "Why'd she make the accusation?"

"'Cause of a scholarship with a morality clause. She'll lose the money if she's caught drinking underage. Some kind of church thing."

Caitlin thought about the desperation of a selfish choice, wondered how desperate the last people to see Chapman had felt.

Greenwood stood, dumped his food in a trash can, and walked toward an unmarked cruiser. "Meet anyone in the sheriff's department yet?"

"Not yet. Something happen?"

"Missing person, female, twenty-four years old." He opened the car door and pointed to the passenger seat. "Interested in a ride along?"

Caitlin got in. Greenwood pulled out and turned right on Tenth Street. "Find anything at Chapman's apartment?"

"You have someone following me, Jerry?"

"Why? Did you think someone was following you?"

"No," Caitlin said, sure no one had. "The cameras at Angela's?"

"That door opens, I get a notice on my phone."

Caitlin thought about Lakshmi's keys and what the BPD thought about her visits.

"Where are we headed?"

"Little town outside of Bloomington called Unionville. Local woman, Paige Lauffer, part-time waitress in Bloomington, part-time student at IU, didn't show up to work yesterday."

"And they called you why?"

He waited for traffic. "Interdepartmental task force. Campus, city, county, state, federal. One from each office, plus the surrounding agencies. Woman disappears, we all get a call."

Caitlin watched the scenery change from strip malls and campus buildings to single-family homes surrounded by trees. The houses looked safe and sturdy in the sunshine, but would a scream in the night reach a neighbor's ears? Would the welcome mats welcome a woman covered in her own blood?

Greenwood brought her back to the moment. "Got another ten miles. Have any other Chapman questions?"

"You know I do." She reached for her phone and started the voice recorder. "How many missing person cases are currently open in Monroe County?"

"Including Paige and Chapman, there are four. Two females and two males."

Like the previous day's meeting in the station, Greenwood's answers came quick and professional. He had a media-ready polish Caitlin hadn't expected to find in a small town.

"What about the surrounding counties?"

"Similar numbers, mix of teen runaways and probable battery victims who don't want their exes to find them."

"Any of them resemble Angela Chapman?"

"This Lauffer girl is five years older than Chapman was when she disappeared. That's all I know so far."

Caitlin guessed there weren't more than one hundred and fifty thousand people in the whole county. "What about murders? How many per year?"

Greenwood glanced over, raised an eyebrow. "You kidding? Maybe two, sometimes none at all."

Five minutes into the countryside, Caitlin saw more trees than buildings, more churches than subdivisions. They passed a farm where two ponies grazed in a bright green field.

"Time for the good stuff, Greenwood. What do you believe happened to Angela Chapman?"

He kept his eyes on the road. "Let's go off the record."

She stopped the recorder. "Is she dead or alive?"

He exhaled. "My guess is she died in the Varsity Villas."

"Murder?"

"Can't think of a motive. I think she overdosed or hit her head on the coffee table—the one Amireau supposedly went through."

"And what? The frat boys disposed of her body? Could they do that?"

"Gets tricky there. Amireau's good for a laugh, but definitely Michelson's toadie."

"And Michelson?"

"Top-of-his-class smart, despite the late nights and bar fights. Didn't waste any time before he lawyered up, and didn't have any financial blocks to the best representation in Indiana."

Caitlin didn't remember any mentions of Kieran Michelson's parents in the articles she'd read. "Rich family?"

"Nope, and far as I could tell, Michelson found his own lawyer."

Greenwood veered right at a fork in the road. Faded letters across a fifty-foot water tower read *New Unionville.*

"Any chance he called this lawyer before Angela was declared missing?"

"Neither his nor Amireau's records show them contacting anyone, but these guys were known for having coke and pot. We never proved it, but I think they were dealing. They could have had prepaid burner phones we never found. As far as hiding a body"—he gestured to the thick woods lining the road—"we've searched forests, fields, quarries, and streams, came back with nothing but ticks and chafing." He slowed, put on a turn signal. "I am one hundred percent sure those frat boys know what happened to Chapman, and I can't prove a damned thing."

He pulled off the road. "Here we are."

Three sheriff's department cruisers were parked on the long gravel drive-way leading to the single-story, red-brick-and-vinyl-siding home. The only unofficial vehicle present, a lime-green Ford Focus.

"If you're sure Michelson and Amireau are the guys, what are we doing here?"

He opened his door. "Could be wrong."

18

T HE BLOND DOLL in nineties plaid had a camera strapped around her neck and a red and silver wheelchair beneath her. According to the box, Becky was not only the school photographer, but Barbie's friend. Though there were over fifty similar containers around the room, Becky appeared to be the only non-Barbie. The rest housed the Mattel namesake herself in various frozen moments of dazzling but impossible anatomy and wardrobe.

Caitlin tapped the girl's plastic prison. "You're better than all these bimbos, Becky."

Paige Lauffer not only collected Barbies, she sold them online. Taped to the wall over a small desk, Caitlin found a spreadsheet with multiple listings.

1920s Flapper—The Great Eras Collection—1993, new in box, $22.00—eBay since 3/22.
1999 Erica Kane—Champagne Lace Wedding—never removed from box—1999—$22.00. Craigslist 3/25.

A bright pink section of wall above the printout, maybe a foot and a half wide by eight inches tall, stood out from the rest of the faded paint. A single drywall screw remained in the center.

Caitlin moved back to the living room and its plug-in air freshener's impression of lavender.

A gray-haired man in a sheriff's department uniform, brown top and tie, traditional five-point star, and gray slacks, held a wide-brimmed hat. "See anything we haven't?"

"Just dolls," Caitlin said. "Maybe something missing from the wall in the bedroom. Besides that, I wouldn't know what to look for, Deputy."

"Actually, it's Sheriff, Miss Bergman." He held out his hand. "I'm Douglas Hopewell, and I doubt your eyes miss anything."

She gave as firm a shake as she could, then gestured toward Greenwood, two county detectives, and the crime scene investigator working the living room. "I'm not in the way here?"

Hopewell shrugged. "New York says you're all right with him, you're all right with me."

"'New York,' huh?"

"Didn't know? Jerry might be a local, but he spent plenty of time away. I've got four detectives total in my department, all great people, but there's nothing like experience. He's handled more violent crime out East than I have in my whole career. Since his wife passed, he's done nothing but work his ass off."

The first time Caitlin had met Greenwood, he'd mentioned his mental state two years back had nothing to do with Chapman. Now she knew why.

Hopewell moved toward the door. "This air freshener is killing me."

Outside, the sheriff leaned against a cinder block wall. "Sweetheart of a day, and you can quote me on that."

Homespun, but apt. Close to five PM and still beautiful.

Caitlin joined him in repose. "You called this a crime scene, Sheriff. Does that mean something they've found suggests Paige Lauffer didn't head up to Indy for a Barbie convention?"

Hopewell put his hat on. "From what we know so far, that would be out of character. She wasn't in a relationship, worked five nights a week at a bar near campus, and volunteered at the nursing home where her mom lives. She didn't show up for work last night, didn't stop by the home this morning. They're the ones who called."

"Her mother?"

"No, her mother's been comatose for two years. The volunteer coordinator reached out. Of course, we'll check her phone, email, and what have you."

Caitlin saw a storm's worth of leaves on the green Ford's windshield. "That hers?"

He nodded. "Last rain was Friday. Hasn't moved since. She's an avid runner, 10K most mornings."

Caitlin thought about the road Greenwood brought them up—plenty of curves, not much shoulder. "So there's a good chance she got clipped by a car."

Hopewell nodded. "Not much a human body can do against a drunk driver. We've started a sweep of the surrounding roads and will have a press conference ASAP. People around here don't ignore announcements about missing girls." He didn't have to say "anymore," or "since the incident," or "because of Chapman." The case of the missing student simmered under the county's collective surface. "So," Caitlin said, well aware of a change in the sheriff's posture, "no chance of a connection to Angela Chapman?"

"God, I hope not."

A large black SUV pulled onto the driveway.

Hopewell straightened his perfectly aligned hat. "Guess we'll see what the feds say."

* * *

Both Greenwood and Hopewell introduced Caitlin to the two male agents, but neither the lanky redhead from the Bloomington resident agency nor the tall superior with the military bearing from the Indianapolis office would comment.

After five minutes in a huddle with his peers, Greenwood moved toward the car. "Ready?"

Caitlin got in, buckled up. "I couldn't hear much from the sidelines. What's the next step?"

"Hopewell's people are setting up a press conference to get the public involved. They'll also get a warrant for Lauffer's cell."

"Can't the FBI access that info, Patriot Act and all?"

Greenwood pulled out and passed a slow-moving pickup truck. "They saw this as a local issue, if it's an issue at all."

"Right," Caitlin said. "A local nonissue that brought out the police, the sheriff, and the FBI."

Greenwood's smirk said she was on to something, but his words moved on in business mode. "Having seen the house, I think Hopewell's theory is the strongest. Woman loved to run, crack-of-dawn type. A tired trucker on a twisty road could have seen her too late. Personally, I'm hoping she started some ecstasy-based spiritual bender and will show up tomorrow with a butterfly tattoo and a newfound love of life."

Caitlin laughed. "You have a butterfly tattoo somewhere, Greenwood?"

He gave her a wink, the good kind, like in the movies. "Boy has to keep a couple of secrets."

Caitlin started to say something about how sexy boys who kept their mouths shut were, but stopped when the image of a butterfly tattoo on Paige Lauffer's ankle morphed into a hummingbird on Angela Chapman's neck.

"What if Paige doesn't wander in from the wild with flowers in her hair?"

Greenwood's eyes went back to the road. "Her phone's GPS data might show where she is. Meantime, our patrols will ask other runners and cyclists if they remember seeing her."

He stopped for a red light. No cars waited at the intersection.

"You can go," Caitlin said. "I won't tell."

He smiled. "Trying to corrupt me, Bergman?"

"We didn't have many Boy Scouts in Los Angeles. I always wanted to see what happened when the neckerchief came off."

His smile crept wider. "Might have to dig up an outfit."

For a second, Caitlin couldn't think of anything but unbuttoning Greenwood's shirt. "Maybe you should." The green light put her back to work. "So, no walking through cornfields tonight?"

"Not yet. Once we get geo tag info, we'll move into the volunteer army phase."

"Is that how it was with Chapman?"

He shook his head. "Poor kid. Imagine a whole campus ready to help."

"That's a bad thing?"

"Forty thousand Lakshmis armchair-quarterbacking our every move with their extensive *Law and Order* knowledge? They could have trampled Chapman with good intentions."

"How do you do it better?"

"Reserves, cadets, call in other counties and ROTC—people who are used to command structure. Average citizens will rally around a cause for three days. That's how much work the everyday employee can justify taking off. After that, the volunteer army dwindles to the family of the missing, and they're fighting about whose fault it is."

Caitlin recognized the buildings on the outside of campus. She pulled out her phone, sent a text message: *Get your people together. Press conference tonight.* "What about Doris Chapman's army of amateur sleuths—the Chapman Chapter?"

"Can't blame the woman for wanting to be involved, but helpful hands often help no one, and sometimes they drag down others."

He stopped at a light near the arboretum. "Anyway, yesterday's underage drunk and today's missing woman might be all the crime Bloomington sees for a year."

"That would be nice," Caitlin said, but thought about the word *sees*. What crimes was Bloomington not seeing?

She studied Greenwood's face, still unsure of his motivation. The man was likeable, good-looking, and obviously gave more of a damn about his job than most people she knew. But he'd been selling her something since the first time they'd met. Was it *Nothing to see here*, or *Look closer*? And if it was *Look closer*, why couldn't he do it himself?

*   *   *

Caitlin and Mary found a spot on the back wall of the conference room. Despite the short notice, the press conference's available seats had been filled by broadcast outlets from Indianapolis, print reporters from surrounding counties, and a single student-journalist: Lakshmi Anjale.

The sheriff's department displayed a poster-sized image of Paige Lauffer taken at the bar where she worked. Sheriff Hopewell started strong in front of a wall of law enforcement—several deputies, Jerry Greenwood, two uniformed BPD officers, and two state troopers. The FBI duo stood near the far wall, removed from the company front of reassurance. Hopewell gave the essentials, and then a female deputy took over. When the standard questions from the pros fizzled, Caitlin sent Lakshmi a text: *Now*.

The girl's hand shot up. "Deputy, do you believe Paige Lauffer's disappearance is related to Angela Chapman's in any way?"

No surprise from the deputy. "Not at this time."

Lakshmi pushed. "I recognize two FBI agents in the room—Agent Mark Christiansen from the Bloomington resident agency—and Special Agent Antoine Foreman from Indianapolis. Can you comment on their involvement in this investigation?"

The crowd's necks craned toward the agents. Caitlin caught the slightest smile on Jerry Greenwood's lips.

The deputy at the podium paused for only a moment. "Of course, the FBI has extended all of their available tools to help bring Paige Lauffer back to us."

"That's wonderful," Lakshmi said, "but it seems unusual that an agent who specializes in the profiling of serial killers would be enlisted to locate a missing person in Monroe County unless there was some evidence, or at least suspicion, of foul play. Could either of the agents comment on their involvement?"

Mary put her arm around Caitlin. "Where did you dig that up?"

If Special Agent Foreman had chosen to keep Caitlin in the loop at Paige Lauffer's house, she might not have spent her five solitary minutes searching for his credentials. The agent worked in the Indianapolis office, but articles showed his participation throughout the Midwest. He'd investigated gangland killings, arrested a notorious hit man, and closed a major cold case after twenty-two years—but nothing at the nonissue-missing-persons level.

The deputy at the podium glanced over to the agents and stepped back. The redhead looked downright uncomfortable, but Antoine Foreman had no problem approaching the podium.

"Someone's done their homework," he said, adjusting the microphone. "While you're correct about my credentials, Agent Christiansen and I are here as part of a standard rotation. The FBI has technology and skills that not every branch of law enforcement can access, and we're here to help Sheriff Hopewell however we can."

Foreman returned to his spot on the wall, and the deputy closed out the session.

Greenwood followed the others off the platform. One step from the exit, he locked eyes with Caitlin and gave that wink again.

19

H E WATCHED THE broadcast live on the NBC affiliate, then opened his DVR menu and watched the ABC and CBS coverage. Then his laptop. He found the entire press conference without edits on the *Daily Student's* website, and clicked "Play."

He laughed at the officers from the different agencies. Helpless behind their badges, clueless despite their guns, pointless in their pants.

And not a single question from Bergman.

A current of excitement throbbed from his toes to his fingertips. They had nothing and he had Paige.

Still, he'd hoped for more from the great Caitlin Bergman. Too soon? She'd just gotten to town. He couldn't expect her to be looking for him, not yet. But she would eventually—if she was what he hoped. The perfect addition to his collection, a public figure, a strong woman with horror in her past, and best of all, the words to describe every second.

Paige awaited, but he couldn't help himself. He opened a new tab and searched for *missing student* and *Bergman.* Exposure at the national level would be dangerous, but the thought of Caitlin's attention got him straight up turned on.

"Deputy, do you believe Paige Lauffer's disappearance is related to Angela Chapman's in any way?"

Who just asked that question?

He clicked back to the *Daily Student* tab to put a face to the ongoing audio. The camera angle hadn't changed, so all he could see was shoulder-length black hair in the second row. He took the video back ten seconds, heard the tail end of the question again from the woman with the slight British accent. He didn't need to see her face to recognize the Anjale girl. In the last two years, she'd tried to tie every crime in the county to the disappearance of Angela Chapman. Just because the stopped clock had the time didn't mean she knew the answers. He watched the rest.

An FBI profiler?

None of the broadcast packages had included the involvement of an FBI profiler. He scrolled down the page, skimmed the two paragraphs below, saw no mention of the FBI. Apparently no one else at the press conference deemed the question germane.

Clueless.

Out the kitchen window, treetops waved with the breeze. He opened the front door, smelled the air, listened to the sounds. Everything hummed with energy, a perfect moment.

Maybe this was what other people felt Christmas mornings. Maybe this was their sex. He shut and locked the door, went down to the basement, slid between the washing machine and the water heater, and felt the warmth of the water behind the metal against his crotch. He rested for a second, enjoyed the sensation, then moved into the one-foot space behind the appliance. He reached to the top of the cylinder, pulled the remote down, and pressed the button.

Behind him, the wood paneling opened to darkness. He moved into the void, pressed the button again. Once the door closed behind him, he found the switch and brought his world to life.

20

Los Angeles

MIKE ROMAN PARKED in the lot south of the Lake Hollywood Reservoir, then hiked down the asphalt road to the smallest of three four-story mansions crammed against the hill. A new silver Lexus sat next to a black Range Rover in an open four-car garage. For a twenty-four-year-old, Kieran Michelson didn't seem to have any trouble with finances. Mike found the call box, pushed the button.

Per Caitlin's instructions, he'd called Rep Repair's office the day before and asked about the Silicon Beach start-up's service—online image consulting, threading, and management. It took a sales call with the CEO himself, Kieran Michelson, to explain exactly what that meant.

For a chunk of money, Rep Repair would find online mentions of a person, monitor and analyze them in real-time for tone, and if necessary, enter conversations using aliases to discredit the *haters*. Kieran's word, not his. In Mike's words, they made bad people look good for money.

Once he understood what Rep Repair did, he knew Caitlin's idea of approaching Kieran undercover was out. Enough people knew Mike's face in Hollywood that it would be a problem, and if not, he was sure the start-up used facial recognition software. He gave his real name and number. Seconds after Kieran ran his info through a search, he insisted Mike come by his house.

The sound of flip-flops slapping on smooth steps grew louder, until the frosted glass door opened. A brunette, nude except for pink bikini bottoms, jelly sandals, and half of the world's tattoos, looked at Mike, disappointed.

He did his best not to stare at her unnatural beauty but couldn't find a part that came with the original model.

"You're not the pizza guy," she said through some sort of Eastern Bloc accent.

Mike smiled. "Maybe someday."

She moved through the doorway. "Did you see him?"

"The pizza guy? Nope. Is Kieran here?"

She sat on the concrete stoop, eyes on the road, and flopped her hand toward the open door. "Up."

Mike hoped the pizza guy was a sixteen-year-old who needed a story to tell. "Fair enough."

He found the stairs, climbed all four levels toward the sounds of the party. The seventy-degree air-conditioning gave way to a blend of the afternoon's eighty-degree breeze and the chlorinated scent of a pool holding the giggles and splashes of inebriates.

"Mike fucking Roman."

Kieran Michelson, tall and athletic, with leading-actor good looks, waved from the trampoline at the other end of the thirty-foot pool, then launched into an irresponsible back flip. He swam his way past a pair of topless blondes floating on either their implants or the pool noodles beneath them. A pale man in a tank top and Rastafarian hat stood behind a DJ setup, tranced out to whatever music idiots listened to.

"Can I get you a drink, sir?"

Mike turned, saw someone in a movie-quality Spiderman costume suspended upside down from the building's roof, five feet over a portable bar.

"What does your Spidey sense tell you?"

The tiny man let himself down, landed behind the bar. "That you need a cocktail, hero."

"Sure," Mike said. "Whiskey and ginger."

Spiderman went to work.

Michelson slapped a wet palm on Mike's sport coat. "Mike fucking Roman."

Mike summoned a smile. "This is quite a place, Kieran."

"I thought I told you to call me K. Did you get a drink?" Michelson's words came out cocaine quick. "Spiderman will make you a drink."

"I got a—"

"Spiderman, get Mike fucking Roman a drink."

"Sure thing, Mr. Michel—"

Michelson yanked Mike back toward the pool. "Fucking Spiderman, am I right?"

"Pretty cool."

"I wanted Wolverine, but you know what they told me?"

"The claws?"

"The fucking claws. Badass as they are, can't make a cocktail with claws. But Spiderman's the man." He turned back to the bar. "Hey, Peter Parker, get Mike Roman a rock-tail."

Spiderman held out Mike's whiskey ginger.

Kieran grabbed the drink, spilled half the goods on the way to Mike's hand. "Hells yes, Spiderman. High-five."

Spiderman left him hanging, but only for enough time to leap up to the overhang's ledge, flip up onto the roof, then reach down and finish the high five upside down.

"Bet Wolverine couldn't do that," Mike said.

"Fucking Spiderman," Michelson said again, oblivious. He put his hand on Mike's shoulder. "You're seriously jacked, bro. We gotta talk workouts."

Mike watched Spiderman crawl across the roof and hide behind an air conditioner. "Does he just stay there until you call him?"

"Who knows? Grab a bathing suit in the room behind the DJ, then get your ass comfortable so we can talk business."

Mike found the stack of bathing suits, all bright red except for the words "Rep Repair" in white across the ass, changed, and rejoined the party.

Kieran came and went, sometimes alone, more often arm in arm with a female. The DJ and Spiderman left around six, the ladies at seven.

In the third-floor kitchen, Kieran ordered steaks from an app on his phone, then cut four giant lines of coke on a marble countertop. "Bro, you ready for the party or what?"

Mike raised an eyebrow. "As in the thing that just ended?"

Michelson filled his sinuses, wiped the powder from his nose. "That's nothing, man. I've got more ladies coming at nine. You want to hit this?"

"I've got a drug test tomorrow, K."

Kieran took rail number two down like a Dyson. "A what test?"

"As we discussed on the phone, my brand will be security for the elite, which means my people have to stay professional, even at the party of the year. That discipline's got to start at the top."

Mike's cover story was based in a truth, or at least the truth of a dream. As a felon, he couldn't legally work as a private investigator in California, but he could start a security firm, and Hollywood didn't seem to mind the shade of his past, given that it was accompanied by notoriety.

Kieran raised a hand to high-five position. "I get it, man. That's sick."

Mike knew he had to accept the offer but wondered if Nazis had the same overdeveloped shoulder muscles as Michelson. He slapped that fascist salute and got to the point. "Of course, discretion will be our thing—the kind of loyalty that comes from nondisclosure agreements and large sums of money."

Kieran wiggled the tip of his nose with his thumb and forefinger. "Man, that sounds like something I might need."

"Maybe we can work out an exchange. You're living the life, K. People will try to find holes they can exploit. Your past, your finances, whether or not your stairs are nonslip in case some low-paid Spiderman wants to slip and fall four stories and sue the trunks off of you."

"Oh, I take care of Spiderman. That guy got blown today."

"Seriously. From my perspective, it looks like you're burning through your investors' cash. Makes you an easy target."

"No way. Rep Repair isn't just a business, it's my dream, bro. Two years ago, I get out of college and people think I'm a drug dealer and a murderer, all because some girl I'm banging gets drunk and disappears. I mean, it was awful. This was my friend, right? But nobody gave a shit. I had people tweeting I should get life in prison. I decided right then I wasn't gonna let those asshats call me a murderer for the rest of my life. I made this thing, raised two million, hired the developers. Every bit of cash I blow is mine, clean and everything."

Mike knew nobody used the word *clean* unless they were dirty.

"Then they're gonna ask the obvious. How can a kid two years out of college afford to run the Playboy mansion?"

"Better than the Playboy mansion. No old balls."

Mike stayed on point. "I know you're familiar with my background. What I used to do?"

"Yeah, bro. Ex-cop, right?"

"That's right. LAPD, narcotics."

"And then you went to prison for corruption. I ripped off a copy of that reporter's book."

Mike wasn't about to get into the whole story. "So I know what I see when I look at this house."

Kieran sobered a bit. "Hey, I lease this place, the cars. Six months of entertaining big-money a-holes in a house like this pays off stacks of cash for what it costs. Got to spend it to make it, man."

"I get it," Mike said. "Who am I kidding? I don't know shit about finance, but like you said, everyone thinks you used to deal. Now you've got a buttload of cash."

Kieran nodded more times than he needed to. "Yeah, I get it, I get it."

He took a few steps toward the balcony, came right back. "Let's say I did hook some people up in college. I'm not saying I did, Mike, but if I did, I sure as hell wouldn't be stupid enough to risk my future by getting caught. Shit, if I was, they would have locked me up two years ago, whether I knew what happened to Angela or not. Here's the answer I give anyone who asks: I saw a niche in the market and filled it. Me and my bros started a farm that grows organic vegetables, certified and everything, then supplies places that don't mind paying way too much for the label. Fraternities, sororities? Shit, colleges are full of people who don't know the value of a greenhouse and some topsoil. Plus they'll pay extra for that hydroponic shit."

Mike smiled. "That's great."

"Yeah, I'm a farmer, bro."

Mike beat Michelson to it, raised his hand. "Up top, K."

A greenhouse, topsoil, and hydroponics—necessary elements for both an organic farm and a marijuana growhouse. Organic veggies might cost an extra buck or two at the store, but no way they added up to a Lexus, Range Rover, and house full of topless women. Mike had everything Caitlin needed. He'd eat the man's steak, then leave before the second wave of strippers washed up.

21

Mary excused herself after an hour of celebratory post–press conference darts and beer, leaving Caitlin and Lakshmi on the sidewalk a block from Kilroy's Sports.

"Well, kid," Caitlin said, breathing in the night air. "First you called out an FBI agent in front of a room full of pros, then you kicked both Mary and my asses at darts. How do you feel?"

Lakshmi laughed. "You were the one who told me to bring up Foreman. It's not like he said anything useful."

"Maybe not, but think of what's *not* being said." Caitlin checked her phone. Five past eleven. "No hot dog cart tonight."

"Not enough traffic on a Tuesday. What's not being said, Caitlin?"

Caitlin thought about Lakshmi and Angela's last text exchange.

F'd up. Going to Sports. Gonna eat some SAUSAGE first.

"It's your body," she said aloud.

Lakshmi looked at her like she'd spoken in tongues. "Sorry?"

"The night Angela disappeared—"

"Of course, our texts. Angela's end of that happened somewhere on this block. The cart was across the street under that light."

"Were you fighting? It seemed like Angela was teasing you."

Lakshmi bit a nail. "We were teasing each other. It was girl's night and she chose to go out with them."

"Dave Amireau and Kieran Michelson?"

"Yes. Apparently she'd made the plans earlier but didn't tell me until they showed up. I didn't want to hang out with a bunch of frat boys and was hurt that she did."

A sensible answer, almost practiced.

"Angela typed the word *sausage* in all caps," Caitlin said.

"I know. The detectives made a big deal about that too. Can you imagine having people analyzing your text messages, even the emojis or typos?"

"Words are my thing," Caitlin said. "I divine a great deal from their usage."

"So do I, but Angela? Not so much." She shrugged.

"Do they still have bands at Sports?"

"Depends on the night. Could be a band, could be a DJ. The place is humongous. According to them, it's the biggest college bar in America."

Caitlin started walking. "Let's find out what happens on a Tuesday."

*　　*　　*

The bouncer looked up from Caitlin's ID. "You don't look—"

She grabbed her driver's license. "Thanks, but don't."

Lakshmi took her into the fray. The downstairs felt familiar: a long bar and two rooms full of booths, a mix of people chowing down on chicken wings and pounding shots. Everywhere Caitlin turned, her eyes adjusted to TV screens showing sports highlights.

"Want to go upstairs?" Lakshmi said, her voice fighting the sounds of dance music.

Caitlin read the sign on the wall. "Sure, let's check out the Jungle."

A wall of humidity hit her as they edged near the crowded dance floor and its mélange of lithe, gyrating women and dudes struggling to keep their tongues in their mouths.

Caitlin pointed toward a patio. "Let's go there."

Plastic chairs circled outdoor tables with closed umbrellas. People puffed on e-cigarettes and spoke at drunk volume.

"It's nicer in the beer garden," Lakshmi said.

"Good God, there's a beer garden too?"

They made their way to a high-ceilinged, glass-walled patio big enough for two hundred. Maybe thirty people Lakshmi's age occupied various parts of the atrium and bar.

Caitlin took a stool.

A male bartender let them know he'd be right with them.

Lakshmi pointed to a raised platform at the far end. "The karaoke scene is big here. Not as big as Bear's Place, but—" Her eyes caught on a table. "Bugger."

"What's going on? An ex or something?" Caitlin saw four guys with two pitchers, four cups, and a board game.

Lakshmi whipped her head back toward the beer taps. "I don't know why he's here. I didn't even know he was in town."

"Who?"

"It's David Amireau and some of his old frat brothers. I have to leave."

"Because you're afraid?"

"Because of the restraining order. I have to stay one hundred yards away, so I have to go right now."

"Interesting." Caitlin pushed away from the bar. "You can tell me all about that on our way home."

"No. You stay. Watch him."

"Why?"

Lakshmi walked toward the door. "You'll see. Text me later."

Caitlin watched her go. Amireau had a restraining order against her, not the other way around. Weird that neither Lakshmi nor the BPD had mentioned that tidbit.

She ordered a beer and then took her drink to a table ten feet from Amireau and company. David Amireau had grown a dark, thick beard, the kind the Special Forces guys wore in Afghanistan. Otherwise, Caitlin didn't see anything out of the ordinary. The narrow bridge between his eyes read "dickhead," and the contrast between his pasty skin and full eyebrows didn't help, but Angela Chapman had called Amireau her friend. She'd texted him, not Michelson, on a regular basis. The guys with him looked sincere enough, laughing when he joked, and bumping fists when points were scored in their game.

Caitlin nursed her beer for fifteen minutes, then walked to the bar for another.

The first group of women appeared before she got back to her seat. College-aged, maybe six, gathered near the doorway. Five minutes later, they numbered fifteen, all shapes, sizes, and races. Five minutes after that, easily two dozen.

Caitlin heard one of the girls say, "Now."

A chant echoed in the patio. "Murderer, murderer."

They started walking. Amireau didn't notice until one of his friends tapped him. The women continued, growing louder. By twenty feet away, they were yelling.

"Murderer, murderer!"

Amireau's friend yelled back. "Dave didn't do anything."

Another of his boys called to the bartender. "Get security in here."

The mob walled in the foursome. Several men in security T-shirts worked their way in, forming a path Amireau could take through the fe-maelstrom, his hands covering his face to keep from being photographed by multiple camera phones. The mob followed him out into the main bar, still chanting. Caitlin went too.

She saw heads turn with recognition and whispers, heard someone behind the bar say, "Hey, it's the guy that killed Angela Chapman."

The remaining stools and chairs pushed back, and the nightclub emptied onto the street, a drunken and angry mass. Their chant continued long after Caitlin lost sight of Amireau, and didn't stop until the wail of sirens replaced words.

22

Twenty minutes and three police cruisers later, the bar had nearly emptied of students. Jerry Greenwood leaned against the railing of the rooftop patio. "Where'd your young journalist friend go?"

"Not quite sure." Caitlin pointed down to the crowd-less sidewalk. "How did the march of the Chapman Chapter end?"

Greenwood laughed. "Most scurried when the lights came on."

"Kind of a weak protest for a college town."

"Well, it's Tuesday." He looked at his watch. "Correction, Wednesday morning. How'd the shenanigans start?"

Caitlin walked him through to Lakshmi's exit. "Because apparently Amireau has a restraining order against her?"

"First time she mentioned it?"

"News to me, and I'm a journalist." Caitlin turned in time to catch a server. "Miss?" She held up her plastic cup, empty except ice cubes. The server nodded.

"Wait a sec," Greenwood said. "Can I have a vodka soda, splash of cran?"

The server took their orders back toward the bar.

They sat. Caitlin picked a plastic votive candle off the table, flicked the tiny switch off and on. "How did Amireau get a restraining order against Lakshmi?"

"How did she behave tonight?"

"She calmly told me she had to leave and that she'd talk to me later."

"Then she's grown. After we released Dave and Kieran without any charges, she followed them everywhere, screamed at them in public, trolled them on social media. Michelson moved to California three weeks after graduation, but Amireau stayed. That summer, someone keyed his car, spray-painted *Murderer* on his front door."

"You think Lakshmi did that?"

Greenwood shrugged. "She didn't go home for the summer, so she had access, but it didn't really matter. Guilty or not, no one proved those boys did anything wrong. Amireau's attorney filed harassment paperwork. Lakshmi showed up in court, tried to present the people's case against Amireau and Michelson without an attorney. Judge not only granted the order, he made her pay their attorney's fees."

Again, Caitlin revisited Lakshmi's age. As professional as she seemed, two years earlier would have made her nineteen. Caitlin hadn't keyed any cars in her youth, but she remembered how out of her mind she'd been the first time she'd switched birth controls. Throw in a best friend's disappearance, and who knows what she could have destroyed? Still, she'd only known Lakshmi for five days. "Do I have to worry about her?"

The waitress returned with their drinks. Greenwood waited until she'd gone.

"From what I can tell, Lakshmi came back that fall, hit the books, and has kept her distance since." He took a sip. "Granted, she bugs the hell out of me, but what would I do if someone killed a woman I loved?"

"Didn't she violate the order by calling the Chapman Chapter out tonight?"

"Technically, Doris Chapman started it all with a tweet, so there's no direct line between Lakshmi and Amireau. I don't see a reason to draw one. This was a fluke. Dave barely comes into town anymore."

"But he stayed close, as in he still lives near Bloomington?"

"Moved to a place near Nashville. Runs a farm that sells organic produce, mostly to sororities or frats."

"So you've kept your eye on him?"

Greenwood took another sip. "Kid knows what happened to Chapman. He'll snap. Only a matter of time."

"And pressure," Caitlin said. "Like a city of women calling you a murderer any time you turn up in public." She tilted her cup back, hit only ice a second time. "Lakshmi and Chapman were lovers."

"You asking or telling?"

"'A woman she loved,' you said. And how about the Friday girl's nights with only two girls, the visits to Chapman's apartment, and the complete lack of love life?"

Greenwood finished his drink. "We never made her say it out loud. I've spoken to her father, and I get it. This might be the town that invented the

Kinsey scale, but everybody has lives back home, and that's their personal journey. But don't go thinking that conservatism is restricted to the Indian doctor. Chapman's parents dwell on the high school version of Angela rather than the college one."

"Then on the Kinsey scale?"

"Lakshmi leans far to one side, but Chapman straddled the divide."

Caitlin crunched an ice cube. "Talk about your college stereotypes."

"Nineteen years old? I didn't know I wanted to be a cop until I was twenty-two, and even then, I probably did it for the wrong reason."

"Which was?"

He laughed. "Ladies love men in uniform. When did you know who Caitlin Bergman was, or were you one of those people who were set at sixteen?"

"I thought I knew before I got to school," she said, then caught herself in a memory, flagging down a mini-van, her torn shorts covered in blood and limestone chalk. "But you're right. Things change us. So you looked at Lakshmi?"

"You know we did."

"And?"

"And that girl loved Angela Chapman the way I loved my wife."

Caitlin held back the next question—if he ever got jealous when his wife went out with another lover.

The server returned and asked if they needed refills. The good-looking detective waited on Caitlin's answer. She'd spent most of the day with the man, and part of her guessed she could spend the night with him as well, but the other part was deep in a tunnel.

"Better call it a night."

*   *   *

After Greenwood left, Caitlin went to the bar to do something stupid. She'd walked the same paths, seen the same sights, but hadn't yet lived in Angela Chapman's moment. Her order didn't shock the bartender, but he stayed to watch her drink the Three Wisemen. One shot of Jack, one shot of Johnnie, one shot of Jim.

Goodbye, balance; hello, night air.

Mary's guesthouse was a mile southeast. Caitlin turned north on Walnut, threw her arms up. "Drunk woman walking, Bloomington, all by herself."

No one yelled back. She checked her phone: 1:08 AM. Slightly earlier than Chapman the night she went missing but in the same tree-lined neighborhood.

New office buildings and townhouses filled the gaps in Caitlin's memory. A few vehicles passed from behind. An off-duty taxi, a city bus, a single Harley Davidson. She felt good but noticed the distance between streetlights had increased. Like the night before, dark patches of green trees, no big deal with buddies at your side, now appeared sinister.

She checked a map on her phone. Only half a mile before a return to decent lighting and the path toward the last place Angela Chapman was seen alive.

She picked up her pace, saw a railroad bridge looming in the darkness. A single streetlight near the rusted steel beams of the wide overpass didn't do anything but blind Caitlin to what lay in wait. She passed under the lonely cone of light, waited for her eyes to adjust. The three shots of bravery now felt like a punch in the stomach. She felt her heart rate increase. Beyond the overpass, another streetlight waited three hundred feet away. She broke into a jog. Twenty feet from the bridge, her jog turned into a sprint.

"I got this," she said.

Her shoes hitting the sidewalk echoed under the bridge, but nothing would touch her. She threw her arms up, yelled again. "Drunk woman running, Bloomington, all by herself!"

She passed under the overpass, didn't slow down. The night air hit her eyes and tears leaked at the corners, but she pounded on until the next streetlight welcomed her back to safety. She leaned over, let her breaths deepen. Her heart stopped punching her. She straightened up, started walking north.

A horn blared from behind. She turned, saw a blue sedan veer far into the left lane toward her spot on the sidewalk.

"Hey lady," a voice yelled, "show us your tits."

A beer bottle smashed against the concrete four feet away, and the car jerked back into the right lane, drove past. Inside the car, five college kids, all women, laughing their asses off.

Caitlin grabbed her phone, ordered a ride, and watched the dot on the map move until a car pulled up to take her home.

23

CAITLIN FOUND SCOTT Canton's office on the sixth floor of the Ballentine building. Lit by morning sunshine, the man sat behind a computer monitor next to a two-foot-tall statue of a smiling Buddha.

She knocked on the open door. "Who's tunneling now?"

He stood with a smile and straightened his rumpled cardigan. "How long were you standing there?"

She claimed the chair near his desk. "You looked deep in thought. Need me to sit quietly?"

"The phrase will reveal itself in time. I am merely the vessel."

"Bull. The computer's the vessel, you're the captain."

"Still, I'm on a sightseeing trip. Lock us up and I'll show you a trick."

"Why, Professor," she said, reaching back to lock the door. "You're not allowed to say things like that to students anymore."

"Sit down, smart ass."

He opened the window, then sat back at his desk and rubbed the Buddha. A drawer in the tummy slid open. He pulled out a plastic bag full of joints and put one between his lips, then pushed the statue's bald head. Buddha spit fire.

"Is that—"

"A fire-breathing Buddha?" Scott took a puff from the lit jay. "You know it. Now let's talk about your troubles, Caitlin."

She brushed her hair back, glanced out the window. "What troubles?"

He smiled politely, handed over the joint. "I have a horrible talent. I can tell the difference between people who like to get high and people who need to get high. I fear you fall into the latter. Plus, you're wearing the same clothes as the last time I saw you."

Caitlin took a hit and mulled over the offer. She wasn't ready to talk to Mary, but she needed to do something, if only to be able to walk the campus at night. Canton was a neutral party with free weed. She let a few words escape with the smoke. "I might be having panic attacks."

Scott's eyebrows went up. "Might be?"

Caitlin closed her eyes, then shook her head yes. "I am."

"Good."

She opened her eyes again, saw him nodding. "Good?"

"Your body's way of telling you you're under attack. How does he come after you?"

"He?"

"Sorry, that's my thing." Scott turned toward his bookcase, searching. "When I came back from Nam, I did all the wrong you could imagine. I drank, I drugged, I fought, I thugged. Lost the love of a good woman and most of my family, ended up spending two years on the street. All the while, *he* kept coming back, and I ran like hell, until I found an outlet."

He turned back, book in hand.

"What you can't tell from my speech, but I assure you would be clear on a page, my *he* is spelled with a capital *h*."

"As in God?"

"Oh no." He handed her a dust-jacketed hardcover of the book she'd studied in college—*Up River: A Collection of Poems by Scott Canton.* "Try the back."

She flipped the book over and met two Cantons. The first, a black and white image of a smiling high school student in a dress shirt and tie. The second, a color shot of Scott with a severe Jim Kelly-*Enter the Dragon* afro, a goatee, and a bright yellow turtleneck, not even a hint of a smile.

He sat back in his chair. "How many years do you guess passed between the photos?"

Caitlin felt the answer was ten. "Eight?"

"Four. That first shot was my senior class photo. My girlfriend took the second a day after bailing me out of jail for breaking a man's jaw."

"Which scared you—the older?"

"No." He tapped on the high school student. "This grinning idiot haunted my every move. I couldn't make peace with the disparity, do you follow? Who I was versus who *he* thought I was supposed to be. Yes, there were flashbacks. Yes, I saw terrible things, did terrible things, but *he* was the one staring me in the face when I got home—the *he* that was never going to be me again."

Caitlin set the book on the desk. "Pronouns are the worst."

"Mine was. Talk about yours. Your assault happened twenty years ago. Were you having these attacks back in Los Angeles?"

Caitlin shifted in her chair, looked out the window, saw a squirrel zip across a branch. Pretty high up, no sign of fear.

"Caitlin?"

She kept her eyes on the squirrel but answered. "Not until last month, when Mary called."

"About this trip?"

The squirrel leapt away, out of sight. Caitlin turned back to reality. "She mentioned the diploma, and I was drunk enough to say yes."

"Then what?"

"I threw up that night. I figured bad roach-coach carnitas, I got what I deserved, but it happened again the next day. Then I had a dream. Mary and I were studying for a test in a bar and ran out of beer, so I went for refills. At the bar I saw a face. His face."

"The man who attacked you?"

"Yes." She exhaled, looked down at her hands. "I tried the old wake-up tricks, but nothing worked. Once again, Troy Woods raped me."

Scott dabbed at the corner of his eye. "I can't imagine, Caitlin."

She tried a smile. "Don't try—it's not fun."

"So after the dream?"

"I agreed to come back to Bloomington."

"Then the real attacks started?"

Caitlin let her head drop to her hands. "Yep."

Scott leaned down to her level. "Any chance you've heard of cognitive behavioral therapy?"

She looked up. "Did we just go from friends talking to friends playing doctor?"

He laughed. "I do have a PhD, but I'm no psychiatrist."

"That would be nice. Got time for one more degree?"

"I am a psychologist, Caitlin. Slightly out of the game, I'll admit. I had a fairly good practice through the late eighties. Lucky me, I found teaching in ninety-one and didn't look back until the wars started. Now I make myself available for those in need, and there are plenty. You might be one of them."

A buzzing broke the moment.

She handed the joint back to Scott, then dropped a hand to her bag. "Yeah, probably."

His eyes followed her reach for her phone. "Did I just lose you?"

"No." She noticed a text message from Mike Roman: *Check your email.* "I haven't spent much time talking about all of this."

"I can tell. You should make the time."

"Looks like I've got some news about Chapman."

"Okay, I can feel the shift. You need to run free." He slid the bag of weed her way. "But think of this as a remedy, not a cure."

He walked to the door, turned the knob. "One last unsolicited thought, Caitlin. Bloomington has become a trigger for you, something that returns you to the helplessness you felt with your attacker. There are ways to recondition you to accept and grow from the events in your life, no matter how awful. Any time you want to grow, you give me a call. Even out of office hours."

She took a breath, found a shaky smile on the other side. "Thanks again, Scott. I will be back."

She walked to the elevator, unsure whether she was more excited to be out of the room or to check Roman's message. The subject line had promise: *Michelson tied to growhouse, probably still active.*

24

T HE NEXT AFTERNOON, Caitlin rang Lakshmi's buzzer. Lakshmi opened the door, mouthed the words *I'm so sorry*, pointed Caitlin to the couch, and continued an existing phone conversation. "You know how much I owe you, Jessica. This will really help with my project . . ."

Photos of Chapman, clippings, and red marker scribblings covered the walls. The smell of burnt popcorn filled the room, and an inkjet printer spit out pages like the press under the *Times* building. Lakshmi grabbed two pages from the expanding stack, walked them and a bowl of popcorn to Caitlin, then ended her phone call on her way back to the kitchen.

"Caitlin," she said over the sound of a refrigerator door opening, "I am so sorry for how things ended last night. I know I should have told you about the restraining order."

Caitlin shook her head. "I got your texts."

There'd been *three* that morning.

A drawer opened and shut. "Sorry about that too, but I believe a proper apology is done in person, preferably with alcohol." Lakshmi reappeared with two topless domestics. "Fancy a beer?"

"Hold that thought." Caitlin fixated on the heading of the pages in front of her: *Initial draft, not for public release.* "What am I looking at?"

Lakshmi set one of the bottles on the coffee table between them and hovered, holding the other. "The executive summary of a campus-wide sexual abuse study that won't publish until the fall. Listen to this." She took the top page.

"'Seventeen percent of the undergraduate women participating reported being the victims of attempted or completed nonconsensual sexual penetration while at college, while twenty-nine percent reported experiencing some type of nonconsensual sexual contact.'"

She drank from her beer, kept going. "'Additionally, thirty-five percent of undergraduate female participants and a similar percentage of graduate students reported experiencing some form of sexual harassment.'"

She handed Caitlin the paper, pointed to a paragraph. "You have to read this part; it makes me too angry."

Caitlin read to herself.

Perhaps most distressing, however, was the revelation that among those participants who did not report an experience of the most serious type of sexual misconduct—nonconsensual attempted or completed sexual penetration—45 percent of the undergraduate women and 29 percent of the women graduate students indicated that they didn't feel the incident was "serious enough" to disclose.

Caitlin reached for the other beer, took a sip. "It's a really great pull, Lakshmi. Awful, but congratulations."

"Maybe it will help with your story."

"Maybe."

Lakshmi joined her on the couch, her hands folded in her lap. "I know I should have told you about the restraining order straight away, but I didn't want to risk losing you."

Caitlin inched away from Lakshmi. "Losing me?"

Lakshmi noticed, leaned back. "Not losing you—that sounds crazy. But maybe crazy's right." She pointed to the wall behind her. "Look at this place. I was almost gone. You being in town, listening to me, talking with me— you've helped me remember the bigger picture. I didn't want to give you any reason to doubt me. Now I see how wrong that was. I should be telling you everything." She put her beer down. "There's something everyone probably knows, but I have to say it. I love Angela, Caitlin, and not as a friend." Her eyes looked close to tears. "We used to joke about it all the time, but I never actually said it out loud. I'm a lesbian." She smiled. "My God, I totally just came out to you. I'm the worst."

Caitlin laughed. "Did you really just come out, like this is *the* moment?"

"I'm the worst," Lakshmi repeated. "I haven't told my father, never said it to Angela. I mean, she knew, obviously."

"Meaning you had sex?"

Lakshmi's eyes brightened. "Yes. I'm sure the police guessed. That's why they treated me like a suspect for so long. Most of the time, when a woman's murdered, the spouse is the one who did it, right?"

"And Angela?" *Was she a lesbian?* Caitlin almost said, then remembered both Doris and Lakshmi's need to keep Angela in the present tense. "Did she identify as a lesbian at the time?"

Lakshmi blushed. "Well, she knew the buttons to push."

"But did she feel the same way about you?"

"When we were drunk or high, we were the only two people on Earth. But when she'd sober up, she'd joke about it, like she was going through a phase."

"And Kieran?"

"Kieran, other guys. She threw herself at them."

"Like she had something to prove?"

Lakshmi shrugged. "Maybe she's gay, maybe just playing. I don't know, but there's one more thing." She took another sip of beer. "The night she disappeared, we got in a fight. It was meant to be our night, a date. We had some drinks, got high, and I told her."

"That you loved her?"

Lakshmi nodded.

"And what did she say?"

"It was awful. She just said, 'No.'"

"No to what? That you loved her?"

"That's what I asked. She stood up and said we should do shots. I got upset."

"Meaning what?"

"Meaning I followed her to the kitchen and said I wanted to know what she thought. She turned to me, vodka in hand, and said she didn't have time to dyke out with me because she'd made other plans."

"With Amireau and Michelson?"

"Yes, those knobs."

"That was it? End of discussion?"

"No," Lakshmi said. "She told me I was being dramatic, that she was too high to process, and that I should go with them to the bars and we'd talk about it later. Well, I couldn't stand the idea of sitting across from Kieran all night, wondering if Angela would choose me or him. I told her to sod off." Lakshmi wiped a tear from her eye. "And she did. I sent the girl I loved to her death," she said, choking on the words, "because she hurt my feelings."

Whatever dam protected Lakshmi's reservoir of tears broke under two years of pressure. She leaned into Caitlin and sobbed.

Caitlin looked down at the mass of black hair shaking against her shoulder and tried to imagine two years of not being able to grieve for a missing lover. She put her arm around Lakshmi and squeezed her tight. Two years, knowing the people responsible for her lover's death were walking around free. Two years of anxiety, fueled by the innocent actions of one night.

"I've got you," she said, patting the girl's back.

Lakshmi nestled in closer, still crying, each sob pulsing against Caitlin's chest. "We're gonna find her," Caitlin started again, her own voice now fighting back tears, "and show the bastard that hurt you he's not untouchable."

Caitlin closed her eyes and shook her head.

"That hurt *her*," she corrected herself, semi-aware that her comforting words might have referred to a different bastard, a different girl, and a different time.

Kieran Michelson or Troy Woods? Angela Chapman or Caitie Bergman?

She wiped a tear away, then pulled Lakshmi's hair back. If there were words that could end their pain, she didn't have them.

What would Scott Canton say?

Caitlin cleared her throat and reached for her bag. "Want to get high?"

* * *

Lakshmi picked through the last of the popcorn kernels. "This pot is great."

Caitlin reached for the remote, turned down the streaming music. "Do you smoke a lot?"

"Oh no, not since the night." She looked up. "Wow, I say that a lot. *Not since the night.* What a horrible phrase."

"Speaking of which," Caitlin said, far from tears and ready to work, "you said you were high that night. What sort of drugs did you girls play with?"

"Mostly weed. I've tried Molly—you know, MDMA? And 'shrooms once, but I puked."

"What about coke?"

"Not me. Angela did occasionally with Kieran and Dave, but I was scared. The first time they offered, it was light green."

"Green? And they called it coke?"

"She said it wasn't quite right but still worked. Other times, it was white, but I didn't trust it."

"Where did they get it?"

"I don't know, but they always had it."

"What about pot?"

"Oh yeah, we got all of our pot from them; so did their whole fraternity. Can we order pizza?"

"I think we have to."

Lakshmi reached for her phone. "Let's get Pizza Monster. I get half off. Meat okay?"

Caitlin didn't care at that point, or remember what they'd ordered thirty minutes later when the driver knocked on the door. She caught the tail end of the exchange with the delivery girl.

"Thanks, and tell Chad I say, 'Hi,'" Lakshmi said, then closed the door.

She set the box on the coffee table, grabbed a roll of paper towels.

Caitlin stared at the happy cartoon monster on the lid. A triangle slice of pizza with big eyes and tiny legs winked over the words "Scary How Good It Is."

"Who's Chad? You know a driver?" She opened the box, saw the disc of greasy goodness.

Lakshmi returned with forks. "Chad Branford. He gave me a stack of coupons."

Caitlin broke a slice free. "The acting teacher?"

Lakshmi joined her, manners abandoned. "Yeah, he bought the Monster when he moved here, gave us all coupons, used to make deliveries himself. He says it paid for grad school the first year."

Caitlin swallowed. "What a great idea."

"Once at the beginning, when business was slow, Angela and I invited him in, and he ate with us, even got a little high. That was the first time I tried Molly."

"Here?"

"No, Angela's. He's got a lot of funny acting stories."

"Did Angela and Branford ever hook up?"

"Oh no, nothing like that. He was just bored."

Caitlin reached for her second slice. "Plus, knowing young women never hurts when it comes to selling pizza."

Lakshmi followed her lead. "We became Pizza Monster evangelists, told everyone. Kieran ordered twenty pizzas for a frat party. After that, word spread pretty fast."

"And Chad rewarded you with half-price coupons?"

"I doubt I'll get through them before graduation. Not without gaining a stone."

Caitlin leaned back into the couch. "You don't have class tomorrow, do you?"

"Why? What do you want to do?"

"Look for a growhouse."

"Growhouse, like pot?"

"Kieran and Dave sell 'organic produce' to sororities and fraternities."

"Another reason to hate them. It's such a good idea."

"Know what a better idea is? Sell weed and call it kale."

25

CAITLIN WAITED UNTIL the waitress left with their breakfast orders, then pulled out her laptop and opened a browser.

Lakshmi moved to share Caitlin's side of the booth. "Wouldn't the police have looked into this?"

"They did two years ago but didn't find anything they could prove. Since then, Kieran and Dave have moved on like no one's watching. We'll start with their farm's web page."

Caitlin found Mike Roman's latest email on her laptop, clicked on the link, and turned the screen toward Lakshmi.

Lakshmi laughed. "Indiana Organic Bro-duce? That's bloody awful." She read a paragraph out loud. "'Located on a twenty-acre farm in Monroe County, Indiana Organic Bro-duce was founded by fraternity brothers from Indiana University, with the goal of bringing farm-fresh organic produce to students across the Big Ten.'"

Breakfast arrived. Caitlin pushed the keyboard back, making room. Lakshmi went for her egg-white omelet. Caitlin looked down at her own sensible fruit and yogurt combo, then back at her computer screen. The phone number in the footer section of the website kept her from impulse-ordering a side of bacon.

She pulled out the cheapest cell phone she'd found at the Bloomington Mall. "Next step."

"Did you get a new mobile, Caitlin?"

"Local number, caller ID disabled, perfect for cold-calling possible sources." She grabbed a pen, jotted the number on her napkin, and slid Lakshmi the digits. "Plus, if I'm in the field and my battery dies, I can use this burner as a backup."

"Smart," Lakshmi said, typing the number into her own phone's address book.

Caitlin bit through an unripe piece of cantaloupe and dialed the farm's business line.

Two rings in, a male voice answered, "Bro-duce."

"I'm a biology teacher at Bloomington South," Caitlin said. "I see you're an organic farm and was wondering if I could speak to someone about a tour of your facility."

"Hold on."

Caitlin heard the voice's owner set the phone on a counter. "Hey, *Lord of the Rings*, Dave here today?"

Someone in the same room replied, "Don't know."

"Fuck it," the voice said, then hung up.

"Oh, good God," Lakshmi said. "This is what happens when frat boys get jobs."

"Not exactly a well-oiled machine, but at least one thread to pull. Did you catch it?"

"The Lord of the Rings." Lakshmi brightened. "Do they mean Frodo?"

"Exactly. Nate Fodor. What's he like?"

"He was a pledge when I knew him, so I didn't get much of his personality."

"And Amireau was his big brother, as in the mentor-slash-torturer fraternity meaning?"

Lakshmi looked surprised. "How did you know?"

"Just a hunch. Let's move on to their financials. We can't see their accounts, like the police, but we can look at their filed corporate structures."

"Corporate structures? This just got really boring. Let's go over there and look around."

"Settle down, Miss Restraining Order." Caitlin logged into a subscription-based legal and financial database. "Cops get to knock on doors. Journalists have to do homework. It's time-consuming, far from glamorous, and most of the time it's boring as hell, but when you find something no one else has seen, it's better than sex."

In three searches, Caitlin had a list of the shareholders in Indiana Organic Bro-duce.

Delta Omega Tau Alumna Philanthropic Association
Organic Foods International
IOBD LLC

"No mention of Dave or Kieran," Lakshmi said. "They're hiding their involvement."

"Not from us."

Although named after their fraternity, the Delta Omega Tau reference had no affiliation with the national chapter and was listed as a nonprofit organization. Instead of officers, Caitlin found another shell corporation.

Organic Foods International appeared to be an import/export business with an office in the Bahamas.

IOBD LLC's ownership broke down into four cells, all other corporations: NF LLC. AF LLC. DA LLC. KM LLC.

Those listings broke down to actual names, each a single-member limited liability corporation.

Nathan Fodor, President
Adam Fodor, President
David Amireau, President
Kieran Michelson, President

Caitlin queried KM LLC. The only other listing linked to Kieran was RepRepair LLC in the state of California.

She drummed her fingertips on the tabletop.

"They may have compartmentalized everything, but they're getting checks. If they're getting checks from a company found trafficking narcotics—"

Lakshmi knew that one. "They're liable for the drugs, whether they're onsite or not."

Caitlin speared a yogurt-covered strawberry with her fork. "And hiding a drug trafficking operation makes a far better motive than covering up the accidental overdose of a friend."

* * *

Caitlin left Lakshmi hunting financials and picked Mary up from the Student Union. "What's with the hippie shirt?"

Mary wore a tie-dyed T-shirt covered in bright-colored, high-stepping bears. "I'm undercover."

"Undercover? You're the dean of the Media School."

"I'm not worried. Half of my staff members don't recognize me, let alone any of the thirty thousand students not in my department. Today, I'm a dirty hippie looking to score. Granola chicks like the Grateful Dead, and who the hell else would ask for a tour of an organic farm?"

Caitlin laughed and aimed for the countryside. Mary worked the console and her phone's music app until Caitlin heard the stoner jam rock of Jerry Garcia and Co. She sang along with her old friend. Neither could carry a tune, but the Dead didn't sound any worse with their help. Their bad voices and giggles carried them to the east side of town. Caitlin caught Mary up on her Chapman progress.

"Even if you catch them selling weed, how does that prove they murdered Angela?"

"It doesn't," Caitlin said, "but if the farm goes back long enough, it's one more place the cops can look for a body. If not, a trafficking charge ought to loosen lips about Chapman."

"Not bad, Caitie. Only two weeks in and you've uncovered a drug ring. Can't believe the BPD dropped that ball."

Caitlin nodded along. "Greenwood is no idiot. I think he thinks he's using me."

"For what?"

She remembered the vibe they'd shared two nights before at the bar and smiled. "Not sure, but I can't wait to find out."

Mary moved on. "What about the other thing?"

"What other thing?"

"You know."

"Why does everyone keep asking me about my rape?"

"Are you serious?"

"That's a joke—"

"Because you got up on a stage and announced it. And now, after twenty years, I'm trying to be the friend you wouldn't let me be back then."

Caitlin stared at the road. "Standing up on the podium, I thought, *No big deal,* but actually staying here in Bloomington, it's gotten harder."

"Well, let's Ya-Ya-sister-pants this bullshit."

Caitlin jerked her thumb toward the back seat. "Want to help? Root around in my bag until you find a police report."

"Okay." Mary found Caitlin's assault folder. "A reading from the rape of Caitlin Bergman." She stared at the contents, flipped a page. "Huh."

"What?"

"I've never really looked at something like this."

"Good for you. What's in there?"

"Okay, the first page looks like a summary document. Next page looks like an initial incident report, handwritten. Was that the sheriff's department?"

"Yes, Deputy Lyle something, right?"

"Oh, that's what that is. Deputy Lyle Sugar."

At no point in the last two decades had Caitlin thought about Deputy Sugar—or his warning: *They're going to tell you to stop, to reconsider, to keep the whole thing quiet . . . Don't let them stop you, ever.* In the end, she hadn't followed his well-intentioned, but unrealistic, advice.

"What else is in there?"

"Looks like the medical report. Oh, Jesus."

"What?"

Mary's hand reached for Caitlin's shoulder, but she stared at the folder. "Pictures."

Another precious moment forgotten until now. The nurse with Deputy Sugar had taken a full spread of photos from the worst possible angles. "Maybe skip the bruised ribs and torn vagina images and get to the written material, Lubbers."

Mary didn't look away. "I can't believe someone did this to you."

"Mary?"

"Right, sorry." She flipped ahead. "Here's a transcript from the interrogation of the accused." She looked over. "Troy Woods . . . Wait, didn't I introduce you two?"

A flash of young Mary's hand tapping Troy Woods on the shoulder in a crowded bar brought a sudden tightening to Caitlin's chest. She gasped.

"Caitie?"

Ignoring Mary, she fought an overwhelming urge to close her eyes. Luckily, a competing urge surfaced—the refusal to pay for a totaled rental car. She checked the mirrors, slowed to a stop in the middle of the road, and lowered her window to let in fresh air.

"Caitlin, why are we stopping?"

Another image surfaced. The ER nurse with the camera trying to maintain her composure but unable to hide the trembling of her hands or the tears she wiped away.

Caitlin unbuckled her seatbelt and looked out the open window. The fresh air helped.

Mary tapped her shoulder, gently, but with worry in her voice. "We shouldn't stop here."

Caitlin took another breath. "Just getting some air."

"Maybe pull over to the side of the road. I see a whole bunch of air over there."

Caitlin forced a smile and turned back toward her friend. "Sorry—just an impulse."

"I know a thing or two about impulses." Mary's eyes had a cloud-before-a-rainstorm look that told Caitlin her fake smile wasn't fooling anyone. "Was the report too much?"

"Mary—"

"I want to help—"

"Tell me how you met Aaron."

"How I *what*?"

Caitlin tried to control the shake in her voice. "You've never told me how you and Aaron met."

Mary started to speak, but stopped, gave an understanding smile, closed the folder on her lap, and moved it to the back seat. "You want the polite version or the real deal?"

Caitlin laughed. "For God's sake, I want the real version."

"Start driving, and I'll tell you the sordid tale."

Caitlin's foot found the pedal. "Spill it, Lubbers. Tell me how the man of your dreams swept you off your feet and out of your pants—and make it dirty."

"First of all, it was a yellow sundress that left nothing to the imagination, and it was summertime in Indiana—the dirtiest summer of my life."

Caitlin let Mary take her away with a carefree story of casual sex that led to deep and meaningful love. No pain, no tears, just pheromones, sex moans, and the collision of home decorating styles.

CHAPTER

26

"GOOD MORNING, PAIGE. I hope you're hungry."

He watched her green eyes find focus. She looked down at the straps around her wrists and jerked against her restraints.

"Easy, Paige. You're safe with me."

She tried to talk. "Who—who are you?"

He reached across the table, touched her fingers. Even drugged, she flinched at his contact.

"Relax." He massaged her hand. "You're mine now."

"'Mine now'?"

"That's right, darling. This is your room. Do you like it?"

From his experience with the gas, he guessed she had another hour before lucidity. His schedule wouldn't permit him to be present—too much to handle in the other world. He had to play with his toy now.

"Since you're not used to the rules here, I'm going to feed you today." He slid a plate in front of her restrained body. "I made you an egg-white frittata. Fresh spinach, a little red pepper, local goat cheese—nothing but good stuff. I also have a green juice I pressed myself. Spinach, kale, micro greens, cucumber, paprika, and ginger. You're going to love it. But first"—he moved around the table and stood behind her chair—"I want to show you your things."

He grabbed a gold cardboard box with a clear plastic front and brought it close to her. "Look familiar? The 1993 Holiday Edition Barbie, mint in box."

The red and gold bodice of Barbie's dress ended at her waist, where flowing red material exploded across her legs, then circled up to each shoulder.

"Must have been hard to sell her, even when I drove the price up to double her value." He set the box near the other things he thought she'd like. "Lucky for you, you've got her back."

He smiled at Paige's vacant face. "And now you can play with her. I know—scandalous. A collector taking a toy out of its box? My collection is different. No matter how the market changes or how bad I need the money, I won't sell you, and I won't give you up without a fight."

He wrapped his arms around her shoulders and squeezed. Her hair smelled perfect. Pantene conditioner, just like she'd bought the day he followed her around the drug store.

He dropped a hand down, cupped her un-Barbie-like natural breast, felt the full, warm goodness under her T-shirt.

"I hope you like it here, Paige. I've got all the things you love. Well, you won't be able to run a marathon, but once you're in a routine, I'll get a treadmill so you can work out. In the meantime, I'll get to know you, and you'll get to know me. The rules are easy and I'm fair, as long as you try to make this work. I want this to work, Paige."

He let go of her breast, lowered his hand further, pressed himself against her. "I want this to work so badly."

His hand stopped at the table, picked up a fork.

"Now let's get some food in you. Egg whites are supposed to keep your hair long and beautiful, just like Barbie's."

27

FROM THE SHOULDER of the narrow country road, Caitlin and Mary could see most of the Bro-duce property. A wide asphalt driveway led to a white, two-story farmhouse surrounded by a patch of ignored green grass. Across the driveway, two delivery trucks and a tractor could be seen through the open doors of a barn. Behind the barn, a field of healthy corn stretched waist high.

"Greenhouses," Mary said, then handed the binoculars over.

Caitlin saw five brick-based hothouses behind the house. "I only see one car."

"Could have parked in the barn. You said twenty acres?"

Caitlin nodded. "According to the map, that row of trees at the end of the lane is the edge of their property. Past that, there's a stream, then someone else's farmland."

"What's that to the right?"

Caitlin swung the glasses west of the farmhouse. "Spinach or kale." She put the binoculars away and lowered the windows. "Cue up that Dead shit, Lubbers. We're going in like your Aunt Tanya."

Mary's Aunt Tanya had spent the last two years of the sixties in a free love camp in western Indiana, and her stories lived on in legend.

"Got it." Mary cranked the stereo. "A couple of *Tanyas* looking for the perfect tomato."

They drove down the driveway blasting "Casey Jones." Caitlin stopped next to the first greenhouse.

Mary got out speaking at full volume. "This is better than Sonoma."

Caitlin followed her to the greenhouse door. "But, Mary, Sonoma had wine."

Mary peered through the translucent glass. "Looks like cucumbers or zucchini."

Down a service road, the land took a gradual descent toward the trees. A clearing beyond the corn hosted a flock of thirty-foot, three-bladed windmills.

Caitlin turned back to Mary. "Anyone in there?"

"Not a man in sight, but with that many cucumbers, who needs one?" She reached for the handle. "Unlocked."

They peeked in. Tall, large-leafed plants ran along both walls. The scent of cucumber filled the humid air.

Mary tapped Caitlin, jumped back into character. "My mother used to have the best tomatoes, or at least, that's what Dad said. He left her when they went bad."

A male voice yelled from behind them. "What the hell are you doing?"

They turned toward a six-foot twenty-something in overalls with a T-shirt underneath, fresh sweat circles under the pits, a scraggly beard, and a pair of plastic carpenter's goggles pushed back onto his bandana-covered forehead.

Caitlin offered her hand. "Hi, we're here for the tour."

He stared at her hand like he'd never seen one. "The what?"

Mary got in the game. "We're organnies."

"What the hell's an *organny*?"

Caitlin looked to Mary. "I told you it wasn't a word."

Mary didn't miss a beat. "Organnies are organic farm lovers, and that's what we are. I write a blog."

His sweaty brow bunched up like it hurt. "Sounds like you steal people's organs, lady."

Caitlin laughed. "That's why *I* call us green girls. Either way"—she held her hand out again—"we'd love to look around the place."

His hand met hers for a clammy squeeze. "We don't do tours."

"But we drove all the way from the Colony," Mary said, way too loud. "What's your name?"

"Gooch," he said. "What's a colony?"

"Mary, he doesn't want to hear about the Colony."

Mary snaked her hand through Gooch's arm, got real close. "The Colony's a hippie enclave in West Baden, where clothes are a choice and people live off the land."

"How old are you ladies?"

"Not that old," Mary said. "But I grew up there. Learned about the earth—and my natural body. You've got a great beard. Can I touch it?"

Gooch blushed. "I guess."

She rubbed his whiskers, looked into his eyes. "A beard like this? You'd be attacked day and night in the Colony."

He looked toward the road. "I can't give you a tour. I'm the only one here."

Mary let go of his beard, took his arm again. "Then who would know? Please, we'll make it worth your while."

His eyes raised four stories. "What do you mean, worth my while?"

Caitlin flashed a few Andrew Jacksons.

"Sixty bucks. You show us around, give us ten dollars worth of fresh greens, and I'll give you three green twenties. Just half an hour, and no one but us three will ever know."

He looked at the cash, then Mary. "But she has a blog."

Mary smiled. "I care more about getting a nice firm cucumber than telling the story of where I got it."

Gooch scratched the back of his head. "Screw it, let's do the tour."

They started at the barn, saw various implements in John Deere colors and the two delivery trucks, no markings other than the word "BRO-DUCE" stenciled on the back doors.

"You guys deliver all across the Big Ten?" Caitlin said.

Gooch kept it tight. "Yep. Let's look at the corn."

He walked them along the edge of the field, mumbling something about an autumn harvest.

Mary looked between each row. "Just checking if you guys farm like we did at the Colony. My dad used to plant weed between the rows."

That got Gooch's attention. "Your dad grew weed?"

"Yeah, until some weird beetle got into everything."

Caitlin pointed toward the end of the field and changed the subject. "Hey, windmills."

"For the power bills," Gooch said. "We gotta keep the greenhouses warm in the winter. Speaking of which."

He took them back to the land of cucumbers, let them pick a few. They moved on to the second greenhouse, a forest of Roma tomatoes. Mary plucked one from the vine and took a bite.

"Good God, these are fresh," she said, wiping juice from her chin. "Who's the farmer around here?"

"This guy Dave. He can grow anything. I just do this for money."

Gooch led them on to eggplant, sprouts, and green beans. In the last greenhouse, he grabbed a cardboard produce box and packaged their haul.

Caitlin read the side. "Nassau, Bahamas? You guys ship outside the country?"

"That's from a supplier," he said. "We reuse the boxes."

"What do you guys import from the Bahamas, rum?"

He shrugged. "Seeds. Let's go."

The house was the only place they hadn't looked. Caitlin noticed the cameras when they got back to the rental car. One near the farmhouse roof facing the road, another near the front porch.

"Can we use your bathroom?"

"Well—"

Caitlin walked toward the house. "Thanks, Gooch."

He followed. "I'd better come with you."

Mary got in line. "I should try too."

Caitlin opened the door to a large kitchen last updated in the eighties. A trash can overflowed near the door, and a case of beer bottles filled a recycling bin. The room smelled like a truck-stop restroom two days past cleaning.

Gooch pointed to a hallway. "Bathroom's right there."

Caitlin saw the so-called bathroom, the padded toilet seat up, a smear of poorly aimed bodily fluids visible from feet away. She went in, shut the door, ran the water, and thanked God she didn't really have to pee.

"Gooch," Mary said in the kitchen, honey in her voice. "Caitie takes forever. There's got to be another bathroom in this giant house."

He gave in. "Oh, yeah, follow me."

Caitlin waited until their footsteps faded, then opened the door.

No better place for a growhouse than a basement. No windows and only one door, usually through a kitchen. She tried a knob and found a dark wooden-slat stairway. She pulled out her phone, turned on the flashlight, and went down.

The unfinished root cellar had a cracked concrete floor, a giant old boiler, a washer and dryer, and a shop sink. Nothing special.

The floor above came to life. She took two steps up at a time, shoved her phone in her pocket, and shut the door behind her, seconds before the return of Mary and Gooch.

"All better," Mary said. "You?"

Caitlin tsked. "You boys wash your hands before you touch the vegetables, right Gooch?"

He laughed. "I don't know about the other guys, but I do."

He showed them out, then watched from the driveway until they pulled back onto the road.

"Shit," Caitlin said. "I thought it'd be in the basement."

Mary bit into a cucumber. "Don't be too hard on yourself. The second bathroom was right next to a stairway. Gooch stood in front of the stairs the whole time I was in there."

"You think it's upstairs?"

She smiled through her crunching. "Yeah, cause he made a big deal about me not being seen on the security camera, said he'd get in trouble if they found out he gave us a tour."

"Mary, you're the best."

"That's nothing, Caitie. Wait until you eat the dinner I'm gonna make with these vegetables. One thing, though—"

"What?"

"We gotta stop somewhere. No way I was gonna pee in that house."

28

Mary had meetings, so Caitlin dropped her off on campus and met Lakshmi in Dunn Meadow for a debriefing. The exposed roots of a tree created natural seats overlooking a creek.

Lakshmi looked up from her tablet. "Wait, what do the windmills do again?"

"Shield power consumption," Caitlin said. "Utility companies monitor for unusual usage, which is why the typical growhouse steals power. Since the greenhouses get their juice from the sun, the rest is getting used by the house. What about you? Find anything else online, or were you *bored* all morning?"

Lakshmi rolled her eyes. "Oh, I was bored, but you were right. I got pretty into it."

"Was it better than sex?"

"I wouldn't go that far." She pulled up a document on the tablet, energized. "So the Bro-duce Corporation didn't purchase the farm until six months after Angela's disappearance, but they were working the land before that. The previous owners were Jack and Linda Fodor."

"Frodo's parents?"

"Correct. Jack and Linda now live in a two-bedroom condo in Fort Lauderdale. I found a retirement newsletter that says they've been there for ten years, so they'd given their two sons, Nate, and his older brother, Adam, control of the farm before the purchase. Adam's six years older than Nate and three years older than Dave and Kieran."

"Which means he's twenty-seven now?"

"Yes."

Caitlin smiled. "And Adam not only went to IU, but he was also in the same fraternity?"

Lakshmi pulled up a picture of young men in matching blue blazers, the entire fraternity from Kieran Michelson's freshman year. She tapped on a clean-cut blond.

"Adam Fodor was Kieran Michelson's big brother, in the fraternity sense. Now he lives in the Bahamas and runs a tourist catamaran."

She opened a browser, showed Caitlin bahamaspartycruise.com. The same man, five years older and tanner, his crew-cut hair now in foot-long, natty dreads, smiled next to two women in barely there bikinis.

Caitlin noticed the sign above him. "Doctor Greenthumb?"

"This means they were growing weed before Kieran and Dave started Bro-duce, right?"

Caitlin nodded. "Probably, but Kieran and Dave saw the chance to make it a legitimate business."

"While Adam went to the Bahamas to grow those awful dreads."

Caitlin remembered the box Gooch gave Lubbers. "Maybe more. The farm's getting something from the Bahamas. Gooch said seeds."

Lakshmi looked confused. "Can't they find seeds in America?"

Caitlin reached for her phone. "Only one way to find out."

Mike Roman answered before the second ring. "Don't make me hang out with that scumbag again, Caitlin."

"Settle down, tough guy. You've earned a vacation. Ever been to the Bahamas?"

He hadn't, but his passport was current. He'd leave on the red eye, touch down in the land of rum the next afternoon, be mission functional by Sunday morning. Caitlin would have to dip into her pile of film-rights money for this one, but that cash had come with a list of producers who might be interested in her next big story. College kids running an international drug syndicate checked more than a few of Hollywood's boxes. She hung up, noticed Lakshmi watching her.

"What?"

"Mike jumps at your command. You two never dated?"

"Me and Roman? You read the book. I put the man in jail."

"Right, but eight years later you teamed up and saved all of those women. Now you work together."

"We don't work together. He works for me."

"You never—"

"Our bond is hard to explain. It's not quite friendship, more like I grew up on a farm hunting a wolf, but then the two of us rolled off a cliff and had to work together to survive, only to find out a mega-corporation threatened both my farm and his hunting land."

"I'm not sure I follow. Is that a film or something?"

"He's like a brother. We don't always agree; sometimes we don't even like each other, but he's there when I need him."

"What about the FBI agent?"

Caitlin felt a blush coming on. "That's more fun than serious."

"Have you ever had anything serious, Caitlin?"

"Sure."

"Were you ever married?"

"God no."

"Engaged?"

Caitlin tried to gauge Lakshmi's direction. "You're getting good at this, Lakshmi, but I'm on to you."

The girl's reaction read innocent enough. "What do you mean?"

"You're establishing the pattern. Caitlin Bergman, successful career woman, uses sex as a casual tool, gorgeous—"

Lakshmi laughed. "I don't remember saying 'gorgeous.'"

Caitlin gave her a wink. "It's implied."

"So the pattern I'm trying to establish is what, exactly?"

"Did the rape make me who I am? Did that one horrible moment change how I looked at men, at sex, at personal relationships? Did that inability to let anyone get close prevent me from finding what everyone else calls true love?"

Lakshmi's smile dropped. "Caitlin, I didn't mean anything like that."

The girl's eyes took Caitlin back twenty years. The deputy, Lyle Sugar, had looked at her the same way from the end of a hospital bed.

"Don't pity me," she said, the words coming out faster than she could control. "I have loved; I've been serious with a man—a brilliant photojournalist with a perfect smile and a better ass. We got engaged before he left for an assignment in Iraq, but he never came back. Well, not all of him." Caitlin felt a line of tears worming their way into the conversation but stopped them at the door. "I've got a healthy sexual appetite, and my schedule means I really need to be into someone to do it on a regular basis, let alone share meals. But it has happened before. I assume it will happen again."

Lakshmi looked embarrassed. "I really wasn't asking about any of that."

One tear got past the bouncer. Caitlin tapped her finger to the corner of her eye. "Guess it was me then."

Lakshmi stared at her nails, or at least made a show of it. "Do you think," she started, delicate, "that Angela, if she's still alive, and if we find her, do you think she'll ever be the same as she was?"

What could Caitlin tell the girl that wouldn't destroy her? If Angela Chapman was still alive—and two years was a whole lot of *if*—she'd have survived unimaginable hell. She'd remember the man's hands, the helplessness, the vivid image of Troy Woods's smile seconds before he knocked her head against a chuck of rock—

Caitlin shook her head. *Not Troy Woods—Angela's attacker.*

Caitlin reached for her bag and got to her feet. "Let's stop for today. It's too nice out."

Lakshmi rushed to pack up as well. "I'm off all weekend. What's the next step?"

Caitlin started walking toward the Ernie Pyle Building. "Before we go to Greenwood, we need to show a correlation between the produce deliveries and the sale of pot."

Lakshmi trailed a few feet behind. "How do we do that?"

Caitlin's chest felt heavy. She kept moving. "We find the weak link, the corner boys. Two years ago, Frodo had to drive Kieran and Dave to parties. Who's driving Frodo around?"

"I don't know. I can't get close. That whole frat hates me."

Caitlin stopped. A version of the questions she'd accused Lakshmi of asking earlier remained unanswered in her own mind. She squeezed her eyes shut, pressed on her temples. "Then we wait for a bit. I need to take care of some things."

When she opened her eyes, Lakshmi looked terrified. "Are you okay, Caitlin? You seem—"

Caitlin grabbed her by both shoulders. "You're a strong, intelligent woman, Lakshmi Anjale. Handle your business."

She left her on the sidewalk and let the tears have their party all the way back to the cottage.

CHAPTER

29

CAITLIN DIDN'T WAIT for the tub to fill. She leaned back against the basin, forced her naked skin to accept the still frigid surface, watched her arms turn to goose flesh.

You must control it.

The steady stream warmed the cold enamel under her bottom.

You must.

She splashed her face.

Control.

When the water reached a foot, she went under, let her hair drift around her face. She opened her eyes and stared up at the white ceiling, lost herself in a wash of color. Warm amber from the light over the sink gave way to the cool blue from the last bits of afternoon diffused by the window.

Same colors as a hospital ceiling.

Twenty years earlier, Deputy Sugar stood at her bedside with the stocky build of a bulldog, a face lined by years of Indiana winters, and a clipboard in his hand.

"Miss, I'm Deputy Lyle Sugar with the Monroe County Sheriff's Department. You're in the hospital." The bass in his voice rumbled like tires over snow. *"Can you tell me your name?"*

The ring of Caitlin's phone brought her back. She sat up, pulled her wet hair away from her face, answered the phone. "Caitlin Bergman."

"It's Jerry Greenwood. Catch you in the middle of something?"

Caitlin turned off the water. "Just taking a break. Any news?"

"Wondered if you had dinner plans."

"Technically, yes," Caitlin said, back in business mode. "But if something's come up—"

"Oh no, just thought you might, you know, want to grab dinner."

"Oh." Caitlin patted herself with a towel. "My friend's expecting me around seven. Why don't you join us?"

She gave him the details, then called Lubbers. Mary had no problem with the extra guest.

* * *

When the doorbell rang, Mary gave Caitlin the boy-crazy look of a thirteen-year-old, then ran for the door yelling, "Hide the drugs—it's the cops!"

Caitlin took two glasses of red wine off the kitchen island. "Your wife is hilarious."

Aaron Gaffney munched a slice of cucumber. "She's a freak, but she makes me food."

Greenwood joined the party. He wore a navy-blue sport coat over a white shirt and gray slacks. Two feet behind, Lubbers did a pelvic thrust.

Caitlin handed him one of the glasses. "Drink this. You're going to need it."

Mary grabbed a large salad bowl from the counter and led them all into the dining room. "I hope you like vegetables, Detective."

"Please, call me Jerry," he said, taking the chair across from Caitlin. "Are you vegetarians?"

Aaron coughed up a bit of water. "Shit, Mary, there's gonna be more than just the salad, right?"

She started the bowl with Caitlin. "Yes, my caveman lover, there will be more than just salad. I have spinach lasagna—"

"As in no meat?"

Mary smacked him on the head, took her seat. "I made chicken too. This salad is special. All organic, all farm fresh."

The bowl got to Greenwood, who filled his plate. "Organic, huh? Somewhere local?"

Caitlin jumped in before Mary could mention their adventure. "She wanted to show me that California wasn't so special."

"Well, she's right," he said, digging into his greens.

Mary launched into matchmaker. "Have you ever lived there, Jerry?"

He looked up with his mouth full, too polite to answer. Caitlin filled the gap. "Detective Greenwood had his big-city time, Mary. New York."

He smiled, swallowed. "Did I tell you that, Caitlin?"

"Not with your words."

"Didn't know you could read so much from my body language."

Caitlin took a sip of wine but didn't dare face Mary. Obvious flirting would only fuel the woman's desire to get her laid. She caught Aaron's eye instead.

Whether lovingly oblivious or picking up Caitlin's desperation, the good professor changed the subject. "New York, huh? I taught composition at NYU for four years. How long did you live in the city?"

"More than a decade."

Greenwood spun the story. His wife had received a scholarship to Columbia Law, and his three years with Bloomington PD had gotten him hired by the NYPD. Six months before 9/11, he'd started in patrol. The table let him move through his time line without opening that wound. He told them how he'd transferred to major crimes, worked his way to homicide. His wife's work in family law had kept them in a Brooklyn brownstone.

Mary found the appropriate opening. "Why did you come home?"

"My father-in-law was hospitalized. Melissa wanted to make peace in case he passed." Greenwood glanced at Caitlin, reached for his wine.

"And your wife?" Lubbers refilled his wine glass. "Do you mind if I ask how she died?"

"Shit, Mary," Aaron said, "is the lasagna ready?"

"I've got a timer. It'll go off."

"How about an awkward meter, babe? Got one of those?"

Greenwood held a hand up. "I don't mind talking about it. Melissa suffered from polycystic ovarian syndrome. It's usually not serious, but she had a cyst rupture."

Mary leaned in. "You can die from that?"

"If the hemorrhage causes an infection, but it wasn't that." He took a breath. "I was working on the south side of town. She was visiting her father at his nursing home, two blocks from Meadows Hospital, out by State Road Thirty-Seven. She'd gone through the pain before. They say it compares to what people with appendicitis feel. Trooper that she was, she didn't want to waste an ambulance, and drove the two blocks. I left work to meet her. She parked in the lot, walked to the ER."

He cleared his throat.

"They were re-curbing around the awning over the ER door. The sidewalk was messed up, so she cut through the construction." He took another breath. "Same time, a cab swings up to the door. Driver's looking at the back seat, where a nineteen-year-old is screaming at the top of her lungs, pushing out twins."

"Oh God," Mary said.

Greenwood nodded. "He thought he hit the curb. Didn't even notice

Melissa until an orderly came out. The bumper knocked her off her feet, her head hit the curb, and—" He made a futile wave with his hand, let the story end. He probably wiped tears away. Caitlin couldn't tell. She, Mary, and Aaron were all busy doing the same.

He broke the silence. "Should have warned you, I'm shit at parties."

Mary got up and threw her arms around his shoulders. "I'm the worst host in the world. What can I do to make this better? You can shoot me if you want. Did you bring your gun?"

Greenwood laughed. "Maybe a slice of lasagna?"

*   *   *

The rest of dinner revolved around tales of the ridiculous. Mary and Aaron's honeymoon disaster in Mexico, the time Caitlin got food poisoning at the mayor's mansion, the various ways women had tried to convince Patrolman Greenwood to ignore their vehicular inebriation.

"Let's have a fire," Mary said, leading the party to the porch. She and Aaron huddled over a firepit while Caitlin claimed a love-seat glider.

Greenwood arrived with red wine reinforcements. "Room for two?"

She took the wine, patted the cushion. Greenwood's body rocked the entire couch.

Mary called over to them. "We're gonna do s'mores. You guys want in?"

Caitlin knew the second she said yes, Lubbers and Aaron would disappear into the house. She'd pulled the same trick on a camping trip their junior year.

She raised her glass. "Why not?"

Mary nudged Aaron, and the two completed their play.

Greenwood laughed. "Wow, Mary's got an agenda."

"Picked that up, did you?"

"Sure, I went to church camp in high school. I know the signs."

"How'd that turn out for you?"

"Dry humping in sweat pants? Not as hot as it sounds."

Caitlin let a loud, manly laugh escape, the kind she reserved for scotch and cigars.

"Wow," Greenwood said. "You okay?"

She reeled in her awkward. "Pretty damned good, actually. You?"

The detective had his top two buttons undone and the right amount of chest hair poked through. No *Magnum P.I.* forest, but not waxed gym rat either. Caitlin already knew Jerry Greenwood would be great in bed—if he didn't burst into tears.

He looked to the sky. "Beautiful night, Caitlin."

She looked up to a full field of stars. It wasn't the time, but she went there anyway. "Any luck with Paige Lauffer?"

He met her back on Earth. "Where'd you and Mary get the organic vegetables? Little farm by Nashville?"

"Maybe we don't talk work tonight."

She leaned in, kissed the man. He met her lips with the perfect amount of pressure and desire—not one single tear.

Who needed therapy?

She touched his shoulder and felt the firm, corded muscle. His hands wrapped around her waist and pulled her closer. He had the grip of a man who could swing an axe. Caitlin loved the push of his lips, the firm, yet receptive play of a good kisser. She stepped up her game, stood, then straddled him. The glider's springs squeaked like a thirty-dollar-a-night motel mattress, and Caitlin rode the wave with the same dirty passion.

Greenwood reached up, held the side of her face with one hand. Caitlin pushed against him, felt the seam of her jeans hit the right place for both of them to know the night's potential.

"Should have worn those sweat pants, Detective."

"Would it be wrong if we left?"

Caitlin kissed him again. "Let's take a walk."

* * *

It only took two blocks to get to Bryan Park.

Caitlin glanced around the dark lawn. "It just occurred to me that you could get in serious trouble if we get caught."

He pressed himself against her. "I could get in trouble just for kissing you."

She felt the urgency of everything great in his slacks. "You've been warned."

She walked him to the place she and Darren Thompson rocked the world, introduced him to the limestone rhino. Pants around his ankles, her panties to one side, Greenwood gave her the best orgasm she'd had in a decade. No tears riding the statue this time.

Nor the time after.

When Greenwood finally joined her, Caitlin had lost count.

Pants reassembled, shirts located, they landed on a park bench, his arm around her shoulder, her feet pulled up beneath.

"Obviously, this won't change anything between us," he said, kissed her head.

"Please, Greenwood. You're not my first officer of the law."

"I could tell. No fear in the line of fire."

She craned her neck, kissed him again. The man's lips tasted like her. She came up for air, stared out to the swaying branches of a maple tree, the sole witness to their session.

Greenwood rubbed his fingertips on her forearm. "Want to get breakfast?"

Caitlin found her phone, checked the time. "At one AM?"

He laughed. "In the morning. You can tell me what you and Mary found at Amireau's farm."

Caitlin kissed the man again. "I'll call when I wake up."

CHAPTER

30

H E WATCHED THE lovers part through the lattice of the park's gazebo, then checked the time. *1:12 AM.* Almost five hours off schedule.

Between his societal obligations, grooming and feeding Paige, and the regrettable human necessity of sleep, he'd only allocated one hour that afternoon to following Caitlin.

Crouched in the bushes outside the guesthouse, hearing her hum, then watching her dress, then change, only to settle finally on her original outfit, he decided to stretch the hour until he saw the person Caitlin wanted to impress. Once he spotted the detective, the schedule went out the window. When the pair reached the park, nothing could drag him away. He was breaking his own rules, reckless.

You're reckless too, Caitlin, but wonderful. Do you know Greenwood's using you? That he'll hurt you? I wouldn't. I'd protect you.

First, he reminded himself there was no room for Caitlin in his collection; then he focused on the reason she'd made the schedule at all.

Self-preservation.

He needed to know if her investigation was getting close.

Fucking the detective seemed pretty close.

Seemed.

But the detective had never found Angela. And if he couldn't find Angela, he certainly wasn't going to find Paige.

31

J UST AFTER TEN the next morning, Caitlin reached for her phone. She'd
told the man she'd call, so she did.

Greenwood answered via speaker. "What can we help with, Miss
Bergman?"

She'd caught him and Maverick walking into a Paige Lauffer task force
meeting. So much for repeat sex. She hung up, reached for her running shoes,
and set out to release endorphins through the less preferable act of jogging.

She'd gone two miles before her phone rang in the middle of Dunn's
Woods, a grove of forested sanctuary in the southwest corner of campus. She
didn't recognize the number but knew the voice.

Doris Chapman sounded agitated. "I can't get a hold of Lakshmi. Have
you heard from her today?"

"Not since last night," Caitlin said, biting back her next thought. *When
I ran away crying.*

"Me either. Maybe she's ignoring me."

Caitlin heard the tinkle of ice cubes in a glass. Maybe Doris was more
than agitated at ten in the morning.

"Why would you think that?" The pause lasted long enough for Caitlin
to check that her phone was still connected. "Doris?"

"I got jealous."

"What do you mean?"

"I checked with her yesterday to see if you'd found anything new, and she
said she couldn't tell me. You see, now that you're involved—"

"I'll call her, make sure everything's okay."

"I can't afford to have her stop talking to me. Angie and I stopped talking. Well, not *talking*, but she stopped telling me real things about her life."

"Doris—"

"My daughter, my husband . . . I can't lose Lakshmi."

Caitlin couldn't let the woman spiral. "Doris, everything's fine. We might have something."

"Something new?"

"Please don't take it personally, but we can't afford to let anything slip. I'll have Lakshmi call you, okay?"

"I'm so sorry."

"Nothing to apologize about."

Five apologies later, Doris Chapman let her off the phone. She sent Lakshmi a text: *Any luck last night? Give me a call when you can.*

A gentle breeze rustled the leaves of the tall trees. Caitlin closed her eyes and counted to sixty, her body swaying with the wind.

She opened her eyes, checked her phone. No reply.

She ran another quarter mile, then stopped and checked again. Still nothing.

In the nine days she'd been in Bloomington, six had started with some sort of communication with Lakshmi. Maybe it was nothing, but Caitlin changed her route, aiming instead for the girl's apartment.

What if something had happened? The last time Caitlin had seen her, she'd told the girl to handle her business. Lakshmi could have gone out to the farm and gotten herself in real trouble.

She got to Lakshmi's building, caught her breath, and knocked on the apartment door.

No answer. Caitlin sent another text: *You around? I'm at your place.*

No sounds of activity in the apartment, no sign of an imminent reply. She checked the parking lot. No Chapman-mobile either.

"Shit," Caitlin said out loud, pacing. "She could be studying, or seeing a movie, or hanging out with friends."

Except Caitlin knew she wasn't doing any of those things. The girl ate, drank, and breathed Angela Chapman. She'd have her phone on and ready for any sort of news. Not just from Caitlin but from Doris as well.

Where the hell are you?

Caitlin's stomach dropped. She'd told Lakshmi to follow the corner boys. The corner boys all worked for Amireau—the guy with the restraining order against her. Lakshmi could very well be in jail. But Greenwood would have mentioned it, right? They had slept together, after all.

She reached for her phone, started to dial, then stopped, dropping her face into her palms.

Slow down, Bergman. You're losing it.

She took a breath, exhaled, then dialed her phone.

The sound of Scott Canton's voice brought a moment of peace.

"Scott, sorry to bug you on a Saturday, but I'm losing my shit."

"I never mind a bee that brings me honey, but what has you in such a frenzy?" He listened patiently as she summed up the situation, then responded in a reassuring tone. "The other day I dropped my phone in a toilet. By the time I got back from the mall with a new one, I had eight missed calls—and I'm seventy. You might be overreacting."

Caitlin kicked the parking lot curb with her trainer. "Apparently that's my thing now."

He laughed softly. "I'm sure she'll call soon. In the meantime, allow me to present a calming distraction for the next two hours."

"Where are you?"

"Fishing, dear girl. Come fish with me."

CHAPTER

32

HALF AN HOUR later, still no response from Lakshmi, Caitlin found Scott
Canton on the south shore of Lake Lemon, locking oars into a row-
boat. He wore a floppy hat, a multipocketed vest, and khaki shorts, but Caitlin didn't see the one tool every fisherman needed.

"Was I supposed to bring the pole?"

"On days like today, I fish for beauty and truth. Same process, less mess."
He nodded toward the folder in her hand. "I don't remember assigning any
homework."

Caitlin held her assault report up to her chest. She'd run back to the
guesthouse, changed clothes, headed for the door, then stopped. She could
have shown up without the folder, but the contents weighed down her every
step. "I'm tired of overreacting, Scott, tired of losing my shit. Do you think
we could—"

He nodded and offered his hand in assistance. "I think we must."

She got into the boat, and he took them into the still sheet of blue. No
more than half a mile across, but twelve miles wide and surrounded by dense
forest, clumps of reeds, and the occasional home. Caitlin dipped her fingers
in the water. Cool, but not frigid.

"I love it here," Scott said between strokes. "Twenty-six miles of shore-
line, hardly any speedboats."

Caitlin pointed to two breaks in the water, covered with a handful of
trees. "I like the little islands."

"You do have a dark side." He pointed back to the shore. "We started at
Riddle Point, which is a cool enough launch for a beginning, but you picked
the one spot on the lake with a literary name. Cemetery Island."

"Better not be any ghosts," she said, tapping on her folder. "I brought my own."

She told him about her failed attempts to read through the contents and her impromptu traffic stop with Mary.

He received the report with the solemnity of a soldier being handled a folded flag, then produced a pair of joints. "Before we begin, might I offer nature's psychologist?"

"Let's share," she said. "Your stuff knocks me off my feet."

He sparked the first, offered it over. "When was the first time you got high, Caitlin?"

"High school." She took a drag. "Classic peer-pressure situation." She handed the joint back. "Two hours later my father picked me up from the principal's office. I hadn't been able to get a full sentence out since my first toke, which was a big deal. I'm a bit of a talker. Dad was a cop, so he took me to the Hollywood station and walked me desk to desk, made me tell everyone he could find that drugs were for losers, laughing his butt off the whole time."

Scott exhaled with a chuckle. "What'd your mother say?"

She went with a variation of the answer she'd given Lakshmi. "There wasn't a mother figure in the picture in those years. What about your first time?"

"In Nam. Pot was the only way I could sleep without nightmares." He sent the weed back her way, then raised her folder from his lap. "I'm ready to face your ghosts, if you are."

Caitlin took another hit. Always a chance that her high could go south, that she'd end up in the middle of a lake, paranoid and miserable, but Scott's pot hadn't failed her yet. She exhaled and nodded.

He opened the folder. Like handing a story in to an editor, Caitlin's urge to watch him read hit strong.

He glanced up and caught her gaze. "I'll give it a look and we'll talk after."

She swallowed and reached for her phone. "No worries."

He gave her a hard stare. "What are you doing?"

"I still haven't heard from Lakshmi."

"And you won't," he said. "No signal out here. Phones scare the fish. Enjoy nature's majesty."

She turned away, watched a heron dip under the surface, then lost herself to faraway sounds. The rolling knock of an unseen woodpecker, the flap of a duck's wings launching into flight, the slight lap of the water against the hull.

Minutes later, Scott tapped her shoulder. "All done."

He folded his sunglasses and hung them on his vest. "What a piece of shit."

Caitlin's tears appeared like a surprise party; unexpected, unwanted, and messy. She tried to fight them back, but Scott's words, so good to hear, so validating, struck deep and true. Her chest ached with each shake.

Scott waited for a gap between sobs, then offered a handkerchief. "Hardly any snot on that."

Caitlin took the cloth and wiped her upper lip. "Not anymore."

"When your tears came, what emotion burst through the barrier?"

She crumpled the handkerchief, squeezed it like it wanted to run away, and bounced her tight fist on her knee. "Anger."

"At Troy Woods, the police, who?"

A word slipped out, barely any breath behind it.

"I have old ears," Scott said. "Too much amazing music and loud sex. Can you say that again?"

She flattened her fist on her knee, tried again. "I was angry at myself."

"What did you do wrong?"

She looked toward the shore, pictured herself getting in the car and driving away. "I trusted someone with a secret, and Woods found out and used it against me."

He gestured toward the file he held. "The part about your mother is true?"

She nodded. "I'd seen her maybe four times in my life up to that point. She had me at twenty-two, gave me up the same day."

"And your father?"

"Who knows? She never tried to pinpoint the accidental donor. Matthew Bergman, my dad, took her to prom years before all of that. When she got pregnant, he was already a cop and a better person than anyone she'd ever known. He and his wife adopted me."

"What did your birth mother's profession have to do with you?" Scott flipped the folder open again. "She's only mentioned in Woods's statement, not in the BPD's reports."

Both of Caitlin's hands drew up into fists. "I guess Chief Hartman left out our little meeting."

33

Twenty Years Ago

WITH HER RIGHT eye still swollen one week later, Caitlin closed it and used her left. Chief Hartman had a certification from a law enforcement union, a picture with John Mellancamp, and piercing Paul Newman eyes.

"Sorry about that." He sat behind his desk. "You need anything? Water, tea?"

She didn't say her first answer. *Less rape.* "No. Will Officer Sugar be joining us?"

"Deputy Sugar," Hartman corrected. "I know Lyle took your initial statement, but he works for the Sheriff's department. Since your incident happened within the city limits, the BPD will take care of you from here on out."

He leaned forward with a smile. "Do you like Bloomington?"

"Is this small talk?"

"No, Miss Bergman. I know you're in a delicate condition."

The bandages over her knuckles strained to prevent her cuts from breaking open as she clenched her fists. "You mean because of my torn vagina?"

He put out a hand, tried to slow her. "Miss Bergman—"

"Or my torn asshole? Is that the *delicate* situation you mean, Chief Hartman?"

"There's no need for that kind of language."

"Sorry," she said. "My torn anus."

He started again. "Bloomington's got to be different from what you're used to, growing up in Los Angeles."

"Well, no one raped me in Los Angeles."

"I want you to know I'm here to help you through this, to make this as easy for you as possible."

Caitlin took a breath, realized she was sweating, wiped her forehead. "Sorry."

"No need to be," he said. "In a big city, horrible things like this happen every day. Small towns like Bloomington? I'm sure you're aware we still have fights between locals and college students over meaningless boundaries and imagined slights."

"Such as what the word *no* means?"

He laced his hands together. "I understand the counselor has gotten in touch."

"Yes."

"And Warren from the prosecutor's office?"

"Who sent me here."

"Yes, good. Have they told you about Troy's account?"

"Let's see that piece of shit talk his way out of DNA evidence."

"People said the same thing about OJ Simpson. Do you know why rape is such a hard thing to prove?"

The tightening in Caitlin's chest prevented her from interrupting.

"It's not like murder. Someone shoots someone, there's a gun. Someone owned that gun, bought bullets. Ninety-nine out of a hundred cases, we find those killers, give a jury enough evidence to send them away. But rape? Most cases of rape happen between two people in a remote place, no witnesses, with no evidence left behind."

"What about his semen, my skin under his nails? What about my face?"

"Horrible, but look at his statement. He says you're into rough sex, that you asked him to treat you this way."

"Who would ask to be beaten to death?"

"You're not the first girl in town to have sex with Troy Woods."

"I don't really care who he finger-blasted after a football game. He *raped* me."

"None of the other women have claimed to have been raped."

"*Claimed?*"

"Don't misunderstand me. He's going to fight this. He already has a lawyer. They're going to find everything they can in your past to suggest this was what you wanted."

"I never wanted to be raped."

Hartman moved some papers on his desk, held up a single sheet. "Do you know Darren Thompson?"

"What are you talking about?"

He read from the paper. "'Last night was amazing, especially when you spanked me. Ever tie anyone up? 'Cause I'd be into that.'"

"Where did you get that?"

He didn't stop. "'Saturday night you should use me however you want. Make me your whore.'"

He handed her the email exchange between her and her ex.

"Darren gave you that?"

He picked up another page from the stack. "Do you know Steve Toblowsky?"

A blow job in his car.

"Tony Jeong?"

A one-night stand after nickel beer night at the Bluebird.

"Ellen Shaub?"

"Good fucking God."

"Him too?"

She looked up into Hartman's blue eyes. "What did you say?"

"The defense will have a lot to work with."

"I like to have sex. That doesn't mean I wanted to get raped."

"Will a jury believe that? A jury of God-fearing Monroe County residents, most of whom married their only lover?"

Caitlin looked at the man's desk, noticed a family picture. "Would you talk to your daughter like this?"

"Would I try to help my daughter?"

"Would you tell your daughter it was okay she was raped because she'd slept around?"

"I'm not saying it was okay if you were raped. But my daughter doesn't have your perclivities."

"Proclivities."

"What?"

"The word is *proclivities*. If you're going to use it to judge me, you should know how it's pronounced."

Hartman raised his eyebrows. "That's the kind of attitude a small-town jury won't feel sorry for. Plus, they'll bring up your mother."

Caitlin's hands shook. "I don't have a mother."

"No, you have an aging porn star so far past her youth that she specializes in double penetration and BDSM. You think that won't come up?"

"I don't know. Does your daughter fuck like your wife, or don't you compare?"

"Miss Bergman—"

She couldn't hold back. "You'd tell your raped and torn daughter what exactly?"

"I understand your father is a policeman."

"LAPD."

"And I can guess why you haven't told him yet. If someone attacked my daughter—"

"Raped."

"If they harmed a hair on her head, I'd drive across the country with a knife, a roll of duct tape, and a sledgehammer, and I'd break every bone in his body, then feed him his own privates, no matter what it cost me. If your father's anything like me—"

"My father's nothing like you. He's the best man on the planet."

"Who you don't want to see spend the rest of his life behind bars because of an overreaction to an unnecessary scandal."

34

S COTT'S ANGER MADE him look twenty-five. "He said these words to you?"
"Hartman presented me with a choice. To prove I was raped, I'd have
to go to trial and publicly air every slutty thing I'd done in my life. But if I
left the rape out of my complaint, Troy would say an addiction to self-
prescribed steroids made him violent, and he'd plead guilty to aggravated
assault, no trial, no press. He'd go to jail and I'd walk away with some bruises
and my dignity."

"You're angry because you chose the deal."

Caitlin nodded. "It wasn't enough to fight for my life. I didn't want to
defend my lifestyle."

"Your lifestyle? When I was twenty-one, I was shooting blindly at men
I'd only meet later in piles of the dead. All you had was a healthy sex life."

"And tits," Caitlin said, looking around the lake. Therapist or not, Scott
was still a man, and even the best men often forgot the world's biggest double
standard. "Have I ruined fishing for you?"

"You're a great fucking woman, Caitlin. Pardon the obscenity."

Caitlin laughed. "Tell me something I don't know."

"Stop being angry with yourself."

"I know."

"No, you don't. You've been dragging this weight behind you. After the
attack, when was the first moment you felt safe?"

"The hospital, I guess."

"You shouldn't have to guess. When did you feel like you weren't under
attack anymore, like Woods, or even Hartman, couldn't hurt you?"

Caitlin closed her eyes, thought about her drive away from campus, her stop in the plains, a walk in the desert outside of Vegas, rolling back onto Sunset Boulevard.

She opened her eyes. "My father's pool. I dove into my father's pool."

Scott nodded. "Good. Was he there?"

"No, I had it all to myself."

"Okay, close your eyes again. Describe the moment."

The gentle rock of the boat helped Caitlin go back. "The water was cold. His pool wasn't heated or anything. I remember my fingertips brushing the grate at the bottom. I sunk down, turned up toward the surface."

"What did you see?"

She pictured the fractured surface, the clouds above. "The sun."

"Why was that safe?"

She opened her eyes. "I don't know."

"Don't you?"

She did but shook her head no.

"Okay," he said, then took off his vest and hat.

"Whoa, Scott, what's happening?"

"How far do you think it is to shore?"

"Maybe a hundred and fifty feet?"

He untied his shoes, set them on top of his clothes. "Are you a strong swimmer?"

"What the hell are you talking about?"

The addition of his wristwatch to the pile left him in only shorts and a T-shirt.

"Something very stupid. I want you to get back to that moment, and we just happen to be hovering over a body of water. I'm going to jump in the water and swim to shore, and if you want to, I want you to swim with me."

"What about our stuff?"

"I have a plan for the boat, so you can leave your things. But I have to warn you, it's only seventy degrees out here, so the water has to be cold, and there are fish, turtles, maybe snakes."

"Then nothing about this is a good idea?"

"Exactly."

"What about you? Any chance you'll have a heart attack?"

"Yes, there's a damned good chance. But if it helps you find that safe spot again, so be it."

He tied a rope into a loop, fastened it to the boat's bow, let it hang in the water.

"Well, shit. I did not see this coming." Caitlin stripped down to her bra and panties. "You sure this isn't just an excuse to get me naked?"

He laughed. "Only your soul, my friend."

She stood on the metal bench, felt the goose bumps on her arms reach for the sun.

"Take a second," he said. "I'll be right behind you."

Caitlin nodded, took a last breath, then plunged feet first into the cold. The bottom came faster than expected. Her bare heels touched a mix of grass and loose soil, maybe eight feet down at the most. She blew out to stay submerged and opened her eyes. The murky water around her melted into the searching sunlight above, not much visibility side to side. Her body's shock gave way to acceptance, and she listened to the distorted sounds of life above. A perfect kind of white noise, a faraway memory, a fetal innocence.

She put herself back in her father's pool and admitted what she hadn't said to Canton. While down there staring at the sun, she'd blown out all of her breath and waited. The oxygen depleted, her chest convulsed, and the overhead sun went wavy. Seconds from collapse, she knew her answer: she could die right then, or she could live. Completely up to her.

That day, the weight of Troy's attack had nothing on the need for one more breath.

Now, on the bottom of Lake Lemon, she made the same choice. She took one last look at the lovely blue above, brought her arms down, kicked to the surface, and broke into daylight.

Scott treaded water next to the boat. "Ready to swim?"

"Try to catch me," she said, then launched into a crawl stroke.

Her body pumped full force, one arm up, the other down, legs kicking, everything in synchronicity, a steam locomotive bound for glory.

No fear, no thought, only experience.

She took a breath, head out of the water, eyes open to the shore. Fifty feet to go. She'd left Scott behind, but nothing mattered. She fought on until her hands touched something reedy, green, alive. She lowered her feet, crawled through four feet of vegetation, hit earth, and didn't stop. She ran twenty feet, jumped, both arms in the air, screamed in pure joy. "Woooooooo!"

She turned to see Scott reaching the shore as well.

"That was really stupid," he said, already shivering.

"So stupid," she said, yelled at the lake again. "Wooooooo!"

Scott joined her primal scream.

When they ran out of air, she turned to him. "Now how do we get our clothes?"

He smiled and pointed out to the boat, breathless.

Caitlin didn't wait for his words to catch up. She ran down the bank and dove back under the surface.

* * *

Later, warming in the car, her head clear, her heart light, Caitlin checked her messages and let out a deep sigh. Lakshmi was alive and well: *I found a corner boy. Want to help me nail these assholes?*

35

Caitlin walked through a clump of aluminum-sided townhouses with uncovered central parking and found Lakshmi hovered over her laptop at a table on the back porch of Unit 3.

"Who lives here?"

"No idea," Lakshmi said, "but there's a week's worth of pizza fliers outside the front door. We should be safe."

Caitlin sat beside her. "Which apartment are we watching?"

"Lucky thirteen." Lakshmi nodded to the two-story unit fifty feet across the parking lot and took a sip from a nearly empty cross-country-trucker-sized iced coffee. "You said to follow the corner boys, so I reached out to the girls in the Chapman Chapter to see if Frodo was still involved with the fraternity, who he was dating, and where he lives now."

"Judging by your caffeine intake, you got a response."

Lakshmi shook her head like a wet dog. "Not much sleep, but yes. So the Sig Eps threw a party last night."

"That's not Frodo's frat."

"No, but his house co-sponsored the event, some sort of STD awareness night, and my friend Deena was going. I parked down the street, and she texted me. Here's a pic."

The selfie of a blonde, presumably Deena, captured two young men in the background—a tall, scrawny guy talking to a younger man dressed in a bright pink robe and a bulbous foam helmet.

"Is that kid supposed to be a dildo?"

"Yep," Lakshmi answered. "The pledges had to dress like sex toys. The dong is Frodo's little frat brother, Chuck Lester. The tall, skinny guy is Frodo. Deena said he handed Lester an envelope and told him to leave."

Caitlin smiled. "And you followed Lester?"

"Kind of hard to miss a walking penis. He ditched his costume, drove to this apartment, and walked around back. That was between midnight and one."

"What's back there?"

Lakshmi showed Caitlin images of a wooden deck, a gas grill, and a window with closed horizontal blinds. "Look at the barbecue."

Caitlin laughed. "No propane?"

"Exactly, and the grill looks brand new. Lester must have put the envelope under the lid."

"You didn't check?"

"Couldn't." She swiped to the image of the kitchen window, enlarged the photo.

Caitlin saw a small black dome in the frame. "A security camera."

Lakshmi nodded. "Indoor, looking out. That's only the first bit. I left for five minutes to move my car down the street. When I got back, there was another frat boy leaving."

"What was he dressed as?"

"A rabbit. It's a brand name for a popular vibrator."

Caitlin sat back. "The case of the backdoor dildos. Take that, Hardy Boys."

Lakshmi went on. "I went back to the bushes and waited. There weren't any more dongs, but around two AM . . ." She found a video, hit "Play."

Caitlin watched shaky video taken through an evergreen. Lanky Frodo opened the grill, grabbed five sealed envelopes, then went inside.

"So we're watching Frodo's apartment?"

Lakshmi nodded. "The farmer's son has three bedrooms all to himself." She pointed to the SUV in the space closest to his apartment. "His car hasn't moved all night. It's the blue Expedition, same one he drove the night Kieran and Dave came to get Angela. Can we call Greenwood now?"

"Since they've separated the sale from the delivery, we can't draw a direct line to drugs. The real question is where the money goes. We know that Kieran, Dave, Frodo, and his older brother Adam are all paid through third-party corporations. How would you get cash to the corporations? Something that no one would question?"

"Could it be a charity?"

Caitlin nodded. "The collegiate Greek system is built on the idea that all sponsored events are charitable in some way. Car washes, the dance marathon—"

"STD awareness?" Lakshmi looked up wide-eyed. "Frodo's the fraternity's treasurer. David was too."

"Great, it all fits together. Say BPD pulls our dildo over and asks why he's got so much cash. Dildo says the fraternity treasurer gave him an envelope after an organized function. Was there a cover charge for last night's party?"

"Two bucks for the STD awareness thing. Would that be enough?"

"The amount wouldn't matter. Our supposition is that they're delivering weed with organic vegetables. The cover charge probably does go to a legitimate cause, but the money in the envelopes pays for the weed. The time between delivery and payment is obfuscated by the collection of money tied to the charity event."

"And the cash gets back to Frodo. Could he launder it through the fraternity?"

Caitlin shook her head. "Risky. Could trigger an audit from the national chapter. Wasn't there some sort of charity associated with the farm?"

"Yes, the Delta Omega Tau Alumna Philanthropic Association. If they send the money to the charity, then the charity must pay out to the farm, or at least the associated corporations."

"Which sends the money to the shareholders. The drugs are the key. We need to follow trucks from the farm to the houses, see which deliveries are followed by events and if the money makes it back to Frodo."

"Then we go to Greenwood?"

"Yep. I only hope we don't have to wait until next weekend. It might be too late for today's deliveries."

"Oh, Caitlin," Lakshmi said, pulling up a calendar on her computer. "We're building up to Little Five. There are parties every night."

The weekend of the Little Five Hundred, an annual student bike race named after the Indy 500 auto race, was advertised as "the world's greatest college weekend." Bigger than homecoming, bigger than graduation, every night leading to the Saturday afternoon event would offer a full spectrum of debauchery—which meant a high demand for narcotics.

They made a plan and parted ways, Lakshmi to sleep and regroup, Caitlin to work out logistics with Mary. She made her way back to the guesthouse an hour past sunset. Tired from the crying and the swimming and the planning, she almost missed the slip of paper stuck in the screen door.

She hadn't left the porch light on, so she picked up the folded half sheet of printer paper and went inside. Throwing her bag down, she flipped on a light and unfolded the note.

Sorry I haven't been in touch. Don't worry, Caitlin Bergman, you're still safe—like a rose embower'd in its own green leaves.

Caitlin smiled, reached for her phone, and typed a text to Jerry Greenwood.

Thanks for the note. Who says chivalry is dead?

She hovered over "Send," then stopped, deleting the response. Replying to the man at this time of night might lead to more than playing in the park, and Caitlin wanted to get up early.

36

THE NEXT DAY, Caitlin watched Lakshmi squeeze a massive black rental pickup into one of the diner's tiny parking spaces and hop out.

"Did you get the stuff?" she asked when Lakshmi emerged.

She nodded. "Easels and everything. Are they here?"

Caitlin pointed to a green Honda sedan at the opposite end of the parking lot. "Here comes Lubbers."

Mary walked over. "Lovely day for a stakeout."

Caitlin didn't realize she'd instigated a hug until her hands closed around her friend. "A boy left me a note."

Mary patted her back, let go. "Like a love note? Let's see."

Caitlin slipped her the paper.

"Wow," Mary said. "Your boy Greenwood's got some penmanship. Weird imagery, though. What the hell does *embower'd* mean?"

"I don't think it's a real word—"

The deafening rumble of a motorcycle interrupted. Behind the wide grips of a Harley, Aaron Gaffney could have passed for an extra in *Easy Rider*. He wore a fringed suede jacket and a white helmet with white stars in a fat blue stripe down the middle, red pinstripes on both sides. He leered at them under raised eyebrows. "Ladies."

Caitlin laughed. "Is that an Evel Knievel helmet?"

He revved his throttle, gave them a metallic, throaty growl. "It gets Mary hot. Right, sexy?"

Mary bounced over to him. "You bet, random biker I just met."

She kissed him like they hadn't seen each other in years, then came up for air. "What's the plan?"

Caitlin gave them the overview. "We need footage of the boys loading trucks, particularly with anything that comes out of the house. We'll set up two spots, front and back, then rotate to follow if anyone leaves."

* * *

Armed with one of two professional cameras borrowed from the *Daily Student*, Aaron parked behind a clump of trees on a service road facing the organic farm. Caitlin, Mary, and Lakshmi drove their vehicles another mile to a public park with a large group of soccer fields, parked, and got out. Kids ages six to fifteen played the game while sidelined parents played games on their phones. Mary, standing by to follow anyone who might leave the farm, set up camp with a canvas chair and a romance novel.

Caitlin left her hybrid and joined Lakshmi in the truck. They drove away from the farm, then turned onto a country road.

Caitlin pointed to a small house on the north side of the street. "That should be the lot directly behind the Bro-duce farm."

Lakshmi parked in the house's gravel driveway, then got out and knocked on the front door. A woman in her sixties, in tan pants and a floral print vest over a red blouse, stepped outside. Lakshmi shook the woman's hand, then gestured toward the land past the house. The woman smiled, even put a hand on Lakshmi's arm. She glanced back toward Caitlin, waved. Caitlin got out.

Lakshmi handled the introduction. "Carol McGovern, this is my professor. Guess what, Caitlin? Not only is she fine with us looking around, *she's a painter as well.*"

Carol shook Caitlin's hand with a firm, eager grip. "Mostly landscapes, all watercolors, but I can proudly say one of my cardinals hangs in an insurance office in Seymour. What are you working on today?"

"Water," Caitlin answered. "It looks like a creek winds through the edge of your property."

"Oh yes, and it's beautiful, especially in this light. Why don't I get my paints, and I'll join you? I can show you the best place to set up."

She turned toward the house, twenty years younger, but Caitlin couldn't paint a smiley face. She dropped their cover story and confessed to the sins of journalism.

Carol looked disappointed, but not angry. "So why come to my house?"

Lakshmi answered, "Because we need to spy on the farm behind the creek."

Carol nodded. "Those boys, huh? Do the police know about this?"

Caitlin knew not to lie. "Not at this time, though I am working with the Bloomington Police Department."

The woman lowered her voice. "Jerry Greenwood?"

Caitlin laughed. "That's right, Mrs. McGovern."

"Does he know you're here?"

"No, and it's for his own good that he doesn't."

The woman weighed the choice, nodded. "Do you want to tinkle first?"

*   *   *

Caitlin pointed halfway up the tallest tree on the bank. "Plenty of leaf cover, nice strong branches—that's my spot."

Lakshmi laughed. "Caitlin, that's like twenty feet."

"I think twenty-five."

Caitlin ran, jumped high enough to catch the first branch, and pulled herself up.

"Badass," Lakshmi said below her.

Caitlin acted like she hadn't pulled something. "You're not the only athlete around here. Toss the bag."

Lakshmi let the backpack fly. Caitlin strapped the gear around her shoulders and climbed to her spot.

Lakshmi called from below. "How is it?"

Caitlin sent a cell phone picture to the group's text thread. She had a good view of the land west of the greenhouses, the road through the back fields, and the space between the main house and white barn. Two cars were parked near the house, but no one came or went, and no one was working the fields.

Aaron replied with his perspective—the main house, driveway, and the barn's front.

Below her, Lakshmi busied herself on her tablet.

Caitlin pulled the school's high-quality camera from the bag. She scanned the farmland with its telephoto lens, snapping shots of a spinach field, the greenhouses, and a brick circle that might have been an old well. She held no illusions she'd find the grave of Angela Chapman, but the act seemed like a productive way to pass the time. After two hours, she and Lakshmi swapped spots, allowing a quick nap against the tree trunk.

She woke to a text alert, swiped her phone to life, found the latest text.

Aaron: *Two guys left main house, walking down road by greenhouses.*

Caitlin called up to Lakshmi. "See Dave?"

"Not yet."

Another text came in.

Mary: *Ready to roll.*

Caitlin saw Lakshmi lower the camera to text her reply.

Lakshmi: *Hold. Walking away from barn. Near last greenhouse now, each carrying something.*

Through the underbrush, Caitlin couldn't see past the rising field. "How far away, Lakshmi?"

"More than a football field—nothing to worry about." She raised the camera again, then texted.

Lakshmi: *One is Nate Fodor. Other could be Gooch. They have a shotgun.*

Mary: *Shit. Get out of there.*

Lakshmi: *No worries. They've got a skeet-shooting trap.*

Caitlin: *Still moving or set up?*

Lakshmi: *Moving. Not far from windmills.*

Caitlin: *Distance from us?*

The boom of a shotgun answered before Lakshmi. Faint male laughter followed.

Lakshmi: *100 yards.*

Caitlin heard a male voice yell, "Pull."

She texted: *Come down.*

Another shot followed. The shooter made contact. "Nice shot, Gooch."

Caitlin whisper-shouted up. "Lakshmi, move your ass."

The voices continued.

"My turn, bro."

"That wasn't even six, Frodo."

"Whatever—it's my gun. Hit the button."

The trap launched. This time, the report came much later. Right after the boom, Caitlin heard a rustle rip through the tree leaves, like sand against a window. A handful of birds shot out of the brush at the edge of the field.

"You could see the thing, right?"

"Who cares? Did you see those birds take off?"

Caitlin looked up. Lakshmi shoved the camera into the bag, put the strap around her shoulder, started climbing down.

"Pull."

The next boom came straight toward the trees. Lakshmi struggled for footing. The camera bag slipped off her shoulder. Caitlin caught the bag before the gear hit the ground, but Lakshmi landed hard. Something made of bone snapped.

CHAPTER

37

New Providence Island, The Bahamas

THE *WAVY LADY*, a red and white catamaran, sat anchored off the eastern shore of New Providence, the island home to seventy percent of Bahamians, and Mike Roman's hotel room. A breeze pushed an aggressive cloud of pot smoke back toward the ship and dulled the steady thud of party music.

Drunk Allison from Chicago touched Mike's arm, her bikini top jiggling enough to be noticed. "Ed?"

Any one of the horny drunks around him on the deck would have appreciated that jiggle, but Mike stayed true to his character—Ed Thompson from Toledo, recently dumped.

"Allison, you're great, but I'm not in a party mood."

"Because of your fiancée?"

"Who told you?" He looked back to the main cabin. A writhing clump danced in front of a bar where Adam Fodor, wearing a Doctor Greenthumb wig and all, dispensed booze in plastic cups, lit joint in his mouth.

Mike had met the elder Fodor the day before, pitched him a sob story about being left at the altar, tried to get a refund for a honeymoon scuba package. Not only did Adam grant the refund, he shared his bottle of dark rum, then guaranteed Ed Thompson a good time on his midnight booze cruise. Compared to Kieran Michelson, Fodor seemed like a pretty good guy.

Drunk Allison grabbed Mike's hand. "Let's go dance."

She pulled him to the cabin, then dove into the meat hurricane. More sweat than standing room. Mike worked his way to the bar, took a corner spot. Fodor approached.

"Big Ed." He tossed his dreads around and slapped the bar with his palm. "Having a good time?"

Mike shrugged. "Good enough, buddy."

Fodor grabbed two cups and a bottle. "I party for a living. I can tell when someone's not having fun. Do a shot with me."

Mike smelled the dark liquor in the plastic cup. His nostrils said no, but Fodor raised his own cup and yelled, "No regrets."

Mike did the shot, regretted everything.

Fodor handed his wig to a second bartender, pointed Mike aft. They climbed up to the captain's deck.

"Adam, you've been cool and everything, but you don't have to look after me."

"Time for my break anyway." Fodor reached into a pocket, came back with a tiny baggy and a ring of keys. "You want a bump?"

He tapped some coke onto the end of a key, did his impression of the eighties.

Mike wanted Fodor to trust him but didn't want to push too hard. "Truthfully, I want to go home."

Fodor sucked through his nostril, wiped the tip of his nose. "Not into the island life?"

"Just thought I'd feel better about everything once I got here."

Fodor handed the baggy to Mike. "Drugs make everywhere better, and the Caribbean has its advantages."

"What, like you just drop by Colombia anytime you want?"

"I do own a few boats." He held out his keys. "You want to hit this?"

Mike Roman had avoided Michelson's coke, but Ed Thompson needed to indulge. He took Fodor's keys, poured a tiny pile onto the end of a standard Kwikset. He did the bump and handed the gear back.

The next part would be tricky. When he'd checked Fodor's web page that morning, two rooms were still available for a Wednesday morning fishing charter from the Bahamas to Florida. Caitlin had told him to look for anything outside of the standard drunk party boat scene. A kid with access to cocaine, taking a one-way trip through international waters the same week as IU's biggest party, had to count. Mike wanted to be on that boat but couldn't look like he wanted to be on that boat. "What I really want is to get to Miami."

"What's in Miami?"

Mike's brain came alive. Lot of dopamine in that dope. "Wow."

"Right? What's in Miami?"

"Sex."

"Shit, we got sex here. You want to go again?"

Mike waved him away. "Picture the dirtiest sex of your life, the kind that you kept in the spank bank at the worst time in your relationship."

"I'm with you."

"You'd better not be," Mike said, "but she will be, and if history repeats itself, so will one of her friends."

"Got an old hookup in Miami?"

"I do. When she found out I was in the Bahamas, she started sending me naked pictures, said get my ass to Florida."

"Bullshit."

Mike pulled his phone from his pocket, swiped, handed the mobile porn machine to Fodor. The photos in the text thread came from the internet, but they looked low budget enough to fit the story.

Fodor handed the phone back. "You don't care about your return flight or hotel reservations here anymore?"

"Would you?" Mike stared at the phone. "Only shitty thing, I can't get another flight for under nine hundred bucks, and that's not till Thursday. The TSA's weird about last-minute one-way shit."

Fodor nodded. "This is gonna sound crazy, but I might be able to beat that. I've got other boats, right? Well, I'm supposed to do a repos to Fort Lauderdale on Wednesday."

Mike fought back a smile. "A repos?"

"A reposition. I'm gonna run a fishing charter over to Florida. We've got four cabins onboard. I can't give you one for free, 'cause, you know, this is a business, but I can get you to Florida on Wednesday night. No TSA. Shit, no customs at all."

"You leave the boat there?"

"Yeah, it needs a little work, and my parents live in Lauderdale. I'll put it in dry dock for two weeks, then charter another fishing trip for the way back."

Mike noticed his heartbeat in his fingertips. The pounding beat worked through his entire body. Dancing didn't sound so bad anymore. In fact, dancing would be required. "You didn't just get me high to make me buy a boat trip, did you?"

"Hell no," Fodor said, "I got you high to get you laid. Either tonight or three days from now."

38

Lakshmi smiled at the red gift bag on her chest. "Caitlin, you didn't have to."

"Normally, I'd have gone full Tiffany's box, but I figured—"

"Gift bags are easy to open." Lakshmi held up her broken wrist. Three signatures on the cast so far—Caitlin, Mary, and Aaron. "It's not your fault I fell, Caitlin. You told me to get down. I can still text and type, and I've got some killer drugs."

She picked up one of the three prescription bottles on her bedside table, sounded out the word. "Nor-co. These are my favorite. Now, my present."

Caitlin leaned forward. "You have to promise me something."

"Like what?"

"I've already talked to your teachers. We've gotten you extensions on several projects, as well as the right to stream your main lectures."

"Caitlin—"

"I've reached out to Doris. She'll arrange any transportation you need."

"I can still drive."

Caitlin got to the point. "I want you to know that we're here for you, that you'll be taken care of."

"What's the promise?"

She met Lakshmi's eyes. "You have to finish."

"Finish what?"

"Promise me you'll finish your degree."

Lakshmi looked confused. "Why wouldn't I?"

Caitlin felt tears in the corners of her eyes, looked away. "Because you got hurt doing my job, less than a month away from graduation."

"Oh, right." Lakshmi raised her good hand. "I promise nothing will stop me from finishing my degree."

Caitlin reached for a tissue, blew her nose. "Good."

Lakshmi looked like she might cry too. "I thought you were a badass."

Caitlin shook away the sadness. "Open your gift already."

Lakshmi tipped the bag over. A slip of paper fell into her palm. "Is this a password?"

Caitlin smiled. "Since your injury will keep you out of the field, that code will let you use my professional credentials on the online financial database."

Lakshmi lit up. "You're trusting me with your password?"

"You've earned it."

Lakshmi clutched the slip of paper against her chest. "Only one thing would make this better. Can we order pizza?"

Caitlin laughed. "Way ahead of you."

*   *   *

Caitlin heard the noise, went to the main room.

Mary stood in the open doorway next to an uncomfortable-looking pizza guy. "Caitlin, tell this young man I'm not trying to steal your pizza."

"She probably was, but she's with us." Caitlin held up a wad of cash. "Remarkable timing, Lubbers."

Mary waved the money away. "I don't mind shelling out for Pizza Monster."

She paid the young man, grabbed the pie, and shut the door behind her. The sweet, oily scent of cheesy goodness filled the room once more.

Lakshmi called from her bedroom. "Is there a monster in my apartment?"

Mary laughed. "That's right, kid. Can you walk?"

Lakshmi emerged from the bedroom and stumbled her way to the coffee table. "Where there's pizza, there's a way." She opened the box and bit into a piece, then looked up at Caitlin and Mary with cheese hanging from her mouth. "Pizza Monster doesn't care that his daughter is a lesbian. That's why he cuts the slices into delicious triangles of bliss."

Mary nudged Caitlin. "Think she'll sell us some pills?"

"Think we'd better move if we want pizza."

They made fast work of the food. Caitlin filled in time-line gaps for Lakshmi—her and Mary's trip back for the abandoned rental car, the surveillance of two Sunday Bro-duce deliveries, the lack of meaningful activity on the farm Monday morning, the fact that it was now Monday night.

The food sobered Lakshmi somewhat. "What about Dave?"

Mary shook her head. "No clue. We've seen Frodo and Gooch make deliveries, and an underclassman drop off money after a party, but no sign of Amireau yet."

Caitlin studied the open spreadsheet on her laptop. "According to our list of sponsored events, they've got nothing for two days."

"Which is good," Mary said. "I have meetings, and Aaron has to teach tomorrow and the day after, so we can't be around for another stakeout. Plus, there's the helmet thing."

"The what-met thing?" Lakshmi said.

"My dumb lover will never be a spy. Gooch flagged him down to ask where he got the helmet, said he'd seen him twice that day."

Caitlin laughed. "Looks like I'm on my own tomorrow."

"I can help," Lakshmi said. "Maybe not drive—"

"Or stand." Caitlin shook her head no. "To go to Greenwood, we still have to document David Amireau at the farm. Broken wrist or not, your restraining order means I'm going by myself tomorrow. I won't do anything stupid."

Mary uncapped two beers. "Famous last words uttered by anyone who ever fell off a cliff."

CHAPTER

39

H E CHECKED THE sidewalk then backed into the gap in the hedge. Sure
that no one had seen, he slid up against the wall, inched toward the
window, heard all three voices. He pulled his hat down further, his jacket
collar up, and glanced through the one-inch gap in the curtains.

Caitlin Bergman, the redheaded professor from the graduation ceremony,
and the Anjale girl—a vocal part of the investigation from the beginning—
all ate pizza beneath a wall of Angela Chapman information.

He stepped back and considered his position. Less than two weeks in
town and Caitlin nearly had all the pieces.

His presence outside the apartment wasn't just playing with fire, it was
walking a tightrope over an active volcano. He had Paige. Paige would have
to be enough. A bird in the hand always beat hiding in the bushes.

He checked the sidewalk again, stepped out, and ran to his car.

CHAPTER

40

C AITLIN PARKED THE hybrid by the fence across from the Bro-duce farm
just before eleven AM and saw only Fodor's blue SUV in the driveway.
She fixed a flexible tripod to the camera, then mounted the rig on her open
window sill. With a video app on her laptop showing the live feed, she'd be
able to get some work done without looking up every five seconds.

She searched her documents for the collegiate sexual abuse study and
found a passage Lakshmi hadn't quoted.

*Women and men, undergraduate and graduate students alike, reported
experiencing sexual harassment or assault before arriving at IU at rates
similar to, or higher than, those they experienced while at IU. These
results speak to a need to better address this issue in our high schools and
communities.*

While presumably accurate, the section didn't address the obvious differ-
ences between high school and college. The maturity gap between ages
fifteen and twenty-one, the availability of alcohol and controlled substances,
the freedom of diving into a freshman class of ten thousand.

The big question: Were men worse now than twenty years ago? A house
full of guys Caitlin knew in college shared two VHS tapes and a stack of
Hustler magazines. Today's youth dialed up pornography on their phones,
where every woman not only enjoyed anal but begged for it.

On the opposite side: Had social media and education empowered victims to find one another, heal together, recover faster?

She opened her writing app and started her piece:

*   *   *

In the spring of 97, my editor at Indiana University's student-published news-paper assigned me the Breaking Away story, an annual fluff piece celebrating the time Hollywood immortalized the sleepy college town in a film of the same name. I remember saying, "This is the worst thing you could possibly do to me."

Two days later, I'd be beaten and raped by Troy Woods.

My best friend had introduced me to the local hero over a drinking game. Everyone seemed surprised I didn't recognize the first-string quarterback with the Disney-prince cleft chin—let alone spend my night flirting with him.

He only piqued my interest when he offered to help with my assignment. A real local, he'd grown up three miles south and could show me spots the usual stories ignored.

That he was four when Twentieth Century Fox made the movie about the yearly bike race, the Little 500, didn't stop my interest. I wanted to tell a story that went beyond the sorority house where the local boy serenaded his girlfriend or the stretch of road where the kid raced the semi.

When Troy proposed a day trip that Saturday, I agreed, even shook his hand when he spoke the seemingly innocent phrase "It's a date."

One thing all victims of sexual assault have in common is a kind of guilt-ridden hindsight, full of self-doubt and self-blame. Twenty years later, the voice inside me repeats the same questions.

Did I lead him on in some way?

Was that handshake the unspoken consent to rip my clothes off?

Troy drove, even took an unnecessary detour past Bloomington South High. No coincidence, a billboard at the end of the football stadium listed Troy Woods—BHS's own Hoosier—among their greats.

High school had been one thing, but IU remained far from the best program in the Big Ten. Troy wouldn't go on to the NFL. He mentioned something about an arena league scout, something else about a coaching opportunity. Two miles from the quarries, I realized his tour had less to do with the town than the townie himself.

Troy knew his way around the massive abandoned stonecutting facility on Tapp Road featured in the film. He and his friends had brought girls to the site in high school—so many he'd lost count.

"This is the place Paul Dooley goes—"

"I've seen the movie, Troy."

"—'cause he doesn't understand his son."

He jumped onto a concrete platform, stepped over a rusted iron beam. Chalk mushroomed where his size 15 shoe landed. Stooping over a pile of small pieces of white rock, he placed a chunk in front of him, pulled a plastic bottle out of his pocket, and took a sip of lemon-lime soda.

"Watch this."

He poured Sprite on the stone, then described the chemical reaction like a fifth grader with a science fair project. The calcium carbonate, aka the limestone, reacted to the carbolic acid in the soda, causing the stone to break down.

He smiled at me the same way previous boys had after pointing out constellations or doing pull-ups. This was his finishing move.

I was no angel. I'd had my share of lovers—maybe more than average—and I'd acquiesced to displays of testosterone less overt or impressive. But not that day. That day I wanted to go home, and I told him so.

He said no.

Unlike my other lingering doubts, I don't question my actions at that moment. I didn't freeze or hesitate.

I started running.

Troy Woods would never play for the NFL, but he caught me in seconds.

* * *

Caitlin's eyes went to the camera feed. The elusive David Amireau stood outside the house next to Frodo. She hit "Record." They went inside the first greenhouse.

Still only one car. Was Dave living there?

She reread her opening. Gratuitous, more therapy than journalism. Either way, she'd started the process. No panic attack, no tears.

Again, she caught movement in the feed. Both men carried boxes from the greenhouse to the barn.

She'd taken the tour. The boxes contained nothing more than crisp Persian cucumbers. Still, she'd documented Amireau at the farm. She started the shutdown process to be ready to follow whoever left. She wasn't ready in time.

David Amireau whipped out of the barn and down the driveway on a bicycle.

Caitlin pulled the camera and tripod off the window.

He reached the road, waited for an oncoming truck to pass.

"Not good," she said.

Instead of turning, he rode straight across the road toward her hiding spot.

She crammed the camera behind the passenger seat, threw a sweatshirt over the pile of surveillance gear.

Amireau's thick beard and beady eyes greeted her through the passenger window. He smiled, knocked on the glass. "You okay?"

Caitlin had no idea if he'd seen the camera. She reached for her phone. "What did you say?"

"Are you having car trouble or something?"

Not exactly the "What the hell are you doing spying on me?" that she'd expected.

"No." She held up her phone, screen locked. "Directions. My phone keeps losing signal, and I'm looking for something."

"What?"

"The soccer fields. My niece has a game somewhere around here."

"On a Tuesday?"

Caitlin tried to lemonade the lemon. "She's twenty-five. She and her friends took the day off for a health thing. Do you live around here?"

"You're in my driveway."

"Oh, sorry," Caitlin said, lost in the thought that Aaron Gaffney had spent an entire day in the very spot.

Amireau looked past her. "Why'd you park like that? All up against the fence."

She tried to force a blush. "I peed in your grass. I wanted to set up a barrier in case anyone drove up all of a sudden. You know, like you just did."

Amireau laughed a little. "That would have been weird."

He pointed down the road. "The soccer fields are a mile to your left. They even have bathrooms. Might be a little nicer than my grass."

Caitlin placed the car in gear. "So sorry."

"No worries, I feel like a dork for sneaking up on you."

She wondered if the smile she summoned looked as unnatural as his. "Thanks for the directions and the rest stop."

"Anytime. Stay safe." He wheeled himself away from the car.

Caitlin pulled out and drove toward the soccer fields. After fifteen minutes of muttering to herself and staring at grass, she retreated to Mary's guesthouse.

CHAPTER

41

ALMOST NOON, CAITLIN grabbed her tennis shoes and ran from her mistake. Her app chimed at the one-mile marker. She did twenty push-ups, started mile two. A block south of the main strip, smells from nearby restaurants called to her. She dug deeper, hit the town square, did another twenty push-ups. She popped back up, headed south. Traffic was light, the sky was blue, and no one but David Amireau and her knew how close she'd come to blowing everything. Her mile three chime came earlier than expected. Apparently, rage took a minute off her usual time. More push-ups, then a turn down a residential street. She'd only planned to run three miles but didn't stop until number five.

Forty-nine minutes. Not her best, but a solid effort.

Fifty feet from the guesthouse, she saw Jerry Greenwood leave the front porch and walk to a sedan.

She jogged closer. "What'd I do now?"

He smiled. "Thought I missed you."

"What's up?" She met him by the car, checked the passenger seat, no Maverick.

"Needed to blow off a little steam," he said. "Looks like you just did."

Caitlin wiped sweat from her nose. "I've got more steam, Detective. Want to come in for a cup of absolutely nothing?"

"More than anything."

She led him to the house. Another folded piece of paper hung from the screen door.

"You can ignore the note," he said. "I'm not as good with words as you are."

"Are you kidding? Most men would have texted."

She grabbed the message. *Want to get together and talk about the city's nicest park?*

No fancy words this time. Maybe Greenwood hadn't written the other note. Could have been Scott Canton. The word *embower'd* screamed poetry.

She opened the door, kicked off her shoes. "How'd you know where I was staying, Cyrano?"

He followed her in. "I'm a detective."

"No one named Mary told you how to find me?"

He winked. "Called the rent-a-car place, said I found your phone and wanted to return it. They gave me the address you gave them."

"My tire store move?"

He moved closer. "Basically."

She stepped back. "I'm gonna rinse off. You can tell me your problems through the shower door."

He laid his sport coat over the back of the couch, loosened his tie. "I'll try anything once."

She got the shower going, undressed, stepped in, and closed the frosted glass door behind her. She'd rinsed the shampoo from her hair when she heard his approach.

"Caitlin, you situated?"

"We're separated by a polite wall of glass. Come on in." She started conditioner. No reason to rush. "Why so frustrated?"

"Besides the wall of glass?"

"Yes, besides this."

She looked over the top of the door, pressed her body against the glass. "Can you see my nips?"

Greenwood sat on the edge of the tub, his tie noticeably absent, top two buttons undone. "Sadly no, but you're rocking out those suds."

"Seriously, what's wrong?"

"Paige Lauffer is completely gone."

Caitlin leaned back, rinsed her conditioner. "That's why you didn't text."

He nodded. "Or call. My phone is really the department's phone."

"Nothing on a running app or GPS pings?"

"No luck with the tech, the tip line, or the searches. Same thing as Chapman. At least this time, no one's made any mistakes."

"Mistakes? What mistakes?"

He backpedaled. "Nothing, but I wasn't involved with Chapman from the onset. Not really a mistake as much as a mishandling."

Caitlin knew Jerry had joined the Chapman investigation late but realized she hadn't met the person who'd started the process.

He changed the momentum before she could ask. "Ready to tell me what you're working on?"

One easy way to dodge that question.

She rinsed the last of the soap from her body, opened the shower door, and stepped out naked, dripping wet.

"I'm working on getting you out of those pants."

*   *   *

Greenwood didn't try to hold her. Caitlin didn't try to stop him from leaving. He'd given her two things—sex and a lead.

She texted Lakshmi. The patient had the munchies. Caitlin appeared at her apartment half an hour later with takeout. She knocked twice, tried the handle.

Unlocked.

She opened the door, set the takeout on the coffee table. "Lakshmi, you here?"

A hoarse groan answered from the bedroom.

Caitlin ran around the corner.

Lakshmi lay star-fished on her back, her maroon panties the only layer between her skin and the puke brown carpet. Her eyes were closed, her breathing labored.

"Lakshmi, are you okay?"

Lakshmi opened her eyes, smiled with her whole face. "I feel great, why?"

Caitlin squatted next to her. "'Cause the door was unlocked and you're lying on the floor with your tits out."

Lakshmi giggled. "I got hot."

Caitlin reached for her un-casted arm. "They said the pills might do that to you."

"So I had a beer," Lakshmi said, propped herself up.

"There's our answer. Let's put a shirt on and some food on top of those pills."

She scoured the apartment for liquor while Lakshmi ate, found a bottle of vodka in the freezer. She tucked it under the kitchen sink, then joined Lakshmi on the couch, told her about her run-in with Amireau.

Lakshmi seemed to grasp the main points but clung to consciousness like a drunk to a toilet. She tapped the satellite map on Caitlin's laptop. "What's that?"

Caitlin moved the computer closer to herself. "Not a tablet, honey."

"Sorry. Does Dave have a swimming pool?"

Overhead clouds partially obscured the body of water behind Amireau's standard-sized mobile home. Much larger than a pool, the area had straight lines around the edges.

Caitlin magnified the image. "It's an old quarry that filled with rainwater."

"That bell-end has a pool." Lakshmi groaned, let a belch escape. "Sorry. That was well rank."

Caitlin zoomed out to see the area north of the trailer. A thick ridge of forest separated Amireau's lot from another, much larger quarry. A massive crater full of green-blue water led to acres of stone piles and a small group of buildings on the far end. The site looked active. Caitlin started a search.

"Let's see who owns the place."

"Let's see who owns your face," Lakshmi echoed. Her eyes-closed time approached.

No luck on the address Caitlin estimated as Amireau's trailer.

She changed subjects. "Lakshmi, what was the name of the detective who started Angela's investigation?"

"Greenwood?"

"No, before him. Do you remember their name?"

Her eyes fluttered. "Uh-huh."

Caitlin relented. "Okay, want to try the bedroom?"

"Uh-huh."

"That's what I thought. Can you stand?"

Lakshmi managed the assisted stumble to the bed under Caitlin's direction.

"Get some sleep, kid."

"Sheep man," Lakshmi answered from another consciousness.

"What's that?"

"Sheep man," she said again.

"Yep, get some sheep, man. I'll be out here when you wake up."

Lakshmi slept away the afternoon. When she woke at ten PM, Caitlin helped her to the bathroom, then another pill.

42

CAITLIN RELEGATED HER Lakshmi duties to Doris Chapman at nine AM, then drove the rented pickup to Frodo's apartment.

Mary knocked on her window at ten thirty with a bag of bagels and two cups of coffee. "You want cinnamon raisin or onion?"

"An onion bagel? Don't you have to talk to people?"

Mary got in. "Anything to keep the horny students away. You've got me for three hours. What's the plan?"

"Caffeinate, sit and wait."

Caitlin added a creamer to her coffee, stirred the concoction with her finger. "Ouch, that's lawsuit hot. I need my tongue to work these days."

Mary swallowed a mouthful like it was an ice-cold milkshake. "Really? You and the detective again?"

Caitlin detailed yesterday's quickie with Greenwood. Mary countered with her and Aaron's nocturnal adventures. They spent an hour over their breakfast, talking about the good world, no movement from Frodo's apartment.

Mary lowered her window, let in another lovely day in the high sixties. "What is it now—noon?"

"Almost."

"Have you been able to open the folder again?"

So much for the good world. "Not by myself, but yes."

"Do you want to—"

"Not right now." Caitlin reached for a pack of gum she'd set in the center console, unwrapped a piece. Maybe if she looked busy, Mary would drop the subject.

"Okay, Caitie. Just so you know, I'm here for whatever you need."

Caitlin popped the gum in her mouth and turned toward Frodo's apartment. *Anytime, kid.*

"Unless you don't want to talk to me about it?"

Caitlin sighed. "Why would I not want to talk to you about it, Lubbers?"

"I don't know." Mary ran her finger along the windowsill. "Did I . . . do something?"

Besides introduce me to Troy Woods? Caitlin pushed the thought away. "No, but it's hard for me to talk about and—"

Mary opened her hands. "Let's talk about that."

"—and I've been able to talk about a little bit, a very, small bit, with Scott Canton."

"Your old professor? As in the poetry department?"

The mint flavor of Caitlin's gum now tasted acidic. She took the piece out of her mouth and looked for a scrap of paper. "Also a trained psychologist, Mary."

Without a word, Mary pulled a wadded napkin out of the fast food bag and handed it over. "But I'm your friend. I used to be your best friend, and you were mine. You were supposed to be my maid of honor."

Caitlin pressed the gum into the napkin and threw it in the backseat. "What are you talking about?"

Mary shook her head. "I'm sorry. I know this is awful. I know you were raped. I get it now. You're the victim here, not me."

Caitlin faced her eye to eye, maybe for the first time that morning. "What are you upset about?"

"I know that *now*, Caitie. Twenty years later. But then, my best friend in the world disappeared without so much as a goodbye."

"Okay, I was—"

"It's not like I didn't make myself available. Emails, phone calls, Christmas cards."

"I got the cards, Mary. I loved the cards."

"That's great. I'm glad." Mary sniffed tears. "But no matter how much time went by, you didn't call me."

Caitlin gripped the steering wheel. "It's not like I talked to anyone else. I buried myself in my work. Shit, it took two years to have sex again."

Tears wanted out. Wadded up napkins wouldn't do the job this time.

She reached for her bag in the backseat, grabbed a pack of travel tissues. She handed Mary a Kleenex, got another for herself.

"Every time I thought about calling you, I found myself right back in the dirt with Woods on top of me. Every email put me back in the hospital or the police station. I was scared, and I was angry, and that had nothing to do with you." Her nose made a slight honk when she blew. "Gross—sorry."

Mary put her hand on Caitlin's arm. "I love you, Caitie."

Caitlin leaned in for a hug. "Love you, too. Sorry it took so long. One thing though—" She broke the embrace. "For now, you don't have to bring it up. There's something safer about talking to a trained professional."

"I'm a good listener."

"I know, but do you remember what you said when you got in the car, about the onion bagels?"

She squinted. "About them keeping horny students away?"

Caitlin nodded.

"That was a joke."

"I know, but my first reaction when you said it was that an onion bagel wouldn't stop some monster from—"

"I'm sorry." Mary looked like she might cry again. "I won't make jokes anymore."

"Yes, you will. And that's okay. That's the difference between a therapist and a friend. I need you to be my friend. Okay?"

Mary smiled. "Okay."

Caitlin looked to the clock. 12:07 PM.

"Who was your maid of honor?"

Mary laughed. "My cousin Ginger."

"Wait, Bible-college Ginger?"

"See? My maid of honor was a sober virgin who thought sex involved an hour of prayer instead of foreplay."

*   *   *

Half an hour later, Nathan Fodor got in his SUV. Mary followed in her sedan while Caitlin drove to a gas station and used the bathroom.

East toward the farm.

No surprise in Mary's text. Back in her car, Caitlin played catch-up. One mile from the farm, her phone buzzed again.

He didn't stop.

Caitlin saw Frodo's SUV parked in the farm's driveway. What did Mary mean?

Her phone rang. She set it to speaker.

"Mary?"

"He just drove by the soccer fields in one of the delivery trucks, headed east. Caitlin, I gotta get to work."

"Don't worry about it. Get going."

She saw the entrance to the soccer fields and Mary's car parked near the gate. "I see you."

"I see you too," Mary said.

Caitlin drove past, watching her rearview mirror. Mary pulled into traffic, headed the other direction.

"How far will you follow him?"

Caitlin gunned the accelerator. "I've got to catch him first."

CHAPTER

43

The Bahamas

Unlike the *Wavy Lady*, a party boat designed to have its nightly sins hosed off, the *Queen of the Waves* was a regal sailing yacht nicer than most people's homes. Mike had been shown aboard by a well-dressed Bahamian mate named John. After ten minutes in his cabin, he found his way topside.

Two billowing sails caught the wind. On the top deck, Adam Fodor and Bahamian John faced the open sea.

Mike joined them behind the captain's wheel. "Now this is a freaking sailboat."

No hangover today, Fodor looked as clean-cut as Bahamian John. "What would you like for breakfast?"

"Got a granola bar?"

Fodor laughed. "For what you're paying? John, make us both a breakfast burrito."

"Sure thing, Captain." John went below.

"Sorry about the fishing thing," Fodor said. "When the other reservations cancelled, it didn't make much sense to spend the afternoon casting lines, especially since you cared more about getting laid than life at sea. You know you could have gotten a ferry for half the price, right?"

Mike figured this would come up. "Yeah, I did a web search yesterday. No worries, look at all this." He gestured out to the water. "Plus, I get a breakfast burrito."

Fodor nodded. "Stretch out on the recliner. I'll send John by with your breakfast."

Mike found a chair, took off his shirt, and kicked off his shoes. Before he could ask for sunscreen, Bahamian John appeared with a bottle of SPF 30, a glass of water, and his burrito.

Mike ate the whole thing, closed his eyes, and let the warm Caribbean sun and wind argue over which would put him to sleep first.

* * *

The waves woke him. Higher than before, choppy even.

"Hey, douchebag."

The words weren't as loud as the waves. He opened his eyes, saw the bright blue sky, afternoon sunshine, a bit of cloud. The world shifted with a swell.

He sat up, bobbing in the unstable body of an inflatable Zodiac.

"Fuck me," he said, realizing he was no longer on the yacht.

"That's right, fuck you."

Twenty feet away, Adam Fodor leaned over the railing of the *Queen of the Waves*, a rope line in hand. Bahamian John stood next to him, holding a rifle. Fodor's rope kept Mike tethered to the catamaran.

"I looked you up online, *Ed*," Fodor said. "I wanted to see this woman who betrayed you. Didn't find much. Know what I found? Try to guess."

A simple web search under Mike's name would bring up his infamous past, but Fodor wouldn't have found Mike's name on anything in his bags. He'd mailed his passport and credit cards to a mailbox store in Miami.

Fodor held his phone up. "Small world, am I right?"

"I can't see—"

"I know, dude. Can't see from that far. John, what's on my phone?"

John smiled. "A very beautiful woman."

"John's being polite. Here's a tip. You want to lie about who you're banging in Miami, don't pick the adult video performer of the year."

Not as bad as Mike thought. "Okay, I lied about the girl. I just didn't want to stay in the Bahamas."

Fodor kept going. "I thought to myself, if you're lying about that, what else? Do I know anyone who'd send a liar to the Bahamas just to check on me? Then it hit me." Fodor swiped at his phone. "I know a psychopath who'd hire someone to check up on me." He flashed the screen again. Mike saw the image this time. Kieran Michelson's face filled the screen.

Fodor pulled the phone back, read, "'Too early to say, but Rep Repair in talks with an elite Hollywood private security firm.' It's got a picture of you and Spiderman, so you must be elite."

Fucking Spiderman.

"So you're gonna leave me out here to die?"

"To die? I'm not Kieran. Look behind you, man. That's Florida. Two miles. You've got your luggage, your phone, all that stuff. Hell, John even slipped a bottle of sunscreen and a few granola bars in your bag." He reached down, held up a silver oar with rubber paddles. "I'm gonna say my shit, then tie this to the end of the line. You pull it in, you can row to shore. You lose it, you're close enough that the tide will take you in by sunset. I'm not the monster here."

Mike eyed Bahamian John's rifle. "Then what's with the gun?"

"You try to follow us, John will put one through the rubber, and you'll have to swim with the sharks."

"Fine," Mike said. "What's the shit you have to say?"

"You tell Kieran this is the last run. I don't want to hear from him or douchebag Dave ever again. As for the business, tell him to get my name off it. I'm out."

Mike took a gamble. "Why don't you tell Kieran yourself?"

"No way. I'll talk to Nate; he can talk to Kieran. If he has a problem with that, remind him that I know things, man. You got it?"

Mike said he did.

Bahamian John climbed up to the captain's deck. Fodor looped the line around the oar and raised Mike's way out of Shit Creek. "You die, it's on you."

The catamaran's engine roared to life, the oar dropped into the water. Mike grabbed the line, started pulling. By the time he held the oar, the *Queen of the Waves* was a dot on the horizon. He dipped the paddle in the water and aimed for America.

CHAPTER

44

CAITLIN ANSWERED HER phone. *"The Daily Student."*

Mary laughed. "I'm on the porch swing with a pitcher of sangria and you're not here. Are you still out at the farm?"

"Oh Mary, the farm is so three-and-a-half hours ago. Also known as the last time I peed."

She checked the rearview. The Bro-duce truck trailed half a mile back. She sped up to eighty. "I'm ten miles north of Bowling Green."

"You followed Frodo to Kentucky?"

She took the Mammoth Cave Parkway exit, saw thick forest to the right and a gas station to the left. Sadly, no time to stop. She pulled onto the shoulder of the southbound on-ramp.

"Technically, he's been following me. Meaning, I pass him, keep him in the rearview, watch for turn signals. When I get somewhere I think he'll stop, I do the highway patrol thing."

"What's the highway patrol thing?"

"I exit, then let him go past me."

She put the truck in gear, drove back onto the freeway. "Then I get right behind him again."

"Does that work?"

Caitlin saw Frodo's truck half a mile ahead. "So far. I think he'll stop in Bowling Green."

"Why?"

"College town. I bet he'll make a delivery. Plus, I really need to pee."

"What if he doesn't?"

"It's a rent-a-car, and pee's mostly water?"

If Mary laughed, Caitlin didn't hear it.

"I'm not gonna rob Fort Knox, Lubbers, but this trip has to be important. The busiest party week of the year, and he drives to Kentucky?"

"Caitie—"

"Hold that thought I assume will be a warning, Mary."

"Why?"

Frodo's turn signal blinked for the next exit.

"I get to pee."

She hung up, watched the Bro-duce truck exit the freeway. She put her own signal on, followed. Two gas stations opposed each other at a stoplight. Frodo turned into the one on the right, parked at a pump. Caitlin crossed to the other, took a spot by the front door. She looked back. Frodo placed the nozzle in the gas tank and walked into the convenience store.

Caitlin ran for the bathroom, lucked out—no line. She opened the door to a single stall, locked the door, grabbed the paper ring, and unleashed the floodgates. Her body went looser than that time she got the two-guy massage at the spa in the Beverly Hills Hotel.

Someone jiggled the door handle. A harsh male voice followed. "Come the fuck on, Wendy."

The man had the kind of Southern accent that made people hate Southern accents.

Caitlin felt her tension return. "There's someone in here."

"Wendy—"

Outside, a female voice answered. "What?"

"Where you been?"

"Looking at the scratchers," Wendy answered. "Who are you bothering?"

Caitlin reached for toilet paper.

"Never mind. Get me a Mountain Dew."

"I gotta pee. Lay off, Darryl."

"What did I tell you?"

The girl's voice cowered, subservient. "You gonna hit me in the store?"

"What did I say, girl?"

Caitlin flushed, washed her hands. The drama continued.

"You said do what you say, Darryl."

"Or what?"

"Or I don't get any Oxy."

"I gotta crap," he said. "Steal me a Mountain Dew and some jerky."

Caitlin opened the door, caught a glimpse of the dickhead going into the men's room. Maybe forty, white tank top with an eagle and an American flag on the back.

She turned the other way and ran into the girl—about sixteen, bad teeth, bad hair, bad bruises on her wrists.

"Sorry," Caitlin said.

The ghost brushed past her.

Caitlin walked to the front window. Frodo's truck still sat at the pump, nozzle in place.

She grabbed trail mix and a bottle of water, then found a travel-sized mouthwash. She looked up, saw bathroom Wendy at the refrigerators. The girl picked two bottles of Mountain Dew, glanced around. Her eyes met Caitlin's, then shifted away. Caitlin went back to the coolers.

The girl tried to walk past. "I'm not stealing."

"Yes, you are. Do you need help?"

"Stealing?"

"To get away from the guy you're with?"

Her eyes shot toward the bathroom. "What? No."

"Is he family, an uncle or something?"

"Please, don't."

Caitlin checked the window. Frodo removed the nozzle from his tank.

"Last chance, do you want me to take you somewhere?"

The girl shook her head no.

Caitlin grabbed a twenty from her purse, handed it to her. "Don't let him know you have this."

She wrestled the Mountain Dews from the girl's hands and walked to the counter.

"Hey, wait."

Caitlin pushed everything toward the clerk, swiped her card. "It's on me."

Frodo climbed behind the wheel of the truck.

Caitlin grabbed her receipt, left the Mountain Dews. "Good luck."

She went for the door. Frodo pulled away from the pumps, put a turn signal on, and waited for traffic.

Caitlin got in her truck, started the ignition.

"Wait."

She looked up. Bathroom Wendy stood outside the gas station door, Mountain Dews in hand.

Caitlin watched Frodo disappear in the rearview and rolled down her window. "Get in, Wendy."

* * *

Caitlin got her to local law enforcement. The deputies tracked down a distant relative, said all the right words about getting Wendy help. She left the girl with the two Mountain Dews and her phone number.

With no hope of finding Frodo, she started the three-and-a-half-hour journey back to Bloomington under a steady deluge. Around ten PM, her dry Los Angeles roots got to her. The Midwest had three seasons more than California, and she was wasting good thunder. She took an exit, parked on the side of a country road. She lowered the windows and listened to the majesty of nature's percussion section.

The ring of her phone disrupted the symphony. She didn't recognize the number or the 786 area code. "Hello?"

"Bergman, it's Mike."

Caitlin closed the windows. "Where are you?"

"According to the nice people whose campfire I'm sharing, I'm in Bill Baggs Cape Florida State Park on Key Biscayne."

"Key Biscayne? As in the Florida Keys?"

"Apparently, and I may have messed up."

He told her the tale.

"So Fodor said he would talk to his brother?"

Mike repeated the exchange. "He said, 'I'll talk to Nate; he'll talk to Kieran.' Does that make sense to you?"

If Frodo drove from Bloomington to his parent's condo with no stops, he could make the trip in twenty hours.

"Mike, how fast can you get to Fort Lauderdale?"

"I have to wait for a mailbox store in Miami to open at nine tomorrow morning. Assuming my credit cards and ID are there, I can rent a car. What am I looking for?"

Caitlin started her engine. "A produce truck. Should be in town around two."

45

"WE'RE NOT HAVING SEX?" Greenwood already had his sport coat off. He hadn't bothered with an umbrella from the curb to the cottage's front door, so his shirt had a small crop of wet spots. According to the forecast, the storm that had dazzled Caitlin in Kentucky the night before wouldn't end until Saturday, two days from now.

"That depends." She turned her laptop his way. "Does this picture get you hot?"

He sat at the kitchen table, looked at her computer screen. "One of the Bro-duce trucks. What does this tell me?"

"This photo was taken two hours ago in Fort Lauderdale."

Greenwood laughed. "As in Florida? No wonder it's sunny."

She showed the next image in the series Mike had sent. "Recognize either of these two?"

Greenwood took a second. "Is that Frodo?"

"He left Bloomington yesterday, drove nonstop to Lauderdale, where he met his brother's boat from the Bahamas—except he didn't stay."

"Okay, I'm hooked. Where'd he go?"

"He spent an hour loading boxes, then turned around, drove north. If he doesn't stop, he'll be back in town tomorrow, just in time for Little Five."

"What's in the truck?"

Caitlin winked. "Getting hot, right? It's time to show you what I've been working on."

She laid out her theories, showed Greenwood the financials she and Lakshmi had been able to retrieve.

Greenwood took it all in. "You still don't know what's in the truck?"

"Look at it this way. Fodor says this is the last shipment. Those boys are getting something from the Caribbean, and whatever it is will be on the truck tomorrow afternoon."

"Caitlin, you are aware I can't just pull someone over because the woman I'm having sex with wants me to?"

"Nate Fodor is the weak link, Jerry. He handles the deliveries; he handles the money. He was there the night Chapman disappeared and you guys didn't look at him."

Greenwood got defensive. "You don't think we looked at him?"

"I'm not saying he's a viable suspect in Angela's disappearance. I'm saying he worked for Kieran and Dave then, and he works for them now. He knows things. You stop him before he gets back to town, find what he's got in the back; he'll do whatever it takes to stay out of jail, and you get your warrants for the farm. That's twenty unsearched acres where Chapman's body could be hidden. Twenty acres you'll have to tear apart when you find their growhouse."

Greenwood shook his head, unimpressed. "Or their cucumbers."

The time for fun and games was over. Sex was one thing, but Caitlin had spent the last fourteen days doing this good-looking asshole's legwork. She stood, pushed her chair back, and slapped both of her hands on the tabletop. "Why are you acting like this isn't what you wanted me to find? Or should I say"—she leaned over, her words slow and direct—"used me to find?"

He tried to fend her off with a smile. "I used you?"

Caitlin didn't buy it. "Yes, Mister Nothing-to-Hide-Ride-Along. You've been playing me since I got to town. Stop acting like we both don't know it."

He started to talk, shut his mouth, took a second, came back calmer. "I can't mess this up, Caitlin. One month after Melissa died, Kieran Michelson made a crack about Chapman being another 'dead slut.' Let's just say I didn't handle it well, and the department lost any leverage it had. They get wise we're on to them, they'll tear everything down before we get close."

She held back a groan. "You had me do all this work because you're afraid of a lawsuit?"

"I'm not afraid of a damned lawsuit." Greenwood looked her in the eyes, intense. "I'm afraid they got away with murder because I couldn't keep my shit together."

Caitlin stepped back, scratched her scalp with both hands, and sighed. She was the last person on earth who could judge someone for losing control of his emotions.

Greenwood shifted in the chair, looked away.

After a few calming breaths, Caitlin sat back down and smiled. "Anyone can have a faulty turn signal."

Greenwood didn't go for it. He pushed the chair back, reached for his sport coat. "What time tomorrow?"

"Between two and three. Does that mean it's on?"

He flung the screen door open and left without answering.

*   *   *

The next afternoon, Caitlin kicked Lakshmi's coffee table. "Bullshit."

"What's it say, Caitie?"

Mary and Lakshmi looked at Caitlin's phone over her shoulders.

"Nothing in the truck but spinach."

She dialed Greenwood. He answered, but she started first. "You've got to be shitting me."

"No problem letting us search. Nothing but eight boxes of spinach and two bags of seeds. Not even a personal joint. They had to cut Frodo loose."

"As in, he's driving back to the farm?"

"Yes, Caitlin, as in they didn't find anything incriminating. It would look weird if they tried harder. I gotta go."

"Wait—"

"Seriously, word of this got to the chief and I might have to tap dance."

"You didn't pull him over? Personally, I mean?"

"No, a patrol car did a routine traffic stop."

"So you didn't see the spinach or the seeds?"

"They sent pictures. I'll forward them. I'm hanging up."

The line disconnected.

"Damn it." Caitlin threw her phone onto the couch.

Lakshmi bit a nail. "So why did Frodo drive to Florida to meet with Adam?"

Caitlin dropped onto the cushions. "No idea."

Greenwood's images arrived. The first showed neatly stacked produce boxes. The next showed an officer's hand two inches deep in a pile of green leaves. A third showed a five-pound sack marked "Seeds—Spinach, Crocodile Hybrid."

Caitlin went back through the photos. "What am I not seeing?"

She stared at the leaves. Slender, one to two inches long, one vertical vein down the middle. "Son of a bitch."

She swiped her phone to the web browser, did an image search, didn't wait for the results. She switched back, dialed Greenwood's number.

He answered. "Caitlin—"

"Why would he drive a truck full of spinach all the way to Florida and not deliver it?"

"Doesn't really matter as far as I can tell."

She swiped back to the browser, copied and pasted the results into their text message thread.

"I'm sending you an image. Look right now—don't hang up."

"I've got Renton on the other line."

She heard his phone ding. "Just look—there aren't enough veins."

He said nothing for five seconds, then came back loud. "I'll call you back."

He hung up, and Caitlin jumped in the air. "That's what I'm talking about."

Mary and Lakshmi rose for the explanation. "What is it?"

Caitlin turned the phone toward them. The screen showed the image she'd sent Greenwood, a group of four green leaves and a search heading— "Coca leaves."

"They're making cocaine."

CHAPTER

46

T HE PLASTIC FORK and knife made the tray look childish. He wanted to impress her, but this was only Paige's second day out of the restraints. He'd been too eager with Angela, and before her, Lourdes, his first. Younger then, less practiced, he'd matured since. Paige would stay; Paige would last.

She'd eaten every bit of yesterday's rosemary chicken. Today's menu—poached salmon, garden salad.

He pulled the tray from the dumbwaiter shelf and carried her dinner toward her room. The need to hide the basement entrance to his collection restricted the ease of use, so one of his first improvements to the old house had been a rope-and-pulley dumbwaiter accessible from the kitchen.

"Shit."

In the hallway, he saw light reflected in standing water. The crushed stone floor of the corridor had been dry the night before. He'd dealt with flooding in the past, but not on this scale, and not since he'd completed Paige's case. He walked the tray back to the shelf, flipped the second light switch. The fluorescents painted the stone-walled hallway a sickly, pale blue. The puddle extended ten feet either direction from Paige's door. The area further down the hall near the playroom looked dry.

"Son of a bitch."

He took off his shoes, rolled the ends of his jeans.

Outside the door, the water pooled well past his ankles. He looked through the three-inch vertical window. Pitch black.

He flipped the wall switch.

Nothing happened.

"No."

He'd tested the room's waterproofing before collecting Paige by dousing the walls and ceiling with a hose, but never with the amount of water that had poured through the soil above after days of nonstop rain. He could only learn so much from the people at the hardware store. They'd believed him when he said he was building a recording studio in his basement, but he'd left out the part about the tunnels he'd dug through the soil, the beams he'd installed, the ten feet of earth between the surface and the display case. He'd sealed the wiring conduit with polyurethane. Apparently, not well enough.

He flipped the top deadbolt, reached for the bottom, stopped. Paige could be standing next to the door. He didn't remember leaving anything heavy enough to be hit with, but hands and feet had worked in the past.

"Do this right."

He walked back down the hallway, clicked the remote in his pocket. The panel in the public-facing basement wall slid open. He worked his way around the water heater and washing machine, closed the door behind him, and climbed the stairs back up to his house.

His laptop waited on the kitchen table. He checked the cameras. Still raining outside, nothing going on in the playroom. Everything else was normal. But Paige's room looked pitch black. He changed the camera to low-light mode, saw Paige in the fetal position on her bed against the back wall.

That much water outside the case meant just as much inside. Paige could already have a cold or infection, maybe even pneumonia, and he was supposed to be keeping her safe. He ran for the bathroom medicine cabinet, found the antibiotics he'd gotten last winter.

He grabbed a flashlight, went back to the basement, hit the remote, and ran down the hallway to Paige's door.

He hadn't wanted the window in the door in the first place, but it came standard in the only door the soundproofing company sold that could fit down the dumbwaiter shaft. Now he was glad he had the option. He shone the flashlight through.

Definitely water on the floor.

Paige lay on the bed, faced toward the wall.

He kept the beam on her, turned the bottom lock. No change.

He opened the door, smelled wet carpet.

"Paige, can you hear me?"

No answer. He swung the beam around the room, saw nothing out of order.

"I'm coming."

His toes dipped into the water inside the room. A foot from the bed, something dragged across his ankle. He aimed his flashlight down, saw the black cord from Paige's bedside lamp caught on the cuff of his jeans. He followed the cord's path from the outlet on the left to the table on the right, where a paperback book weighed down the stripped and exposed ends of copper wire.

"No," he said, reaching out.

Too late. Paige's hand reached out of the darkness and knocked the book off the edge of the table. The exposed end of the cord fell into the water.

The shock knocked him off his feet.

*   *   *

He woke in darkness, his face wedged against the wall. Every hair on his body stood on end, every muscle tight. The sharp tang of ozone overpowered the smell of soil-rich water.

"Paige?"

His fingers searched for the flashlight, found nothing. He stood on shaky legs, felt his way back to the doorway, went toward a light coming from the left. But the light couldn't be electric; the entire grid had blown when the cord hit the water. *Stupid*. He'd wired a ground fault circuit interrupter into his collection's circuit box, but not into each circuit. Paige must have watched him shake until the breaker tripped, then ran safely out the door.

Daylight spilled down from the kitchen through the dumbwaiter's shaft. She'd climbed out.

Too big to risk getting stuck in the shaft, he limped to the basement entrance and worked the manual crank. The door inched open.

He ran around the water heater, up the stairs, and into the kitchen.

A mess of wet footprints led outside where Paige Lauffer ran through the field in the pouring rain.

47

CAITLIN HADN'T HEARD from Greenwood in forty-five minutes, and not from lack of effort. "Mary, get the camera."

Lakshmi handed Mary the gear. "Me too?"

"Sorry, the restraining order might—"

"Sod it," the girl said, the implications understood.

"Don't worry, we'll need you here, ready to break this story. Stay by the phone."

They got to the Bro-duce farm twenty minutes later. A police cruiser and blue-paneled truck blocked the view. Across the street, another car blocked the road to Amireau's trailer.

Caitlin and Mary walked toward the cruiser, the rain now only a slight drizzle. A male officer in a rain slicker stopped them.

"Excuse me ladies, no press."

"That's funny," Caitlin said. "I don't recall identifying myself as press. Do you, Lubbers?"

Mary had the camera out and at eye level. "Weird that you'd just assume something like that, Officer."

"Bizarre." Caitlin saw two additional BPD cars near the farmhouse, a sheriff's van, and a dark SUV. "Since you brought it up, please tell Detective Greenwood that Caitlin Bergman is here."

The officer keyed his radio, relayed the message, got a response. "Wait here."

An unmarked sedan came down the drive and parked behind the cruiser. Mary raised her lens.

Detective Jane Maverick passed between the vehicles, lit cigarette in mouth. "Are you kidding me with that camera shit?"

Caitlin moved closer. "Not feeling a lot of gratitude here, Jane."

"This is bigger than your feelings, Bergman."

"Like we don't know?" Mary said. "You guys wouldn't even be here if Caitie hadn't figured this out."

Maverick gave Mary her eat-shit stare. "Who's this?"

"Mary, relax. What's the deal, Jane?"

"You may have started this, but the feds are here. They're going to grab Michelson in LA. Right now, this is contained."

"You think I'm gonna talk? I just want to know what's happening."

"Sure, and you happened to bring the head of the journalism department with you."

Mary snapped another photo. "So you know who *this* is."

Maverick flipped her off. "Here's what's gonna happen. You've got the exclusive—"

"Which I'm going to use through the *Daily Student*," Caitlin said.

"Fair enough. But not until we have all the players. Off the record, you're my hero, Bergman."

Caitlin looked to Mary, got the nod. "Fine. We agree to keep this quiet for now."

"Including your protégé?"

Mary got out her phone. "Yeah, we can control Lakshmi."

She made the call on speaker. Lakshmi promised no word without clearance under penalty of obstruction of justice.

Caitlin looked back to Maverick. "Off the record, is it the jackpot or not?"

Jane's stern lips broke around the edges. "Most of the top floor is a grow-house, just rows and rows of plants, then a drying room. Even better, they've got a little coke factory in the works, special for Little Five."

"What about arrests?"

Maverick went back into protection mode. "Lots of pieces in motion. Do us a favor—get lost before the feds figure out you're here." She walked back to her car.

Mary lowered the camera. "Lots of pieces. What's that mean?"

They'd picked Frodo up on the traffic stop, and Gooch was small-time. That only left one piece in motion. "They don't have Amireau."

In the car, Caitlin called Mike. "Roman, where are you?"

"In a cab, fifteen minutes from home. What's up?"

She filled him in.

He laughed. "As much as I'd love to take more of your money, I'm not sure I can do much in Friday rush-hour traffic back to Hollywood. Plus I'm not getting in the way of the feds."

"I don't need you to get in the way, just get eyes on Kieran."

"I'll let you know," he said and hung up.

Caitlin stared out at the wet soccer fields while Mary talked Lakshmi through a rough draft. She finished and ended the call. "Now what, Caitie? We wait?"

"Where is everybody? No soccer in the rain?"

"Field's too wet."

Caitlin grabbed the steering wheel, leaned forward. "I hate waiting."

Her phone rang. She didn't recognize the local number, but the female voice sounded familiar.

"Is that you?"

"Is what me?" Caitlin said, close to attaching a name to the woman.

"Someone's in my back field. I thought maybe you and your friend were painting again."

Carol McGovern, the woman with the farm across the creek.

Caitlin started the truck. "Carol, I'll be there in two minutes. Can you see who it is?"

"Let my check my birding binoculars," the woman said.

Caitlin switched the phone to speaker and spun the truck toward the road.

Carol returned. "Looks like a young man traipsing around in the mud near the trees."

Caitlin thought back to their stakeout, shot Mary a look. "Does he have a shotgun?"

"A shotgun?" Carol answered, amused. "Oh no, looks like he has a ten-speed, but he's not going anywhere fast."

Caitlin pulled out and sped toward the woman's house. "What about you, Carol? Do you have a shotgun?"

*   *   *

They ran from Carol McGovern's door, got back in the truck, Mary at the wheel, Caitlin riding shotgun.

Mary pulled out, the spinning tires flinging mud into the air. "You sure we shouldn't call the police?"

"Both Carol and I called Jerry directly," Caitlin said, loading a second shell into Carol's Remington. "He didn't bother to answer."

Mary turned the rental truck down the muddy field road leading toward the Bro-duce farm. "And you know how to shoot one of those things?"

Caitlin laughed. "You forget who my dad was?"

Mary pointed to the tree line. "Jackpot."

A mud-covered man facing the trees struggled to get a red bicycle through the bushes.

"Get us there, Mary."

Lubbers swung to a stop thirty feet away. Caitlin hopped out, shotgun up and ready.

David Amireau, dressed in a once-white T-shirt, a mess of brown where pants should be, and bare feet, turned her way.

His eyes narrowed. "You?"

"Stop there, Pig-pen. Hands up and all that shit."

He dropped the bike, started running for the trees. Caitlin shot once into the weeds, ten feet to his left. He stopped, raised his hands.

Mary yelled from the truck. "Now do you want me to call the police?"

Caitlin smiled. "I just did."

48

Two hours and a whole lot of questions later, Chief Renton offered Caitlin the chair in front of her desk once again. "I understand you've played a significant part in today's events."

Caitlin sat. "My work took me in a direction your department hadn't been able to go. Of course, once I found evidence of a criminal enterprise, I called your detectives. Thanks again for that level of access, Chief."

"I thought I asked you to call me Abigail." Renton's words carried the same underlying stink as her strained smile. "Now you'd like to watch the interrogations?"

"Observe only, from a camera feed or two-way glass."

Renton nodded. "With the understanding that nothing heard can be used, either on or off the record, in print, web, broadcast, or any other conceivable form of media on this planet until the completion of the trials of all parties involved."

"I don't need to tell this story, Chief. Your detectives did promise me the scoop on the bust, and I choose to give that access to the *Daily Student* when appropriate."

"You'll sign something to that effect?"

"On two conditions." Caitlin shifted forward. "The first—obviously, if I see evidence of abuse or violation of due process I will not hesitate to go public."

Renton looked offended. "That won't happen."

"I'm just reminding you I consider my work as a journalist to be a calling rather than something I do for money. I'll make this compromise in exchange for my second condition."

"Which is?"

"I get a copy of the Chapman files. Again, with the caveat that I will not publish any abstract from the contents."

"For what purpose?"

"To find that girl, Abigail. To see if anything, no matter how small a detail, has been missed. I might see things in a different way from your detectives. I promised Doris Chapman I'd try."

She didn't remember seeing gum in the woman's mouth, but Renton's jaw moved with a sideways grind.

Caitlin threw one last jab. "Small price to pay for the largest drug bust in your department's history, all under your command."

The woman's stress lost to her pride. "Now that's a story you can cover."

*   *   *

Caitlin found Greenwood and Maverick in the lunchroom huddled over salads. "Congratulations, Detectives."

Jane smirked. "Who let you in here?"

Greenwood started to get up.

Caitlin pulled out a chair, sat at the table. "Don't even. I'm not trying to mess up dinner."

Greenwood's shirt collar was unbuttoned, his sleeves rolled up to the elbows. "A dinner that happened to be delivered from Lennie's before we even realized we were hungry."

Caitlin snuck a piece of chicken out of Greenwood's salad container, popped it in her mouth. "I figured you'd be too busy to eat. Why the break?"

Maverick got up, refilled a coffee cup. "Amireau refuses to say anything until his lawyer gets here. Should be tomorrow morning."

"What about Frodo?"

Greenwood found a gap between bites. "Complicated. He said he wanted Amireau's lawyer."

"How's that complicated?"

Maverick sat back at the table. "He doesn't know the guy's name. We told him we couldn't be sure who he meant. So he asked for the public defender. It's Friday night, so a public defender won't be in until tomorrow morning, which means we leave him alone until then."

So much for watching an interrogation. "What about the scene?"

Greenwood smiled. "Hundred plants, various stages of harvest. Over two hundred pounds of packaged weed."

"Half a million bucks," Maverick said.

"And the coke?"

Maverick pulled out a tablet, showed Caitlin an image. The windowless room could have been a chemistry lab on campus except for the ingredients stacked in neat piles. She swiped through the images. Bags of Portland cement, a gas can, a jug of sulfuric acid, potassium.

Caitlin pointed to a beaker full of white powder. "Is that coke?"

"Sodium bicarbonate," Greenwood said. "Technically, we didn't find any cocaine. But there was a row of coca plants in the grow room, mostly dead or dying."

Caitlin got the picture. "So the shipment was fresh seeds for later and enough leaves to crank out a batch for Little Five?"

"Looks like," Maverick said. "How did you know they were playing Pablo Escobar?"

"Lakshmi told me Amireau had offered her green cocaine once. Only time I'd heard of something like that was back in LA. LAPD found three club kids, all dead. They settled on bad chemistry."

Greenwood nodded. "The kind that comes from a self-taught cook. What else?"

"Adam Fodor's reluctance to stay involved in a pot business he probably started. The Bahamas aren't Colombia. Weed's one thing, but they don't mess around when it comes to cocaine trafficking."

Greenwood looked smitten or at least horny. "Damned impressive, Caitlin."

She tried not to blush. "What about Gooch?"

Maverick nearly spit her coffee. "Who now?"

"Big guy, beard, overalls?"

Greenwood laughed. "Randall Gutcherson. Got him too. Same thing, waiting on a lawyer."

Caitlin reached for another piece of chicken. "So no one's talking tonight?"

"Unless you've got an idea."

She reached for her laptop. "Maybe Frodo doesn't know how much he has to lose."

*   *   *

Munching the remains of Greenwood's salad, Caitlin watched the detectives play with Nate Fodor via the observation room's video feed. Chief Renton and two detectives stood behind her.

Frodo tapped a photo printout on the interview room's table. "So I met my brother at my parent's house."

"My bad," Greenwood said, pulling out three more of Mike Roman's shots from Florida. "I was supposed to show you all of these."

The first, Nate and Adam loading a crate into the back of the delivery truck. The second, a wider shot of the boys at work and an older man, their father, twenty feet away. The third, the coca leaves found in the back of the Bro-duce truck.

"So what?"

Maverick touched Greenwood's arm. "We shouldn't be talking to him without his lawyer."

Greenwood pushed her hand away. "This kid should know how much jail time his dad faces for his bullshit."

Frodo took the bait. "My dad? What are you talking about?"

"Nothing," Maverick said. "Greenwood, outside, now."

Greenwood left the folder and images. "We'll be right back."

Seconds later, they joined Caitlin and the others at the monitors.

Greenwood smiled. "Anything?"

"Not yet," the chief said.

Maverick took a seat. "Shouldn't take long."

Frodo shifted in his chair, rolled his neck. Caitlin watched the timecode on the monitor. The wait felt like minutes, but only thirty-two seconds passed before he leaned forward. He pushed the images aside to look at the documents below. Caitlin had chosen the order:

1. The title to the farm and the Bro-duce corporation's financial structure docs
2. A listing of payments made by both Nate and Adam Fodor to their parents
3. A summary of Florida's drug-related property seizure statutes
4. A spreadsheet that correlated the earlier payments to the Fodor parents' accounts and the mortgage payments received on the Fort Lauderdale retirement property

Caitlin could see Frodo's hands start to tremble.

"Oh no," he said, the words barely audible through the monitor.

The entire room broke into applause.

Maverick got up. "Let's go get him."

Greenwood gave Caitlin the quickest of smiles on his way out. Seconds later, he reappeared in the interrogation room and reached for the folder. "My partner was right. We can pick this up tomorrow when your public defender shows up."

"Wait, let's make a deal."

Maverick stood in the open doorway. "Why? Your name's on the farm and the bank accounts. You were found with enough coca leaves to manufacture a kilo of coke. You transported those ingredients across state lines. Your brother, across international waters. In addition, people have been making cash deposits into the grill in your backyard right after huge deliveries of pot to local frats, often in trucks driven by you. Exactly what kind of deal do you think we need to make?"

Greenwood closed the folder. "Back to your cage."

"But I know things you don't."

Maverick laughed. "We know everything about your bullshit drug empire, Frodo."

"I know about Angela Chapman."

Chills ran up Caitlin's spine.

Greenwood shook his head. "You'd say anything now."

"Seriously," Frodo said, "but I need to know you'll leave my parents out of this."

Maverick laughed again. "Kid, this thing crossed state lines. You're organized crime. Your parents too."

Frodo's voice kicked up a register. "I'm serious. They had me bury something."

"Bury what?"

"The morning after everyone went out, you know, the night Angela disappeared—they called me on one of the burners, said to get to their apartment, get rid of some garbage."

Maverick clucked her tongue. "We went through all the garbage within two miles of the Villas—city dump too. Nice try."

"At the farm," Frodo continued, "I buried four bags. Weird, lumpy shapes. I don't know what was in them, but they stunk."

Greenwood kept his tone even. "You're telling us you didn't look in the bags?"

"I didn't know Chapman was missing. I just did what they said. But I can take you to the bags, at least tell you where to dig."

CHAPTER

49

Los Angeles

MIKE PARKED AT a trailhead between Kieran's house and the Hollywood sign and flashed his lights once. Michelson emerged from the darkness and got in the passenger side with a duffel bag. "You got here fast."

Mike drove west. "I was in Hollywood. Where are we going, Kieran?"

"TJ, bro."

"Why Mexico?"

"I just need to get there. Maybe cut over to Durand Drive up here, stay away from my place."

Mike understood Kieran's concern. He'd been outside the mansion for the last hour, watching twenty of the FBI's finest pick the place apart. Not only were the agents unimpressed when he pointed out the absence of Kieran's off-road scooter, they told him flat-out to leave the premises.

We don't need help from a dirty ex-cop, they'd said. A decade after his conviction, only one person in Los Angeles saw Mike as anything other than a criminal, and she waited by the phone in Indiana. Pissed off, he'd started the drive home. Michelson's call came seconds after.

Now, less than a mile from the feds, Mike continued to play dumb. "Something you want to tell me, Kieran?"

Michelson dug through his bag, came back with a wad of cash. "I'll pay you five grand."

Mike pointed to the glove box. "In there."

"Sure, can we get going?"

"Yeah, one more thing." Mike popped the trunk. "You're going in the back."

"The trunk?"

"You called for my expertise, K. You've gotta leave town and don't want to be seen. It's a world of cameras, understand?"

Kieran got out, followed the doctor's orders. Wedged in the trunk, the tall twenty-four-year-old looked like a kid in a couch fort. "Any chance we can stop for tacos, maybe hand them to me through the back seat?"

"Sure," Mike said. "I know a place downtown."

He shut Kieran in, took side streets south and west. Thirty minutes later, he came to a complete stop in Westwood.

"K, I'm getting out for a bit. I'll be back with food. Don't go anywhere."

"See if they have carnitas, bro."

Mike got out and walked toward the man waiting beyond the concrete barriers that protected the tall gray and black Wilshire Federal Building from vehicular attack. "What is that, seventeen stories?"

The well-built man in a tailored charcoal suit looked up, the same direction.

"That's a state secret," he said, offering his hand. "Special Agent Jim Martinez. Caitlin said you had something for me?"

Mike shook the agent's hand. "In the trunk."

"Out of curiosity, why didn't you drive him back to the agents on the scene?"

"Caitlin says you're one of the good guys."

Martinez smiled. "And she knows?"

Mike shrugged, walked him to the car. "She knew about me."

CHAPTER

50

TRUE TO THEIR word, the BPD kept the Bro-duce bust under wraps. Their press release announced a conference at ten AM the next day, no details. Under Mary's supervision, Lakshmi worked all night, writing and rewriting the piece. Caitlin refused to read the drafts, opted instead for eight gorgeous hours of sleep back at the guesthouse.

She woke early, showered, checked her email. Lakshmi's draft read better than pieces written by twenty-year veterans. Caitlin's favorite part—she'd left Angela Chapman out entirely. According to Mary, they'd wait until the press conference to loose that arrow.

Caitlin sent a text to Scott Canton. *Want to go fishing?*

A reply came quickly. *At Denny's. Come now.*

*   *   *

"The young lady can write." Scott's glasses reflected the bright phone screen. "So why are you here instead of at the press conference?"

Caitlin munched her last piece of celebratory bacon. "My ladies know what to ask."

"You must be very proud."

"Lakshmi's come a long way in sixteen days."

"Have you ever done that before, been a mentor?"

Caitlin didn't have to sift through her twenty years of experience. "I usually work alone."

"Why does Lakshmi get your attention?"

"Because she brought me wine and told me I'm amazing?"

"I gave you weed and told you you're amazing. You didn't invite me on any stakeouts."

"Well, I want to find Angela Chapman."

"Why? Three weeks ago, you didn't know she was missing."

"Damn, Scott. What'd I do to you?"

The curvaceous waitress in her fifties returned, coffee pot in hand. "How you doin', Professor?"

Caitlin grabbed a cardboard table tent covered with glossy pictures of desserts and gave the pair their privacy.

Age didn't weaken Scott's charms. "Kind of in the middle of something, Charlese. You know I'll reach out when I have needs."

Charlese winked. "Thought I took care of your *needs* last night." She smiled at Caitlin. "You want something else, hon?"

Caitlin let go of the treat tent. "Still debating."

The woman's perfume trail overpowered the kitchen's cloud of fried eggs, even when she walked away.

"So you didn't sleep at home last night, Scott?"

Scott winked. "Back to business. Now I'm on my third cup, so the caffeine might be confusing my tongue. I think I know why you're helping this girl."

"Fine. Why am I helping this girl?"

"She's an intelligent, hard-working young woman with no mother."

"I see what you're getting at."

"What am I getting at?"

Caitlin sighed. "I didn't have anyone in my corner. I mean, it's totally different with Lakshmi. She didn't get attacked—her friend did. She's got Doris Chapman and her Chapter friends. Plus, she didn't run away. And I could have had someone in my corner. My dad, Mary, other friends—"

"But you didn't."

Caitlin pushed her greasy plate to the side. "It's not just for Lakshmi."

"For who then?"

"For Angela Chapman. For Paige Lauffer. For the seventeen percent, or however many girls there are who have to deal with shit like this and are too scared to ask for help."

"That's a lot of weight to carry."

"You asked. Is that what you thought I'd say?"

"Yep, those exact words. Every one of them. I'm kind of a genius."

"Oh, I knew that the second you told me." Caitlin waved at Charlese, got a smile and a right-with-you finger.

Scott followed her action. "Please tell me you're ordering more bacon."

"Better." She pulled the cardboard tent over, awaited the woman's return.

He tried once more. "It'd be okay if you were helping Lakshmi for yourself."

"For me?"

"Helping Lakshmi find Angela Chapman might be a tangible way to deal with what happened to you twenty years ago. That's not evading, Caitlin. That's empowering."

"You're damned right it's empowering," she said, pointing to the mint Oreo milkshake in advance of Charlese's return. "This one, please. I'm celebrating."

Charlese got the point without closing the distance.

"Excellent choice," Scott said. "What about the rest of the weekend? Going to the Little Five Hundred?"

"They ride bikes in the rain?"

He nodded. "I believe so. Should cut down on the drunks in the stands. Could be fun."

"No way," Caitlin said. "I lived that one too. I'll start with a run, see where that takes me."

An hour later, her feet took her through the rain-soaked campus, her mind free, clear, and content, until in her third mile she passed a kiosk topped with a blue light. She stopped and stretched, examining the slender gray tower stenciled with the word "EMERGENCY" and its call box below. Not only could a student report an injury or crime, but the built-in camera would record the whole thing.

She shook her head and exhaled. *Too bad Chapman hadn't been on campus when she disappeared.*

Another exhale brought another thought.

Too bad you weren't either.

She wiped a mix of sweat and rain from her brow, and the brief flashes of regret from her mind, and ran back to Mary's cottage.

Rather than track mud in, she peeled off her shoes and wet running gear and piled them near her bag, noticing the protruding corner of her assault report that she still hadn't faced.

Empowering, Scott had said. Did she feel empowered enough to try again?

Her naked skin rippled with gooseflesh. *Maybe shower first.*

Robed and warm post-shower, she set her bag on the kitchen table and reached for her report, but the buzz of her phone and Lakshmi's subsequent invitation to happy hour led Caitlin back to celebration mode and clothing. They met five staff members from the *Daily Student* at Bear's Place and fought the tiny pitchers of liquor destruction until everyone lost.

* * *

She woke the next morning on Lakshmi's couch, saw the young woman working at her desk. "Anything new?"

"I want to die," Lakshmi said, "but the AP picked up the post-conference piece under the headline 'Drug Bust May Solve Mystery of Missing Student.'"

Caitlin found her phone, skimmed the article.

Detectives refused to comment on possible ties to the disappearance of Angela Chapman, despite the involvement of former schoolmates David Amireau and Kieran Michelson, both persons of interest in the unsolved disappearance.

"Well done, Lakshmi." She found her rental car's key fob under an open Pizza Monster box. "Did we order again last night?"

Lakshmi laughed. "That was your idea. You kept saying, 'Let's kill the—'"

"Right." Caitlin remembered chanting the words *Let's kill the monster.*

She excused her hungover self, left for the guest cottage. By two PM she felt hungry; by four, the rain had stopped; by five she felt human.

Greenwood texted at six forty-two PM. *Amireau wants to talk deal.*

CHAPTER

51

J ANE MAVERICK OFFERED Caitlin the same observation room chair from two nights before. This time the monitor showed two men at the table—David Amireau in a Monroe County jumpsuit and his fifty-year-old rent-a-friend lawyer.

"Okay, everyone." Renton addressed the full room. "For those who don't know, Caitlin Bergman is here, with my department's approval, acting as a consultant."

She pointed out the two FBI agents next to Greenwood. "Caitlin, these are—"

"Christiansen and Foreman, I believe."

Renton nodded. "There's a copy of the Chapman file on Greenwood's desk if you still want it."

Caitlin nodded. "Yes, ma'am."

"Here's the situation. We have Amireau on schedule-one felony narcotics distribution and production, with racketeering options if Justice chooses to prosecute at the federal level. We also have an unsubstantiated assertion by Nathan Fodor that he buried several bags on the property the day after Chapman's disappearance."

Caitlin interrupted. "Unsubstantiated, Chief? As in, there's nothing there?"

Greenwood took the question. "We haven't arranged a deal with Frodo's attorney to let him point out the spot."

Chief Renton rapped the tabletop. "No deals. These boys are going away. All of them. I'll take down their damned fraternity if I can."

"Right," Greenwood continued. "If Chapman's buried on that property, we'll find her with or without Frodo. Forecast says the rain's done for now, so we'll be digging by tomorrow."

Maverick jumped in. "Not Channel Two. They think we'll get another thunderstorm tonight."

"Either way," the chief said, "we don't need these boys to dig."

Caitlin pointed everyone back to the monitor, where David Amireau whispered with his lawyer. "So what's the dog and pony show all about?"

Greenwood smiled. "Panic."

*   *   *

The scene on the monitor felt straight out of a one-hour cop show. Caitlin didn't mind this episode. The lead detective looked good in bed.

Greenwood stood, addressed the attorney. "Call us when your client wants to tell us something we don't know, Richard."

Amireau's handcuffs rattled against the tabletop. "I didn't kill Angela Chapman."

Maverick hovered by the door. "Anyone say you did?"

The young man looked sick under the fluorescent light. "I know Frodo told you something."

"He told us everything. We don't need you." Maverick walked out.

Richard, the lawyer, whispered to Amireau, who started talking. "She was high when we picked her up."

Greenwood sat back down at the table. "Who was?"

"Chapman. Who else?"

"Not Paige Lauffer?"

If Amireau recognized the name, he didn't give anything away.

"Angela. And not coke high. Like Molly or a roofie or something. She kept saying it wasn't her idea."

"So? You said she left your apartment on her own accord."

"I was passed out, man. Blackout drunk. I wake up, Kieran's got three trash bags full of shit. He says, 'Help me clean up.' I cleaned up."

"Are you saying Kieran Michelson killed Angela Chapman?"

"All I ever wanted was to sell a little weed. Kieran wanted to be Scarface. Angela knew we were making coke. She knew about the growhouse. If anyone killed her, it had to be Kieran."

"Bullshit," Greenwood said. "You know exactly what Frodo buried, which makes you an accessory, unless you can prove something."

"I've got the phones."

Greenwood adjusted his tie. "What phones?"

"The burners we were using back then. K texted Frodo. I've still got that shit. I'll give it to you."

The lawyer tapped him. "You've got his attention, David. Stop now."

Amireau didn't. "I didn't kill Angela, and I wouldn't have helped anyone bury her. She was my friend."

Greenwood let the moment hang for almost twenty seconds, then leaned in. "What do you want?"

The lawyer laid out the deal. Amireau would plead guilty to distribution and production, but any conspiracy charges would fall on Kieran's shoulders, and if they found Chapman's body, that was between Frodo and Kieran.

The detectives rejoined the team in the observation room, all smiles.

Chief Renton ended that. "No deals. Get Frodo to give up where they got the burners. We can get the text exchanges from the telecom companies."

Greenwood started. "But Chief—"

"These frat boys made this department look like small-town hicks. If we can't make the case without them, I'll consider a deal, but for now, we work the farm. Anyone have a problem with that?"

Agent Foreman stepped forward. "Let us know what you need, Chief."

Renton looked at Maverick and Greenwood. Jerry looked like he might say something, but she didn't give him the time. "And put that piece of garbage back in his cell."

The crisp chime of a mobile device interrupted. Greenwood reached for his phone.

Renton continued, "I want crews out on the site twenty-four-seven until we find—"

Another phone chimed. Maverick's this time, followed by Foreman's, followed by Christiansen's.

Renton threw her hands up. "I left mine on my desk. What's happening?"

Greenwood showed the chief his screen.

Renton drew a sharp breath, then snapped into action. "Jerry, put Amireau back in the tank, then catch up. Everyone else, let's go."

Caitlin followed the flow of law enforcement into the hall, overheard whispered words.

Where?

Who found her?

At Greenwood's cubicle, she found a large white document box. Fully loaded, the Chapman case materials weighed more than she'd expected from a problem without a solution.

She hefted the mass toward the door and nearly ran into Greenwood, who moved like he was on the hunt. From what she knew of the BPD's case-load, there could be only two *hers* that made the entire department shift into high gear. Since the box in Caitlin's hands meant she was privy to all aspects of the Chapman investigation, this rollout had to be about the other missing student.

"You found Paige Lauffer, right?"

He hesitated. "I can't—"

"You don't have to. Call me later."

52

Caitlin, Mary, and Lakshmi weren't the first press on the scene. Two broadcast trucks from Indianapolis marked the perimeter. A sheriff's cruiser blocked the entrance to the soccer fields where they'd parked days before, and a law enforcement swarm moved under work lights revealing the nearest goal box. Flashlights danced in the darkness beyond.

Mary sent Lakshmi to spy on the other journalists, then rejoined Caitlin. "Looks like BPD, the sheriff, and those SUVs, is that—"

"The FBI? Definitely."

They turned at the sound of a passing truck, saw the emblem of the Monroe County Coroner.

Lakshmi rejoined them. "That means Paige Lauffer's dead, right?"

"Gotta be," Caitlin said. "What'd you learn?"

Lakshmi quoted one of the broadcasters. "'Officers on the scene refuse to speculate about the identity, though eyewitness reports claim the naked female body found resembles missing student Paige Lauffer.'"

Mary snapped a photo of the workers under the lights with her phone. "Lakshmi, start writing."

The girl reached for her bag. "Okay, what do we know?"

Mary reviewed her photo on the camera's screen. "Same as the competition's report, enough for a good tease."

"We know more than that," Caitlin said. "You ready?"

Lakshmi had her laptop out. "Shoot."

"Though awaiting official confirmation by the Monroe County Coroner, an unnamed source working with the Bloomington Police Department said a body found in a soccer field is believed to be that of missing student Paige Lauffer—"

Mary interrupted. "Who's the source, Greenwood?"

She didn't let Lubbers stop her flow. "Authorities believe the woman was killed elsewhere before being dumped sometime between Friday and Sunday night."

"Caitie—"

"When asked if the suspects arrested in the Friday raid of the nearby Bro-duce Organic Farm had anything to do with the girl's death, officials from the FBI refused to comment."

"Caitie, we haven't even spoken to anyone yet."

"I know, Mary. Lakshmi, email that to the Indianapolis FBI tip line."

Lakshmi typed away. "What subject?"

Caitlin smiled. "'Special Agent Foreman—please confirm.'"

She heard the swoosh sound of Lakshmi's electric volley being bumped into the ether.

"Think it'll work?" Mary said.

A far-off boom announced the superiority of Channel 2's weather predictions. Definitely more rain on the way.

"Time will tell."

Caitlin glanced back at the coroner's van. Two techs carried a collapsible awning toward the penalty area.

Five minutes later, Lakshmi pointed toward the parking lot. "It worked."

Special Agent Antoine Foreman jumped over a fence. "Who talked, Bergman? Your boyfriend?"

"I don't know what you mean. Are you confirming Lakshmi Anjale's story?"

"'An unnamed source working with the Bloomington Police Department?' If your fuck buddy Greenwood said something to you about this case, I'll make sure he loses his badge."

Caitlin nullified Foreman's anger with calm. "Wasn't Greenwood, but I'll give you a hint. It's a journalist working with the Bloomington Police Department who just happens to have an amazing ass and several awards to her name."

"Who told you the body was dumped here between Friday and now?"

"Mary and I were sitting here Friday afternoon; Paige Lauffer's body wasn't. There was no break in the rain until today, so no one played soccer or cut the grass."

"That doesn't mean this isn't the crime scene."

Caitlin shrugged. "Kind of a weird place to kill a girl. Easy enough to dump her, though. Pull in, back up, toss the body. Sloppy, like someone was in a hurry. Maybe the police were raiding their property. Can you speculate whether the boys from the Bro-duce Organic Farm had anything to do with Paige Lauffer's death?"

Foreman shook his head. "You're done with the BPD. Renton may feel like eating your shit, but I don't have to."

"So you're confirming that Paige Lauffer's death is related to David Amireau and possibly the disappearance of Angela Chapman?"

Foreman stopped, his lesson learned. "There'll be a press conference tomorrow morning. I don't want to see you until then."

Lightning flashed over the parking lot, filling in the shadows as Foreman walked away. Caitlin started counting. Seven seconds before the thunder.

Mary let out a sigh. "Go ahead and print, Lakshmi. You've got your confirmation, from the FBI no less."

Lakshmi started giggling.

Caitlin looked over. "What's so funny, giggle-puss?"

"He said 'fuck buddy.'"

That accent got her again. The trio laughed all the way to the car.

C H A P T E R

53

THE NEXT MORNING, Mary's toes nudged Caitlin from the opposite end of the couch. "Remind me why we're here instead of at the press conference with Lakshmi?"

Caitlin opened the box of BPD Chapman files on the coffee table. "That girl can handle the conference with one arm tied behind her back, or at least in a cast. This is the Chapman mother lode, and judging from Foreman's attitude last night, our access is on borrowed time."

The massive, unbound volume made Caitlin's sexual assault report look like a cautionary pamphlet. Whatever the BPD had done wrong in their investigation, they hadn't neglected their paperwork.

"You think Amireau killed both girls?"

Caitlin shook her head. "I think Chapman overdosed, Michelson disposed of her body to protect his drug empire, and Amireau suffered a life of public shame for two years, only to finally snap and kill Paige Lauffer."

Caitlin flipped through her pages. She had Greenwood's initial reports, basic summary info, pictures of Chapman's apartment, and full schematics of Michelson and Amireau's place at the Villas.

Mary dove in as well. "What are we looking for?"

"Detectives look at the pieces to string together a narrative. Chapman goes missing, they assume she's run away. No personal items absent, the story changes to foul play. We're looking for anything that didn't follow that narrative, or did but was omitted from common knowledge."

"So everything?"

"Relax, Lubbers. You've got two hours and then you're free to go teach or whatever it is you do with your days."

Mary stuck her tongue out. "Usually I grade the homework, not do it."

They read in silence for ninety minutes.

Mary broke the silence with a guttural "Huh."

Caitlin looked over. "Got something?"

"Greenwood's got a note here. Only two words: *See Shepherd.* That mean anything to you? I haven't found anyone in the interviews named Shepherd."

Caitlin felt a flutter in her chest. "Shit, I might know."

She opened a browser window, typed a query. "The other night, when Lakshmi was all high, I asked her who she talked to at BPD before Greenwood."

"Jerry wasn't the first detective?"

"No, his wife had just died and he was on leave. They brought him in as soon as they knew it was something serious, the second day, maybe the third. I asked our little doper who the first detective was, and she said, 'Sheep man.'"

Mary dove back in the box, started flipping through pages. "'Sheep man,' as in high talk for Shepherd? If he was the first detective on the case, shouldn't there be something in here, an initial report or something?"

"Sure should." Caitlin joined her, going through the box from the other side. She stopped, pulled out a sheet of paper. "Here it is, an initial investigation report." She scanned through the typed document. "No way."

"What?"

She handed the sheet to Mary. "It's signed by Chief Renton, not Shepherd."

Mary took the page, started reading. "Have you ever even talked to a Detective Shepherd?"

"That'd be kind of hard." Caitlin swung her computer Mary's direction, the results from her search at the top of the screen. "Detective Chris Shepherd died almost two years ago from a self-inflicted gunshot wound."

Mary dropped the report to read the obituary in front of her. "There's no mention of suicide here."

"Maverick let it slip the first day I met her. Greenwood tried to play the whole thing off, something about an older cop facing down early-onset Alzheimer's."

"Did he really have Alzheimer's?"

"As in, did the initial investigator on the biggest case in the history of the Bloomington Police Department have issues with his memory that may or may not have affected his job performance? If so, did a possible mental lapse allow crucial evidence to become corrupted, go missing, or be overlooked entirely?"

Mary's juicy secret smile had to match Caitlin's own. "And how did every news outlet, from the tiny student paper to the national broadcast networks, miss this little gem of a story?"

"Only one way to find out."

54

BESIDES THE ADDRESS, two things told Caitlin she'd found the right place—the sign next to the driveway that read "Piano Lessons" and the beautiful sound of live music marching out the open window.

At one minute till the hour, the music stopped and the front door opened. A good-looking woman in her mid-sixties waved. Caitlin grabbed her sheet music and hurried up the driveway.

Isabelle Shepherd had the kind, patient eyes of a woman no doubt loved by everyone she met.

Caitlin handed her a stack of cash and four pages of music. "Thanks for squeezing this in."

She looked at Caitlin's beginner rock series. "You say you played when you were younger?"

"Up through middle school, then a little at college."

"Well, 'Imagine' should be a piece of cake."

Caitlin followed her into a stylish great room centered on a black grand piano. Various framed happy-family images covered the fireplace mantel. A large color print of Detective Chris Shepherd in his uniformed prime occupied the central spot of honor.

Isabelle placed Caitlin's sheet music atop the piano and took a chair next to the bench. "Now, why are we desperate to imagine there's no heaven?"

Caitlin sat at the keys and built upon the story she'd told the woman over the phone. "I made a bet with a man that I had more talent than I may actually possess, and I'm not about to lose for lack of effort."

"You have a date tonight?"

"Yep, someone I've met recently who is single, has a great job, and has a piano in his living room that he cannot play."

Isabelle flashed those kind, understanding eyes. "Well, in one hour I think we can get you to the point where you can play and sing without stops."

Caitlin found middle C, tried her first attempt at greatness. She remembered how to read the notation and what the finger placement guide numbers meant, but faked some bad choices. Isabelle stopped her, explained the perceived mistakes, and Caitlin tried again. Five more passes, and she could get all the way through without stopping.

"You're doing great, Caitlin. Ready to try singing?"

Caitlin took the opportunity for a break. "Not yet. I think my need to pee might be making me better than I am."

She excused herself to the bathroom, returned to find Isabelle coming out of the kitchen with a cup of tea.

Caitlin stopped in front of Detective Shepherd's photo. "Is this your husband?"

"Yes, that's my Chris."

"He's with the BPD? My date's with a cop. Maybe they know each other."

"They might have," Isabelle said and sipped her tea. "My husband died two years ago."

"Oh, I'm sorry."

Isabelle picked up a Kodachrome-colored image of a college-aged couple in formal wear from the late sixties and handed Caitlin the frame. "Here we are the year we met. He'd just pinned me."

Caitlin noticed a trio of matching Greek letters over the door of a familiar local building.

"Were you a Tri Delt at IU?"

Isabelle nodded, walked back toward the piano, and placed her hand over her heart. *"Let us steadfastly love one another."*

Caitlin returned the frame to its home and went back to the piano.

Isabelle watched her. "Out of curiosity, have you ever dated a police officer?"

"No, but I like when they wear the uniforms."

The woman's once-welcoming eyes now looked tired and distant. "It's a strange kind of life, even in a town as small as this. They'll never tell you everything they do, and you'll never be sure they'll come home at the end of the day."

"Oh God, was your husband killed on the job?"

Isabelle set her tea aside. "My husband shot himself."

"I'm so sorry." Caitlin paused and gave the woman a chance to stop her, either by words or body language, but saw nothing. "Was he sick or something?"

"They said he might have had some plaque on the folds of his brain, but I don't think that would have scared Chris. I think he was haunted by something he saw or did. He never told me. The police have their own fraternal secrets." Isabelle must have noticed Caitlin's stunned expression. "Now I'm sorry. Here you are ready to go on a date, and I'm depressing the heavens out of you. Which officer do you have the date with? I may know him."

"Jerry Greenwood."

The woman's pleasant smile returned. "Oh, Jerry. I'm sure you know about his wife. She passed two months before Chris."

Caitlin nodded. "We've talked about her some."

"As far as I know, he's a great guy."

Caitlin suddenly wanted out of the house. Sharing sheets with guys like Greenwood or Martinez to get preferential treatment had never bothered her, since both sides knew the score and got to enjoy the benefits, but lying to a widow felt cheaper somehow, dirtier. If Chris Shepherd had indeed shot himself because he'd let Chapman's murderers get away, the public would soon find out, and innocent Isabelle would have to deal with his mess all over again.

Isabelle nudged Caitlin's arm. "You know what? Jerry's got a great voice. You should say you'll play if he'll sing."

Relieved, Caitlin shut her sheet music and stood. "That's a good idea, and that saves me half an hour to get ready."

Caitlin thanked the woman for her time, moved across the room, but stopped for one last look at the smiling girl who'd just been pinned—as in given the pin of her boyfriend's fraternity. She couldn't see the design without magnification, but a simple web search in the car validated her hunch.

In his last bio on an archived copy of the BPD's website, Detective Chris Shepherd included his status as both an alumnus of Indiana University and a brother in Delta Omega Tau—the same fraternity as David Amireau and Kieran Michelson.

CHAPTER

55

CAITLIN FOUND LAKSHMI in the *Daily Student* newsroom. "Walk me through Saturday morning, when Angela disappeared."

"Again?" Lakshmi looked up from her keyboard, distracted. "I've got deadlines on both Paige Lauffer and the Bro-duce farm updates."

"They can wait, Lakshmi. The initial report is gone."

Lakshmi turned her way. "Wait, what report?"

"From Chris Shepherd, the detective on the scene. There's a typed version, but it's signed by Chief Renton, not Shepherd, so who knows if he even wrote it. I have the whole Chapman file—"

"What does it say about me?"

"Focus up, Miss 'I've-Got-Deadlines.' Greenwood and Maverick gave me a practiced lecture, then you gave me the time line of the night before, but I need to know your version of what happened from when you calleSd the cops until when Greenwood took over."

"My version? You mean the truth."

"Yes, sorry if—"

"Whatever." Lakshmi swiveled her chair toward Caitlin. "So I woke up around ten, felt bloody awful. Basic hangover aches and pains, but a horrible feeling that stayed around no matter how much coconut water I drank."

Caitlin knew the rejuvenating power of coconut water, but Lakshmi's low feeling sounded more like a chemical side effect. Maybe she hadn't been lying when she told the BPD she'd been too high to go out with Angela, Kieran, and Dave. Caitlin tried to remember: Had Lakshmi told her they'd been smoking pot, or had she just assumed that?

She made a note to circle back if it mattered. The rest of Lakshmi's story matched the BPD account: the texts, her visit to Angela's apartment, her confrontation with Amireau and Michelson.

"They played dumb, so I called the cops and they gave me Shepherd."

"Describe him."

"Just an old white man who didn't care. I yelled, threatened him with social media. When that didn't work, I played the girl card."

Caitlin laughed. "You cried?"

"That he responded to. He even agreed to let me ride with him."

"Anything to reassure the little lady."

"Exactly, so he sends a squad car over to Angela's, and we drive to the boys' apartment. At this point, Kieran and Dave were both there."

"How did they act?"

"Like I was mental. But Shepherd saw Dave's black eye and said it'd be easier on everyone if they told us about the night before."

"Did Shepherd write anything down?"

"No, he accepted everything they said, which was that Angela walked home around two AM. They didn't mention being high the night before."

"I'm sure you didn't either."

Lakshmi looked like she'd just taken a slap.

Caitlin moved on. "Then what?"

"We walked through the woods to Angela's. At this point, I'm freaking out, but Shepherd's easy-breezy beautiful. He even put his arm around me." Lakshmi must have caught the look on Caitlin's face. "Not in a sexual way, but like—"

"Like a father would do, comforting his little girl?"

"Not *my* father," Lakshmi said, "but yes, I suppose. Either way, it made my skin crawl."

"Because he sounded like he didn't believe you," Caitlin said, well aware of the feeling, "and worse, like he felt bad for you."

"Right. So we get to Angela's and she's not there. Shepherd checks with all the neighbors, none of whom have seen her."

Caitlin made a note. "So he finally took you seriously by five-thirty."

"Not at all. He drove me home, said he'd let me know if they found anything, but to keep calling Angela's friends and family to see if she turned up."

"Which you did?"

"Nonstop. Doris got in her car, drove to the station, and screamed bloody murder until they took action. I got called back into the station around ten PM that night to give an official statement."

"When did Greenwood get involved?"

"Monday morning. At least, that's when he asked me back into the station."

"Almost two days missing at that point."

"And no one was watching Dave and Kieran. They could have done anything they wanted to Angela."

* * *

"Caitlin." Doris Chapman's seven-thirty voice had a started-at-three boozy slur. Her T-shirt and sweat pants combo shouted abandonment, not fitness, a stark contrast from their first meeting. "You didn't have to drive all this way."

Caitlin took to the couch and watched the broken woman refresh her tumbler from an ornate bar cart.

"Can I get you something? I'm tired of drinking alone."

"Whatever you're having."

Doris poured eight fingers of whiskey into a second glass and wobbled back to the couch. "What's going on? Did Amireau kill Paige Lauffer?"

Caitlin took a polite sip. "I don't know. The FBI is in charge of the Lauffer investigation."

"Guess I'm not the only one out of the loop." She visited her glass like she lived at the bottom.

Caitlin noticed a stack of packed moving boxes next to an empty china cabinet. "So the unofficial separation became official."

"Bruce and I are done." Doris looked up to the dark second-story landing. "I've got boxes of things, but no daughter and no husband."

Caitlin moved closer. "I'm sorry."

Doris put up a hand. "What do you want to know?"

"Your interactions with Detective Shepherd." Caitlin put her phone between them, started her voice recorder. "When did you find out Angela was missing?"

"Oh." Doris looked at her now half-empty glass. "Too late is the answer. Too late to do anything useful."

"Doris, I can't find Angela without your help right now."

The lawyer whispered into her drink. "No one's going to find Angie."

"Give it here, Sweat Pants." Caitlin took Doris's glass and set it on the coffee table. "I've been in Indiana for eighteen days—only eighteen—and now Michelson and Amireau are in jail, probably for life, unless one of them cuts a deal to tell the police what really happened that night with Angela. Since the cops are happy getting them for drugs, you may never know what happened to your daughter unless you help me tonight."

Doris reached for the glass Caitlin removed. "I'm so lost."

Caitlin stopped her and brought the woman into her arms. She felt the warmth of Doris's face against her shoulder, the tickle of tears against her neck.

"You might be lost, but you're not alone."

In time, she got Doris through the list of questions, then crunched through two mints that hid nothing for the drive back to Bloomington.

Twenty minutes north of the city, she got a text message from Jerry Greenwood. *Did you have to use my name when you talked to the widow?*

56

CAITLIN COULDN'T FIND a parking spot close to the guesthouse. An FBI SUV and an unmarked sedan lined the curb. Mary stood on the porch next to Chief Renton and Special Agent Foreman.

Caitlin climbed the steps and broke the ice with a smile on her face. "Is this about the weed? 'Cause it's medicinal, and it's not mine, and it's oregano, so who's the pothead now? Also, can we order pizza?"

Mary was the only one who laughed.

The dour federal agent held out a document. "Caitlin Bergman. This is a court order for the return of all files related to the Bloomington Police Department's Angela Chapman investigation."

Caitlin let him hold it in the air like a paperboy. "Whoa there, Foreman. Chief Renton should have told you that our agreement grants me full access to the files in question."

Chief Renton gave the slightest smile. "The FBI doesn't recognize our agreement. My hands are tied."

Caitlin grabbed the document from Foreman's hand. Nothing like a court order to tell her she'd found the real story. Of course, this meant the open door policy with the BPD had ended. "Fine, this gives me carte blanche to write about the fine job your department's doing."

Renton shook her head. "Actually, our lawyer says that's not quite true. You see, your agreement with the BPD stands. It's simply been superseded by a federal investigation."

Caitlin hated Renton's smug expression. "You dirty bitch."

Mary's jaw dropped. Renton might have pooped. Foreman looked like someone had just punched his mother. "Miss Bergman, do you really think you can address a chief of police with that word?"

"That was for you, you inept bag of limp dicks. I know my rights." Caitlin pushed past the agent. "Let's get your files and get you the hell out of here."

"The team's already inside," Renton said.

Caitlin turned back. "You went in without a search warrant?"

"We had the owner's consent."

Caitlin looked to Mary. Maybe it was the remnants of Doris Chapman's whiskey, but a fire burned in her gut. She threw up her hands. "Did you screw me again, Mary?"

Mary stared back at her, confused. "Again?"

Jerry Greenwood came through the door with the box of Chapman files. "That should be everything."

Another betrayal. Caitlin shook her head. "You too?"

He gave an apologetic shrug and handed Foreman the box. Foreman and Renton headed down the steps to their cars. Greenwood stayed up top, next to Mary.

Caitlin's fire burned hotter and wild. She and Mary had anticipated losing the files, so this visit wasn't a surprise. But having the BPD violate her safe space and treat her like a criminal?

No way in hell.

She took the three steps down to the sidewalk in one leap. "Special Agent Foreman, one quick question."

Renton and Foreman turned to face her. The chief smiled. "It's really nothing personal, Miss Bergman."

"And this is purely professional, Chief. According to our agreement, I can't write about the Bro-duce brothers, but there's a much better angle to cover. Special Agent, can you confirm the presence of an active serial killer in Bloomington, Indiana?"

Foreman slid the box into the back seat of the SUV, shut the door. "No comment."

Caitlin didn't stop. "Is that because confirming the presence of an active serial killer would not only reveal your own agency's incompetence, but might also show how the BPD's handling of the Chapman disappearance allowed the killer to evade detection for two years, to then hunt and kill Paige Lauffer?"

Foreman walked around to the driver's side, got in.

Renton came back, ready to fight. "How dare you? Are you saying that Detective Greenwood was anything but professional?"

"Not at all. It wasn't Jerry Greenwood who mishandled the investigation, possibly even disposed of evidence."

Mary came down by her side. "What are you doing, Caitie?"

Caitlin shrugged Mary's hand off her elbow. They didn't get to walk away with their shame in a tidy box. "Chief Renton, is it true that Detective Chris Shepherd treated Angela Chapman's disappearance as the inconsequential worry of a female friend, rather than a missing person's case, ignoring obvious physical evidence?"

"Not at all."

"Is it possible that the three-day window caused by the man's patronizing of female student Lakshmi Anjale allowed Kieran Michelson and David Amireau ample time to dispose of any and all evidence that might have led a competent investigator to Angela Chapman's remains?"

"Detective Chris Shepherd was a great man with an exemplary record."

"Who just happened to shoot himself two months after being removed from the Chapman investigation?"

Renton dismissed her with a wave. "Shepherd's suicide was the result of a personal medical issue."

"That he withheld from his wife?"

"You're talking out your ass, Bergman. Greenwood, let's go."

Jerry walked down the steps, stood next to the chief.

"Maybe not," Caitlin continued. "The lack of paperwork from Shepherd is highly suspect. Either he didn't bother to fill out an incident report or else someone in the BPD chose to omit his version, going so far as to put a typed revision in its place, not signed by the officer on the scene, but by you, Chief Renton."

Jerry put a hand up, started to open his mouth.

Caitlin didn't wait for a response. This was the tenth round, time for the knockout. "Here's something more significant. Did you know that both Detective Shepherd and the last two men to see Angela Chapman alive, Kieran Michelson and David Amireau, were all members of the same college fraternity?"

Renton pursed her lips like someone with a rotten tooth who'd just smelled her own breath. "Forty years apart? Who would care?"

Caitlin crossed her arms. "I think Doris Chapman would care that members of the same fraternity recently arrested for running a massive drug operation had the opportunity to conspire with the initial investigator into her daughter's disappearance."

"There's no proof of that."

Like she'd done with so many before, Caitlin had Renton on the ropes. She took one more verbal swing.

"Just how long did the Bloomington Police Department allow members of Delta Omega Tau to manufacture and distribute narcotics under your command?"

Renton looked ready to burst. "Do you know how hard I've worked to get where I am, you self-serving bitch?"

"You kiss the FBI's ass with that mouth, Abigail?"

"Stop it, Bergman." Greenwood said. "Chief, we have what we need."

Renton pointed Caitlin's way. "Write that shit in a public forum, and you'll spend the rest of your nights in Bloomington in the drunk tank."

Caitlin's heart raced, all adrenaline, but she wasn't going to back down. "You think you scare me? You're not half the asshole Connor Hartman was."

"I didn't rape you, Bergman, but I'll fuck you over if you get in my way."

Caitlin heard the words, but didn't see Renton anymore, only Connor Hartman's beautiful, but uncaring, blue eyes. She felt her fingers make a fist, her arm fly forward. Lucky for all involved, Greenwood's last-minute dive kept her from connecting with Renton's jaw. He took Caitlin's punch in his ribs.

"That's it, Bergman," Renton yelled. "Assaulting an officer. You're going in."

Greenwood kept them apart. "Chief, the last thing you want is this reporter in your jail. Let's go."

Renton ground her teeth, opened the passenger side of the unmarked sedan. "This is my town, Bergman. My town."

Greenwood shut the chief's door, walked around to the driver's side. "Calm down, Caitlin—take a bath. This will all work itself out."

"*Take a bath?* Are you shitting me, Jerry?"

"No," he said, then got in the car and drove away. The SUV followed.

"Caitie, are you okay?"

Caitlin had forgotten Mary was standing there. She took a short breath. "I'm fine."

Mary put a hand on her shoulder. "You don't look fine."

Caitlin turned fast, knocked the hand away, stuck her palm out, and pushed. Mary stumbled backward. Hitting the rock wall kept her from falling on her ass.

"Illegal search and seizure mean anything to you, Mary? You let them in my house."

Mary held her wrist like it hurt. "Your house? You need to calm down."

"You did it again," Caitlin said, the image of Hartman's eyes now replaced by Mary standing next to Troy Woods in a bar.

"Did what again? Chill out, Caitie. You didn't even have those files a week ago."

Caitlin felt her chest tighten. "That's not the point. They can't just—"

The pounding in her chest drove her words away. She couldn't finish the sentence.

"Caitie?"

She tried to breathe, heard the rush of waves. Mary's face morphed, flew up and sideways, ended perpendicular—or maybe that was her.

* * *

"For a skinny girl, you're pretty heavy."

Caitlin saw Mary's face, felt water. She looked down, found her naked body in a foot of water.

"How did I get in the tub?"

"Unicorns, Caitie. How do you think?"

Mary stood in the bathroom doorway. "Do you need to go the hospital?"

"No, I guess I had a panic attack."

"Duh."

Caitlin leaned forward. "Mary—"

Lubbers put a hand up. "Don't. Are you going to drown if I leave you?"

Caitlin took a deep breath. "I'll be fine now. I'm so sorry."

"You might be tomorrow. Between the BPD and the FBI, you might be really sorry. I'm going home. I've got a whole bunch of work and three classes tomorrow. Your boyfriend left you some towels."

"Mary—"

Too late. Caitlin heard the front door slam. She sank into the water, closed her eyes.

Had she really tried to punch a police chief?

"Stupid, stupid, stupid."

"Take a bath," Greenwood had said. *"This will all work itself out."*

What a crock of shit. No one cared about finding Angela Chapman. Not compared to covering their own asses.

She turned the hot water handle and put her hands under the pouring spout. The water in Lake Lemon was nowhere near as warm. She took another deep breath and sank beneath the surface, remembering her daytime plunge— the feel of the underwater grass, the mud floor of the reservoir, the calm glow of the sun at the top of the dark water. She stayed in the deep until her mortal need for breath brought her back to the light. She sat up, brushed the water from her eyes, found herself back in the bathroom.

A robe and two thick towels waited for her on top of the closed toilet seat. She reached over, found one of the smaller files from the big box of Chapman tucked between the towels. She grabbed the file with wet hands, read the handwritten label.

Possible Suspect—Lakshmi Anjale.

Caitlin jumped out of the tub and read the file, sitting wet and naked on the cold tile floor. After her second pass of the ten-page document, she shuffled into the living room, found her phone, and sent a text: *We need to talk right now.*

57

Half an hour later, Caitlin met Lakshmi on the sidewalk outside Angela Chapman's empty apartment. She held back the assault of questions on the tip of her tongue, not because Lakshmi looked like she'd been crying for the last hour, but because she didn't want the BPD's cameras to capture a single word. "Why are you hanging out here tonight?"

Lakshmi zipped up a hoodie. "After you asked about Shepherd, I got mad and drove over. You want to come in?"

"Let's walk." Caitlin turned toward the opposite end of the complex, her still-wet hair sticking to her neck. "Mad about what, me bringing up Shepherd?"

"What? No, I was mad at myself." She laced her fingertips and pushed back and forth with nervous energy. "I'm having a hard time remembering Angela. The real her. Does that make sense?"

"Sure."

Caitlin stepped into the forest on the path that Chapman would have walked to the boys' apartment. Headlights of cars on a road to their left flickered through the leaves.

Lakshmi started up again. "I came up here to talk to her, you know? I sat in her room and tried to hear her voice."

"And?"

"Didn't work. I mostly cried." She pointed toward the road. "Look, there goes the Monster."

Caitlin saw a lit red and orange sign strapped to the top of a pizza delivery car. The Monster-mobile's light passed behind tree trunks, fading into the darkness.

Lakshmi turned back to Caitlin. "Not Chad, though. He's got an old white SUV."

Convinced no one else was around, Caitlin went to work. "Memories can be fuzzy, Lakshmi. Sometimes they change over time." She squared off facing the girl. "What do you remember about Ruth Davis?"

The night hid much of Lakshmi's face, but Caitlin caught the ripple of tension on her forehead.

"'Jesus' Ruth? As in my freshman-year roommate?"

Caitlin nodded. "'My roommate went mental,' you said. Almost three weeks ago, we were talking about how you and Angela met—"

"I remember. What are you asking me?"

Caitlin watched her eyes. "Did Ruth Davis file a complaint against you with the student housing administration?"

Lakshmi stepped back like she'd been shoved, her mouth open in disbelief. "Ruth Jesus-is-the-only-man-I'll-get-on-my-knees-for Davis was the spawn of a Bible-thumping evangelist who thought girls went to hell if they danced, even in Zumba class. She was a lunatic with a ten-year-old's understanding of human sexuality."

Caitlin took a step forward. "A lunatic who swore her roommate harbored a lesbian crush on her, bordering on obsession. Did she file a complaint?"

Lakshmi gave a sharp, single laugh. "Yes, she alleged that I tried to seduce her with my lesbian wiles."

"Did you?"

Lakshmi threw a hand up. "Second week of school, I told her she'd look great in a skirt. The girl dressed like the Amish. She needed all the encouragement she could get. A month later, she comes home, walks in on me having 'personal' time. She filed a report about me showing her my fanny, all because I thought she'd be gone for another hour. The poor girl didn't know the difference between her urethra and her vagina. Masturbation might as well have been sodomy."

Like the reasoning behind Lakshmi's restraining order, the answer sounded believable, but Caitlin had more. "Tell me about Pratima Siddal."

Lakshmi's voice dropped. "Those documents were supposed to be sealed."

Caitlin crossed her arms. "You attended a public high school before you went to Hackley. Did you have a relationship with a teacher named Pratima Siddal?"

Lakshmi met Caitlin's posture and came back angry, her voice doubled in volume. "Sounds like you know what I had with Mrs. Siddal, Caitlin.

I want to know how the sealed record of a juvenile victim of sexual assault got in your hands."

"The feds profiled you, Lakshmi." Caitlin quoted a line from the FBI's report. "'From a young age, Anjale has exhibited tendencies toward obsession with female love interests.' They say you stalked Chapman, that you harassed Ruth Davis, that you cost Pratima Siddal her job and her marriage."

"*I* cost Pratima her job?" Lakshmi threw her head back, then returned with fire in her eyes. "I was a fifteen-year-old who'd never been kissed, and she was the twenty-four-year-old grammar teacher who coached the girls' soccer team, and the only other woman of Indian descent within twenty miles. Did I have a crush on her? Yes. Did I lose my virginity with her? Yes. Did I start it? No bloody way."

She ran a finger under an eye, pushed back a tear. "I was fifteen. I'd never smiled so much in my life, so I called her, way too many times, even waited outside her house to try to talk to her. That's what teenagers do. Her husband called the police, my dad got involved, the next thing I knew, they arrested Pratima for statutory rape and my father shipped me off to private school. That record is supposed to be sealed."

"It is," Caitlin said. "Your father shared the story with the detectives."

"Fuck my father." The girl's voice trembled. "I mishandled my time with Pratima, and for that, I'll always be sorry. But I didn't stalk her or Jesus Ruth or Angela."

Caitlin let Lakshmi's words hang in the air. "But you did drug her."

Again, Lakshmi's mouth dropped open. "What? Who did I drug?"

Caitlin pointed a finger at the girl's chest. "The night Angela went out with Kieran and Dave. You told me you got high."

"Yes, we got high. I told you that."

"On Molly," Caitlin said. "You woke up with aches and pains, felt horrible, drank coconut water to feel better. Those are the next-day side effects of Molly, or Ecstasy. You got high on Molly."

"Yes," Lakshmi repeated. "I told you that."

"No, you just said you got high. Everyone, myself included, assumed you meant high on weed. Angela Chapman was rolling when she left your apartment."

Lakshmi looked lost. "Okay, so?"

"No one knows where you were between your last text with Angela on Friday night and ten AM Saturday morning."

"Because I was asleep, Caitlin."

"Maybe, but you could have been right here, waiting in the woods to talk, just like you waited outside Pratima Siddal's house seven years ago."

Lakshmi's shoulders hunched forward. "I wasn't."

Caitlin pushed. "You could have met Angela on this very trail. She could have died in your hands. You could be the one who disposed of her body."

Lakshmi bounced back. "Why would I go to the police the next day? And how would I have disposed of a body?"

"Are you saying you're not smarter than Kieran and Dave?"

Lakshmi palmed her forehead. "Is this really happening?"

"The police didn't check your apartment for five days. You could have done everything you've said Kieran and Dave did. Either way, you're the one who slipped Angela the Molly."

"I didn't *slip* Angela the Molly. She knew we were doing it." Lakshmi tried to grab Caitlin's wrist, but Caitlin brushed her away.

"David Amireau says otherwise."

"And you believe him?"

Caitlin poked Lakshmi in the chest with her finger and yelled, "You lied to me."

Lakshmi took a step back. "Caitlin—"

"Every day I've been here," she continued, her finger punctuating every sentence in the air, "you've done nothing but use me, lie to me—the whole time. People ask me why I work alone? Because you can't trust anyone but yourself."

Lakshmi reached for her again. "Caitlin—"

"No." Caitlin pushed her away. "This is done. Don't talk to me, Lakshmi. Don't call me ever again, or Amireau won't be the only one with a restraining order."

She turned and walked back toward the parking lot.

Lakshmi trailed behind, pleading through tears. "I never did anything to hurt Angela, Caitlin. We'd done Molly a bunch of times. She loved it."

Caitlin unlocked her car, didn't look back. "Keep telling yourself that."

58

AT NINE AM the next morning, Caitlin walked into Scott Canton's office, still shaking the effects from a bottle of wine and a trio of Benadryl the night before. "Professor, I need Buddha's wisdom."

A young man in the kind of vest only a grad student could pull off choked on his coffee.

"I'm sorry," Caitlin said. "I'm looking for Scott Canton."

The man's face forecast a thunderstorm. "You haven't heard?"

* * *

She considered a space near the ER, remembered Jerry Greenwood's dead wife, and drove to the main lot instead, passing three narrow-looking spots close to the entrance. As scatterbrained as she felt, she'd rather walk two extra rows than scrape the car of a doctor who was trying to save Scott Canton's life.

A nurse showed her into the ICU. "Mister Canton's daughter-in-law is here."

A female voice answered. "Daughter-in-law?"

Caitlin recognized the woman in the Denny's uniform next to Scott's bed. "Sorry I'm late, Charlese."

Charlese took the hint. "Oh, his daughter-in-law. Hi, darling."

The nurse left them alone, and Charlese gave her the latest. Scott had suffered a stroke between love-making strokes, possibly due to the little blue pills made popular by those commercials on the Golf Channel. The doctors had induced sleep but expected him to wake in the next hour. Overall prognosis, alive and expected to recover, possibly some damage to his center of speech. Caitlin said she'd stay while Charlese found a cafeteria breakfast. She took the chair next to the bed, faced Scott, and forced a smile.

"Two trips to hospitals in three weeks."

She saw no movement from his eyelids, no wiggle from his nose, despite the oxygen tube in each nostril. A piece of tape kept an IV stuck into the man's wrist.

"Once for a girl I can't trust anymore—and now you, Professor."

She took a breath, shook her head, and tried not to cry again, unable to even pinpoint the primary cause.

He's expected to recover. You're crying for yourself.

She groaned the thought away and leaned in to whisper, "I've heard this happens to people in therapy, Scott. Just like going to chiropractors, I got hooked. Now I can't imagine doing this without you."

She stood, pulled a curtain from the wall to the end of his bed, sat back down, and recapped her last two days out loud. After five minutes of listing every detail she could remember, she still didn't have the missing piece.

"I have absolutely no proof that Lakshmi drugged her girlfriend. I'm going on the last-minute claim of a kid looking at twenty years in prison, a kid who may very well have killed both Paige Lauffer and Angela Chapman."

She noticed a shake in her pointer finger. Her heart rate clicked along like a roller coaster on a steady climb toward its apex, with inevitable drops, twists, and turns on the other side.

"Can't talk to Greenwood 'cause I blew up on the BPD and the FBI. Can't talk to Mary—may have botched that too. And why couldn't I keep it together with the chief? I've dealt with tougher gatekeepers than Renton. Is this what I am now? Some sad woman who loses her edge and talks to herself?"

Her pointer finger shook harder. She grabbed her knuckle with her other hand, pressed both down against her leg. She heard rustling but didn't look up. The roller coaster, ready to fall.

"I'm scared and I hate it."

She heard a sound, something like a whisper, something like her name. She took a deep breath, leaned forward, exhaled. Not only was she headed for another panic attack, this time she ran the risk of having to pay a hospital bill if they found her on the floor.

The whisper repeated, louder this time. "Caitlin."

She closed her eyes, shook her head. "Not gonna happen."

The voice came back. "Caitlin."

She looked up, saw Scott Canton's open eyes, one finger in the air.

A smile broke across her face. "Scott, you're awake!"

His finger motioned to come closer. "Caitlin."

His voice sounded hoarse. Caitlin saw a squeeze bottle of water next to the bed, squirted some into his mouth.

"You had a stroke. Do you need anything?"

"Molly," he said, the word barely air over teeth.

Caitlin looked for the nurse call button. "Who's Molly?"

Scott shook his head, motioned again.

She leaned in. "I'm here. What about Molly?"

He continued, each word a labored effort. "Were—"

She nodded. "Were?"

"—did see—" He stopped, shook his head like the words were wrong.

Caitlin found the call button on the side of the bed, hit the control.

"—get—"

"I'll get the nurse, Scott. People are on their way."

He shook his head again, frustrated.

"You don't want the people?"

She felt his fingers ring around her wrist, looked up to his eyes. He took another breath, gave the whole thing a run. "Were did see get the Molly?"

Caitlin sounded out the words. "Were did see—" She laughed at her own stupidity. Not only had Scott heard her entire recap, he'd found the missing piece. "Where did Lakshmi get the Molly?"

The room filled with qualified medical professionals, all with questions of their own. Caitlin gave them room to work. She'd gotten what she came for.

59

CAITLIN FOUND A blue bike with a faded Pizza Monster sticker locked to the theater building's bike rack. She checked the time. *2:58 PM.* According to the schedule posted online, Chad Branford's class ended at three.

Her phone chimed with another text from Lakshmi.

The first had arrived at 10:02 AM: *Pls call me when u get a chance.*

The second, 12:37: *I would gladly take a lie detector test.*

The latest: *I can't believe u would trust the BPD over me.*

The girl had a point.

"Caitlin?"

She turned around, saw Chad Branford, bike helmet in hand. "Professor Branford, I was hoping to run into you."

He flashed a smile. "Please, call me Chad. Are you here with Lakshmi?"

"All by myself," she said. "I'm surprised you remember me."

"Are you kidding? I spent some time in LA, so *Fallen Angels* was right up my alley. I'd read your book way before we met. Is it out of line to assume you're helping look for Angela?"

"Why would you assume that?"

He put his helmet on and tapped the plastic with his finger. "Lakshmi and you together? Had to be retracing Angela's last day. How can I help?"

"I'm trying to get another angle on Chapman's personality, and I know she thought of you as a friend. If you have some time—"

"I'd love to," he said, unlocking his bike, "but I've got to run home, then drop by work. Can I call you tonight, or maybe even tomorrow?"

Caitlin couldn't wait another day. She helped him back his bike out of the rack. "This won't take long. What if I give you a lift?"

His smile returned. "Great idea."

"Tell me about your time in LA," she said, leading him toward the parking lot. She wanted him distracted until they were on the road. Branford gladly covered his part-time work in a Hollywood pizza place, his makeup gigs on independent horror films, and the two touring acting gigs that shaped his decision to attend grad school—a children's theater tour of the southwest and a national tour of *Oklahoma*.

Once they'd wedged his bike into the rental's hatchback and pulled out, Caitlin started with a few entry-level Chapman questions: *What was Angela like in class? Did she ever seem sad or afraid of anyone? Had she spoken about a boyfriend?*

Each of Branford's answers sounded authentic but hummed with nervous energy. He stopped to give a direction. "Turn south here—when the light changes, obviously."

Caitlin looked over, saw him staring at her, amused.

"You're building up to it, aren't you, Caitlin?"

She checked the traffic signal, still red. "Building up to what?"

He shook his head. "We met two weeks ago, but you've come to find me now, which means you must have discovered something you need an answer to, something only I can give."

The light changed and Caitlin turned the corner. "Maybe."

He wagged his finger. "Then you hunted me."

"Hunted you?"

"Sure, cornered me outside my class, offered me a ride, killed time with small talk, then played with me in your lair until I couldn't escape."

Caitlin pulled over to the side of the road. "Whoa, Chad, I hope you don't feel like my hybrid is a *lair*. If you'd like to get out—"

He laughed. "Are you kidding? This is great. I love being hunted."

"Never thought of myself as a hunter before," Caitlin said, pulling back into traffic. "No offense to you, but you might be the smartest actor I've ever met."

He drummed his hands on his thighs. "Let's get your question out of the way."

"Fair enough." Caitlin went back into work mode. "I know that you, Lakshmi, and Angela used to get high together. The night Angela disappeared, she and Lakshmi both took MDMA."

"And you want to know if they got the pills from me?"

She nodded.

He sat back in his seat, his smile fading into resignation. "I'm glad someone finally asked. The cops never did. Not that I felt bad about it. I mean, it looked like that Michelson kid killed Angela, and obviously Lakshmi knew, and no one came after me. I was afraid if I brought it up out of the blue, it wouldn't help the cops, but I'd get fired for some sort of teacher–student violation."

"Understandable," Caitlin said patiently.

Branford pointed at the coming intersection. "Turn right up here."

She took the turn, glanced his way. "Want to tell me about the pills?"

He spoke with a slight tremble. "First off, I'm not a dealer. I keep a little pot around for stress, but I inherited the Molly from a guy in a French clown troupe who couldn't take his stash on a plane. The second I found out Angela went missing, I doused the rest of the pills with a hose." He held up a finger. "But I didn't sell the pills. The girls helped me so much when I started the Monster that I gave them Molly whenever they asked. I am *not* a drug dealer."

"No judgment," Caitlin said. "I wouldn't have made it through the last three weeks without a friend's weed stash."

Branford smiled. "I knew I liked you, Caitlin Bergman."

She laughed, then got back to the point. "Who asked for the Molly the night Angela went missing?"

"Lakshmi."

Caitlin's stomach turned. Another omission from the girl's version of events. "Did she call or drop by your classroom?"

"She dropped by a few days before, said she and Angela wanted to party that Friday."

Damn it. Lakshmi hadn't just procured the pills, she'd planned the whole night. As in premeditation.

"And when did she come by and get the Molly?"

Branford looked confused. "She didn't. Angela grabbed the pills that Friday at the end of class."

Caitlin slowed for a stop sign. "Wait, Angela grabbed the pills?"

"It didn't make sense for Lakshmi to make an extra trip."

Caitlin leaned back against her headrest. *If Chapman knew about the pills, then Lakshmi was telling the truth.*

Someone in a car behind them tapped the horn.

And I accused her of drugging the woman she loved . . . after I accused her of stalking the teacher who'd seduced her as an underage high-school girl . . . and brought up the whole load of homophobic roommate bullshit.

The horn honked again, longer.

Branford cleared his throat. "I think it's your turn."

"Right, great." Caitlin drove through the intersection, both guilty and relieved. She'd have to beg Lakshmi's forgiveness for shaming her, but at least now she knew the truth. "Wait, where are we?"

"Near Bloomington South High." Branford pointed past the intersection. "You want to keep going straight. It's only another mile."

Caitlin glanced back at a street sign. "Is this Tapp Road?"

"Yeah, Winslow turns into Tapp at Walnut. I don't know why."

Caitlin tightened her grip on the wheel.

"Are you okay?"

She realized Branford was watching her and fixed her eyes on the road. "Just got kind of queasy."

The structure loomed in her peripheral vision. Set far back from the road on the passenger side, the long, three-story, sheet-metal shed still stood. She forced herself to remember Lake Lemon, the chill of the water, the light of the sun above.

Branford's voice brought her back. "Take the next left."

She turned south onto a dirt road and checked her rearview mirror. She'd passed her past by half a mile.

Branford pointed to a solitary duplex on an acre of grass surrounded by cornfields. "That's me."

"Why the hell does a charismatic, business-owning young man like yourself live way out in the sticks? I know there's no money in teaching, but I've never heard of pizza failing in a college town."

Branford laughed. "It might not look like much right now—"

"It looks like corn."

"—well, there's land under all that corn. In five years, this will all be housing subdivisions—and I'm sitting on twenty-two acres."

"Definitely the smartest actor I've ever met," Caitlin said, pulling onto his asphalt driveway. She parked between the house and its detached garage.

Branford didn't reach for his door handle. "I know I never said 'off the record' or anything, but I'd love to stay out of the whole mess."

"No reason to bring it up. I'm working this all on my own," Caitlin said, conscious of the many smoldering bridges she'd left in town.

"Well, riding with you saved me an hour. How can I repay you?"

"No need." Caitlin pressed the trunk button and got out.

Branford met her at the tailgate to retrieve his bike. "I insist. Any chance you like pizza?"

Caitlin shut the trunk. "Some might say too much."

"I've got a stack of free pizza coupons in the kitchen. Can you wait like two minutes? I'll hook you up." He pulled his house keys out of his backpack. "That is, unless you have some hot date you need to run to?"

Caitlin's only plan was to head back to Mary's guesthouse. A free meal wouldn't hurt anything. "Lakshmi says your pizza is pretty good."

"Liar. Lakshmi says my pizza's the *best*. Don't go anywhere."

Caitlin watched him jog the bike to the house's kitchen door and slip inside.

Where would she even go? At this point, it might be easier to drive her rental car cross-country than turn around and face Greenwood, Mary, or Lakshmi.

She shook her head, stretched, then walked over to the back patio, plopped down on a deck chair, and filled her lungs with country air. Since the nearest residence was an old farmhouse at the other end of the cornfield, maybe three quarters of a mile away, there'd be no distractions until Branford's return. Caitlin closed her eyes and went into her tunnel.

If Lakshmi hadn't drugged Chapman, Caitlin had nothing new to bring to the story. With access to the farm, the cops would find Chapman's body, which meant Caitlin would have to read it in the paper like every other jerk. What to do?

She looked up at the waist-high, bright-green rows of corn, watched the tassels wave in the light breeze.

There was the other story. The *real* story. She'd driven past the spot. She could drive back, walk the area—or she could go back to the house, pack her stuff, and leave town.

For the second time in the nineteen days she'd been in Indiana, her dad's singsong voice came back to her.

"Could *don't mean* should, *but* would *won't mean* did—*unless you let it. Otherwise, you'll never forget it.*"

She took another look at the cornfield and nodded.

It's just a building. Troy Woods won't even be there.

She'd drive over to the old limestone mill, see what there was to see, then let her emotions tell her whether to go back to Mary's place or drive aimlessly across the country.

"There you are."

Branford's return brought her out of her head. He walked over with a plastic shopping bag in hand. "I thought you ran away."

Caitlin stood. "Just clearing my head."

"Good, I come bearing gifts." He pulled three business-card-sized coupons out of the bag, each marked "Free Pizza by Owner."

"May you never go hungry," he said.

She pocketed the cards. "Or thin. I thank you from the bottom of my stomach."

"The second item isn't really a gift," he said, reaching back into his bag. The familiar cover of *Fallen Angels* appeared. "Told you I was a fan."

Caitlin reached for the hardcover book. "Have a pen? For once I don't mind signing a copy."

He leaned in next to her. "No, that's the surprise, Caitlin. Open the cover."

She opened the book, saw her own signature in blood red—the same color pen she'd used at every signing. "I don't remember seeing you at the bookstore."

"What can I say? Nobody in casting remembered seeing me in Hollywood either. Maybe it's why I teach." He took the book back, brought out two more items, a glass pipe and a metal tin. "Now, I know you have to run, but you mentioned a penchant for the forbidden plant. I was gonna smoke a bowl before I went to the Monster. Care to join me?"

He unscrewed the tin's lid, and the smell of dank pot wafted her way. "Sounds like a good way to burn a pizza."

"Oh no," he said, pinching a bud from the tin. "It's a gentle sativa, mellow, but not mind-numbing. I've performed *Hamlet* on this strain."

Again, she thought about her upcoming visit to the old mill. For the first time since she'd been in Bloomington, she wasn't worried about walking the spot sober. "No thanks, I'd better get going."

She dug for the rental car's key fob in her pocket, started walking.

"Are you sure," he asked, trailing behind her. "It's really good stuff."

"I've got a lot of work to do." Still fifty feet away, she hit the fob, unlocked the car with a beep. "That's my ride."

He sped up and stepped in front of her, planting his body between her and the car. "I'm super-bummed. What are the odds I'll ever get a chance to chat with an award-winning author at my own house?"

His mouth offered a perfect toothpaste-commercial smile, but his eyes gave off something else, something dark and intense. For the briefest of seconds, Caitlin was reminded of Troy Woods. Although way under Woods's towering six and a half feet, Branford still had a few inches on her. Caitlin moved her tongue against her cheek, her mouth suddenly dry.

"Gotta go, Chad," she said, not challenging, but firm.

His eyes opened wide, and the dark intensity she'd seen disappeared. "Of course. Sorry if that sounded creepy." He moved aside. "It was really great sharing a moment with you, Caitlin."

"You too," she said, continuing her walk to the car.

Woods is on your mind. Of course he is, but Branford's just a teacher.

Her tension dissipated with each step.

Lakshmi's favorite teacher, she reminded herself, *and a fan of your writing. Who could blame him for wanting to get to know you?*

Now only ten feet from the car, Caitlin smiled, remembering Lakshmi sitting at the signing. The girl had waited politely for her turn to talk about a body buried in a field; a safe, noninvasive distance away, maybe twenty feet at the most. About the distance Branford was behind her now, standing back near the patio chair.

Caitlin's smile disappeared.

But if Branford had a copy signed, how the hell did Lakshmi not see her favorite teacher at the table?

"Hey, Caitlin." His friendly voice called out from behind her. "I think you forgot your phone."

She turned, saw him jogging toward her with a mobile device in his hand.

Lakshmi's favorite acting teacher, the one who did makeup on horror films in Hollywood.

She turned back to the car, saw her phone sitting in the center console.

Her heart dropped into her stomach. Branford *had* been at the signing.

The guy with the goatee darker than his hair and the kind of horrible scars people looked away from.

"Must have slipped out of your pocket when you sat in the chair," he said, only seconds away now.

She could be misreading coincidences, wrong, or just plain crazy, but every hair on her arms stood on end. No time to get to the driver's side of the car or to crawl in through the passenger's door, not even keys to scratch with—only the fob in her hand. Fuck it, if she was wrong, she'd apologize.

Caitlin planted her left leg and kicked straight back waist-high with her right foot.

Her kick made contact, full-force.

She spun around, saw Branford stumbling backward holding his ribs, eight feet away, the phone still in his hand.

Ready with an apology, she waited for some sign of outrage, or even surprise, but Branford shook his head and stood up straight, no more smile.

"What gave me away?" he said, the charm in his voice replaced with cold calculation, the welcoming light in his eyes now dark.

Caitlin shifted to her right.

He matched her position, fast, like Peter Pan's shadow.

She shifted back left, he did the same, then smiled and pressed the button on the side of the phone. Sparks arced between two contacts at the tip of the anti-rape stun device.

"This doesn't have to hurt," Branford shouted over the frantic snapping.

"Yes," Caitlin said, "it sure fucking does."

He lunged forward, stun gun out.

Caitlin ducked left, threw a roundhouse kick toward his side, made contact again, but weakly, a push instead of a snap. He swung the phone toward her leg. She pulled away, avoiding the shock, but tumbled backward and landed close to the front of the parked car. She got up fast, put another five feet between them, her hands in fists.

"Shit," she said, her eyes stuck on the key fob sitting in the dirt where she fell.

He followed her gaze, quick-stepped closer to the fob, and reactivated the stun gun.

No way she could get to her key or her phone. With that thing ready to shock the daylights out of her, no way she could beat Branford in a fight. She caught her breath. The only good thing about all that time she'd spent running from her past was that now she could run very, very fast.

She turned and sprinted into the cornfield.

The waist-high corn whipped across her jeans as her canvas deck shoes sped through the mud, but she pushed hard, full-speed. She glanced back, saw Branford following behind her, but slower. She'd beat him to the farmhouse, find help, a witness or even a phone. Anything to buy time and distance. On a lazy day, she ran a ten-minute mile. A good day, an even eight. Caitlin guessed she cleared the distance between Branford's driveway and the farmhouse in six. Lungs burning, she ran into the grass surrounding the farm and checked behind her.

No sign of Branford. Maybe he'd crouched in the corn, maybe he'd gone back. If he knew what was good for him, he'd run back home, get his car, and get the hell out of town before Caitlin got back with the cops. She inspected the farm, saw a partially collapsed garage with nothing inside and the two-story house with a long front porch. No cars in the driveway.

"Help," she screamed, running toward the front door.

She climbed onto the porch, flung open a screen door, and pounded on the solid inner door. "Help me, please, anyone."

She looked back, still no sign of Branford.

She knocked again, then grabbed the door handle. No give. Stepping away, she looked into a window, but saw nothing but curtains. She smacked her hand on the glass and shuffled down the width of the porch. "Please, anyone."

In the far corner near the porch ceiling, a modern security camera aimed toward the door. She took a step back, looked directly into the lens, and screamed. "If you can see me, please send help. The man's name is Chad Branford."

She turned back to the corn.

Damn it.

Maybe he'd been hiding earlier, maybe she'd been blinded by adrenaline. Branford was three-quarters of the way through the corn and getting closer.

Caitlin jumped off the porch and ran around the house. A small set of cinder block steps led up to a screened-in patio. She reached for the screen door. Held in place by a hook and eye latch, the flimsy barrier shimmied in place. Caitlin put a foot against the porch frame and pulled again, full strength. The tiny lock gave way.

She scrambled into a well-kept garden of spices and vegetables, jumped over a lawn chair toward a door, and tried the knob.

Unlocked, thank God.

She opened the door into a kitchen, turned and slammed it shut behind her. Not only did it have a simple knob-lock, it had two deadbolts. She turned all three, then backed away until she bumped into a counter.

Find a phone.

She spun, inspecting the room. The cabinets and appliances looked well used but unchanged since the seventies. She scanned for a wall phone.

Nothing. No old AT&T standard. No cordless charger.

How about a knife?

She checked the counters, saw a microwave, a toaster oven, and a stack of newspapers, but no knife block.

"Are you kidding me?" she yelled, stepping toward an opening that led to a large staircase.

The loud creak of movement on hardwood floor froze her in place. She dropped into a squat, held her breath, and waited for another sign of life.

Seconds later, a weak voice called from somewhere past the stairs. "Is there someone here?"

Definitely in the house. Hard to say whether it belonged to a male or female.

"I saw you on the camera," the voice continued. "I've called the police."

Relief washed over Caitlin. "There's a man chasing me," she said, following the sound toward the right, now definitely feminine, maybe a senior citizen. She moved toward the stairs, saw a room on her left full of older furniture with vinyl dust covers. "Where are you?"

"I'm on the phone with the police, just inside the parlor."

Caitlin turned another corner, saw the house's front entry lobby and a wainscoted opening leading to a side sitting room. Caitlin entered the parlor, saw an open laptop on a TV dinner table with a live security feed of the outside porch, but didn't see a little old lady.

She definitely didn't see whatever struck her in the temple, only the blossom of hot pain that drove sight from her right eye.

She collapsed onto the hardwood floor, her hand clutching at the point of impact.

Chad Branford walked out from an unseen corner. "He's not outside, dear," he said, his voice mimicking a little old lady, his hand once again clutching the stun gun. "He's right here."

Caitlin tried to stand, but a sharp kick to the jaw knocked her over again, the pain spreading everywhere. She reached out with her hands, tried to crawl.

The violent snap of the stun gun returned. "I guess you were right," he shouted over the sound of superheated air exploding. "This does have to hurt."

CHAPTER

60

MOLD, MOIST EARTH, mildew, urine. The smells sank into the back of
Caitlin's mouth.

She opened her eyes, saw only a sliver of light. She tried to turn her head,
but a strap held her down against a mattress. Same with her hands and feet.

How long has it been? Hours?

Her jaw was on fire, and her shoulder ached, probably from Branford's
stun gun, but the pain battled something narcotic that kept her thoughts dull.

Hours then.

She couldn't see her clothing but felt the difference between what she'd
been wearing and the pajama-like fabric now covering both her top and
bottom—wet below her crotch. Unconscious, she'd pissed the bed, probably
some dirty mattress in Branford's second house, the farmhouse she'd run to
for help.

*Idiot. He told you he owned twenty-two acres of land, which means no one
saw you running, no one heard you scream—and you didn't tell a single person
where you were going.*

She let out a whimper. A restraint below her breasts kept her breath
shallow.

*This is the man who killed Angela Chapman, probably Paige Lauffer too.
Not Amireau or Michelson, definitely not Lakshmi Anjale. A fucking acting
teacher.*

Her chest shook and she gasped, letting out a longer but somehow weaker
noise, and a single thought echoed in her head.

This is how I die.

Something else made its presence known. A sound—rhythmic, excited, familiar. A mix of heavy breath and the slight slapping of skin.

A high whine escaped the back of Caitlin's throat. She took another gasp, let her first scream out. She knew the sound of a man masturbating. The steady pace turned feverish.

His soft voice came through, almost serpentine. "You're safe now."

She screamed again, but still heard his breathy whispers. "You're mine, Caitlin."

She lost herself, screamed until she saw nothing, felt nothing. His own scream joined hers, an unbridled chorus. Her voice gave out; her tears did not.

He gave his own whimper. His voice sounded softer, further, perhaps turned away. "Oh, Caitlin, I'm so glad you're here."

She heard movement, then a zipper.

"So glad."

The air pressure in the room changed. She heard a whoosh, then a footstep onto crushed stone.

"I'll be back tonight," he said, even further away.

A soft thud was followed by the metallic slide of a deadbolt being turned, then another.

Then silence.

CHAPTER

61

Los Angeles

Mike had checked his phone first thing each morning. Still nothing from Caitlin.

On Monday, he'd had a follow-up call with Agent Martinez, who'd handed Michelson off to be transported to the Midwest, but Martinez hadn't heard from Caitlin either. That afternoon, Mike emailed her an invoice for his Bahamas expenditures, the last line a stand-alone item labeled "Manure Transportation (Kieran Michelson)." Her lack of reply didn't faze him, but he spent the rest of the day skimming news coverage of the Bloomington drug busts. Nothing mentioned Caitlin's involvement.

A weekend without a debrief wasn't unusual.

Not hearing back by Monday after a big story's release wasn't exactly unheard of either but did strike Mike as out of the ordinary. Caitlin often followed up for additional details she could use in supplemental pieces. That or she'd meet him somewhere to brag over cocktails.

By Tuesday night, almost seventy-two hours after he'd turned in Michelson, Mike got worried. Scrolling back through the Bro-duce stories, he found a trend, dialed the *Indiana Daily Student*, and left a message.

A young woman with a slight British accent returned his call Wednesday morning.

"Is this Mike Roman? My name is Lakshmi Anjale."

The Anjale girl hadn't spoken with Caitlin since Monday night. She didn't go into detail, but Mike could tell they'd ended on less than friendly terms. Also, she'd gotten a text from Caitlin on Tuesday at 5:47 PM.

Fuck this town.

Cryptic, but more reply than he'd gotten. Lakshmi gave him another number and name—Mary Lubbers-Gaffney.

When Weird-Last-Name Mary returned his call, she told him Caitlin had cleaned her stuff out of the guesthouse on Tuesday and disappeared without so much as a thank-you note. She also filled in the details regarding Caitlin's dalliances with Jerry Greenwood and the BPD confrontation.

A quick conversation with Detective Greenwood revealed he also hadn't heard from Caitlin since Monday, but he did mention pointing her toward Lakshmi.

A full loop. The only off-ramp a text that read *Fuck this town*. Mike tried to go about the rest of his week, but sleep couldn't beat his instincts.

Thursday morning, he searched for flights to Indianapolis.

Friday, he landed and rented a car.

That afternoon, he placed a copy of Caitlin's book in front of the Bloomington Police Department's desk sergeant and pointed to the photo on the jacket.

"My friend is missing."

62

CAITLIN'S EYES FOUGHT to focus on the mess of pink and white halfway up the nearest wall. Her brain filled in the gaps between the low light and whatever drugs Branford had forced into her system.

Barbie.

Wait, not *Barbie*, but cursive pink and white letters in Barbie's trademarked style, abused for vanity art: *Paige.*

Caitlin had found the missing wall art from Paige Lauffer's doll room.

She was still restrained, but not in a bed. Straps kept her upright on a metal chair, arms at her sides, knees and feet together, no wiggle room. Her body reported aches and pains, but no violation below the waist. The clothes felt the same as last time, some sort of pink cotton pajamas. Her bare feet touched cold stone, smooth but unpolished.

She sat at a wooden table big enough for two across from an empty chair. Underneath Paige's Barbie sign, the twin-sized bed she'd woken on earlier waited with neatly applied sheets, also bright pink. The off-white wall looked smooth and slightly reflective. The ghostly tint of fluorescence lit the room from behind. The air felt humid; her skin, sticky.

She looked at the ceiling. Smooth, off-white like the wall, possibly metal. A faint column of air moved against her face from a single darkened light fixture made of round translucent plastic with a one-inch ringed gap around the edge—a bathroom light and fan combo.

To the right, another smooth wall, maybe two feet from the table's edge. To the left, a cheap plastic shelving unit held a stack of clothing and three unopened Barbie dolls.

She'd seen walls like this before. A reporter she knew from National

Public Radio had installed a similar soundproof room in her garage for home recording, minus the Barbie dolls, mattress, and threat of endless rape.

Caitlin shuddered. *I'm gonna die in here.*

The light above came on.

She took a deep breath. *Not without a fight.*

Two deadbolts turned behind her, then the door opened. Caitlin saw the profile of a man shadowed on the wall. He paused, shifted to one side, then back again, almost a small dance.

She wouldn't let him control the moment. "Either murder me or come around where I can see you, Branford."

"Looks like you're awake," he said. No movement.

"Is this where you tell me how much power you have over me, or are you jacking off again?"

He laughed, then brushed past her, pulled out the other chair, and sat. "Welcome, Caitlin Bergman, to the rest of your life."

His black V-neck T-shirt and blue jeans seemed innocent enough. His leather gloves did not. Caitlin hadn't memorized Branford's face, but his toothy grin lacked the former shiny toothpaste-commercial goodness.

"Jesus, Branford, you wear false teeth?"

"Not I, Caitlin. Chad has a set that would blind most people. Part of his appeal."

"You're not Chad Branford? 'Cause you look just like him."

He shook his head no.

"Okay, who the hell are you?"

He smiled. "Now that's the real question, isn't it?"

"Maybe I don't want to know." She flexed her arms against her straps, found no give. "What day is it, anyway? How long have I been here?"

"All in good time. I'd like to teach you the rules."

"What's to know? You come in, rape me until I die, then dump me in a soccer field."

"I'm not going to force myself on you, Caitlin. I'm certainly not going to kill you."

"Right, ask Paige Lauffer."

"I didn't rape Paige Lauffer."

"Still ended up naked and dead in a goal box."

"Paige didn't listen to the rules."

"Chad Branford's secret dungeon rules?"

"I told you," he said, his voice steady but with an electric current buzzing below the surface, "I'm not Chad Branford."

"What should I call you? Dungeon master? Barbie doll enthusiast?"

Branford put both elbows on the table, rested his chin in his palms. "Are you done?"

"Not in the slightest, you wannabe actor. I can do this all day long."

"And I want to hear every precious word, Caitlin. This is why you're here."

"To ask questions about your obvious narcissism—despite the inevitable micro-penis or downstairs mix-up you've got going on that makes you the sicko you are, Not-Chad-Branford?"

He held up a hand. "Rule one, when I raise my hand, you stop talking."

"That crap didn't work for my first-grade teacher, and you're not half the woman Mrs. Browning was."

He stood. "Caitlin, my hand was raised."

"And you can shove that right up your—"

His sharp punch connected with her left cheek. Her head snapped to the side, a mix of white hot pain and instant dizzy.

"When I raise my hand, you stop talking. Do I need to repeat myself?" She rattled her head no.

"Good." He sat back down. "It brings me no joy to hurt you. Rule two— eat what I give you, then place your empty plates and things in the drop."

"What drop?"

"You haven't seen the room yet, but you'll be able to move around soon. Eventually, you'll be allowed in the playroom as well. So follow rule two. Eat what I give you."

Caitlin worked her jaw around, tasted blood.

"I know," he said. "You have so many things you want to say, but I've got you hooked, right? You're already considering logistics. It's not just one room, but two. If there are two rooms, there must be a way out. You're a smart woman. Sorry, not merely smart, you're a genius, Caitlin. You'll stop asking questions, and you'll listen to my rules, placate me, bide your time. How am I doing—close?"

"Close."

Branford looked pleased. "Do you know why I know what you're thinking?"

Caitlin locked eyes with him. "Because you're a genius too."

He clapped once, rocked back in the chair. "Exactly, and you're really going to take me to task."

"By talking back while you torture me?"

"At first," he said. "But we'll get through this phase quickly if you accept the inevitable."

"That I can't escape?"

He shook his head no.

"Paige escaped."

"If Paige *escaped*," he said, leaning across the table again, "how come you're here in her room, and she's lying in pieces in the morgue?"

If Branford wanted to brag, she'd let him. He was right: she had hope.

"Fine," she said. "I live in this room now, I follow the rules. You and I have talks until you decide to hit me or drug me to sleep so you can do whatever."

"Your sarcasm doesn't bother me because you're on the right track. See, this was the problem with Paige. She didn't get me."

"And I do?"

"Oh Caitlin, I know you do. Go ahead, tell me."

"Tell you what?"

"Who I am."

"Don't you have a class to teach?"

"Called in sick," he said. "I'm not going anywhere until you tell me who you think I am."

Caitlin thought back. Once she'd left Scott Canton's hospital room, she'd looked up Branford's teaching schedule. He taught on Tuesdays, Wednesdays, and Fridays. If he'd really called in sick, that made it one of the three. She'd been taken on Tuesday, and was fairly certain she'd been there more than one night. Today had to be Friday. Missing for three days.

The tapping of his gloved fingertips on the tabletop reminded her of heavy raindrops hitting a window, like the night she'd driven back from Kentucky. She took a breath, cleared her throat, and humored him.

"Fine. You're a high-functioning psychopath, possibly of genius-level intelligence."

"Not possibly," he said. "I have certificates to prove it."

"I'm sure, though the bragging buries the lead."

He raised an eyebrow. "Which is?"

"You need to be recognized. You need someone to appreciate your genius."

He stood again, paced behind the chair. "Exactly."

"Which means you'll be caught soon. You need the world to know, to share your secrets. Who was it, by the way?"

He stopped, obstructing her view of Paige's pink sign. "Who was what?"

"The parent who didn't care. Your father or your mother?"

"Ouch," Branford said, his hand clutching his heart in mock pain. "What else?"

"You've gotten careless. The decorations in the room, the room itself, all show a level of meticulous planning worthy of a choreographer playing to the single audience of Paige Lauffer—yet here I am in her place."

"You have no idea how many moving pieces there are."

"Maybe," Caitlin said. "More likely, part of your need to dominate is fighting with your need for respect."

He wagged his finger at her. "That's where you're wrong. I don't need the rest of the world to know. I've got Caitlin Bergman, right here, part of my collection."

Jesus. His collection.

She looked away from his smug smile. "How many? Me, Paige Lauffer, Angela Chapman?"

"Antoine Foreman, eat your heart out." He sat again, leaned across the table, and reached out, touching her arm near her elbow. "Two years. Can you imagine that?" His gloved fingertip slowly traced its way up her arm, the exploration of each new inch causing Caitlin to flinch against her unyielding restraints. "I didn't expect the local hicks to have a chance, but they assigned an FBI special agent, a profiler no less, and he hasn't come close in two whole years."

He stopped at her shoulder, looked directly into her eyes, smiled, then pushed some of her hair behind her ear. "You've been here what, a month?"

Caitlin swallowed hard, but didn't look away. "If today's Friday, I've been in town for three weeks. It is Friday, isn't it?"

"Nice try." He pulled back and slapped the table. "I'm hungry. Are you hungry?"

Caitlin let her breath escape. "What about the rest of your rules?"

"Fuck the rules," Branford said, already up and moving toward the door. "This is fun."

No way to gauge time, no clue when he'd return. She noticed a black camera dome in the corner above the bed. What did it matter if he watched? Surely he expected her to test her restraints.

Four seatbelt-like nylon bands kept her pink-pajamaed torso against the chair. One over each shoulder, one across her ribs below the breasts, one around her waist. Her arms, pulled together behind the chair, lay over the straps, bound at the elbows and the wrists, her fingertips pressed together.

Three days and no cops. Hardly any memories of the time so far. Who knows what he's done to you, what he'll do to you.

Her chest shook. She shut her mouth, kept the breath in.

Don't lose control, not yet.

A similar strap crossed her thighs and flattened her legs against the seat. She tried to move her feet. Another set near the ankles restricted any movement other than side to side.

Lose control? Who are you kidding? You have absolutely no control.

Her chest heaved again. "Not now."

Words couldn't stop the looming attack. Fighting against hyperventilation, she tried to remember Scott Canton's advice.

The rush of the water. The sunlight above. The run to the car. Dinner with Mary and Aaron. Sex with Greenwood.

For a second, she felt calmer, but then she remembered the photos of Angela Chapman on her missing person's poster.

Which of Caitlin's photos would they use? After all the years of getting the story, she'd be the story.

In Bloomington.

Where it all began.

Her short breaths couldn't compete with the straps. She lost her air, her sight, and her consciousness.

*   *   *

She smelled rosemary and garlic, opened her eyes.

Still in her chair. A plate on the table held a sizable mound of potatoes, steamed broccoli, and a grilled chicken breast.

Branford held a plastic forkful of food inches from her face. "Here comes the airplane."

She turned aside. "No way."

"Caitlin, do you remember rule two?"

"The drugs you're forcing into my body have clouded my memory. Was rule two 'Screw yourself'?"

She braced for another punch, but Branford placed potatoes into his own mouth and swallowed. "See? No drugs in the food." He forked a piece of broccoli. "No hormones either, and the veggies are organic."

She ignored the angry chorus warming up in her belly and changed the subject. "Nice touch with the scars. That was you, right?"

He smiled. "I've found the key to a convincing disguise is an uncomfortable visual disfigurement, which I know sounds awful—"

"You kidnap and imprison women."

"Right? I might be a monster, but I'm not a jerk." Branford used the edge of his fork to break off a hunk of chicken. "A skin disorder, a facial scar, a handicap. No one wants to face a victim. What's that about?"

"The fragility of mortality," she said, staring at the plate. The chicken looked tender and juicy. "To acknowledge someone else's impediment is to face our own weakness."

Branford's eyes narrowed. "Well said."

The pulsed buzz of a cell phone somewhere on Branford's body broke the tomb-like silence. She'd guessed they were underground, but the phone's active signal meant not too far down. He ignored the alert.

"Try some chicken."

She turned away. "Not hungry."

"Haven't I shown you that the food isn't drugged?"

As long as he wanted her to eat, she'd starve. "Maybe I don't want to have to sit in my own feces."

"This is only temporary," he said. "Follow my rules, and you'll be free to move around. Eat."

The fork came back her way. She denied entrance once again.

He set it on the plate. "I can force-feed you. I'm horrible with the IV, but I've done it before."

His phone buzzed again. He reached into his pocket, looked down at the screen, slipped the phone back, continued.

"Or we can go liquid diet, which involves my hands on your throat, you gagging and spitting up baby formula. Does that sound better?"

Caitlin met his eyes. "You want me to eat, Branford, untie one of these hands."

His phone chimed, a different tone altogether. Whatever the two church bells back-to-back meant, Branford's demeanor changed.

"Shit." He reached for his other pocket, came back with a folding knife, and opened the blade. "I don't have time to play this game anymore."

He walked behind her. She heard a crisp snap, then felt the restraint around her right wrist loosen. Another snap freed her arm at the elbow.

His lips brushed her left ear. "Don't go anywhere."

She heard the door close, the locks turn.

She reached behind her, found a thick plastic loop around her left wrist, maybe a zip tie, and another near her elbow. Both were looped around the straps keeping her body against the chair. The straps met at a metal ring near the small of her back, but there was no release mechanism. She followed the material to the underside of the chair, where the straps fed into a junction box that allowed excess material to pass through. She tugged on a hanging strap, tried pushing the tail back through the slot, but couldn't find any give.

She dropped her head. *This monster has this down to a science.*

Fine. If she couldn't break the straps, she'd break his plan. She reached for the plate, set the dinner on her lap. The scent of rosemary overpowered the garlic, and Caitlin loved rosemary.

She picked up the plastic fork, tucked it under her right leg, then grabbed a handful of mashed potatoes. No way she'd give Branford the satisfaction. He'd already changed her clothes once, and not for her comfort. He wanted her neat and clean.

She smeared the white goodness across her chest, careful to get both the straps and the pajama top. She reached back to the plate for a handful of broccoli florets, crushed them against her pants until she felt the wet paste through the material. She finished up with the chicken and remaining potatoes.

Caitlin didn't know what damage she could do with a plastic fork, but she wanted to find out.

63

H E SHUTTLED THE footage backward until he saw the BPD cruiser in the driveway of the duplex.

They've found me. Taking Caitlin was a mistake.

He changed feeds, checked the front door at the same time stamp. A uniformed female officer knocked, peered through the glass, and left after a minute.

He switched back to the driveway cam. The officer sat in the cruiser for two minutes, then drove away.

He ran to the kitchen door, grabbed his binoculars, and stepped outside. No sign of the cruiser near the duplex registered to Chad Branford. He replayed the voicemail.

"Mister Branford. This is Detective Jerry Greenwood from the Bloomington Police Department. Please call when you have a moment."

He took a breath, calmed himself. *Not a mistake. An opportunity.*

He dialed the detective's number. Greenwood answered after two rings.

Chad Branford's pleasant voice went to work. "I was on a bike ride and didn't hear my phone ring. How can I help, Detective?"

"Won't take long, Mister Branford. I'm looking for a woman named Caitlin Bergman. Know who I mean?"

"Sure, the reporter. Does this mean there's been a break in the Chapman murder?"

Greenwood didn't answer right away, but Branford hadn't overplayed the part. His dialogue followed the natural curiosity a college professor might have.

As if on cue, Greenwood broke the dramatic pause. "Why would you say that?"

"She stopped by on Tuesday and asked me questions about Angela that no one else ever had."

Greenwood took the bait. "What did Miss Bergman ask?"

"I'm not sure I feel comfortable talking about that."

"Do you mean over the phone?"

Branford gave a little laugh. "Actually, I mean talking to a cop without some sort of, you know, common understanding. I guess you could ask her what we talked about, and anything she says I said would be hearsay."

"That's the problem. No one's heard from Caitlin Bergman since Tuesday."

Branford slapped his face in mock disbelief. "She didn't get to Los Angeles?"

"What do you mean?"

After the right amount of hemming and hawing, Branford said he'd told Caitlin about Angela Chapman's MDMA pills. When Caitlin learned about the Molly, she said she'd done all she could and that the FBI had the case. Then she'd asked about the fastest way to the airport. Branford told her to take state road 37.

Greenwood followed up with questions about the timing of events, details about their route from the school to the house, then thanked Branford for his time.

"Not a problem, Detective. Please, call anytime. There's not a day that goes by that I don't think about Angela Chapman."

He hung up and returned to his laptop. The feed from Caitlin's room showed the mess she'd made. He rewound, watched her tuck the plastic fork under her strap.

What a woman. So much smarter than Paige Lauffer. He smiled at the thought until the inevitable followed. *And Paige escaped.*

Caitlin would fight him, maybe even to her death. He had no desire to watch her die, but she had to be taught.

He went back downstairs. Outside Caitlin's door, he opened a wall panel and turned a small plastic valve, then twisted a knob clockwise to the five-minute mark. Then he went back to the shelves and pulled the manila BPD folder from Caitlin's laptop bag. Five minutes. More than enough time to learn the details of Caitlin Bergman's personal hell.

64

GREENWOOD HANDED MIKE Roman a page still warm from the laser printer. "That shows the path of Caitlin's rental from campus to Professor Branford's house."

Mike leaned against Greenwood's bullpen cubicle and stared at the map, a solid line with marks every mile or so. "The dots are the GPS pings from the car's tracking system?"

"Right." Greenwood handed him another. "Next trip went from Branford's house to the guesthouse."

Mike compared the two. "How much time between trips?"

Greenwood handed him a third. "You mean sitting in Branford's driveway? Thirty-seven minutes."

A patrol officer passed by, slower than necessary, another set of screw-you eyes. Mike had received the same cold look from every cop he'd met in the station house until they'd placed him with Greenwood. He was used to it. Like the FBI agents at Michelson's house, nobody still on the job liked someone who'd gone dirty anywhere near their shop.

Mike smiled and waved. "It's not contagious."

The officer sped up and walked away like it was.

Ignoring Greenwood's latest page, Mike looked back down at the second sheet. "Long time to sit and talk after the drive across town. Is pot legal in Indiana?"

Greenwood laughed. "Nope. Why do you ask?"

"I spent a lot time working narcotics in Los Angeles, never once met an actor who wasn't holding something. And I don't know how well you got to know Caitlin," he said with a smirk, "but she doesn't mind the occasional puff."

Greenwood turned away, maybe to hide his blush. "Makes sense."

Mike moved on to the third page, a much larger map with four times as many dots—the drive from Bloomington to the Indianapolis airport.

"How long was she at the guesthouse?"

"Hour and fifteen. Started driving to Indy around five twelve, got to the rental return at six thirty-five."

Mike set the maps on Greenwood's desk. "You got any traffic cams or footage from the rental return or airport?"

Greenwood shrugged. "The maps suggest she left town."

Mike noticed an older woman in a beige blazer perched at the edge of the room, arms crossed, standing next to a no-nonsense man in a government suit. "Airlines confirm that?"

Greenwood looked like he hated the words coming out of his mouth. "I've got calls out, but nothing back yet. Same with the cell company."

Mike nodded toward the woman. "You got a female captain?"

Greenwood smiled. "Chief, actually. That's Renton's way of saying we're done here. Other guy's FBI."

Mike knew the look. "Because all signs point to Caitlin leaving Indiana. And even if she's missing, she didn't go missing in Bloomington. Who'd she piss off the most?"

Greenwood turned away from Renton's gaze. "You were on the job, so you know I'm not gonna bad-mouth my department to a complete stranger. I'm in the middle of some major shit and can't do much more for Caitlin, but I'll let you know if I get any replies." He offered Mike the pages again.

Mike grabbed the maps. "When and if you get any."

"Unless you've got some way to speed up the process, something with a bigger dick than the FBI."

Mike thanked him and walked away under the chief's hawk eyes. Five feet out the door, he called the bigger dick.

"Special Agent Martinez, this is Mike Roman."

CHAPTER

65

CAITLIN SNAPPED AWAKE, her brain embracing the sensation of unbound movement. Nothing held her down to the mattress.

Alone again in the bedroom. The overhead light gave a warm daylight wash, but was it really daytime? Was this Saturday?

She smelled something familiar. Caress body wash, the same scent she used at home, and something else—Aussie brand shampoo. Her hair was wet. Branford had bathed her, yet she had absolutely no memory of the process. What else had he done during her mental gap?

Something felt off between her legs, awkward and foreign.

She reached for the sheet, felt immense, hot pain at both of her wrists. Both ankles felt tender as well, ripped skin rather than muscle damage, like she'd strained against straps.

She pulled the sheet. Another pink pajama top, this time with a word across the front: "Princess." Further down, white cotton underwear she didn't recognize.

She took a deep breath, pulled the fabric aside, and saw the end of an oversized sanitary napkin.

"Thank God," she muttered, removing the mega-pad slowly. No damage done other than the monthly murder of cotton. Still, Branford had been between her legs without her knowledge, permission, or even the flash of a memory.

She tossed the pad on the floor.

Which was worse? Paige Lauffer on a soccer field or this hell?

She shook the thought away and took inventory of the rest of her life. Only one chair at the table, the one bolted to the floor facing the bed. From this angle, she saw bolts holding the table legs in place as well. On top, a small plastic caddy played centerpiece.

Beyond the table, she saw the fourth wall and the door for the first time. The door had a vertical window. Two flat metal discs filled the holes that would normally house locks or handles.

A closed, rectangular metal panel, similar to a post office parcel drop, sat to the left, halfway up the wall. Below the drop, a camping toilet, lid closed. A stack of four plastic milk crates split the difference between the wall drop and the door to the outside world. Each functioned as a shelf for plastic bottles of water and soft drinks, boxes of granola bars, tissue, and toilet paper. A stack of additional pajamas had been placed on the shelves to the right, all pink.

She lowered her bare feet to the floor. Her ripped ankle skin made her want to melt, but she forced herself to stand. She got one step before she slipped and fell toward the table. Worse than a banana peel, she'd slipped on her bloody maxi.

She inspected the caddy on the table. Tampons, sanitary napkins, gauze, Neosporin, extra strength Tylenol, wet wipes, more cotton underwear.

She worked her way around to the door, looked through the window's thick glass, saw only a rough white stone wall. The same stone as her bedroom's floor, and the same chalky stone she'd tried to throw in Troy Woods's eyes to get away. Indiana limestone. Made sense: they'd driven down Tapp Road to get to Branford's house. He'd built an underground lair in the remains of a quarry.

Caitlin hobbled over to the toilet. She pushed the pedal to flush, sat on the closed lid, and reached for the caddy. Two pills in the Tylenol bottle, no way to overdose. She grabbed a bottle of water, took the pills, loosely wrapped her wrists and ankles with Neosporin and gauze, then applied a tampon and slid on a fresh pair of underwear.

One last look around the room revealed something under the bed—a metal rectangle in the wall, ringed with thick, hardened yellow foam at the same height where a power outlet would be, or once was.

Caitlin couldn't see any weakness in Branford's prison.

"Genius," she admitted, then collapsed on the bed.

* * *

A noise woke her. The wall-panel drop box clanged open, and familiar smells attacked: grease, cheese, oregano.

She stumbled to the drop box, saw another bottle of Tylenol, the smiling face of the Pizza Monster, and a message on a yellow Post-it note: *Eat what I give you.*

She took the pills and box to the table, sat in the chair she'd been strapped in the day before. With help from a Diet Coke, she got three Tylenol and two slices down.

Behind her, the locks turned and the door opened.

"Put your hands behind you," Branford said, close in seconds.

No way she could fight him yet. "I tried to eat it all, but I'll vomit if I eat another slice."

"Caitlin, your hands."

She lowered her hands behind the chair, flinched when she felt the cold steel of handcuffs latch wrist to wrist.

"Get up."

She rose.

"If you move, I'll hurt you. Do you understand?"

She nodded.

He covered her face with a black cloth bag. It wasn't tight, but offered no visibility other than the light below.

His hand touched the small of her back. "I'm going to take you to the playroom, the place where I was forced to wash you."

A shudder ripped through her body.

"Don't ruin your clothes," he continued. "Don't throw away the food I worked so hard to prepare. Don't hide a plastic fork so you can try to attack me later."

"I won't—"

"Stop talking. You're mine, Caitlin. Say it."

She hesitated. He tugged on the handcuffs. "Say it."

"I'm yours," she muttered, aware of the cuffs digging into the flesh of her wrists through the airy gauze.

"Now you know me, Caitlin. My name is Embower and I'll keep you safe. You're going to walk backward. If you make any sudden movements, I will hurt you."

She looked down, saw her feet, and stepped backward. Five more steps took her through the doorway.

"Take a step down."

She did, felt damp crushed stone under her feet.

"Stop here."

He turned her ninety degrees to the right, then pulled. "Let's go."

She counted the backward steps in her head.

Sixteen.

"Turn to your left, then walk forward until your toes touch a wall. Go slow."

She turned, took two cautious steps, then reached with her foot until she made contact.

"Step up, Caitlin."

She did, felt another smooth stone floor.

"Five steps forward."

She watched her feet land on the floor and stopped. His hands touched hers, then the cuffs came off. Seconds later, she heard a door close behind her, then two deadbolts.

A burst of electronic static filled the room, followed by his amplified voice. "Take off the bag and turn around."

She did. No window in this door, but two large glass cases in the wall filled the room with soft light, one on each side of the door. To the far right, Caitlin saw Branford through an aquarium-thick three-foot-wide window.

He spoke into a wall-mounted microphone. "I'm going to leave now. If you'd like to watch a movie, place the case on the table and I'll start it when I can. Do you understand?"

She nodded.

He smiled, then pulled a curtain over the window.

She rubbed her wrists and stared at the glass, waiting to see if he returned. Not that he needed to; Caitlin noticed a camera in the corner above the window. She turned around and inspected the room.

The off-white wall to her left had a wooden bookshelf full of paperbacks and DVD cases. Two red beanbag chairs slumped together near the end of the shelf closest to the door. At the opposite end, Caitlin found two laundry baskets, one empty, the other the keeper of four neatly folded white towels, and a pre-fab fiberglass shower and porcelain toilet in the far corner. Both looked clean. She saw no plumbing, but a light gray strip of concrete ran diagonally across the smooth limestone floor from the bathroom corner to the wall on the far right. If her math was correct, that right-hand wall, lined by a long stainless-steel industrial table, was the barrier between this room and her own soundproofed chamber.

Between the two walls and opposite of the entrance, the wavy pattern of galvanized sheet-metal roofing panels covered the remaining wall, except for a dark flat-screen TV sealed behind thick glass. Caitlin padded over to the TV area, found a rust-brown love seat on top of a remnant cut of beige Berber carpet. For the television to work, it would need a power source, and with the right odds and ends, electricity could be weaponized. Caitlin inspected the metal panels and thick glass, but rivets held the sheet metal together, preventing access to the TV cabling.

"Caitlin?"

Branford's voice returned through a different speaker. Caitlin stepped back, looked up at the TV and saw his self-important smile through the frame. He sat at a table. Caitlin noticed the corner of a toaster oven stacked on top of brown cabinets a few feet behind him. Definitely the farmhouse kitchen.

"You don't look like you're relaxing. Can I put a movie on for you?"

She said no.

He shook his head, frustrated. "I'm sorry, I've had electrical problems recently. April showers bring May flowers, as they say. I can't actually hear you."

Caitlin shrugged, shook her head side to side.

"By now you've intuited there's no way out of the playroom unless I release you, yes?"

Caitlin nodded, but her mind drifted to the other room, trying to picture the sealed power outlet under the bed frame. The story of Paige Lauffer's escape lived under the fragments of things she'd seen.

"Fine," Branford continued. "I'm going to leave you alone for three hours. Since you haven't chosen a movie for today, any choice you make will be for your next time in the playroom." He gestured toward the bookshelves. "I also have a fine mix of plays and popular fiction, even the recent memoir of a famous journalist."

The screen switched to a second-story video feed looking down at a cornfield. At the far end of the green, Caitlin could make out Branford's duplex, but saw no sign of her rental car.

She sat on the couch and spent all three hours watching the wind barely move the world.

CHAPTER

66

H E CHECKED THE feed. Caitlin was still watching the TV.
Not bad, considering yesterday's lesson. How long will it be this time?
Angela, his Angel, had fought for a month before relenting. He'd tried a kinder approach with Paige, his Barbie, and paid the price. Still, Embower hoped Caitlin would understand soon. He had so much to share with his Writer.

Back to the purse. He'd gone through Caitlin's bag on the first day, found her wallet, minimal makeup, and not one, but two cell phones. The iPhone had been powered on, so he incorporated that into his plan, but didn't dare turn on the cheap black model until he knew why Caitlin had it. He needed to understand every move she'd made. No false steps, not with a piece this valuable. He rifled through a wad of credit card receipts, smoothed each, and typed the date, amount, and vendor information into a spreadsheet on his laptop.

Seven slips in, he found a receipt from Bloomington Cell in the mall that listed an 812 number.

So the iPhone is your personal device and the second is a burner you bought to appear as an anonymous local number. In disguise like me, Caitlin.

The police would hunt for his Writer unless she'd dropped off the grid on purpose. He needed to close their file.

Embower ran upstairs and checked his costume closet. Dropping the rental car off had been easy enough. He'd thrown on one of his brown pageboy wigs, a black sport coat, and Caitlin's sunglasses. But to really make the woman disappear, she needed to be seen in public, safe and alone. He dug through his bins for five minutes, then returned to the kitchen, convinced he had the necessary ingredients.

He consulted Caitlin's rape report. Even at twenty-one, her intelligence outshone all parties involved, but his favorite part was the recent note she'd added at the top of Troy Woods's statement.

Miami Correctional Facility. Kokomo, IN.

He opened a web browser and typed in his search: *Miami Correctional Facility visiting hours.*

67

"Y OU HAPPY NOW, Roman, or do you want to call the president?"
It'd taken a day, and no one was happy about being there on a Saturday night, but Mike was back in the BPD's station house with Greenwood and Foreman, thanks to a few phone calls from Special Agent Martinez. Chief Renton scowled in the back of the observation room.

"Unless you're a total dumbass," Foreman said, pointing at a monitor, "you can see Bergman right there, driving into the rental return lot."

Jerry Greenwood managed a smile somewhere close to pity and leaned over Mike's shoulder to move the footage back. "Does look like Caitlin, doesn't it?"

He played the clip for the fifth time. Three seconds at the gate showed the front license plate and the hood. Two seconds showed chin-length brown hair, sunglasses, and a black sport coat.

Mike tapped on the tabletop. "Find anything at the counter?"

Foreman answered. "Bergman didn't go to the counter, only had to leave the keys in the drop. The automated system did the rest."

Mike kept his eyes on Greenwood. "But nothing in the airport?"

Greenwood shook his head no. "Could have changed her mind. Does she know anyone in Indianapolis who might have picked her up?"

"Hell if I know. What about her phone?"

Again, Foreman interjected. "Last usage ended at the car lot. Nothing on her financials after that or since. Does Miss Bergman carry a lot of cash?"

Mike thought about the time she'd handed him five hundred bucks to buy fake IDs and Social Security numbers in MacArthur Park. "For certain stories. Still, she's definitely a missing person."

Renton spoke from her dark corner. "Since she's obviously left Blooming-ton, the FBI will handle Bergman's disappearance from here on out."

Foreman stepped forward and turned off the monitor. "We've mobilized the Indianapolis office and are coordinating with IPD, in case you need to relay that information back to anyone."

"Great." Mike put on his team player face. "What's our next move?"

Foreman planted his feet and crossed his arms. "*Your* next move is to leave this to the professionals."

Mike stood up and gave the agent the old thousand-yard stare from inches away. Greenwood's hands came up, open palms, cautious.

Mike smiled at the room full of ego. "And that's who you guys are? The professionals?"

Foreman nodded. "Damned right. You can tell because we all still have our badges."

Mike chuckled. "Let me share something I've learned from personal experience. Failure follows you whether you've got a shield or a shovel. The important thing is to deal with your shit before it blows up in your face. Tell Kieran Michelson I say hi, you hard-working professionals."

He brushed past Foreman and left the station. He got two blocks on foot before an unmarked sedan pulled up beside him. The female driver rolled down the passenger window and leaned over. "Get in."

Mike caught her cigarette smoke from the sidewalk. "Why do I have the feeling I'm gonna get a ticket for a broken taillight?"

The driver threw the car in park, got out. Mike watched the squat woman with the ponytail toss her cigarette only to reach for a fresh one.

"Greenwood can't get away," she said, "but he's sorry for how they're treating you. Long story short, no one in that room's gonna look real hard for Bergman. She tore up this town like a tornado."

"Sounds like her." Mike caught a strong whiff of the detective's latest exhale. "Got another one of those?"

She handed him her lit cigarette. "Reporters, am I right?"

He took a drag. "Especially her, with all that quest for the truth BS."

"Know who likes reporters? Other reporters, especially stories about missing reporters. You know any?"

She took the cigarette out of his hand, popped it back in her mouth, and walked back to her car.

Mike leaned into the open passenger window. "I didn't get your name."

"You sure as shit didn't," she said, and drove away.

68

From the puppy-dog look on his face, Caitlin knew Branford wanted a compliment.

"Good enough," she said, reaching for her water bottle.

He ate a forkful from his own plate, made a yummy noise. "So tender, how could it be better?"

He'd come into the playroom, cuffed her, bagged her, and led her back to the bedroom where dinner for two waited. Straps bound only her thighs and abdomen this time, leaving both arms free.

She controlled a plastic fork, her plastic plate of food, and a water bottle. Enough to throw a good fit, but not a defense.

She shrugged. "I like to eat outside."

"Maybe we'll get to that point."

The mere possibility sent her mind jumping through the fields of hope. Another manipulation. She pushed a stalk of broccoli around her plate.

"I've got twenty years on Chapman, same with Lauffer, maybe even twenty pounds. Why am I the lucky girl? People like you are supposed to have a pattern."

He shifted forward, excited. "Do you know Shakespeare?"

"The guy who works at the smoke shop in the mall?"

He quoted, "'There is a tide in the affairs of men, Which, taken at the flood, leads on to fortune; Omitted, all the voyage of their life is bound in shallows and in miseries.'"

Caitlin stabbed another piece of chicken. *"Et tu, Bruté?"*

"You know *Julius Caesar?*"

She popped the meat in her mouth. "Brutus loses in the next act."

He shook his head. "I simply meant, the moment was perfect and I grabbed you."

"Like with Angela?"

He gave a concerned grandma smile. "You're not eating your broccoli."

"If I'm going to die soon, I might as well go full of this chicken."

The smile disappeared. "Eat a piece of the broccoli."

Caitlin took a chance. "If you tell me how you got Angela."

His fingers curled into fists. "I'll tell you how I collected Angela *and* Paige if you eat all of your broccoli. How's that for a bargain?"

She reached for a stalk, started chewing. "Angela first."

Grandma's pleasant smile returned. "Okay. Chad had known her for some time. I'd already found my house and had a list."

"A list?"

"Of possible pieces to collect and protect. My Angel and I kept running into each other. Like me, she was reinventing herself. I kept myself involved tangentially."

"The coupons," Caitlin said.

"That's right, though I really did need the business to take off in order to build all of this."

"Such methodical madness. So Lakshmi asked you for Molly?"

"Amazing, right? I know you don't see it yet, but this is all about the timing, the congruence, the perfect moment—"

"The tide and affairs, sure. You were saying how Lakshmi asked you for the Molly?"

"Correct. At this point I knew all about Angela and Lakshmi's sexual relationship, the boys Angela had been with too, especially Kieran Michelson."

"How?"

"Because I'd watched for months," he answered, matter-of-fact. "The girls always ordered pizza on their nights together, so I drove by Lakshmi's apartment that Friday and waited for the call."

"But you had no way of knowing when they'd be done or if Angela would leave. How would you have gotten her alone?"

"You see? That's what I mean by *the moment*." He drank his last sip of water and crinkled the bottle.

Caitlin pushed. "But the moment didn't happen. So then what?"

He tossed the bottle over her head into the drop box. "The frat boys showed up, and I followed them to the bar. Drunks make it easy. I assumed Angela would end up at either her place or Kieran's. When they started their walk, I dropped by the Monster."

"Already creating an alibi."

"Mostly investment management. I pop in and out whenever, make sure no one's slacking. I even delivered two pizzas in the Villas. We always do a fair amount of business there, especially on the weekend."

His switch between the minutia of running a business and the hunting of a college girl had no change in tone, all logical steps down the psycho path.

"I'd almost given up, but then I saw my Angel stumble out of Kieran's apartment all by herself."

He laughed. "All I had to do was flash my lights and wave. She walked over, asked if I'd take her home, and passed out. I put her in the back seat and threw a blanket over her."

Caitlin shuddered. "That easy."

"The perfect moment, Caitlin. A moment like no other. My moment."

"And Paige?"

He pushed Caitlin's plate closer. "One more vegetable, please."

Another forkful kept him going.

"As you can imagine, I didn't dare look for another piece for some time. There's nothing like having a prize everyone wants, being so close to the edge."

"Of getting caught?"

He ignored the question. "I met Paige three months ago."

"Another one of your students?"

"Passing ships," he said. "Chad Branford's bike rides intersected Paige Lauffer's running routes."

Caitlin's stomach turned. The road to a woman's death started with a disciplined workout regimen. "And you what? Asked her out?"

"Not I, Caitlin, Chad Branford. And he didn't ask her out; he noticed her T-shirt from a five-K charity run to help a local nursing home and asked how to make a donation. She directed him to her Facebook profile."

Caitlin wanted to tear into the seam between Chad Branford and whoever he claimed to be, but she'd unleashed the story he had no one else to tell and couldn't interrupt the flow.

"I learned more from her online auctions than her social media accounts. Such detail, such attention paid. I saw a kindred spirit, and one so different than Angela—soft-spoken, introverted, isolated. I knew I could take her. Then you came to town."

Caitlin flinched, reached for the last piece of broccoli.

"I knew your story, Caitlin. I tend to notice news articles about men who manipulate women."

She started to say something, stopped.

He noticed. "Yes, I am self-aware, have been since my teens. *Different, distant, disturbed.* They called me all the good *D* words. I fought them at first but then broke the words down. Different? Yes, gladly so. Distant? I have no respect for people who don't see society for what it is, a construct we use to enforce an arbitrary moral code. Disturbed? Well, who isn't? Where was I?"

"I came to town."

"You sure did. I had to attend the ceremony. Right away, I was smitten. You were so strong, but also damaged and lonely, even in a room full of people there to celebrate your greatness. I left a note so you wouldn't feel alone."

The notes. Caitlin had forgotten completely. Once she'd realized neither Mary nor Greenwood had left the two handwritten notes, she'd assumed it'd been Scott Canton, but never got a chance to broach the subject. Mary knew they existed. Maybe that would help someone find her, assuming anyone wanted to.

"Dangerous, sure, but I had to help you. I even had my copy of your book signed the next day, but I didn't let you distract me. I still wanted Paige and I got her. But a week later, you showed up with Lakshmi, looking for my Angel. I'd been careful, and so much time had gone by, but there you were, picking up long-forgotten threads. I kept tabs on your progress, in case you got close. I saw you take chances, walking campus by yourself, drinking to excess, smoking your brilliant mind to mush, fucking the detective in the park—each action an unanswered cry for help that no one but me seemed to hear. Then, Paige complicated things by forcing my hand, ruining everything I'd built."

He spread his hands. "Well, the sky may have poured rain, but I found a moment of sunshine. You'd exposed the Bro-duce boys and Paige was dead. Since the police would never find my Angel in the Bro-duce farmland, I muddied the waters with my Barbie. That chain of events led us here. Tell me I haven't taken the tide at the flood."

Caitlin forced herself to meet his eyes. "So why me? Why keep me *safe*?"

"Oh Caitlin. Only you can understand what I've become." He picked up the dishes and walked them to the metal drop box behind her. "And let's face it, between your panic attacks, drug use, and reckless sex life, how much longer can you survive on your own?"

She knew not to interrupt him, but after all his genius-intelligence bravado, Branford was just a clueless dickhead who couldn't handle an independent woman.

He came up behind her and leaned his head against her shoulder. "No matter how this ends, I'm glad it was you."

His grip loosened. The air moved, the door closed, the locks turned.

Caitlin pushed against her straps. "So what? I'm just gonna sit in this chair?"

A loud metal clang behind her answered. He'd taken the dishes from the wall drop box. The soft whir of the overhead fan followed.

In seconds, Caitlin found herself Thanksgiving-meal tired. By one minute, she couldn't fight the weight of her eyelids.

CHAPTER

69

"WHY DID YOU drug me again? I feel like I'm missing ten points off my IQ."

"Walk, Caitlin."

Ten steps so far, bagged and cuffed, dressed in pink pajamas once again. She felt him tug, continued walking backward.

"And it's gotta be morning, right? As in twelve or so hours after our last talk?"

No answer. At fourteen steps, she heard the jingle of keys.

"Seriously." Her *s* words slurred like a drunk's. "I get that you're a genius—"

"Stop."

She took step seventeen, passed him.

"—but a legitimate doctor gave Michael Jackson propofol, and we all know how that turned out."

"Caitlin."

She ignored the alarm in his voice, counted steps nineteen, twenty. "What, where?"

"Now," he yelled. She heard him shift in the stone, felt his hand grab her pajamas. She took a chance, fell backward.

Her shoulders hit the loose stone first, her head a second after. She did quick math from her twentieth step, added her height. Thirty steps from her cell door and she still hadn't hit a wall.

He dropped onto her chest, knees first, took her breath.

"Don't fucking move."

She gasped through her bag. "What happened?"

"When I say *stop*, you stop."

She panted. "I can't breathe."

"You can die in this place, Caitlin. Today, right now."

His weight shifted, doubled the pressure. She spread her feet as wide as she could, touched walls on both sides, maybe four feet across.

"Can't breathe," she repeated.

The bag came off her head. She blinked twice, but still doubted what she saw towering over her. His body blocked the overhead light, but she could tell he'd changed his hair. Still short, but feminine, familiar.

"If you try something like that again," he said, "I will kill you."

"The drugs made me dizzy."

Jesus, he's wearing a wig.

"I'll bury you right here. No one will know the story of Caitlin Bergman."

The realization set in.

A wig that looks like my hair.

"I'm so high." She panted harder. "I just fell. Please, help me up."

He held her face, squeezing her cheeks against her teeth. "When I say *stop*, you stop. Understand?"

She let out a garbled *yes*, and he let go. She rocked onto her side, dropped her head back, and gasped. The bag returned, and he pulled her to her feet.

"Accidents happen," he said, his voice back to an untrustable calm.

He marched her to the playroom, shoved her inside, undid the cuffs, locked the door, and left her alone.

She raised her hands to remove the bag, winced at the pain in her arm. One more bruise would be a small price to pay for what she'd learned from her brief glimpse down the hall. Ten feet further, the hallway ended at an exposed rock wall, but five feet away, on the right, there was another door.

"Caitlin?" The crackle of the speaker turned her around. He didn't appear in the window this time. "I'm leaving. There's food, water, and drinks on the table, and towels near the shower. If you behave, I'll have a special treat for you tonight." Another quick burst of static ended his announcement.

Caitlin looked around. Scrambled eggs, bacon, and a plastic cup of orange juice waited on the right-hand table next to a stack of granola bars and bottled soda. She ate the world's worst continental breakfast, then cried her way through a shower. She needed to recover soon.

She might die in Branford's underground lair, but she'd die fighting.

She wrapped herself in a towel, limped to the bookshelf, and started looking for a weapon. Could you cut someone with the edge of a DVD? She found a copy of *Tommy Boy*, opened the case.

Empty.

She reached for *Fargo*.

Also empty.

He kept the discs somewhere else, left the cases for ease of selection. She moved on to the books.

She needed something heavy. She thumbed through a stack of plays and magazines, found nothing. The paperback romance novels and cheap mysteries came next. Caitlin loved both but couldn't dig out of hell with a summer beach read.

"Hello, stupid," she said, touching the spine of Branford's copy of *Fallen Angels*, now placed alongside the rest. She sighed, then moved on for something much bigger—*The Riverside Shakespeare.*

Caitlin's freshman-year roommate had owned a copy of the massive hard-covered book that contained every work attributed to William Shakespeare. They'd used the heavy tome for arm workouts.

She lugged the book over to a beanbag chair, opened the cover. *No good.* Someone had removed almost half the pages. A chill tickled her body.

Caitlin saw words in yellow marker, nearly invisible against the tan binding of the inner cover.

My name is Angela Chapman. I think it's April but can't be sure. If you find this, Embower killed me. Tell my parents I love them and that I'm sorry.

Caitlin flipped through the flimsy outcropping of preface pages before the substantial missing chunk but didn't find any more handwriting. Instead of page 1, the remainder opened to page 707, a list of footnotes and attributions for *Henry VI, Part 3*. The next page opened to *Richard III*. Branford must have found her messages, destroyed the altered pages, and left the cover as a warning. Whatever she'd meant to leave behind he'd taken, gone forever.

Where did Chapman get the marker?

Caitlin searched the shelf but found no sign of a writing utensil. No doubt Chapman did what Caitlin would have if given a pen, and went straight for Branford's eyes.

"Good for you, Angela."

Chapman's words repeated the name Branford had given himself: *If you find this, Embower has killed me.*

Caitlin dropped into a squat at the bookshelf; she'd seen a pocket-sized Webster. She found the dictionary, flipped to the *E*'s, saw nothing for *embower*. The pocket-sized edition wouldn't list every permutation or rare origin. *Embower* hinted at an older world, but *bower* rang familiar. She flipped to the *B*'s.

Mr. Webster delivered.

Bower—from Old English būr, from Proto-Germanic *būraz. Cognate with German bauer "birdcage," Old Norse bar (Danish bur, Swedish bur "cage").
Noun **bower** (plural **bowers**)
1. A bedroom or private apartments, especially for a woman in a medieval castle.
2. (Ornithology) A large structure made of glass and bright objects, used by the bower bird during courtship displays.

Verb bower (third person singular simple present bowers, present participle bowering, simple past and past participle bowered, obsolete embower)
1. To enclose.

Caitlin closed the dictionary. "Son of a bitch."

Branford's chosen identity was a man who enclosed women in cages. How long did kept animals survive? How long had Angela? They found Paige Lauffer twelve days after her disappearance.

Embower had held Caitlin for five days. She didn't want to know what he'd try once her monthly visitor left town.

She slid Shakespeare back in place, started at the far left of the bookshelf.

What else did Chapman try?

Caitlin spent the next three hours going book by book, page by page.

CHAPTER

70

RATHER THAN FACE a restless night in Bloomington's cheapest hotel room, Mike followed the nameless female detective's advice and filled Mary and Lakshmi in on his interactions with the BPD. The trio convened in Lakshmi's apartment and spent Saturday night into Sunday morning behind computer keyboards. By nine AM, the *Daily Student*'s online edition had published one article under the headline "Famous Reporter Goes Missing in Bloomington" and another titled "Did BPD Drop the Ball?" By noon, both stories had been picked up by the Associated Press, and the student paper was fielding calls from national broadcast outlets.

At four o'clock that afternoon, Mike woke on the couch, with Lakshmi standing over him. "Caitlin called when I was asleep."

He sat up, saw Mary stretching through a yawn nearby, and took the phone from Lakshmi's hand. "Slow down. What am I looking at?"

"The call history," Lakshmi said. "I had my ringer off, and the phone was on the charger. I didn't look until now."

Mike scrolled through the list. The last incoming call came from a local number at 12:37 PM. He handed the phone back. "Three hours and twenty-three minutes ago. How do you know it was Caitlin?"

Lakshmi told them how Caitlin had given her the number before they'd called the Bro-duce farm for the first time. "I'm not sure if she used it for anything else. She told me she'd only use it when her main phone's battery was dead."

"No voicemail?"

The girl shook her head. "I tried calling the number back, but she didn't pick up, and there's no mailbox."

Mike took his own phone out, tried the number, but got no answer.

"I never turn my ringer off," Lakshmi said, lowering her head.

Mary put her arm around the girl. "Everybody has to sleep."

"But why would she call and not talk right after both stories went out on the wire services?" Lakshmi said. "Is this Caitlin's way of telling us to lay off the Bro-duce coverage, let her work undercover?"

Mary laughed. "Too late for that. You went national, girl."

Lakshmi's hand went to her mouth. "Ohmigod. Will they have to print retractions? Is this her getting back at me?"

Mary cornered the pacing girl. "For what, trying to help?"

"She was so angry when she left—at both of us. Would she do this just to ruin my future? Or make the BPD look stupid? Or the FBI?"

The professor laughed, but Mike saw something in her eyes, something unsure. Both women turned his way.

He grabbed the keys to his rental. "Bergman's got her own kind of code, but she wouldn't mess with a story. First things first: we find out where she called from. Let's go see Greenwood."

They moved toward the door but didn't get far. A black FBI SUV blocked Roman's rental in the parking lot.

*　*　*

"I don't know how else I can tell you go to hell, Roman." Back in the BPD conference room an hour later, Agent Foreman gestured at the image frozen onscreen. "That is Caitlin Bergman walking through a metal detector at Miami Correctional Facility, five short hours ago."

He slammed his hand down on the table. Mary and Lakshmi jumped. Mike shifted uncomfortably. Chief Renton, behind them with arms crossed, laughed.

"Here's a copy of the visitor log complete with time stamp, a copy of her driver's license, and her signature." Foreman grabbed a stapled stack of pages. "Here are the GPS pings from her burner phone, showing her location directly outside the prison complex at the same time she called Lakshmi Anjale's phone. And yes, in case you were wondering, we knew about her second phone since it was one of the many numbers we discovered and traced back from the Bro-duce farm's records. I don't know what you've read in the *local press*, but we're taking both the Bro-duce bust and Caitlin's disappearance seriously."

He tossed the pages, grabbed another sheet, held up a printed image. "Last but not least, here she is in the visitation room, speaking to a prisoner.

Caitlin Bergman is not missing—she just doesn't want to be found. If you continue to waste the time of the BPD, the FBI, or myself, I will destroy all three of you. Do you understand me?"

Mary and Lakshmi promised to print retractions in the *Daily Student*, spin the story as a misunderstanding.

Chief Renton approached with a smile. "Mr. Roman, you're awfully quiet."

Mike kept mum. He could understand Caitlin cold-shouldering Lubbers and Anjale, but he hadn't done anything wrong—not this time at least.

Eating that much crow turned his stomach. "Sorry to waste everyone's time."

71

"CAITLIN." EMBOWER APPEARED on the TV once again, his face freshly scrubbed and pink. "Put the bag on."

Caitlin left the couch, found the bag, and pulled it over her head. She'd spent three unsupervised hours going through books, then God knows how long napping. She hadn't even considered poking eyeholes through the thick muslin. *Dumbass.*

"Stay where you are." She heard him push his chair back.

After a ten count, she reached for the bag. No televised voice told her to stop. His kitchen was up at least one floor, but it wouldn't take long for him to reach her.

She worked the fabric. Her nails didn't catch. She pulled the bag back over her head, caught the cloth in her teeth, and started grinding. A pinhole of light appeared through the wet spot.

"Caitlin." His voice returned through the wall speaker. "Clasp your fingers behind you."

The locks turned, the door opened, the cuffs went on.

"Come."

He tugged her backward. She aligned an eye with the hole, saw the bright image of the kitchen on the TV screen.

"Step down," he said.

They moved into the hall. Past the open door to her bedroom, the hallway veered left. Pale blue light came from the right.

"Walk."

He marched her back to the bedroom, sat her down, strapped her in, unlocked the handcuffs, removed the bag, then set up his folding chair and sat across from her. A pizza box waited on top of the table.

"Which do you want first? Dinner or story?"

"What's so great about this story?"

He wrote the headline with his hands, excited. "'Missing Reporter Alive and Well.'"

Caitlin felt her chest tighten. "Better eat first."

He opened the box and slid two pieces onto Caitlin's plate. "Fine. I have other news. I'm making improvements to your room."

"Like a tunnel out?"

"In a way. You're getting a drain. That may not seem important now, but this rainy season has been unpredictable. There used to be carpet in here."

"Hence the smell." Caitlin forced a mouthful of pizza down.

Embower looked pleased. "That brings me to the other improvement. I'm going to reduce the usage of drugs."

"How?"

"You'll see tomorrow. Be prepared to spend most of the day in the playroom."

Caitlin shrugged. "Bigger in there anyway."

He stood, put the pizza aside, then reached under the covers of Caitlin's bed. His hand came up with her laptop. He placed the computer in front of her, powered up and waiting for a password.

Caitlin's fingertips met the keys like a lover. "Why are you giving me my laptop?"

"In case you wish to take notes."

She remembered the camera in the corner, covered each hand with the other as she typed her password. No Wi-Fi networks available. No Bluetooth either.

"Ready for story time, Caitlin?"

She met his eyes. "Knock yourself out."

He paced as he dictated. "'At twelve thirty-seven, Caitlin Bergman called Lakshmi Anjale from an unlisted cell phone outside the Miami Correctional Facility in Kokomo, Indiana.'"

Caitlin typed along, but her words had nothing to do with his showboating.

If you're reading this, you've found the place of my death. The man who calls himself Embower, known locally as Chad Branford, is responsible for the deaths of Angela Chapman, Paige Lauffer, and myself.

She copied the date and time from the desktop calendar.

Sunday night, 8:53 PM, the fifth day of her captivity, her twenty-fourth day in Bloomington.

Something he said stopped her typing. "Wait, what?"

Embower nodded his head. "That's right. Woods said he was ashamed for what he'd done to you."

She tried to process the fragment of his story her subconscious had retained. "What the hell are you talking about?"

"He was sorry. Those were his words."

"Wait." Caitlin shut the laptop. When she'd seen him in the hall that morning, she'd assumed the wig was part of his kink. "You dressed like me?"

He raised his eyebrows. "Impressed?"

Impressed wasn't the word. "You dressed like me, visited a men's prison in drag, and met with Troy Woods?"

He tilted his head to one side. "I like to think I became you—"

Caitlin threw her hands up. "Bullshit."

Embower smiled, reached into his pocket, swiped at a phone, then showed Caitlin a photo of herself, taken from the back of *Fallen Angels*.

"Before," he said, then swiped again. "And after."

The second photo resembled her back cover shot in both framing and wardrobe. Taken as a selfie, the woman in the photo wore a black sport coat and a white collared shirt. Her hair, brown, straight, and chin-length, looked beauty-parlor good, and better than Caitlin's real hair any day of the week. More makeup than she'd ever owned coated the face, completely balanced and Photoshop-quality flawless. Even the lips were done. The second face didn't look like Caitlin necessarily, but the whole package resembled a real-life woman. At least, a woman dressed for a male-dominated industry where sexuality was a weakness.

"Jesus, what the hell's wrong with you?"

"All it takes is practice and an airbrush." He put the phone away, smug. "I can't say I came close to your natural beauty, but I did convince a room full of strangers. And Woods, of course."

Blood rushed to her cheeks. Caitlin shook her head, violated. She'd known some of the best drag queens in West Hollywood, so it wasn't the proficiency of the disguise that pissed her off, or the assholes who fell for it. Embower had done much worse. He'd taken her identity and presented himself to the man who'd scarred her for life. "You saw him? Talked to Troy Woods?"

He nodded. "Sat in the chair with the phone and the glass and everything. At first I was surprised he couldn't tell, but it makes sense, doesn't it? He didn't see you as a woman then. Why should he now?"

Caitlin fought back a scream. A scream could get her hit or worse. She grabbed the thumb of her left hand with the fingers of her right and squeezed. "And you do, Embower? You see me as a woman?"

"Such a woman, Caitlin. A strong, intelligent woman who doesn't take shit from anyone."

She shook out her hands and met his eyes. "I thought I needed to be saved."

His smile dropped instantly. "From yourself, yes. The things you do and say."

She bit the inside of her cheek, anything to slow down the eruption. This wouldn't be a panic attack. This was pure rage. "And what did you say to Woods as me?"

Embower set his feet shoulder-width apart, looked down to the floor, then raised his head with both altered posture and voice.

"'I don't accept your apology, Troy, nor do I need it.'"

"I don't sound like that."

He continued, "'You may have taken my body, robbed me of my halcyon days at IU—'"

Caitlin hated the word *halcyon*. *Hated*.

"'—but you didn't take anything I couldn't replace. While your life spiraled out of control, I built a career.'" One hand went to his hip, the other punctuated his words. "'While doors locked you away, I broke through walls, soared through the sky.'" His voice thundered. "'I do not need your apology, just as the world does not need you. Your crime, inconsequential; your mark on the world, invisible. I am Caitlin Bergman. Who the fuck are you?'"

Embower hung up an invisible phone, dropped his hands to his sides, and raised his eyebrows.

Caitlin looked down at her hands, both white-knuckled from squeezing the tabletop.

"I didn't expect applause," he said, leaning down over the table, "but not even a smile?"

If he came a foot closer, even bound to the chair, she could strangle him or gouge out his eyes or pull the tongue out of his sick fucking mouth. "Are you that delusional, Branford?"

His expression darkened. "That's not my name."

She leaned forward, straining against her straps. "Do you really think I'm over what Woods did to me?"

"You're a strong woman, Caitlin," he said, as if that would put out the fire in her chest.

"Do you know what it meant to leave everything I cared about, to be ashamed of who I was"—the straps moaned under her movement, and her voice left the volume of polite conversation—"to be afraid to tell my father why I left college weeks before graduation?"

"Caitlin, you're upset, but you shouldn't raise your voice at me."

She couldn't hold back anymore, wouldn't even try. "I couldn't have sex for years after that. I couldn't even masturbate without crying. I tried to kill myself twice, chickened out at the last second. And now, twenty years later, every time I have sex, I flash back to that afternoon with that asshole on top of me. I have to fight through that memory every time a man touches me. Every damned time."

Embower pulled Caitlin's laptop out of her reach and raised his hand. "Stop talking."

"But I'm a strong woman," she yelled. "Strong women yell, and they swear and they fuck and drink and get high, and yes, they cry and sweat and grow hair everywhere, and that's totally up to them. But every day, some asshole tries to change that because that's not his idea of what a strong woman is." She leaned her face as far forward as she could. "Hit me—I don't care. You want me to live in your bullshit dollhouse? Fine, but I'm not going to follow your script."

He slapped her hard.

Her head flew back. A mixture of blood and snot flooded her sinuses. She blew a pink bubble out a nostril and laughed. "Is that all you've got?"

He pulled back again but stopped mid-swing, composing himself. "You're upset. You don't mean what you're saying." He nodded, apparently in agreement with himself. "You'll be happier when you see the changes."

He picked up the laptop and walked out. Caitlin heard the fan above come to life.

So much for cutting down on the drugs.

CHAPTER

72

CAITLIN'S FACE FELT raw, maybe from last night's slap, maybe from the pattern of the playroom couch she woke on. The TV showed the outside world, overcast but sunny.

He'd left breakfast on the steel table once again. Still in last night's pajamas, she shuffled over, found a note in a paper bowl next to a single-serving box of cereal.

I don't want to lose you the way I lost Paige, so I'll give you a day to consider your situation. I think you'll enjoy the changes.

She crumpled the note and opened the cereal. A sound stopped her, the first she'd ever heard in the room that hadn't come from the TV or the wall speaker. It sounded like a muffled jackhammer.

Something else was new. He'd cut a rectangle into the door, like a mail slot, but for putting on handcuffs.

She inspected the foot-wide, six-inch-high panel. A metal slab filled the gap from the hallway side. She poked the steel, sensed a little give. Her finger caught the cooler air of the hallway.

The sound returned. Definitely a jackhammer. A drain, he'd said. Not just an evil genius, but handy too.

She took breakfast back to the couch, went to the bookcase, grabbed the *Riverside Shakespeare*. She could always count on Bill Shakespeare for a tale of revenge, and a pound of Embower's flesh sounded like the perfect inspiration. The table of contents remained intact on a wispy page preceding the missing block, but all of the comedies and the first three histories had fallen victim to the great removal. She double-checked the first page after the gap.

709.

She stared at the number with the eye that didn't hurt. "Hold on."

She looked back at the table of contents. *Richard III* started at 708. Yesterday, the first page she'd seen had footnotes for *Henry VI, Part 3*. Now, she looked at 709, the second page of *Richard III*.

Someone had ripped out page 707–708.

Someone had ripped it out last night.

But why would Embower do it? The page hadn't showed any notes from Chapman.

Caitlin shut the book and looked around the room with fresh eyes. Two beanbag chairs sat near the door. Maybe in some twisted reality she and Embower were supposed to sit and read to each other. But why were there two laundry baskets?

She got up and checked the pair of plastic baskets near the shower. One wet towel on the left, three clean and dry on the right. She'd used one yesterday, so it could be her own, but even in this subterranean hell, it would have dried by now. She grabbed the terry cloth, felt enough water to wring out.

Two chairs, two laundry baskets, 708.

365 × 2 = 730 days

She couldn't remember the exact date Chapman had disappeared, but the rough math worked.

She factored in a week or two of disorientation, guesstimated the difference between her arrival and Chapman's last night, got slightly less than two years.

Embower hadn't discovered and torn Chapman's notes from the *Riverside.* Angela had found the biggest book she could and tore out one page a day to keep track of time.

"The police would never find my Angel in the Bro-duce farmland," he'd said.

Caitlin had thought that meant he'd buried Chapman somewhere else.

He had—in a cell behind the playroom bookshelf—and she was still alive.

After two years, Angela Chapman is still freaking alive.

Caitlin's heart wanted to explode, her mouth wanted to scream, but her brain wouldn't allow either.

Stop . . . breathe . . . think.

Caitlin needed to get her a message.

There were no writing utensils in the playroom, but the two shelves held hundreds of thousands of words, and Caitlin knew the text in one of those books better than anyone on the planet.

She took *Fallen Angels* and the dictionary to the torture table and worked with her back to the camera.

She opened a breakfast bar. Just as she'd hoped, bits of chocolate and granola stuck to the inside of the wrapper. She wet her fingertip, put it against the bar's sugary cement, touched the first ripped piece of paper, then pushed down against page 709 of the *Riverside Shakespeare*.

Seven bars later, she felt confident Chapman would get the message.

Angela
My name Caitlin Bergman
I am prisoner too
I know your parent
I know your friend
Will get us out soon
Be ready
Leave message here

Her back still to the camera, she set the books aside, picked up the black walking bag, and bit a second eyehole.

Once she could see with both eyes, she returned the books to the shelves, then went back to the couch and studied the TV's cornfield.

Caitlin hadn't run in a week. Even bruised and beaten, her body ached for a workout.

*   *   *

Sometime near sunset, the wall speaker crackled. "Caitlin, it's time."

Embower appeared in the front window. His black T-shirt had dark circles around the neck and pits, patches of powder everywhere.

"Get the bag and walk to the door."

She picked up the bag, faced the eyeholes the right way.

"No," he said. "Don't put it on yet."

He left the window. The steel panel in the door slid open. Caitlin saw his body through the opening.

"Put your hands through the hole," he said, no need for the mic now.

"What about the bag?"

"Fine, put it on," he said, impatient.

Caitlin did so, then fumbled toward the door like she couldn't see. "Found it."

Her hands went through the hole and the cuffs went on. She pulled back. The panel closed and the door opened.

He tugged her out. "Walk."

With the clarity of two eyeholes, Caitlin saw a large opening with a tray full of plates to the right past the door to her room.

"Stop," he said. "Turn left, walk forward."

She went into her bedroom, heard the door shut and lock behind her.

"You can take the bag off."

Caitlin did, saw him watching through the window. He motioned her toward the door. She put her hands through and he unlocked her cuffs.

"What do you think of the changes?"

She looked around the room, impressed. "This makes the process so much better. Thank you, Embower."

His lips curled into a smile. "Anything for you."

He slid the metal panel closed, latched something, then walked away toward the playroom.

He'd left dinner on the table, teriyaki salmon with rice and cooked carrots. Caitlin grabbed a bottle of water and dug in.

Her feet felt a rough patch in the otherwise smooth floor. She looked under the table. Like the playroom, the bedroom's limestone floor now had a strip of gray concrete that led toward the outside wall. Unlike the playroom, Caitlin's line ended in a circular metal drain under the table. Two Phillips-head screws kept the four-inch steel disc and its waffle-pattern holes in place.

She remembered the camera and decided to wait to investigate the drain. From the vantage point of the camper toilet post-dinner, she stared at the brand new drain and worked out a plan.

There were only two ways out of the room—handcuffed with a bag over her head or drugged and unconscious. She needed to be both conscious and have her hands free—and Embower hated a mess.

Caitlin had a new drain and enough tampons and maxis to destroy an entire dorm's plumbing.

CHAPTER

73

MIKE STARED AT the big man in the orange jumpsuit on the other side of the glass. Troy Woods had forty pounds on him, two inches of height, and shoulder muscles swollen from hours on weight benches.

The inmate reached for the phone, showing the faded ink swirled around his right wrist. The institutional blue complemented the recent red wound over his cauliflower ear.

Mike spoke into the handset. "You in the Aryan Brotherhood, Woods?"

"Who the fuck are you?"

"Who do you guys even beef with? I figured everyone in Indiana was white."

Woods snorted. "Then you don't know shit. We got Mexicans like everywhere else, except in here they don't even mow the grass. You a cop?"

"I understand you had a visitor yesterday. Caitlin Bergman?"

Woods smiled. "Yeah, you're a cop. Fuck you, cop."

Mike watched Woods puff up, typical jailhouse bravado. "Fuck me, but you're not getting up? You that bored?"

Woods rolled his shoulders back. "Seven out of fifteen, I got spare time. Guess whose fault that is?"

"The Mexicans'?"

"Caitlin Fucking Bergman's."

"Thought you had some sort of car accident," Mike said. "Something about a family of four and a fourth DUI."

"Links in a chain, Cop."

Mike stared him down. He'd met a hundred guys like Woods in prison, tough guys who believed they wouldn't have been there if someone else hadn't failed, never owning up to their own stupid mistakes. Having been one himself, he knew the best way to get them to talk was to treat them like the victims of circumstance they claimed to be. "You're right. I used to be a cop, but then I ended up on your side of the glass, thanks to Bergman."

"Bullshit."

"Four years in Corcoran, all because that bitch reporter had to prove she was smarter than me. Sound familiar?"

He watched Woods process the mix of truths and lies. Woods's hard-case act dropped a level. "Corcoran? That's where Manson was, right?"

Mike nodded. "Protective Housing Unit. Never saw him. What'd you and Bergman talk about yesterday?"

"Why do you care?"

Time for the big sell. "What kind of job do you think an ex-cop can get with a felony in his jacket? Nothing on the books, I can tell you that. So when I got out, I dove in dumpsters, sold scrap metal—all that shit not fit for a white man. Then I met a guy."

"Who?"

Mike looked around. "Do they record this shit?"

Woods leaned closer to the glass. "Video only, no audio."

"No names," Mike said, all lies at this point, "but the guy worked for a big PI firm and needed some muscle. I spent two years taking pictures of cheating husbands, planting bugs on cars, and throwing the occasional scare into would-be snitches. Then we got a client, I'm talking big money, the kind of money that makes rules, not breaks them."

He had Woods on the edge of his seat. Every con loved a conspiracy.

"You think you and I are the only ones Bergman fucked with? This rich guy has a real hard-on for her. Not only that, he's got juice too. I don't believe in God or anything, but all of a sudden I'm getting paid to dig up dirt on the woman who ruined my life. Might not be a miracle, but that's what I call justice."

Woods nodded along. At this point Mike could sell him a timeshare. "So why are you here?"

"She's down in Bloomington trying to take on an old police chief named Hartman who's still got some friends." Mike raised his eyebrows. "She didn't tell you about your part in her big exposé?"

Panic flashed through Woods's prison-yard-heavy routine. "No. She sat down yesterday looking like a freak show—thick-ass makeup, weird dyke haircut, said, 'You remember me?' I didn't recognize her, so she said her name. I told her to fuck herself."

"What'd she do then?"

"Bitch ran out in tears."

Not the reaction Mike expected. "Bullshit. You made Caitlin Bergman cry?"

Mary Lubbers-Gaffney had told him about Caitlin's panic attacks, but he'd seen the woman laugh with a knife to her throat. That this washed-up convict had a hold over her made Mike want to slip a guard five hundred bucks for a minute without the bulletproof divider between them.

Woods smiled. "I tried to cheer her up, asked if she wanted to sign up for a conjugal, relive the old days."

Mike's fingers strangled his handset. "When you raped her."

Woods shrugged. "So what are you gonna do to that bitch?"

"Oh, I'm gonna take care of her."

"You won't say what?"

"You seem solid, but I knew plenty of stand-up guys who ratted to cut their sentences in half."

"Not me—ask around."

Mike smiled, finally able to speak truth to this asshole. "Know this, Woods. You'll get your payback, and you'll know I was the one who made it happen."

*   *   *

"Agent Martinez said to give you anything you wanted." The prison guard with the shaved head cued up the footage on the computer, two camera angles, side by side. "Here's your happy couple," he said, letting the video play.

"No audio?"

The guard shook his head. "Blame the ACLU."

The cubicle dividers blocked most of Caitlin's visit with Woods, but Mike caught a glimpse of her face when she exited.

Her hand went up to her eyes, blocking her nose and lips, and stayed there until she left the frame, like a celebrity avoiding the paparazzi outside a rehab center.

"Could you play that at half speed?"

The kid turned, revealed his impressionable twenty-year-old face. "You want the whole thing?"

"Just the walkout."

"Okay. What's that like, working for a Martinez?"

"How do you mean?"

"We don't get a lot of *ezes* or *itas* around here, not on this side of the bars."

Mike didn't bite. "You gonna hit 'Play'?"

The footage played in slo-mo. Still hard to get a good glimpse—almost like Caitlin didn't want the camera to see her face.

"Freeze it there."

Mike stared at the image. Caitlin's hand froze right below her lips on its path to her eyes. "Can I get a copy of this?"

"I'll get you a file."

Mike didn't know everything about Bergman. They weren't lovers, didn't share hopes and dreams, talk about God, or exchange Christmas cards, but Woods's words didn't make sense.

"Thick-ass makeup."

Mike had only seen Caitlin wear makeup when she'd been a TV reporter, and then, only because someone else applied it. She certainly never wore bright pink lipstick. But then, he'd never seen her cry either. He pointed to the upper-right corner of the screen, a bright yellow height strip along the doorjamb.

"Is that thing accurate?"

The guard leaned in. "Far as I know."

Mike shook his head. He didn't know Caitlin's measurements, but he'd have noticed if she was five feet ten.

The guard handed him a thumb drive. "This is the whole visit. Anything else I can help with?"

Mike pocketed the drive. "Who's Woods been scrapping with?"

"Big turf war between the Aryans and the beaners in the last two months."

Mike nodded, headed for the door.

The guard followed. "Hey, Agent, maybe you'll clue me in, since we're both in law enforcement. From what I saw, it didn't look like Woods said anything useful, either to her or you."

Mike stared at the bald kid's hairline. Full and dark, no sign of recession, probably shaved daily. If the Aryan Brotherhood had a friend on staff, Mike stood close enough to smell his swastikas. "Law enforcement to law enforcement?"

"Yeah, Woods seems like a real badass. Tells every cop he meets to go to hell."

Mike gave the youth Nazi his money's worth. "Troy Woods gave me more than I needed to close my case. Hell, he offered to rat on everyone he knew—anything to shorten his sentence. You might as well put him in a stadium, 'cause every cop in the Midwest is gonna show up to listen to him sing."

The guard looked like Mike had just pantsed Hitler. "You're shitting me."

"Don't let that get around. People hear something like that, you'll find your badass dead in a shower."

74

"You'll stay in your room until nighttime."

Caitlin watched Embower's lips through the window, heard his voice through the handcuff slot.

"I have two classes. There's breakfast in the drop and a sandwich for lunch. Also a stack of books."

He slid the panel shut and left. If he'd be away most of the day, he wouldn't be watching the camera feed. He'd have recordings, but Caitlin would work on the presumption he only checked past footage when something went wrong.

She downed some Tylenol and ate breakfast. After her last bite, she casually knocked her open water bottle off the table, swore dramatically, and dropped to her hands and knees.

The bottle landed inches from the drain. She poured the remainder in, listened, but didn't hear anything, then tried to turn a screw with her fingertip. No luck, but something seemed unusual. Usually, a cover plate like that sat inside a grooved ring, its screws sunk into predrilled holes. From what Caitlin could see, Embower had tapped metal anchor bolts into the limestone, rather than the strip of concrete, then rested the cover on top of the hole, probably to save time while the concrete hardened. Either way, her focus now was how to clog the holes in the cover.

She got up, dropped the empty bottle in the metal drop, and inventoried the shelves. Twenty-three bottles of water, twelve Sprite, twelve Coca-Cola, eight Diet Coke, two boxes of maxi-pads, and three boxes of tampons.

Too big to squeeze through the openings, she took each tampon from its applicator and split the cotton in two. When she had ten disassembled, she went under the table and thumb-fed the material down the drain.

She needed to make a wad. She grabbed a paperback copy of Steven King's *It* from the stack of books, tore out twenty pages, rolled each, and fed them down as well. She repeated the process with another box of tampons, another chunk of a different book.

Time to test the dam. She grabbed a bottle of Sprite, poured some down. The liquid hissed its way down the tube, but the last two pages she'd dropped didn't move. She poured a little more, missed the drain.

"Shit."

Sprite splashed on the limestone floor. She expected a little bubble from a soda, but the liquid turned into foam instead. A chemical reaction.

"Are you kidding me?"

Troy Woods's fifth-grade science fair project had taught her the basics. The carbolic acid in the soda caused the unsealed limestone to break down.

She poured the rest of the Sprite where the screws entered the stone. She had no idea how much soda it would take to loosen the screws but needed to fill the drain regardless. She emptied another two bottles then returned to tampons and books. She stopped for lunch, put one of the empty Sprite bottles in the metal drop, replaced the caps on the other two, and tucked them into her bed sheets.

After lunch, she risked another hour under the table. Overall, she squeezed one hundred pages, twenty tampons, three granola bars and their wrappers, and the bread from her sandwich down the drain before climbing into bed to await playroom time.

* * *

Hours later, the metal slot clanged open. Embower stood outside Caitlin's window, handcuffs in hand. "Who's hungry?"

Caitlin walked over. "What time is it?"

"Seven."

She bagged herself, put her hands through the slot. They walked to the playroom, no discussion. She heard the door lock behind her, found the hole, put her hands through once more.

"You're not eating with me tonight?"

No window in this door. She couldn't see his reaction, but his hands stopped moving on the handcuffs. "Not tonight."

The cuffs slipped off. She left her hands in the hole. "Embower? Can I have a clock?"

His answer came slow. "Why a clock?"

"It's like Vegas in this place. My circadian rhythm's gone crazy. Nothing big, maybe a little alarm clock."

He squeezed her hands gently, then pushed them back through the door. "We'll see."

The metal slot slid shut.

She reached up and removed the bag.

A takeout container waited on the torture table next to a crisp copy of the latest *Daily Student*. Her own face stared at her from center page, above the crease. The headline—"Missing Reporter Found."

He'd be watching—no doubt in her mind about that—but she couldn't wait. She picked up the paper.

FROM MARY LUBBERS-GAFFNEY, DIRECTOR

In response to this publication's weekend coverage, representatives from both the Bloomington Police Department and the FBI Indianapolis field office have confirmed that journalist Caitlin Bergman, believed to be missing, has been located.

Although the IDS works to ensure all stories adhere to the highest journalistic standards, this weekend's coverage illustrated the danger of supposition and opinion in the digital age.

Not a blatant apology, but Caitlin could imagine how Mary felt. She'd risked the career she loved by taking on the cops, lost, and had to reward them with a front-page victory lap. No doubt, Lakshmi had done the same. Caitlin wouldn't let their sacrifice go without recognition.

Tears were coming, but she wouldn't fight them. She threw her head back, cried for her friend, for her pain, for years of silence. She'd look pathetic for the camera, but Embower's gambit had only steeled her resolve.

After twenty minutes of waterworks, she tossed the paper on the table and walked to the bookcase. She stared at the books, pulled a few, returned them, opted finally for the *Riverside Shakespeare*. She took her dinner and her hope to the couch.

Don't open the cover yet. Eat the food.

Caitlin got the container's chicken salad down, drank some water, then finally reached into William's insides.

Page 709, gone. Caitlin's message, gone.

She turned to 711, 713, 715, flipped the pages with her thumb, watched the words of the Bard pass by unaltered, 953, 1175, 1233.

Near the end, her finger caught a dog-ear.

Wedged between pages, she found five of the cutout words she'd used to make her message for Angela.

Caitlin Bergman
ready
Angela

Caitlin allowed herself a tiny smile, then wadded the words, dropped the ball into her salad, and scooped a forkful of lettuce and paper into her mouth.

After dinner, she walked Shakespeare back to the shelf and found a play by Tennessee Williams she'd seen the day before, *I Can't Imagine Tomorrow*. She folded the blue paper cover so the title displayed as *Imagine Tomorrow* and shoved it into *Riverside* like a bookmark.

Maybe Embower'd seen the whole thing. Maybe not.

Caitlin set the DVD case for *Tommy Boy* on the counter facing the camera and returned to the couch to finish her salad. Chris Farley didn't appear on the TV for an hour. She sat back and enjoyed the movie.

Whatever Embower'd been doing, he hadn't checked on her until now.

75

THE NEXT MORNING, Mike studied the duplex from the passenger window of his rental. "Might be cameras. Keep driving."

Greenwood slowed but didn't stop at Branford's house. "Roman, people
are gonna notice if this takes more than an hour."

"You're not allowed to get breakfast with a friend?"

"Sure I am." Greenwood let out a chuckle. "Just not one of Caitlin's
friends. We didn't even get breakfast."

"You didn't have to say yes," Mike said, his eyes on the property. "What's
down the road?"

"Old quarry."

"Like the *Flintstones*?"

Greenwood nodded. "Gotta turn around anyway. I'll show you."

Mike used his side mirror to see the back of Branford's garage. Decent
siding, well-kept grass. "Shouldn't a single acting professor be close enough
to campus to let his good-looking students make some mistakes?"

"He's a teacher; maybe it's all he can afford. This is stupid. I thought you
had something to show me."

"I do," Mike said. "I just haven't seen it yet."

He turned and faced Greenwood. "Branford was the last person to see
Caitlin."

"Except for the prison staff and Woods."

"Who hasn't seen her in twenty years. Besides, Caitlin doesn't wear
lipstick."

The road ended at a high fence topped with razor wire. Greenwood
stopped the car at the gate, shifted into reverse. "Not sure that will hold up
against GPS, cell phone records, and security footage."

"She sure as shit isn't five feet ten."

"Maybe she wore heels."

"Bullshit," Mike said. "She wears black pumps or running shoes every day of the week, because she's the kind of person who chases after a story. I thought you got to know her while she was in town."

Greenwood looked away. "Yeah, we worked together."

"Yeah, I heard what you did together." Mike noticed three "No Trespassing" signs and two cameras. "What's with all the security?"

"A lot of the old quarries fill up with water. Kids go swimming. Once a year, someone breaks a neck or a leg, has to be medivaced out. Hole back there is deep, but dangerous. No easy way to climb out once you get in the water."

Mike smiled. "So you've totally gone swimming in that thing?"

Greenwood drove back toward the house. "Just one of the reasons I'm lucky to be alive."

Mike bumped his armrest with the back of his hand. "I owe the woman, Greenwood. I know this shit doesn't make sense, but I'm not ready to see what everybody wants me to see, not when it feels so wrong."

He groaned. "I guess all I have to show you right now is that I'm serious about this."

Both men stared at Branford's house as they passed.

Greenwood finally nodded his head. "Okay, Roman. You find anything besides uneven makeup, I'll come running, Chief Renton be damned. One more thing—"

"Don't do anything illegal?"

"Didn't think I had to say that, but yeah, don't. I was going to say that this rental might not be the best tail car."

"Two-door, salmon-colored Korean jobs aren't the shit in rural Indiana?"

Greenwood laughed. "Locals are partial to old American pickups. My father-in-law's Chevy is parked in the lot of his nursing home. He keeps it there just to look at, but he won't miss it—and he owes Caitlin Bergman in a big way."

CHAPTER

76

EMBOWER LOOKED AT the forecast: showers off and on all day. Not a great morning to bike to campus. He checked the video feeds. Outside, rain fell in steady sheets. Inside, Caitlin looked content at her bedroom table, breakfast nearly finished. He opened his spreadsheet, made a note under favorite meals.

2 eggs scrambled, maple bacon, avocado, potatoes, salsa.

He scrolled through the tabs, clicked on "Compliance," started typing.

DAY 7—NIGHT. Newspaper had desired effect. No resistance after play-room time. Has fallen into habitual pattern for transition between playroom and bedroom. First compliance benchmark met much earlier than with Angel.

DAY 8—MORNING. Gave her alarm clock. Seemed grateful. Left her with promise of quality time after third class. If alarm clock undamaged, consider surprising with laptop again. Rain in forecast. 75% chance, three sources. Shouldn't result in flooding, but watch rest of week.

He saved the document, opened another, scanned through the "Compliance" tab.

DAY 27—NIGHT. Consensual, reciprocated sex.

He skipped the details, looked to the end of the entry.

Escape attempt.

It made sense in hindsight. His Angel lived a sexual life and knew the power of sharing her gift. She'd tried to manipulate him. He'd mistaken the action for acceptance and had had to punish her.

Would Bergman make the same attempt?

He typed one more note.

The Writer doesn't understand yet. Take no chances.

He noticed the time. 9:26 AM.

"Shit."

Time for Branford to go to work.

*   *   *

The rain worsened. His tires spun when they met the asphalt.

He wasn't the only one fighting the weather. A quarter of a mile from his place, a beat-up red and white pickup shot mud into the air pulling into traffic.

Fifteen minutes later, he stopped at the four-way intersection near the theater department, let undergrads with umbrellas pass, wondered if Caitlin would use the treadmill he'd bought for Paige. He wanted her healthy but wasn't sure he should encourage her to run.

A horn honked. He looked up, saw the red and white pickup still behind him, the male driver pointing toward the intersection.

Embower turned and parked. The truck sped away in the opposite direction.

Ten minutes later, Professor Branford had his students in a circle, giving one another warm-up massages. After two hours, he stepped out the front door to a dry but still ominous sky. He wanted to spend the hour between classes monitoring his collection, but a lighting designer needed to talk about the summer schedule over lunch at the student union.

Mid-walk, Branford paused to greet two of his students and noticed a man behind him. Over six feet tall, broad shoulders stretching the corners of a lightweight rain jacket, his dark sunglasses and fifties buzz cut made him look like Central Casting's impression of a soldier or a cop.

"No," Branford said, his attention back on his students, "I will not be bringing a date to the drama prom. Will you, Tammy?"

He listened politely to sophomore Tammy's plan for the theater department's year-end banquet, but something flashed in his mind. He'd read Caitlin's book eight times. How had she described Mike "Babyface" Roman?

A cop built on the frame of a marine, grown from a Boy Scout.

He glanced back to where he'd seen the muscular anomaly.

Gone.

Branford excused himself, met his associate for lunch, and saw no further sign of the man. The only thing he noticed after his second class was the arrival of another thunderstorm. His last class finished at five, but the rain did not. He spent the drive home wondering if the new drain in Caitlin's room would prevent a repeat of the Paige debacle.

He'd given his Barbie a lamp, which she'd plugged into the jack under her bed. After a week of nonstop storms, groundwater snuck in where the wall met the floor. Paige took advantage of that opportunity.

Caitlin had neither lamp nor outlet, and her drugstore alarm clock ran on a double A battery.

You're worrying about nothing. Worst-case scenario, you gas her, let her wait out the storm in the playroom.

Despite the urge to run across the field to the farmhouse, he parked in the Branford garage, went in the house, and loaded up the live feed on his computer. Caitlin shifted in the chair like she couldn't get comfortable, a paperback open on the table. Her hair looked messy, but the floor looked dry.

Embower exhaled, sat back. Still, something was wrong. Not in the collection, but there in Branford's house.

Smells fresh.

He switched his camera feed, checked the driveway and front door. Nothing unusual. He got up, walked the first floor. The dining room he never used felt colder than the rest of the house. He pulled back a curtain, found one of the windows open half an inch.

He couldn't remember the last time he'd opened that or any other window in the house.

He went back to his laptop, rewound the day's footage, saw nothing at the front door, nothing at the driveway.

He went outside, walked the backyard. The dining room window wasn't high off the ground, but Embower didn't see any footprints or sign of forced entry.

You're being paranoid. Remember the tornados in March? You opened the windows to depressurize the house.

He felt better, but not good enough. Something pink caught his eye where his land met the quarry's fence. He walked over, picked a soggy plastic bag from the weeds. Inside, two more bags, both muddy, and wads of paper towels. He looked back at the stretch of grass from the fence to his back window and saw faint depressions in the grass every three feet. Someone had covered their shoes to avoid leaving discernible footprints.

"Shit," he said, ran back inside.

He'd checked the feed from the Branford house, not the farmhouse. He scrolled through the second-story camera's feed, stopped the time line at 1:45 PM, almost halfway into his second class. A big man in a rain jacket ran from behind the garage to the dining room windows, two bright pink plastic bags over his shoes.

Embower thought back through the day.

This man knew I was in class because he followed me to work.

"The truck."

He returned to the Branford feed. Earlier, he'd looked for someone coming up the driveway. This time, he kept his eyes on the road. At 1:12, the red and white pickup passed the house going toward the quarry. At 1:56, the same truck went the other way. Embower loaded the front-door feed again but watched the interior in front of the staircase this time. 1:38. A dark shadow walked from the foyer onto the staircase. Halfway to the landing, his face passed the camera.

This idiot thinks he's smart. He has no idea who he's messing with.

Embower picked up his phone, dialed the Bloomington Police Department. "Someone broke into my house, and I can identify him."

CHAPTER

77

AT BREAKFAST, HE'D told her he'd be gone all day. Caitlin had been working since nine AM, starting with the handcuff slot in the door. The wad
of toilet paper she'd wedged in the corner of the sliding panel wouldn't stop
the slot from functioning, but the extra half inch of space might let some
fresh air in, or Embower's gas out. Next she attacked his airborne delivery
method; the overhead fan. The camera over the bed tilted down, so he could
see toward the fan, though not the ceiling unit itself. Any move she made in
that direction would have to look natural, or at least motivated.

For half an hour, Caitlin went stir-crazy, starting on the bed. She stood
on the sheets, walked back and forth, then hopped down and paced around
the table. Then she climbed up the chair to the tabletop, running her hands
through her hair, reaching up, touching the ceiling. She hopped down,
walked toward the bed, then the door, then climbed back on the table with
items from the storage shelves tucked into her pajamas. More crazy arms,
more why-God-whys toward the ceiling, her hands working off-camera.
After five more trips spread over an hour, she'd done all she could to the
fan. Every action in the five hours since had focused on loosening the drain
cover with her foot while appearing to read.

She poured the last bottle of Sprite under the table and checked the
alarm clock.

5:42 PM.

She pushed the ball of her foot against the drain. The carbonation bub-
bled around her toes in the half inch of standing liquid.

Two hours back, she'd felt her first wiggle. She shifted her focus from clogging the drain to getting the cover off its mount. Now she felt the metal disc slide back and forth, maybe a quarter of an inch worth of give.

The groove of the metal bit into her skin. Her left foot bled freely. She switched feet. The fizzle stopped, she didn't.

She'd done all she could from above the table. But if Embower checked the camera, he'd see her crawl under the table, come running. She had to take the chance. He said he'd be back for dinner. Either way, he'd come soon.

She knocked the remains of her paperback onto the floor, went down after it, reaching into the puddle of garbage and blood. She wrapped her fingertips around the cover's edge, and pulled. The cover slid to one side, the anchor bolts below straining against the weakened limestone. She put both hands around the loose edge, pulled again.

Her right hand slipped. "Holy shit," she said, clutching her fingers. The nail from her middle finger floated in the mélange.

She grabbed the cover again, pulled back, and screamed.

Something gave. She fell backward. The cover and its two screws, anchor bolts and all, dripped the stink of cola onto her face.

She tucked the rounded metal under her shirt, crawled out from under the table.

If Embower was watching, she'd hear the fan motor. A minute passed on the alarm clock. Nothing happened. She climbed onto the bed and tucked her new weapon under the sheets.

Another minute passed. Then ten, then twenty.

At 6:22, Caitlin knew what was wrong. Not only had Embower not seen her with the drain cover, he didn't know the drain had backed up. The pool she'd made didn't show past the table, and she'd used every bit of liquid in the room.

He would come with dinner and have her put her hands through to be cuffed.

"Shit."

She looked at the crates near the door. Nothing left but the camp toilet.

"Shit," she repeated, smiling.

She got herself to the toilet, flipped the lid up and peed. But instead of putting the lid down, she pulled the open toilet onto its side, then climbed onto the bed as the dark blue mix of treatment chemical and fecal matter spread across the floor.

78

MIKE PACED IN his hotel room, phone in hand. "I know the story got you in trouble, Lakshmi, but Caitlin needs your help."

The Anjale girl sounded seconds away from a hang-up. "Call Greenwood if it's so bloody important."

"Can't reach him."

She gave a frustrated laugh. "Welcome to my world."

"You know Branford, Lakshmi. You partied with him."

"Like twice," she said, "and always at Angela's place."

"You've got to know something about him or his business that will tell us more. There's no way he lives in that house."

"How can you tell?"

Mike laughed. "Nothing in his laundry baskets, nothing in the washer and dryer, and both bathrooms were stocked with brand-new rolls of toilet paper."

Someone knocked on Mike's door, three firm raps. A gruff female voice followed. "Mike Roman. BPD."

"Lakshmi, I gotta go. I'm getting arrested."

"You're what?"

"Do what you want, but remember—whatever I'm up against, Caitlin's dealing with worse, and she wouldn't have been involved if you hadn't asked her for help."

He switched the phone to speaker, placed it on a table, and opened the door to the female detective who had given him the cigarette.

"Mike Roman," she said, "you're under arrest."

"What for?"

She held out a photo of his face going up Branford's stairway. "Breaking and entering and grand theft auto."

Mike held back a smile. She didn't mention the pink plastic bags, but someone must have noticed.

"Greenwood said I could use his father-in-law's truck."

Maverick shook her head. "That old son of a bitch saw his parking spot empty and called it in. Hands on the wall, please."

Mike assumed the position so the detective could frisk him. "Greenwood know about this?"

"Pretty sure that's why Chief Renton suspended him."

79

THE STATEMENTS STOLE hours from Embower. First with the officers who came to the Branford house, then the trip to the station to off-load his security footage, then back to the house—but the attention paid off. Both Greenwood and Roman would be out of his world. Embower didn't understand what had stopped Greenwood's involvement—something about the red and white truck—but Roman's face in Branford's house would be enough to file for a restraining order once they released him from custody.

He watched the last two officers pack up in the shelter of his dry garage. "As far as you can tell, the only thing missing is the hard drive?"

The older of the two nodded. "If you hadn't noticed the drive missing—"

The other one closed the trunk. "Or had the video."

"Right, if you hadn't noticed the missing drive, then checked your footage, we wouldn't have been able to tell he'd been inside. What was on the drive?"

Branford shook his head. "Stuff for my classes. I'd only bought it a month ago. Don't know what he'd want with it."

Mike Roman hadn't found anything. After Embower's own wall-to-wall search, he'd tucked his work hard drive under the passenger seat of his SUV, then set its padded carrying case in the upstairs bedroom amid a pile of random financial papers pulled from his filing cabinet and thrown on the floor. Anyone watching Roman climb the stairs on the video would assume he'd found the pile important.

"Sounds like he thought you knew something about that reporter. Don't worry—he won't bother you again."

The officers turned their car around, drove away.

Embower went to the kitchen, opened his laptop, and shuttled through the three-and-a-half hours the house had been full of police. Convinced they'd found nothing, he switched to the farmhouse network.

He clicked on the exterior camera that faced the Branford house, looked through the same time frame. No one so much as glanced toward the farmhouse.

They don't know. Your collection is safe and ready to be played with.

He clicked on the feed from Caitlin's room. She lay on the bed, facing the wall. The floor looked dark, wet. Rain still fell outside but couldn't have filled the room that fast.

"Not possible."

He switched the camera to the low-light setting. Caitlin looked normal.

How did the drain fail, and why isn't the sump pump pulling the water out?

He switched back to the normal exposure.

And why is the water dark?

He rewound the footage. Almost three hours back, the dark stain receded under the table. He hit "Play."

Caitlin knocked over the toilet, limped to the bed, and got under the covers as filth spread across the floor.

CHAPTER

80

C AITLIN WATCHED THE alarm clock under the covers. *9:58 PM.*
She'd been facing the wall for twenty-eight adrenaline-pumping minutes. Her muscles anxious, she fought the urge to wiggle. Two more minutes and she'd shift slightly to her left. She didn't need for Embower to believe she was sleeping, but didn't want to have to rearrange the items hidden in the sheets.

The light above her turned off.

Time to go.

She put her head under the sheets, breathed in deep.

The next sound would decide everything. If the fan turned on and ran smoothly, she'd end up on the torture table, or worse.

She held her breath, started counting.

The fan came to life, but not in a healthy way. A series of clicks ended in a low hum—the sound a motor made when blocked by three tampons, five wet wipes, and the covers of two Tom Clancy thrillers.

She reached for the first of five bottles. At a thirty-eight count, she raised the empty Sprite bottle, twisted the cap off, and shoved the opening against the spread-out cotton of a tampon in her palm.

No way to know if Embower's gas would get up her nostril faster than the air from the bottle, but she moved the cotton and inhaled.

After five seconds of lemon-lime smell, she set the empty between her legs and held her breath again.

9:59 PM.

She counted seconds in her head. The clock hit 10:00 PM before she reached for her second bottle. So far, the only effects she felt were from holding her breath.

Twenty years ago in her father's pool, she'd held her breath for more than three minutes. That time, she'd wanted to die. This time, she wanted to live.

her second burn
re are open in
three minutes

CHAPTER

81

THE TIMER STOPPED. He'd followed the usual math, two minutes of gas, three minutes of dissipation. Embower looked through the window. Caitlin hadn't moved. He opened the door, smelled the mix of treatment chemical and decay.

"Caitlin."

He stepped in, watched the filth swirl around his shoe.

"I know this was you lashing out, testing me."

He moved past the table, kicked a pair of empty Sprite bottles.

"But I have to teach you. This time, you will learn."

He picked a paperback off her pillow, threw it behind him, then pulled back the sheet.

"In time, you'll thank me."

Caitlin lay in the fetal position, one hand tucked into her chest, her other under the pillow. He pulled her shoulder, set her flat on her back.

Her eyes snapped open.

"Thank you," she said, then struck his head with something sharp and metal.

82

CAITLIN'S FIRST SWING broke the skin. The jagged corner of an anchor bolt cut Embower's cheek, inches from the eye.

He reached for his head. She reached for his crotch, twisted three hundred and sixty degrees.

Embower fell toward her. Caitlin used the closing distance to attack again, this time bringing the edge of the metal disc down against the base of his skull. He collapsed onto her lap. She shoved him to the side and ran for the open door, hearing movement behind her.

"Caitlin, wait—"

The raised doorjamb snagged her left foot going into the hallway. The drain cover fell from her hand, but she caught herself on the wall and turned around. Embower staggered around the table, his face a mix of blood and blue toilet water. Caitlin slammed the door and turned the top deadbolt. Through the window, she saw him throw his body against the door as she flipped the second lock.

"Caitlin." His face left a smear of blood against the glass. "If you don't open this door, I will tear you in ways Troy Woods never imagined."

Caitlin looked around, found a light switch panel with a timer next to a pipe with a valve. She turned the valve, twisted the timer, and ran down the hall to the door past the playroom. There was no window, but she turned the locks and opened the door.

A woman wearing pajamas, pink like Caitlin's but with the word "Angel" across the front, stood three feet away, arms at her sides, bag over her head.

The bag tilted to one side. "What's going on?"

"Angela Chapman, take that freaking bag off your head."

The girl pulled the black bag away, revealing the ghost of Angela Chapman. Two years in captivity had stolen more than time's entitled toll. Angela's tired, dark-circled eyes dared only a second of connection before darting into the room's corner. Her defined, athletic muscles had dissolved into the gaunt, pulled skin of an anorexic. Her hair held neither the youthful bounce of her high school photos, nor the rebellious spike of her college days, but hung limp in a dishwater bob. A severe scar crossed her right forearm. Another on her neck, where the remains of her hummingbird tattoo had been lost to raised pink tissue.

Caitlin reached her hand out. "I'm Caitlin Bergman and we're getting out of here."

Angela flinched away. "Why are you doing this?"

Not the reaction Caitlin expected.

"I don't want to rehearse tonight," Angela whimpered. "I just want to sleep. Take off the wig, Embower, please."

"Rehearse?"

Christ, the wig.

Three days ago, before he'd impersonated Caitlin at the prison, Embower must have visited Chapman as well, workshopping his character on his captive audience.

"This isn't rehearsal, Angela, and I'm not Embower. I left you the note."

The girl backed closer to her bed. "This isn't funny."

"Isn't funny?" Caitlin looked back down the hall. No movement, yet. "Angela, I know he dressed like me, but I am the real Caitlin Bergman. I'm a reporter from Los Angeles. I'm working with Lakshmi Anjale and your mother, Doris. I wrote a book—"

"Fallen Angels," Angela said.

"Right, like in the playroom. That's me. He had me in Paige's room on the other side. He killed Paige, and he'll kill us both unless we leave here right now."

The girl's eyes shifted back toward Caitlin's face, daring another look.

Caitlin reached for her own hair, pulled. "See? Not a wig."

Chapman's head cocked to the side.

Shit, this is like talking to a puppy.

"Angela, I know you need sensitive handling right now. After everything he's done to you, I know you need time to trust. But time's the one thing we don't have. How can I prove it to you? How can I get you out of this fucking room?"

Caitlin searched her knowledge of Angela for anything Embower wouldn't also know but realized Angela's disappearance had defined her.

Missing student, Angela Chapman.

Sainted daughter to Doris.

Black eye to the BPD.

Fuck buddy to Kieran.

Lesbian lover of Lakshmi.

Prize to Chad Branford.

What did Caitlin really know about her? What did she have in common with this young, wounded woman?

"Angela, look at me."

Chapman's eyes met hers.

"Right now you're dead. You might feel alive because you're breathing and you're scared and you're in pain, but you're not *living*. You're trapped at the bottom of a pool, looking up at a world that doesn't know you're there and can't help you until you swim to the top." Caitlin shook her head. "I don't have the words to make this pretty. My hands are raw, my feet are covered in piss and shit, and I don't know how long . . ."

She stopped, checked the hall again, turned back to Chapman.

"He's killed the real you, Angela, so you could be his *Angel*. And when you dared not to be, he hit you, and he cut you, and he raped you. That's his sickness. Men like him want you to live out their fantasies on a pedestal, to define you according to some image they've built in their messed-up minds. And I can't say this isn't going to define you—"

Caitlin's chest spasmed with the need for a sharp breath, and her voice came out with a tremble. "Some Neanderthal did the same thing to me twenty years ago, and sometimes it still feels like I'm dead." She sniffed up the tears clouding her sinuses. "Like every good thing in my life died right there in the dirt." She wiped the corner of her eyes and fought through. "But it didn't. I'm still alive and I'm ready to get back to the surface with everyone else. And you can be too, Angela, if you come with me right now."

Angela took a sharp breath, then another, then tears came. She moved closer. "You're real?"

Caitlin nodded and threw her arms around the girl. "In all my fucked-up glory."

For the first time since Caitlin had opened the door, Chapman's face broke into a smile. "Is Embower dead?"

"No." Caitlin put space between them and pulled Angela toward the door. "He's locked in my room."

Angela recoiled. "Did you get his keys?"

"His keys?"

She took another step back. "He has a remote for the locks."

Caitlin looked back down the hall. The door to her room was still closed. She'd started the gas, and Embower didn't have the benefit of air trapped in Sprite bottles, but with the fan too messed-up to circulate, Caitlin had no idea how long the effects of the gas would last.

She took the girl's arm, felt nothing but bone. "Chapman, come with me or we both die today."

"He'll catch me," Angela said, shaking. "He always catches me."

Caitlin grabbed her hand. "Last time you were alone."

Angela jerked to life, went through the door with Caitlin, then took the lead. "There's a dumbwaiter on the right."

Caitlin winced through the feeling of the rocks on her bare, torn feet and passed her bedroom without looking. "What about the tunnel to the left?"

"No good," Chapman answered, already climbing onto the shelf where the topless dumbwaiter waited. "His remote does that door too."

The folding chair Embower would bring into Caitlin's room rested against the wall. She ran back, wedged the chair under the doorknob, and glanced through the window. Embower lay on the floor facing the bed with his hands over his mouth, but he wasn't moving.

She ran back to the dumbwaiter opening in time to see Chapman's feet disappear through the ceiling. Next in line, she climbed the shelving, grabbed the rope on the side, and jumped up until she could wedge her foot on a support beam. Above her, Chapman kicked her way out of the shaft, eight feet up. Caitlin reached for another beam, then froze.

The distinct chime of a timer dinged in the hall below.

So much for the knockout gas.

No going back now, Caitlin pushed off a support and pulled her way up into the kitchen, clamoring over a countertop and landing on the linoleum.

Angela helped her up. "There's no phone."

"No knives either," Caitlin said, turning back to the counter. "Help me lift the microwave."

The large appliance hadn't been moved in years. Caitlin knocked a stack of plates off the top and grabbed the cord. They each took a side, then stopped.

Though distant, there was no mistaking the crisp shots of deadbolts being turned echoing up through the dumbwaiter shaft.

"He's awake," Angela said, her eyes wide.

Caitlin swallowed hard. "Well, he's not getting up the way we came."

They pushed the microwave through the dumbwaiter opening. It fell three feet before getting lodged, blocking the shaft.

"He'll just come up the other way," Angela said.

"Do you know where it comes out?"

Angela shook her head no.

Caitlin considered their options. They could try to fight, two against one, but she'd already lost one fight in the farmhouse. "We run."

"We won't make it. He has cameras."

Caitlin saw Embower's laptop on the kitchen table and smashed it against the counter. His surveillance fell in pieces onto the linoleum. "Back door," she said. "Let's move."

83

"NOT THAT WAY." Chapman pulled Caitlin toward the corn. "The main road's closer."

Under the light of a full moon clouded by a steady drizzle of rain, Caitlin looked across the field to the Branford house, then in Chapman's direction. Even in the dark, she could tell the girl was right.

"How many times have you done this, Angela?"

"This makes thirteen."

"Lucky number thirteen? Let's go."

Mud coated her feet, rain soaked her clothes, and cornstalks sliced her skin, but Caitlin ran the quarter mile without flinching.

Chapman stopped for breath at the country road. "This is the farthest I've gotten. Which way?"

Past the cornfield, trees lined both sides. Caitlin didn't see lights in either direction. "Left, toward State Road Thirty-Seven."

"But don't we want to get to town?"

Caitlin thought back twenty years, remembered the woman in the van who took her to the hospital after Woods's attack. She'd come from her job at the hospice down the road.

"That's what he'd expect, Angela. We go left."

"Okay."

Angela took off in a sprint. This time, Caitlin struggled to keep up. Half a mile down, the girl looked back, stopped in the middle of the road with her arms up, and yelled, "A car."

Caitlin pulled her down against the embankment. "What if it's him?"

She caught her breath, soothing her bloody feet on the wet grass. "I don't know how much more I can run, Angela. You hide and I'll flag down the car. If it's safe, I'll wave you over. If it's him, I'll run the other way."

"I can't leave you," Chapman said between breaths, her face glistening from raindrops. "He'll kill you."

Despite the little light there was, the young woman's face looked different than it had under the subterranean fluorescents. Flush with life, renewed by water, Caitlin saw Doris Chapman's daughter Angie, and Lakshmi's best friend Angela, ready to win a two-on-two basketball tournament and down a few beers with her friends.

Caitlin squeezed the girl's hand. "Wait until there's no way he can see you, then run until you find someone. Tell them you're Angela Chapman and that Chad Branford kidnapped you."

The girl shook her head. "Embower said no one knows who I am, that no one ever even looked for me."

Caitlin moved closer, her thin pajamas wicking the rain from the grass, and grabbed Chapman's shoulders. "Angela, your mom, your dad, Lakshmi, the whole campus, the FB-freakin'-I—everyone in Indiana—is looking for you. Don't let anyone tell you otherwise."

Now Caitlin heard the distant buzz of the car's tires on the wet asphalt. She raised her head. The car had split the difference—maybe half-a-mile away. She leaned back, let the rain soak her face.

"And don't call him Embower. He's Chad Branford. The police know where he lives."

Chapman nodded, took a deep breath.

Caitlin joined her, the bellows of their hard-working lungs the only sounds audible in the country night besides the falling rain and approaching car.

Angela broke the silence. "I read your book."

"What?"

"In the playroom. I read *Fallen Angels*."

Caitlin laughed. "What'd you think?"

Angela looked down at her wrist. "That men take what they want, and women don't get anything but scars."

Caitlin touched Chapman's shoulder once, then stood up. "Scars just prove you lived through something, Angela. Get ready to go home."

She walked into the road with her arms up. The headlights caught her, the vehicle slowed. One hundred feet away, she knew she'd made a mistake.

She stood there until Branford's white SUV came to a stop, his bloody face glaring behind the steady beat of windshield wipers, then she ran around the passenger side and sprinted toward town.

She looked back, saw his headlights swing around. She left the road for the forest, heard his brakes squeak, and his door open.

"Caitlin," he yelled. "Time to come home."

She didn't stop running. "Come and get me, Branford."

The ground sloped downhill. She hit a patch of wet leaves, slipped, fell on her ass. The momentum took her another twenty feet. She came to rest at the bank of a creek.

I should be scared, she thought, her eyes on the treetops and the night sky. *I should be terrified.* Even as Branford scrambled down after her, one thought drove away Caitlin's fear: *At least Chapman will get away.*

"Roman, you're out."

Mike rose from the holding cell bench. "Just like that, Detective? What happened?"

Maverick opened the cell door. "Greenwood's father-in-law dropped the grand theft complaint. Funny thing, his nurse said he never made the call in the first place on account of his having a tube down his throat."

"That is funny." Mike followed the woman out into the hallway. "Maybe Greenwood talked some sense into the old man."

"Who knows? We haven't heard from Jerry since he blew up on the Chief this morning after having breakfast with a friend." She handed him an envelope of his pocket things, then wheeled a rolling suitcase out from behind a counter. "Oh yeah. I went back to your hotel to let them know you might be staying with us instead. Oddly enough, the clerk already had your bag stowed behind the front desk."

"Convenient." Mike had checked out of his room and left fifty bucks and the bag with the kid fifteen minutes before Maverick had knocked on the door. "Guess they needed to turn the room around. As much as I appreciate the bellhop service, Detective, what about the breaking and entering at Branford's place?"

"Call me Jane." She pulled a cigarette out from behind her ear. "Technically, I didn't get around to filing any charges yet. I couldn't wrap my mind around how you slipped into Branford's house without disturbing a thing but managed to give a camera the cleanest face shot I've seen in years."

Mike held back his smile. "I've done some stupid stuff in my lifetime, Jane."

She shook her head side to side. "Like impersonating an old man and calling in a stolen truck, or getting yourself arrested for breaking into a house on purpose? What the hell were you thinking?"

Mike reached for his suitcase. "No one here was going to look at Branford, not without probable cause." He gave the tiniest of smiles. "But if he invited you guys into his house, you'd have to look around. So what did you find?"

Maverick walked toward the exit and opened the door with a chuckle. "You risked B&E charges just to make us look at Branford? You could have spent a year in jail for Caitlin Bergman, maybe more with your record."

"I had to shake something loose." He inhaled the fresh air pouring through the opening. "I've done time, Jane, and I've got enough regrets to fill a thousand photo albums, but I don't have a lot of friends. Now are you going to tell me what you found or not?"

She lit her cigarette and stepped out into the parking lot. "Nothing."

A light sprinkling of rain hit his face when he followed her out into the night. "Then why am I outside?"

Maverick walked toward a row of police cruisers. "You can thank your call to Lakshmi Anjale for that one. I don't know what you said to the girl, but she spent the last few hours logged into Bergman's financial database. And, as is her style, she called the station every five minutes in the last hour until we took her seriously. Turns out Branford owns the farm behind his house, all through another name tied to his pizza company. Also, it looks like the name Chad Branford is an alias."

She opened the door of a detective special. "That and Angela Chapman turned up at a nursing home two miles past his place fifteen minutes ago, said she'd last seen Branford chasing your girl through the woods." She pointed to the passenger side. "You coming?"

CAITLIN DODGED BRANFORD for as long as she could, dipping in and out of the creek, up one ridge, down another, drawing him a rugged country mile from the road, but she lost the fight when he tackled her trying to climb uphill and lost consciousness shortly after. She woke once to the sound of swearing as he dragged her up a forty-five-degree incline, a welt pulsing on the back of her head.

She woke the second time on the floor of a moving car, in less pain, but with her hands zip-tied behind her, her ankles bound. She saw bench seating behind her, a bucket seat in front.

Branford's SUV.

The canted view from the side window changed from dark, rain-filled night sky to the white siding of the farmhouse.

She heard him yell from the front, "Not like this."

A chorus of sirens answered, proving Caitlin's gamble had paid off. Angela Chapman had not only found help but rallied the troops. Caitlin pulled her knees in and pushed up against the door, her mud-and-rain-soaked pajamas now more skin than fabric.

"It's over, Branford."

The sudden thuds of cornstalks folding under the SUV drowned her weak voice out. She twisted around, saw Branford's duplex surrounded by red and blue flashing lights.

"Your turn to live in the cage."

Still no reaction. She raised her hands to the unlock button on the door but couldn't override the child locks. She twisted her wrists, wiggled her feet.

No give there either. She tightened her abs, pulled her legs through the loop made by her bound arms. Still zip-tied, but her hands were in front now.

They took another turn. Something hard hit her ankle, a portable hard drive, no case. It slid to the side and got caught in the passenger-side seat belt assembly.

She heard sirens in pursuit, shouts, a loudspeaker. "Branford, stop the vehicle."

The SUV lurched forward, and he screamed his reply. "My name is Embower!"

Caitlin felt an impact, saw pieces of a chain link fence scrape past. The SUV took hits—rocks, not bullets. *They're not shooting him because you're in the car. They won't be able to help.*

She got herself onto the bench seat, saw large piles of stone outside beyond the frantic windshield wipers.

"My name is Embower!" he shouted again, his eyes on the road.

Caitlin yelled back, "Sure it is, genius!"

His eyes flashed to hers in the rearview, manic.

He turned the wheel. Caitlin fell to one side, and the car came to a stop.

She worked her way back onto the bench. "There's nowhere to go, asshole. Your moment is over."

Out the windshield, she saw two cop cars with an opening between them. Beyond the opening, nothing but darkness. *The quarry.*

He revved the engine, then smiled in the rearview mirror. "*Our* moment, Caitlin. Our moment is over. Gone with the tide, but what a story it will be."

He gripped the wheel and the SUV screamed forward. Caitlin heard gunshots, the impact of metal on metal. A tire blew. The SUV swerved but didn't slow. She threw her arms over the driver seat headrest, pulled her zip-tied hands against his throat and yanked hard. "My story's not over."

Branford didn't fight and she saw why. For a few seconds, the headlights lit nothing in the darkness ahead. Then, the car tilted forward and the hi-beams reflected off the fast-approaching water at the bottom of the quarry.

The SUV's grill met the surface first, but the windows stayed intact. The driver's side airbag hit Branford. Bits of powder, metal, and fabric peppered Caitlin's face and hands. The car's rear dropped into the water and Caitlin fell backward—her hands, still around his throat as water started pouring in through the open driver's side door.

The airbag deflated and she lost hold of him.

"No!"

Too late, he slipped out. The water filling the void came in fast, and the SUV sank inches in seconds. Caitlin jumped between the two front seats and pulled the door shut as the exterior water level reached just below window height. What little light remained came from the headlights shining into the aquamarine water and the instruments of the dashboard console. She reached up and tapped on the overhead lights.

Her jaw trembled, her hands shook. *Think, Caitlin. Stay in the game.*

The outside water level neared the roof, the indoor up to her waist. To open the door, she'd have to equalize the interior and exterior pressure. Only way to do that, break a window, wait for the car to fill, then swim out.

She beat her fists against the windshield. Pointless. She needed something solid, something with a corner.

The hard drive in the backseat.

Before she could turn, the overhead lights dimmed, then went out, followed by the console instruments, then the headlights.

"No," she said, the water level now just below her bra line. "Please, no."

The only answer, the popping of metal under changes in pressure.

She'd have to do without the light or do without light forever.

Leaning back between the seats, she squatted in the dark water and felt for the hard drive still wedged in the seat belt assembly, working her fingertips through the murk. She sat back onto the bench seat then bashed the hard drive's corner against the rear passenger window. No cracking sound, no rush of water. She screamed and struck again. This time a torrent of water poured through the crack onto her lap.

She dove for the front and worked her way into the passenger seat. The back window caved with a noise like crumpling plastic, followed by the roar of a waterfall. The water level, last at her breastplate, rose to her chin in seconds. She took one final breath and pulled the handle.

The door opened and Caitlin frog-kicked her bound legs and hands through the aquamarine toward the distant lights of the surface. After fifteen feet, she broke through.

"Help," she screamed before bobbing back under. With her feet still bound, she couldn't tread water, had to settle for the dead man's float. She turned her back to the air, let her hands and feet dangle beneath her. She exhaled again, threw her head up above the water.

"I'm here," she said, grabbing another breath before she went back under.

A pale stream of light moved her way and a ringed shadow appeared in front of her. She pulled her head above the water, saw a white circular preserver, and grabbed for the edge with her fingers.

"She's got it," someone yelled.

Caitlin clung to the buoyant foam, coughed. "I'm here."

A male voice came through a speaker. "We're coming for you, Caitlin. Stay on the preserver."

"I'm here," she repeated softly. Just this once, she'd accept help.

She felt the hands before she heard the angry voice. "So am I."

Branford pushed down on her shoulders.

Caitlin lost her grip and went under.

Ten feet down, his hands let go and his feet kicked Caitlin's shoulders. His last act would be to drown her.

You don't know how much time I've spent in the deep, asshole.

She reached up and grabbed his shoe. He kicked again, but Caitlin got his other foot, pulled down. Both sinking now, Caitlin got her hands around his head and put the zip-tie back to work. His body bucked against her, his hands fought against her grip, but she pulled back harder, and looked up. Once again, she saw the light of the world from the edge of darkness.

Not a bad sight, she thought. *The end of my tunnel. At least I'm in control.*

Her chest ached, her muscles gave way, her heart wanted to stop.

But Branford's stopped first.

When she felt him go limp, Caitlin pushed off his shoulders with her hands, then off his head with her feet.

CHAPTER

86

Two Days Later

"**A**RE YOU SURE you should be up and about, Scott?"

Scott Canton lowered the guardrail of his hospital bed, smiled with the functional seventy percent of his lips. "If you can, I can."

Only ten days into his recovery, Scott moved well, but his words took effort.

"Good," Caitlin said, "'cause I won't spend one more minute strapped in a bed."

She leaned back on her crutches. They'd bandaged her ankles and wrists, sewn up the gash in her head. Nothing permanent except the nightmares.

Mike Roman wheeled a walker in Canton's direction.

Scott accepted it and then waved him away. "At ease." He got his weight over the walker, winked at Caitlin. "Let's g—" He struggled with the *g* sound, then started over. "Let's roll." Ten feet down the hall, he pointed at a green space out the window. "Beautiful day."

Mike beat both of them to the door, did the honors.

Scott looked to Caitlin. "He have to be here?"

"You try getting rid of him," she said. "He's like a stray dog I gave bacon to."

Scott shot Mike a nod, pushed past. "Best kind of dog."

Roman stayed by the door, giving them space. He'd been at the quarry when they pulled Caitlin out of the water, in the room when the cops questioned her, and by her side as much as she'd allowed since. For this conversation, she only wanted Scott.

By the time the invalids crossed the twenty feet to the stone bench, Caitlin smelled like a sweaty Band-Aid. She didn't mind. She smelled alive and the view was nice. A path between two flower beds in full bloom meandered to a grove of birch trees centered on an ornate limestone cross. Singing birds mixed with the distant hum of a gardener mowing a field beyond the trees.

Canton tapped her knee. "Talk."

Caitlin watched a flurry of green fly from the riding mower. "I killed him."

"They say he drowned."

She shrugged, felt a twinge of pain between her shoulder blades. "I choked him until the water took him."

The mower finished a row, swiveled around for another pass.

Scott gave the expected response. "Self-defense."

"I'm not worried about legal charges." She met his eyes. "You've killed, Scott." She looked over at Roman. "He's killed. I've killed."

Scott took a second, replied. "We've killed."

She saw his mouth open wide in joy. "Jesus, did you just make a conjugation joke?"

He tipped his hat. "Teacher."

Caitlin's laughter joined his. Her many points of pain gave way to relief.

She wiped a tear away. "I'm gonna be so messed up."

"So much *more*."

She laughed again. "So much more messed up."

The gardener finished another row, kept right on going. Nothing stopped him.

Scott reached for her hand. "Therapy?"

She took the offer, squeezed him tight. Another tear fought its way out. "You know it."

"You talk. You friends," he said.

"Sure. You Tarzan, me friends."

Scott didn't look pissed, but he put extra prep into his next sentence. "You're not alone, smart ass."

"No," Caitlin admitted, tears now rolling from both eyes. "I'm not alone now."

He let go of her hand and pointed to his chest, then to Mike Roman. "You therapy, you talk, you friends."

"Okay, Scott. I promise. Therapy, talk, friends, I promise."

She had him crying now. He took another hard breath. "You help."

"I'll help myself, Scott. I will."

"No, help her."

"Her?"

He nodded. "Help her, Caitlin."

She swallowed hard. "Chapman's already gone. She's with her parents, not that they're still together. The police, the doctors, they'll help her."

He poked her arm. "They don't know."

"Shit," Caitlin said. "If they don't know, who does?"

"You do."

Caitlin had spent nine days in Branford's collection. Chapman, over seven hundred. She'd suffered multiple fractures from repeated abuse and showed signs of habitual rape and constant mental reprogramming. Caitlin hadn't seen media coverage yet but knew the world of exposure the girl would endure.

She found a smile. "Okay, Scott."

Mike Roman came closer. "Probably time to go."

Caitlin turned and saw a throng of media badgering a pair of security guards.

Mike pointed across the field. "Help's on the way."

A BPD sedan drove across the grass, Jerry Greenwood at the wheel, Maverick riding shotgun. Mary Lubbers-Gaffney's green Honda followed, windows open, radio blaring the Grateful Dead's "Casey Jones." Greenwood and Maverick got out.

"Don't you hate reporters?" Jane said, before passing them to go on the offensive.

Greenwood knelt at Caitlin's feet. "How are you?"

She grabbed her crutches. "Why are you down on one knee?"

He looked flustered. "I'm so sorry."

"Get up. A cop begging a reporter's forgiveness on one knee is a journalist's money shot."

He stood and helped her up. "Mary's gonna get you out of here."

"Great. Get the door for a lady?"

Greenwood ran to Mary's car, opened the back door. Caitlin saw Mary behind the wheel, Lakshmi at her side.

She called back to Scott, "You gonna be okay?"

Canton smiled again. She couldn't be sure, but this one looked like eighty percent. "Go. Therapy, talk, friends—"

"Help," she said. "I promise."

87

"CAN WE GET some air in here?"

Mary lowered the rear windows. "Anything you want, Caitie. We won't be in this car long."

Caitlin let the fragrant breeze fill her lungs. "Why not?"

Lakshmi leaned over the front seat. "The press saw Mary's car. We've got to switch. Get those crutches ready."

"The hospital made me take them," Caitlin said. "I'm fine. I ran barefoot through a cornfield two nights ago."

She sat back, closed her eyes, saw Angela Chapman sprinting ahead of her through the rain. She opened her eyes, sat forward. "Lakshmi, how's Angela doing?"

The girl's expression darkened.

Mary fielded the question. "They're keeping her under observation, Caitie. No one's really allowed near—"

Lakshmi cut her off. "She doesn't want to speak to me, or see me. Ever."

"You don't know that," Mary said. "It's early."

Lakshmi shook her head. "She screamed when she saw me, Caitlin. Said it was all my fault, said she never wanted to see me again."

Caitlin touched her shoulder. "Lakshmi, you can't imagine what Branford did to her. You don't know her reality. You're a good friend. Someday Angela will thank God you were there for her, even if she didn't know you were. Take it from me." She caught Mary's eyes in the rearview.

Lubbers blinked away a tear. "Here we go."

They pulled into a lot and parked next to Lakshmi's graphic-wrapped Toyota.

Caitlin reached for her crutches, then laughed. "Guess it's time for a paint job."

Lakshmi helped her into the passenger side of the Missing-Chapman-mobile. Mary handed Lakshmi keys and walked around to the driver's side.

"Lakshmi's not coming with us?"

"You kidding? She's got a story to write."

Lakshmi drove Mary's car back toward campus while Caitlin and Mary took 37 South.

"Not sure what your plans are, Caitie, but you're welcome to the cottage again, if that's not weird. Otherwise, Aaron and I would love to have you."

Caitlin stared at the signs for the next three exits. "Could we go down Tapp Road?"

"Seriously? I don't think we can go to the crime scene, even if you lived it."

"I want to go to where Woods raped me, and I'd like you to go with me."

Mary shook her head. "You're the patient."

She turned east on Tapp Road, pointed out the nursing home that Chapman ran to for help, almost two miles from Branford's house. Caitlin looked through the clumps of trees on the other side of the street, trying to guess where she herself had run from him, but everything looked different under the sunshine.

Mary warned her half a mile from the farm.

"I'm fine," Caitlin said, "for looking, at least."

"Then here we go."

Even two days later, law enforcement vehicles surrounded the farmhouse. Embower's keep looked small, maybe a quarter of the size of the Bro-duce compound.

"Lakshmi found the deed, you know, under the name Chet Watkins."

The cornfield passed by them, happy as corn could be, all ears, no sounds.

"Branford's real name was Chet?"

Next came the road to the Branford house and the quarry beyond.

"He showed up as a Pizza Monster shareholder. She backtracked from there, just like you taught her."

"That's a shame," Caitlin said. "It was really good pizza."

Mary laughed. "I thought that yesterday and felt like the worst person on Earth."

"Are you kidding? You're the best."

Mary went somewhere sad. "I'm sorry I let the FBI into the house."

"Don't be. I'm sorry it took me twenty years to come back. I'm sorry I missed your wedding."

Mary nodded. "Well, you're here now."

They crossed a bridge. Caitlin pointed toward the familiar sheet-metal shed of the old stone-cutting mill, and Mary turned onto a recently paved road. A new two-story building with a large parking lot took up the area in front of the old mill. A sign displayed the hours of the *South Bloomington Gymnastics Center*.

Mary took a spot, reached for the door. "Need me to let you out?"

Caitlin grabbed her hand. "Hold on, I'm not done apologizing."

"And I said you don't have anything to apologize for."

"Fine, then let me thank you."

"Well, in that case." Mary sat back, relaxed.

Caitlin started with the easy stuff. "Thank you for being there for me, for not giving up on me after twenty years."

"Caitie—"

"Just listen. Thanks for offering me your home, for hugging me like no one else, for your lipstick—"

"My lipstick?"

"If you hadn't given me that hideous pink lipstick the first night I got here—"

"Which you didn't wear."

"Exactly. If Branford hadn't found that in my purse and put it on, Roman wouldn't have noticed his disguise."

"We would have kept looking."

"I know, even after twenty years of me being an asshole."

"You weren't an asshole—"

"I hated you."

Mary didn't try to interrupt. "Okay."

Caitlin looked down at her fingers and pulled on the bandage over her missing nail. "You asked why I didn't come to you after I was attacked. I couldn't. I was so mad."

"At me?"

Caitlin had to get it out, and she owed it to Mary to look her in the eyes. "I love you, Mary Lubbers-hyphenate-Gaffney. I'm saying it now so you don't feel bad or take any guilt on yourself in any way, but I hated you."

Mary looked away for a second, bit her bottom lip, then returned to Caitlin's eye contact. "Okay. Why?"

"It's the dumbest thing in the world." Caitlin let the words out with a sigh. "You were the only one I told about my mother's profession."

Mary's eyes opened wider. "As in, the porn star thing?"

"Troy Woods knew." Caitlin looked up, tilted her head back. "He told Chief Hartman, and Hartman used it to embarrass me. The only way Woods could have known—"

"I am so sorry."

"Don't be."

Mary put her hands on the steering wheel at ten and two, then ran them to eight and four. "I don't even remember telling him."

"We were at Nick's English Hut. He said something about how we looked like virgins."

"Ohmigod." She dropped her head into her hands. "I was trying to get you laid."

Caitlin reached over and touched her leg. "Stop, Mary. I didn't tell you that to make you feel bad. I need you to understand how alone I felt and why I didn't come to you then. I was looking for someone, something to blame, like how Angela Chapman reacted when she saw Lakshmi."

Mary threw up her hands. "I am the world's worst friend."

Caitlin put her arms around her. "No, I'm the world's worst friend, or at least I was. That ends today. Look at me: I'm a hugger now."

Mary laughed through her tears, squeezed Caitlin back. At some point, Caitlin's need to blow her nose broke the moment. She reached into the door pocket, pulled out a missing persons flyer with Chapman's face on it and blew.

"Let's go see the place," she said.

They walked around the new gymnastics center and faced the old mill. The machines, limestone powder, and chunks of discarded stone were all gone. Recent construction had filled in the broken windows, added walls to the main building, and paved a sidewalk. Still, Caitlin found the old walkway where Woods had showed off his Sprite trick. The row of remaining eight-foot blocks divided a strip of grass and a hedge.

"Here," she said.

Mary stood beside her, said nothing.

Caitlin looked at the new strips of sod, the pressure-washed rocks, the blossoming shrubs, and saw nothing of Troy Woods.

"Hey, Mary?"

"Yeah."

"What's your second-favorite pizza place?"

CHAPTER

88

Seven Days Later

ROMAN'S EYES HID behind sunglasses. His rental at the curb was still running. "So you're staying?"

Caitlin stood in the open doorway of Mary's cottage. "Come in, if you want."

"I gotta hit the airport. Just wanted you to know I got the check. You didn't have to do that."

"Are you kidding? You flew to the Bahamas while I got kidnapped. Totally worth the money."

Roman smiled. "Not sure your timing's accurate. Your head wound might have been worse than we thought."

"Oh, it's definitely worse," Caitlin said. She started to reach toward him, stopped herself.

He raised an eyebrow. "What, do we hug now?"

"You wish. So you came by just to say thanks for the check?"

He looked past her, into the house. "How long are you staying?"

"Why? Need the work?"

"I was thinking of going south."

Caitlin knew what he meant. "Mexico?"

"It's time, but I need to know you're safe."

"Mike, you don't have to worry about me."

"You're right. I don't have to. So you'll be here for a while?"

"Maybe the whole summer."

"Writing your story?"

"No," she said. "Just living. Mary's trying to get me to teach a fall-semester guest intensive. We'll see. I'm pretty messed up."

Roman looked her up and down. "You look nice enough. You and Greenwood got a date?"

"Are you kidding? It's only been a week since I left the hospital."

"Doesn't sound like something that'd stop you."

"The man used me, Mike."

Roman smirked, repeated himself. "Doesn't sound like something that'd stop you."

Caitlin shook her head. "When Chapman disappeared, Greenwood blew up on the Bro-duce boys, basically had to let them go. So when I showed up, he pushed me toward their drug empire, knowing damn well Chief Renton would be afraid of the big-city journalist with an axe to grind against the BPD. Haven't heard much in the way of an apology from that bitch, by the way."

"Don't think you will. She's taken a medical leave. The interim chief is alright, though. Really has her shit together."

"Maverick?" Caitlin laughed. "Jane better quit smoking. A job like that will stop a heart, stress alone. What about your best friend?"

"Aren't you my best friend?"

In the past, she would have given him shit for that one. "I'm talking about the frat-boy kingpin, Kieran Michelson and his bros."

"Amireau and Frodo have trial dates in six months. The feds are still working on the K-man. You know how that process goes. Could be a year, could be more. My boy Adam gets to stay in the Bahamas. They can't really prove he did anything sinister."

Caitlin remembered her stash of weed in the other room—and the description of Angela's face the night she and her unoffending friends were kicked out of Kilroy's Sports.

Sixty sheets to the wind, but laughing.

"I'm not sure the others did either," she said through a sigh.

Mike raised an eyebrow. "Maybe pot will be legal by the time they get to trial. So why are you all dressed up if you don't have a date?"

Caitlin laughed. Roman didn't miss much. "Angela Chapman's in a facility thirty miles from here. I'm gonna go talk to her."

"For a book?"

She shook her head no. "Thanks for stopping by. Let me know if you go down to Mexico."

"Are you kidding? I expect an update every day to make sure this state hasn't killed you."

"Come here, Roman." Caitlin reached out for the hug. This time he didn't resist.

She whispered in the big man's ear. "What did you really want to tell me?"

Mike spoke softly. "I got a call this morning from a prison guard in Kokomo. Troy Woods died from wounds sustained in a riot."

Caitlin swallowed. "Do they know who killed him?"

"They're pretty sure the Aryan Brotherhood thought he helped law enforcement find a missing reporter."

She let go, looked him in the sunglasses. "Wow. I didn't expect that."

"Karma, right?"

He stepped back, waved. "Stay safe, Bergman."

She waved back.

He walked down the sidewalk, got in his rental.

Watching him go, Caitlin tried to decide how she felt about Woods's demise.

Sunshine, a cool breeze, grass, trees, flowers, a beautiful college town, new friendships, no deadlines or headlines, nothing but time on her side—she decided not to give a damn one way or another.

ACKNOWLEDGMENTS

This novel, and the *one and only* Caitlin Bergman, came to life thanks to the love, support, and daring of a whole village of professionals, friends, and family—all of whom deserve a standing ovation, open bar, and/or lifetime supply of pizza, depending on their personal preference.

My agent, Eric Myers, had the patience and prescience not only to see a diamond in the rough, but to stick with me until the manuscript was polished and shiny. A million thanks—and sushi at SugarFish—and tacos at El Sitio—for making my dream a reality.

My editor at Crooked Lane Books, Chelsey Emmelhainz, was the first complete stranger to fall in love with Caitlin Bergman. Her notes and suggestions, as well as the hard work of the rest of the amazing team at Crooked Lane, transformed a nearly there manuscript into this finished book in your hands.

My trusted beta readers, including those brave souls who conquered the sizable original drafts, put up with typos, sloppy imagery, and radical misspellings, and still provided insightful and constructive criticism (apologies if I'm missing anyone): Travis Betz, Shulie Cowen, Charli Engelhorn, Ara Grigorian, Jeremy Kryt, Christine Logsdon, Derek Miller, Ward Roberts, Hilary Ryan Rowe, Wes Rowe, Rebecca Stevens, and Robin Winter.

In 2011, I attended my first writer's conference—the Santa Barbara Writer's Conference. Between the workshops, guest speakers, happy-hour appetizers, and late-night pirate sessions, I found a family of established and aspiring writers who encouraged me at all stages, including, but in no way limited to Lorelei Armstrong, Barnaby Conrad III, Avery Faeth, Toni Lopopolo, Matthew Pallamary, Andrea Tawil, Laura Taylor, Robin Winter, my wolf pack of Ara Grigorian, Chase Moore, and Trey Dowell—and, of course, the powers who bring the magical week together every year, Grace Rachow and Monte Schulz.

In addition, Ara Grigorian and Janis Thomas's Novel Intensive helped me pare a sprawling plot down to a compact and marketable story. On the subject of Ara Grigorian, whose name has already appeared three times, I cannot thank him enough for the many hours spent delving into this challenging industry and for his support from inception to publication. Together, we will keep Porto's in business.

Likewise, author and journalist Jeremy Kryt has supported me from college until now, spending hours exploring life and the literary world over email exchanges, phone calls, and Skype sessions, even while embedded with foreign armies or *autodefensas* in South and Central America. Thanks for your friendship, wisdom, and the use of your MFA by proxy. Actor-writer-producer Derek Miller has also been beside me since my sophomore year. I can't imagine my path without his talent, advice, and sense of humor.

The character of Caitlin Bergman began in a screenplay in 2007. Although based on several of the strongest people this author has known, the part was written specifically for my college friend—and later Broadway, TV, and film actress as well as wife and mother—Karen Walsh Rullman. Whenever I write a line of Caitlin's dialogue, Karen's voice fights on.

Unlike Caitlin Bergman, I've been blessed with fabulous parents and a supportive family who love the arts, problem solving, and a mean game of *Clue*. Thanks Norm, Barb, Pete, Cami, Logan, Zach, and the extended Norman-Michalek-Rusnak-Thoemings for all of your support—despite the swearing! Same goes for my in-laws, Jim and Ruthann, and all of the extended Stevens-Burns, who weren't quite sure what I meant when I said I wrote crime fiction. Thanks for being more proud than scared.

Indiana University, the city of Bloomington, the Bloomington Police Department, and the FBI all play parts in this fictional episode of Caitlin Bergman's life. Although all four have dealt with horrible real-world events, in no way is this work meant to denigrate the hard-working police officers, federal agents, college professors, or local businesses of a beautiful college town. This Indiana native and IU alum chose the idyllic location to show that suffering is universal and that no one place is immune from corruption and abuse, no matter how lovely. My longest lasting friendships began in and around the creative jewel of the Midwest and continue to this day.

This work also touches on sexual assault, drug use, trauma, and psychology. My personal therapist, Annie Armstrong, was instrumental in the handling of this material, but in no way does this author claim ownership or expertise in the subjects presented. If you or someone you know is suffering, please seek help from a trained professional.

Finally, actor-comedian-writer Rebecca Stevens, also known as my wife, has been my inspiration, harshest critique partner, and biggest fan. Thank you for understanding that sometimes writing means searching for ways to commit murder, eating a basket of steak fries, or staring at a computer screen instead of doing laundry. Every day with you by my side is a sexy, fun-filled thriller, and every day without you is a mystery that must be solved.